Waiting to Begin

ALSO BY AMANDA PROWSE

Novels

Novellas

The Game
Something Quite Beautiful
A Christmas Wish
Ten Pound Ticket
Imogen's Baby
Miss Potterton's Birthday Tea
Mr Portobello's Morning Paper

Memoir

The Boy Between: A Mother and Son's Journey From a World Gone Grey
(with Josiah Hartley)

Waiting to Begin

AMANDA PROWSE

LAKE UNION
PUBLISHING

Text copyright © 2021 by Lionhead Media Ltd.
All rights reserved.

Published by Lake Union Publishing, Seattle

www.apub.com

Amazon, the Amazon logo, and Lake Union Publishing are trademarks of Amazon.com, Inc., or its affiliates.

ISBN-13: 9781542023436
ISBN-10: 1542023432

Cover design by Ghost Design

Printed in the United States of America

Waiting to Begin

PROLOGUE

1984

Ordinarily it would have been exciting, travelling somewhere by train, but there was nothing ordinary about this trip or this day. Bessie's limbs felt leaden, her spirit even more so. Philip stowed her big suitcase in the overhead wire rack and slid into the seat facing her on the other side of the table. His Adam's apple looked huge, rising up and down like a lift, carrying conflicting emotions from his brain to his mouth and then back again.

'I brought some snacks. Sandwiches – cheese and tomato,' he said.

He placed on the table between them the square Tupperware container with the faded green lid and the small piccalilli stain in the corner. The sight of the box, something from home and touched by her mother's fingers, was enough to bring on her tears. She shook her head.

'I'm not hungry.'

'Well, not now, but maybe later.'

'Are you actually turning into Mum?' she asked, more sharply than she had intended.

'God, I do hope not.' Philip drummed his fingers. 'I'll leave the thermos in the bag then.'

She felt the sting of guilt. Her brother was her single ally right now, her confidant and only friend. He deserved better.

'Sorry, Philip, I can't seem to . . .' The words ran out.

'It's okay,' he nodded. 'I understand.'

Regardless of his reassuring words, he avoided catching her eye, staring instead at the back gardens along the route as the train picked up speed.

She looked away, knowing that he didn't and couldn't understand. Not that she did herself entirely. Despite her best efforts, tears gathered at the back of her throat and nose and slipped silently down her face.

'Please don't cry, Bessie.' Philip's tone was calm and kindly, and his sweetness only encouraged her to cry all the harder.

'I can't help it.'

He pulled a few folds of toilet tissue from his jeans pocket and pushed them across the table. Gathering them gratefully into her hands, she blotted her eyes.

'No matter how hard I try, I can't see my future,' she managed, her voice low, wary of waking the old man on the other side of the aisle.

'Well, none of us can – that's why it's called the future – unless you've got one of those crystal balls or a time machine!' he said, in an effort to make her laugh.

'I wish I did.' She blew her nose. Of course, he was right – no one knew what lay ahead, but Bessie had had a plan where she could see the shape of her life, and now?

'Nothing has changed so far as the world is concerned. You can still have a great life; you can still make your dreams come true.'

'You don't understand, Philip.' Staring at her brother, she wrung her hands on the plastic tabletop between them. 'Everything has changed because *I've* changed. It's only months since I was celebrating my sixteenth birthday with the whole world at my feet and now . . . I'm not the person I thought I was.' This was true – everything she had thought she knew about herself had been erased. Somewhere along the line, the coating of confidence that had made her feel like she could take on the world and win had been wrenched violently from her without her consent, and she was left soft and fragile, unable to survive a fall.

'That's just how you feel right now, but you won't always. You will be strong again, bright and ready to face the world.' Again Philip's Adam's apple rose and fell, as if swallowing a lie.

Bessie looked away. Someone had scrawled the word *courage* on the window frame. She let loose a small, ironic sigh of acknowledgement.

The elderly man across the aisle snorted in his sleep. Grey tufts sprouted from his wide nostrils, and he sat with his head tipped back and his hands clasped across his chest. He had placed his cap, wallet and keys on top of his coat, which lay neatly folded on the table. Trusting.

'When we get there, I'll come with you, see you settled. Stay for a bit,' her brother whispered.

Bessie nodded, trying not to think of the dip in the mattress of her childhood bed, that comfortable crawl space where she had succumbed to sleep nearly every night of her life, knowing she was safe, with her parents and brother just along the landing. The smell, feel and weight of the blankets were all the more familiar and comforting because of it. But not tonight.

'I'm scared, Philip,' she said in a small voice.

And there it was, the phrase that encompassed all of her feelings.

'I know.' He tried out a weak smile. 'Why don't you write one of your postcards? Take your mind off things?'

She watched as he unbuckled his satchel and pulled out the small pack of white postcards, bought from the post office on the high street. He clicked the end of his ballpoint and pushed that across the table too.

Bessie gripped the pen and turned the card to the angle at which she was most comfortable writing – in physical terms at least, because it was mental torture to scribble these lies to the people she loved.

> *Dear Mum and Dad,*
> *How are you both? How is Nanny Pat's cat? Still*
> *hanging on, I hope.*

She paused and looked out of the window.

> *The weather is cold, but lovely. The sky is clear and*
> *blue and, if it wasn't for the frost and the chill, it*
> *could be summer, it has the same colour. The sky . . .*
> *where in just a few weeks I will be flying. Can you*
> *believe it? I am so excited. Me, an air hostess. All my*
> *dreams come true . . .*

'Tickets, please! All tickets, please!' the conductor shouted, slamming the carriage door behind him. Bessie put down the pen. The old man opposite started and sat up abruptly, blinking.

'I don't know what's going on!' he chuckled, as much to himself as to his fellow travellers.

I know how you feel . . . Bessie turned again to the world rushing by beyond the window. *I know exactly how you feel . . .*

CHAPTER ONE

The vicar had told the whole RE class that prayers were not meant for personal greed or the fulfilment of desires, and this Bessie adhered to, mostly. Often her requests were for famine relief in Ethiopia, Nanny Pat's cat, Tiki, who was clinging on to life by a whisker, and her best friend Michelle's dad, who was out of work and had been for the last two years on account of his dicky back.

But today was a special day. Bessie woke a second or two before her alarm, as she always did, and with her eyes clamped shut, she broke the rules, fairly confident that one selfish prayer, slotted in among the many for the masses, was probably allowed on her sixteenth birthday.

Hey, God, please make this a good year for me. Please help me get out of this town. I want to see the colour of the sky in California. I want to chat to people who don't know every square inch of this place like I do. I want to have a life like I see on TV, where people live with big, big kitchens, good tans and great hair. I want an amazing life – and I want Lawrence to fall in love with me, like I have with him.

Even the thought of Lawrence was enough to send her a little cuckoo, as if her excitement was more than she could contain. It burst from her like fireworks.

And of course, I also want world peace and an end to all hunger. Thanks. Oh, it's me by the way, Bessie Worrall.

She kicked off her duvet, jumped out of bed and stood like a star with her hands over her head and her legs splayed. Filling her lungs, she shouted out, 'It's my birthdaaaay!'

'Shut up!' came the muffled reply from her brother, Philip, whose room was along the hallway. 'No one cares!'

'You shut up!' she hollered in reply, with the express intent of irritating him. 'And actually, you're wrong – *I* care!'

Nothing, not even his foul mood, could dampen her spirits. She walked to the mirror above the chest of drawers in the corner of the room, where an irritating sticky splodge of glue from some long-discarded sticker sat in the corner. She studied her face, figuring she looked pretty much as she had done last night when she'd gone to bed, which was both a disappointment and a relief. Her boobs, she noted, were still no more than small buds, which she cursed, and there was sadly no visible improvement on the crop of spots fighting for space on her chin. She pulled a pouty face, very much liking the way her hair bouffed up when she first woke and disappointed at the prospect of it falling flat over the coming hours. The long-layered lengths with a hint of blonde, courtesy of a generous squirt of Sun-In, gave her a bit of a Bonnie Tyler vibe, although her brother, whose comments she largely ignored, said she looked more like Bon Jovi – but what did he know? She pulled it back into a scrunchie. Her eyebrows were freshly plucked into thin, high arches over her hazel eyes. She ran her finger over the little red dot of crusted blood where she had nicked the skin with a misplaced tweeze. Hours could be spent this way, staring at her face, prodding it, and comparing it to the pretty faces of the girls at school.

It was going to be a fantastic day, and anything could happen! She was sixteen. *Sixteen!* The kind of age where adults took you a bit more seriously, realising that you were properly emerging from the chrysalis of teenage years and were within snatching distance of adulthood. An age where all sorts of delights were now available, and not only those of a carnal nature, because at sixteen she could, if she so chose, leave school, join the army, get married, work full-time and drive a moped . . . The possibilities felt endless. Not that she intended to join the army or indeed drive a moped – her sights were set on the skies. There was something about the TV adverts for big jumbo jets with their coiffed and lipsticked attendants that fuelled her imagination and spoke to her. They offered the glamour and escape she was looking for. She wanted to fly around the world as an air hostess. She wanted that fitted red uniform and a little suitcase on wheels that she dragged along behind her. A life of freedom and exploration called, and just like her alarm clock, it felt well within her reach.

'You up, Bessie?' her mum called up the stairs excitedly.

'Yep! Coming!'

About to leave the room, Bessie went back to the mirror for one quick check on her teeth, running her tongue over her straight pearly whites, which she considered to be one of her best features.

'Bessie, for the love of God! Are you coming down or what?' her mum called again, but with more of an edge this time.

She took the narrow stairs two by two, leaping into the little square hallway by the front door. The summer morning light filtered through the dappled glass of the door and pooled on the green carpet, which, where the sun touched it, had gone a paler shade than the edges. When they had visitors, her mum always moved the rag rug from the bathroom and put it over the lighter spot.

'Here she is!' she heard her mum whisper, and knew exactly what to expect next, by long tradition. Bessie paused for a beat, swinging around the corner with her hand on the top of the newel

7

post. And then there it was: the sound of her dad's harmonica, playing his own version of 'Happy Birthday'.

Her parents, Jeannie and Eddie, stood side by side in their pyjamas, her mum looking simultaneously happy and emotional and her dad with the cord of his red and black tartan dressing gown tied tight across his burgeoning tum, the harmonica raised to his lips in readiness. The instrument had been a gift to him from his own dad, who had apparently fought in World War II with his trusty instrument secreted in a pocket, whipped out as and when required to lift the spirits of his comrades. Bessie hoped her Grandad Arty had been better at playing than her dad or it might have had quite the opposite effect on his poor comrades in dire need of a boost.

Bessie conducted with her index finger, trying not to let her grin slip into laughter as her dad did his best to get the tune of 'Happy Birthday' right and her mum, bless her, sang along in an earnest attempt to keep up with whatever he was now playing. As if this wasn't bad enough, her brother decided to bang his disapproval on his bedroom floor, the thuds coming through the ceiling. After an excruciating thirty seconds, it was over.

'Happy birthday, Bessie.'

'Yaaaaaaaay! Happy birthday to me!' she roared in return.

Her mum took a step forward and wrapped her in her usual brief awkward hug – a throwback, her dad had explained, from her own childhood, where hugs were in very short supply. Bessie loved that she tried and gripped her tightly in return, whereupon her mum did what she always did and patted her on the head and tousled her hair. Her dad pulled her into a close hold and kissed her on the forehead while her mum scurried off to grab four plates from the shelf in the kitchen cupboard, Bessie and her dad following on behind.

'Sixteen, baby girl. It doesn't seem possible,' her mum said.

'Do you feel sixteen?' her dad asked, as he always did.

Bessie touched her head with both hands and then her chest and finally her forearms. 'Do you know, I do!' She and her dad laughed.

'Mind you, it wasn't exactly the happiest day for me,' her mum interjected. 'I mean, of course it *was* – I got you!' she corrected, giggling, as she went to the fridge to grab the milk and eggs for pancakes, the only breakfast available on birthdays in this house. Every other day Bessie ate cereal and watched with a look of disgust as her parents tucked into toast and marmalade with chunks of orange peel in it. What was it about old people that made them like the bit of the fruit that in every other orangey scenario was thrown away! She shuddered at the very thought.

'I was smitten the very moment I saw you, but my goodness, it wasn't what you might call an easy birth,' her mum said, wincing at the memory, as she cracked eggs into the Pyrex bowl that had belonged to Bessie's nanna. 'I wasn't ever the same again, not down below.'

'For the love of God, Jeannie! She doesn't want to hear about the state of your lady bits on the day you gave birth, do you, Bessie? Not today!' Her dad took a seat at the kitchen table and popped the harmonica back in his dressing-gown pocket.

'Actually, Dad, I don't want to hear about my mother's lady bits on any day.'

'Yes, good point!'

'Can you please tell Philip that I'm making the pancakes and he should come down so Bessie can open her pressies.' Her mum smiled at her, letting the excitement build.

Her dad rocked back in his chair until he was balancing on the rear two legs and then leant his head away from the table before shouting, 'Philip, your mum's making pancakes and you need to come down so your sister can open her pressies!'

9

Her mum shook her head with a look that was so well practised her dad took little notice.

'I give up, I really do! Go and get her presents, Eddie!' her mum said, nodding her head towards the lounge.

Bessie sat down and patted the tabletop in front of her as it filled with gifts wrapped in a wide assortment of paper, carefully harvested after each birthday, smoothed and returned to the drawer. Philip came loping down the stairs in his underwear.

'Couldn't you put some clothes on for your sister's birthday?' Her mum tutted in his direction.

He glanced down at his hairy legs and pigeon chest. 'I'd say not, judging by the look of things.' He sat down and flicked his fringe from his eyes.

'Why do I bother?' Her mum gave her umpteenth hefty sigh of the morning.

Philip looked at the open egg box next to the cooker and folded his arms across his chest with a look of disgust. 'I can't believe I'm being forced to sit at a table where you're giving people animal products to eat, Mum!'

'What are you talking about?' Their mum whipped around to face her son, whisk in hand.

'Philip's a vegan now.' Bessie nodded to show she had been paying attention.

'Is that right?' Her dad looked more than a little perplexed. 'What's a vegan, exactly?'

'It's like a vegetarian.' Her mum sounded proud of her knowledge on the matter.

'Yes, like a vegetarian, but we don't eat any animal products at all,' Philip informed his father condescendingly.

'So, no bacon, no sausage, no roast lamb?' her dad queried.

'No, none of them – pig, pig, sheep, obviously.' Philip stood his ground.

'What about cheese?'

'No, no cheese – that's a by-product of milk, cow juice, dairy, and therefore no.'

'Humph.' Her dad scratched his chin. 'What about proper gravy with juice from the roast?'

'No, Dad.' Philip sounded exasperated.

'Eggs?'

'No.'

'A Cornish pasty?'

Philip chose not to answer but breathed heavily.

'I can't think what you'll survive on, boy! Lettuce?'

'It's really not that difficult, Dad. Carmen and I refuse to eat the flesh or by-products of innocent animals. If it has a face, I will replace!' He lifted his hands as if spewing wisdom.

'Are you sure you don't want a pancake?' Her mum shook her head, cracking more eggs into the Pyrex bowl.

Philip looked a little frustrated.

'So what is it you eat, son? Lentils and potatoes and stuff?' Her dad inadvertently wrinkled his nose.

'Yes, when I can get lentils.'

Bessie recognised her brother's veiled dig at their mother's store cupboard, which was largely full of alphabet spaghetti, boxes of Frosties, tins of corned beef and Cup-a-Soup.

'I saw you outside Wimpy two days ago, scoffing a burger,' she said, blowing his cover.

'Shut up, Bessie!' he yelled, and she instantly felt bad for the revelation, but not enough to ignore the tender bait that dangled. It was too good an opportunity to have her brother on the back foot.

'Don't get mad with me just because I saw you consuming the flesh of innocent animals! And anyway, you should be extra nice to me today – it *is* my birthday.'

'You think you're so clever, Bessie, but I've heard it on the grapevine that there are far worse things to be doing after school than scoffing a Wimpy!' he said, looking her right in the eye, his chest heaving.

She felt the cold wrap of fear around her head – did Philip know about her and Lawrence?

'Anyway,' she said, drawing breath and deciding to get the next jab in, 'you're only a vegan because *Carmen* is a vegan, and I honestly think if *Carmen* said run around the marketplace with your pants on your head eating a raw chicken, you'd do it!'

Her dad's head drooped. 'For the love of God, your mother is cooking pancakes, you're supposed to be opening your gifts and this is *not* the atmosphere we want on a special day. Please, please, try and be nice to each other.' He looked at his wife. 'I can't believe I've been saying that since they were babies! Why can't they be friends?'

'Just give her her bloody presents, Eddie.' Her mum rubbed her forehead, where Bessie had no doubt the beginnings of a headache lurked.

'Here we are, little love.' Her dad pushed the gifts closer to her, along with a small bundle of envelopes in the colours of sugared almonds.

'Thank you!'

'Don't get too excited.' Her mum did this – put the lid on any potential joy, as if it were better to quash any shoots of happiness before they took root.

'I won't,' Bessie reassured her. She picked up a square package and pulled the wrapping off to reveal the traditional Terry's Chocolate Orange.

'Your favourite!'

'It is. Thanks, Mum.'

'Can I have some?' Her brother reached out his hand.

'Sure.' She pushed it towards him and he smiled.

12

'I'm only kidding. I wouldn't eat your birthday chocolate.'

'Well, of course you wouldn't – it's made of milk . . .' Bessie grinned at him and tore the paper from a tube of lip gloss, the one she had wanted. 'Thanks!' she said, unscrewing the top and inhaling the peach-scented goo that she intended to slather over her lips later before hopefully transferring it on to Lawrence Paulson's face and neck. The thought sent a shiver of want right through her.

Next she opened a pair of fluffy ankle socks and then a box of Maltesers, and finally a book token from Nanny Pat and Grandad Norm, and an Our Price token from Auntie Nerys, enough for her to buy the new Spandau Ballet album she'd been hoping for.

'So how do you get your exam results?' her dad asked. 'Are they coming in the post? Can't remember how we got Philip's!'

'They put them up in the school hall today.'

She felt the first flicker of nerves at the thought, which had overshadowed all others in the last few weeks. The exams had gone okayish and she knew that with a clutch of decent grades she could complete the sixth form and then head to college to become anything she wanted!

'You'll have done fine, sweetie – you take after your dad. Brains.' He tapped his forehead.

'It's quite a day for you, missy. We'll have your cake with tea later, half of it to celebrate your birthday and the other half to toast your success.' Her mum had made a Victoria sponge, of course.

Philip stood and loped over to the bread bin and reached behind it to retrieve his own gift to her, neatly wrapped in white tissue paper.

'Ah, Pippin, you little sweetie!' her mum announced, in the same tone with which she noted all of his achievements: *Pippin is out of nappies, the little sweetie, joined Cubs, the little sweetie, got his yellow belt in judo, passed his cycling proficiency exam and now managed to buy his sister a birthday present all by himself . . .* Her tone and nickname embarrassed her eighteen-year-old son, and in response he threw the gift on to the table in front of Bessie, who knew enough not to make the same level of fuss as her mother as she ripped at the tissue.

'Leg warmers!' she yelled. They were fabulous, hot pink with lime green stripes.

'What in God's name are leg warmers?' her dad said, wrinkling his nose as his mouth fell open.

'They're like socks but without the feet in,' her mum, the oracle, explained, as she grappled with the heavy frying pan and flipped a pancake high in the air, before watching it land on the floor in a sorry-looking wrinkled heap. 'First one's for the bin, anyway!' she chuckled.

'Socks without the feet?' her dad said, looking utterly perplexed. 'Whatever will they think of next?'

Bessie smiled at her brother. 'Thanks, Philip, they're mint.'

He tried to look cool but his big smile told her he was chuffed. She knew he would have spent a chunk of his wages from his Saturday job at the petrol station on them. These were the moments when he felt like the brother who used to play with her in the garden, the brother who helped build her secret den under the privet hedge, the brother who snuck her into the cinema to see *Flashdance*, and not the brother who ignored her, clearly irritated by her very presence.

'You'll have to write all your thank you's, and I'll post them for you. I've got a packet of notelets you can use.'

'Thanks, Mum. I love my pressies.' She was not about to let the dreaded thought of writing thank-you notes to her aged relatives spoil the moment.

The phone rang in the hallway.

'No doubt that'll be Nanny Pat to see if you like your book token. Don't forget to ask how Tiki's doing!' Mum nodded towards

14

the hallway, prompting as she always did, while ladling more of the pancake mix into the frying pan and swirling it around. Her dad let out a loud and unexpected blast on the harmonica and her mum jumped and yelped, dropping the pan on the stove. The thick batter sloshed out and dripped down the front of the oven, before pooling on the carpet tiles.

'For the love of God, Eddie!' she screeched, clutching at her chest with her one free hand and staring at the mess of her kitchen.

Bessie figured breakfast might be a little late. Running to the phone, she grabbed it, and before she had the chance to say hello, Michelle started singing.

'Haa-appy birthday to yooooooooo!'

'Thanks.' She sat back on her favoured step, about a third of the way up, knitting the long, curly wire around her fingers.

'So whaddya get for your birthday?' her friend said, cutting to the chase.

'Can't remember. Not much,' she lied. It had been Michelle's birthday last month and she hadn't received any gifts apart from the bubblegum-flavoured lip gloss Bessie had bought her. Her best friend's family, she knew, had no spare money for presents. They had no spare money for anything much. To relay the long list of all the lovely bits and bobs now nestling in a pile on the table would seem a little mean.

'Some Maltesers,' she offered casually.

'Save me some!'

'I will,' she promised.

Nothing was half as much fun if Bessie didn't share it with Michelle. They had sayings, quotes and comments known only to the two of them and heavy with hidden meaning. For example, if something was lame or not up to scratch, they said it was a bit 'Ronnie', cruelly inspired by Ronald Booker, a boy in their year whose name, they figured, neither of them would recall when they

15

looked at school photos in years to come. He was a walking under-achiever, bland, vanilla, forgettable. If they liked a boy, however, and wanted to subtly announce this, they would say they were *hungry* and use his initials related to food, a basic code but one they thought was foolproof.

'God, Michelle, I'm starving!'

'Really? What do you *fancy*?'

'Ooh, I'm thinking . . . *L*iquorice and *P*opcorn . . .'

Lawrence Paulson . . .

'Ah, yes, liquorice and popcorn sounds good!'

It was almost like having their own language. They so loved each other's company, they often laughed until they cried or needed a pee. The two events were not always mutually exclusive. And these fits of laughter could happen anywhere: in school, on the sofa, at the cinema, at the school carol concert – or even at an ice rink, where Bessie had collapsed on the grubby grey slush as Christmas skaters whizzed past her head and she, weak with laughter, lay crying and close to hysteria on the cold wet surface, powerless to stand, despite the shouts and moans of all of those whose path she blocked. She and Michelle made plans for all the things they would do when age and funds allowed: travel, live in a flat together (one with a balcony and a fantastic view), get their hair dyed profes-sionally, and go out with and possibly marry different members of Duran Duran.

'Results day!' Michelle took a sharp intake of breath. 'I couldn't sleep last night. I'm freaking out a bit.'

'I'm not,' Bessie answered truthfully. 'I mean, there's not a lot we can do about it now, is there?'

'I s'pose not. Plus, you're smart. I worked a zillion times harder than you and I bet you still beat me.'

'It's not a competition,' Bessie reasoned, although secretly she quite liked the idea of getting good grades and using her brains.

'So you reckon you're going to do it with Lawrence tonight?' Michelle whispered.

'I think so,' Bessie whispered back, looking up the hallway to check her family were still safely gathered in the kitchen.

Michelle squealed.

'Shhhh!' Any overexcitement was sure to be investigated by at least one if not both sets of parents.

'Oh my God! Are you scared?'

'Not really.' She spoke the truth because she *wasn't* scared – she'd already *had* sex with Lawrence Paulson.

It was the only thing she hadn't shared with her best friend, partly out of embarrassment and partly because at fifteen she knew there were some folks who would take umbrage and might get involved. And by 'some folks', she meant Michelle's parents. It didn't feel nice to have this secret from her mate. Not nice at all. In fact, she generally avoided the topic of Lawrence altogether, figuring this was easier than having to skirt around a lie.

She became aware of her brother's footsteps, and then there he was in his pants with his arms folded over his chest, looking like some skinny irritating genie that had popped up without being beckoned.

'Come on, Bessie! Carmen's probably trying to get through!'

She found it impossible to fathom how *anyone* could find her dorky brother attractive, no matter how much she loved him. It was quite nice for her, though, as Carmen was head girl at their school and the fact that she was her brother's girlfriend gave her a little status by association.

'I'd better go, Michelle. Philip says Carmen's probably trying to get through.'

'Okay, well, I'll see you in about twenty minutes.'

'Yep, see you in a little bit.' Bessie hung up and slunk from the stairs.

'What do you mean, "see you in a little bit"?' Her brother looked perplexed and furious in equal measure.

'It was Michelle – she's coming over in a minute. And after we've got our results we're going to hang out and get ready for tonight.'

'So, what was so important that you had to hog the phone if you knew she was coming over to talk to you face to face in a matter of minutes?' His voice had gone up a few registers.

'Just stuff,' she said softly. *Like the fact that I'm planning to have sex – legal sex – with Lawrence Paulson tonight and she thinks I'm a virgin and therefore it's a big deal . . .*

'God, you kids have no idea!' He shook his head and she stared at him, knowing for a fact he had not had sex with Carmen, as she had heard them talking about it in the front garden through her open bedroom window. He had said he thought they were ready to get physical; she had said that in the eyes of God it would be better to wait until marriage for sex. He had said he'd ask God to put a blindfold on or if he'd mind turning away, just for a minute or two . . . and then Carmen had left a little abruptly.

'Be nice to your sister! It's her birthday!' their dad called.

Philip gave his sister a look of pure dislike.

'Come on, pancakes are ready!' her mum called.

Bessie slunk past her scowling brother and took a seat at the kitchen table. Her dad was eating a pallid and rather wrinkled pancake and winked at her, the corners of his mouth drawn down in distaste. She picked up her fork to tuck into the cool, greasy lump that sat on her plate, sloshed generously with lemon juice and sugar.

'Thanks, Mum.' She smiled meekly and used the side of her fork to cut a mouthful.

'You're welcome.'

'You were on the phone for an age!' her dad said suddenly.

She didn't want to look him in the eye, not when the topic under discussion had been S-E-X. 'I guess we have a lot to talk about.'

'Well, I guess you need to find a way to have less to talk about or, better still, wait until you *see* your mate. It'd be bloody cheaper! There's no money tree in our back garden.' Her dad was fond of telling her this, and yet, compared to Michelle's family, they lived like kings. And if they did have a money tree, she'd give it a big shake and, with whatever dropped out, buy a ticket to California.

'We are so proud of you. We can't wait to see your exam results. This is just the start for you, the start of your big adventure. Our little girl . . .' Her mum ran her palm over the tousled pineapple of hair on the top of her head and Bessie thought it odd how they saw her as a little girl and yet she knew she was a big girl with big ideas. 'I can't wait to see them either.' She couldn't wait for her adventure to begin.

CHAPTER TWO

August 20th 2021

The alarm pip-pipped its infernal noise. Bess screwed her eyes shut, reluctant to greet the day. The blanket of melancholy that wrapped her shoulders and held her tight felt as unpleasant and restrictive as it always did on days like these, weighing her down.

Reaching for her phone, she jabbed her finger on to the button that would silence the alarm, having no choice other than to admit she was awake: her face squashed into the soft pillow, the pull of her bladder, which needed emptying, and her husband's rumbling snore, which ended with the smack of his lips. And yet she lay perfectly still, hoping pointlessly for five more minutes of escape.

Admitting defeat, she opened her eyes and rolled on to her back and, with her nightdress rucked around her middle, stared up at the ceiling and the three-arm ivory-coloured chandelier decorated with snaking leaves. The addition had seemed like a good idea when she thumbed through the interior design magazine in the newsagent's, looking for inspiration, convincing Mario that it was all the rage. Now, though, with its bare candle bulbs and plastic droplets that from a distance looked like glass, she thought it a bit too grand and out of place in the cosy bedroom of their dormer bungalow. Not that she would ever admit this to her husband, who had taken a bit of persuading that at one hundred and fifteen quid it was what the article had described as 'an investment piece' – money he felt would have been better put towards a new mattress. A year or so back they had considered a replacement, but she had fallen at the final hurdle at the mere thought of giving up her beloved bed, refusing to upgrade because she knew it was the little imperfections and familiarity that gave her the best night's sleep. A new, firmer example without the comfortable dip in which her hip lodged and without the lingering essence of its history would not be the same at all. Mario didn't get it, but then Mario didn't get lots of things.

She smarted at the resounding fart that now poisoned her atmosphere, making her jaw tense and her nose wrinkle.

'Was that you or the dog?' She nudged her husband with her right foot, her toes sliding against his wide, hairy calf.

'I know it's an awful thing to say,' Mario mumbled, 'but I honestly don't know.' He chuckled until the duvet shook. Bess did not find it so amusing and felt the squeak of her back teeth as she ground her upper and lower jaw with irritation. She looked at Chutney, their dark, leggy mongrel, snoring peacefully in the wide space between them on the bed.

When Chutney was a pup, they would on occasion breach the gap, scooting him to the bottom of the mattress and reaching over to make contact skin-to-skin as they indulged in quick, satisfying sex on a Saturday night, with the promise of a lie-in on Sunday. It had been a while since they had shifted the dog for this purpose, using him as both an excuse and a foot warmer. It wasn't Mario's fault. Newly married, Bess would have laughed at the fart, leapt on top of her husband, chastised him, kissed him and buried her face in the chest of this man who had pledged to love her for better, for worse, for richer, for poorer, in sickness and in health. She tried to recall when she had stopped behaving that way, tried to remember exactly when it had first felt easier to curl up and reflect, harder to laugh and be silly. When she lost the baby, certainly. That was one marker.

It was the turn of Mario's alarm to blast its greeting, and her heart sank.

How she hated the sound. Hated it more than the scratch of something on a chalkboard, more than the squeak of cutlery across the cheap metal trays of the kids whose lunches she served every day in the school canteen and more than bloody Smudge's piercing yap. Smudge being the small Jack Russell that lived with Mr Draper (*'Call me Jonathan!'*) over the way and who harassed Chutney at every given opportunity – the dog, that was, not Mr Draper. 'He wants to be friends!' Mr Draper would trill, while Smudge did his best to snap at Chutney's one remaining testicle with his teeth bared.

'Come on, lazy arse!' her husband chortled. 'Time to get up!'

'I am many things, Mario, but I'm not lazy.'

'I was joking,' he sniffed, 'or trying to. You're not still a bit down in the dumps, are you?' His intonation was heavy with judgement and impatience with her.

Her silence said more than any fake denial or forced smile that might have helped smooth the start of the day.

'The thing is, Bess,' he said eventually, 'I don't know if you know this, but your mood is catching – it's a joy hoover. It makes me feel like shite; it even makes Chutney feel like shite!' He ran his hand over the head of their beloved mutt.

It wasn't news. Her moods balled the sunshine and lobbed it into the back yard to land with the weeds growing up through the patio and the discarded wood stacked in the corner, loitering without purpose. It put the house in permanent winter, which made her feel both powerful and guilty.

She watched him rise and stretch, his fringe sticking up at all angles, the grey hair of his chest wiry and long and his eyes bleary, picturing the man she had fallen in love with when he had come to talk to the manager of the supermarket in which she had been working. He, a young salesman, and she, a girl trying to find her place in the world, keeping her head down, working with tins of beans instead of flying the skies. The man who had held her hand as they fell asleep each night, as if contact was vital. The man who would creep downstairs in the morning, returning with a cup of hot tea, steadying it on her bedside table for when she woke. *That* man, who had thrown her a lifeline . . .

'Do you know, I sometimes wish we could go back to those years when we were first married and you were so much nicer to me,' she said. 'You wouldn't have dreamt of saying something like that . . .'

His response was slow in coming. 'I'd like to go back to then too, when I was three stone lighter and you were fun – remember fun? When I had the energy for great sex, and you had the inclination. And when you were much nicer to me too.'

'I am nice to you!'

He scratched his chest. 'You are, but that's the issue, I guess, love. You're *nice* to me in the way you are to anyone else, but you used to be . . . you used to be . . .' He looked up and his mouth moved, but no words came. 'I don't know.'

'I used to be what?' On some level she wanted to hear it, like expelling a splinter or spitting out poison.

'I don't know what the word is, Bess. I don't know how to describe it.' He shook his head. 'What I do know is I haven't time to sit down and analyse it right now – time and my foreman wait for no man, as the saying goes.' He laughed drily.

She watched him leave the room and remembered her husband, when the gold band on her finger had been shiny and loose, crawling up under the duvet, kissing her foot, her leg, mad for her and so in love, like she filled him up, like she was enough. She swallowed the lump in her throat, knowing she had felt that way too. It had been enough. But they had started married life as a couple heading out hand in hand on a great adventure, joint captains at the prow of their ship – now it was as if they were tethered, but slightly adrift, bobbing on a vast, endless ocean without direction and on a lilo that was slowly deflating. And the hiss of escaping air filled the quiet moments when words were wanting.

It was impossible not to think of Jake and Daniel, intoxicated with the first flush of love and all the expectations of the newly wed. Their faces had split with joy as she and Mario waved them off on their honeymoon only a week ago. Their wedding had been a hastily organised and intimate affair at the local registry office, followed by a party for their nearest and dearest, here in their modest home in St Albans, where they had drunk Prosecco and danced barefoot on the kitchen floor until the sun came up.

And of course she was happy that Jake was happy, but how she wished she could go back to when Natalie lived in her pink-themed bedroom, running home from school to fret over homework or boys and Jake lived in his own pink-themed bedroom, running home from school to fret over homework or boys. How she had loved sleeping with her children just along the hallway, calling out when they needed her. And the four of them, sitting at the kitchen table, passing the ketchup, laughing over silliness and feeling in those moments like they were safe behind their front door, where just being together meant they kept the real world at bay. It was all she had ever wanted, a life she loved.

It was as if, when the kids were young and at home, she had recreated the happy home of her childhood with Philip and her parents around *their* breakfast table, her mum fussing, her dad going along with it all and with love – deep, unshakeable love – as their glue. But now Jake was a married man and Natalie a busy woman and they had homes of their own, which were slick, grey, glossy and uncluttered. Homes where she had no hand in the decor and no say in bedtimes or what food was put on the table.

Chutney jumped from the mattress and followed Mario into the bathroom along the hall. Bess, like Chutney, had no choice other than to listen to him pee. She sat up, swallowing the bitter tang of nastiness on her tongue, caused by teeth that needed cleaning and, she suspected, not helped by the crumbling molar at the back of her mouth on the right.

The sound of Mario's footsteps now going down the stairs and the pit-a-pat of Chutney following drew her from her thoughts. She took her time, swinging her legs over the side of the bed and reaching for the pink fleece dressing gown that her daughter had put into the charity box a year or so ago. Bess, having retrieved it, had been wearing it ever since. It might have been the summer, but she liked the snug feeling of the soft fleece on her skin.

The bathroom floor was pleasantly cool under her feet. Staring at the bowl of the toilet, she wondered how it could be so hard for Mario to remember to pull the chain. When confronted, he said it was environmentally preferable and that there was no need to unnecessarily waste water.

'What a load of old bollocks!'

She touched her fingertips to the thin wisps of straggly hair that constituted her eyebrows. Daily, she stared at the high arches and wished she had never plucked them, especially now that full, youthful brows were all the rage – whatever had she been thinking?

'You look old, Bess,' she whispered, pulling her skin this way and that, watching it bag and sag beneath her touch and patting the small pouch under her chin. It was rare for her to study her face in this way, preferring not to be reminded of how she looked.

'You coming down, Bess?' Mario yelled from the kitchen.

'Yep. Coming.' Bess pulled her hair into a scrunchie and went downstairs, hoping coffee might lift her mood.

Mario stood by the kitchen sink, beaming. He pointed to a large cellophane-wrapped orchid that stood proudly in a fuchsia-coloured pot on the draining board.

'Happy birthday, love.'

'Ah, thank you. I didn't know if you'd remembered.' She walked forward and kissed him quickly on the cheek, feeling the graze of whiskers beneath her lips.

'Of course I remembered!' He pointed again at the plant.

'That's . . . that's lovely. Pretty.'

'I got you a card, a really, really nice one, but I've lost it.' He shook his head.

From anyone else, she might think of this as a poor excuse for not having bothered, but for Mario, who daily lost his car keys, a shoe, his glasses, the newspaper . . . she knew it was most likely to be genuine and that the card would be stashed somewhere safe and unpredictable, like in the fridge, on a shelf in the garage or in the space by the side of the telly where old magazines liked to gather.

'It's got a duck on the front.'

'Oh! A duck?'

'Yes, Bess. A duck.'

'No doubt it'll turn up.' With a duck on the front. She didn't confess to feeling a little indifferent as to whether it surfaced or not, picturing something garish, cartoon-like and very, very yellow.

Her phone buzzed with a text alert.

HAPPY BIRTHDAY MUM! LOVE YOU! SEE YOU LATER X

'Ah, it's from Nat, bless her.' She put the phone face down on the tiled countertop and opened the back door. Chutney popped his head out into the sunny morning and looked back at her as if to say, *Do I have to?* 'Go on, Chuts, go and have your wee and then I'll get your breakfast.' He waddled out reluctantly.

'I love the way you think he knows what you're saying.' Mario grabbed the ham sandwiches he'd made the night before from the fridge and put them in his red plastic lunch box, as he always did. It meant he didn't have to leave the building site to grab lunch and could get more hours in each day. He worked hard, always with one eye on his monthly bonus.

'Actually, he knows exactly what I'm saying! He talks to me properly when we're on our own.'

'Is that right? So what does he have to say?' he asked, with the twitch of a smile about his mouth that she fixed on, knowing what he was thinking: *This is more like it . . . the old Bess . . . the funny Bess . . .* He clearly missed her; what he failed to grasp was that she missed her too.

Bess harnessed the moment and tried to recapture some of her old sass, tried to emulate the woman who remembered fun. The woman who was enough. 'Well, just what you'd expect, really. What he likes and dislikes for his breakfast, how he doesn't like the lady groomer who nipped his leg that time with the clippers, his views on Brexit – that kind of thing.'

'Talking of breakfast, how about I make you something special before I go?' Mario rubbed his hands together, keen and eager, as if he could take this upturn in the atmosphere and spin it into something bigger, something more – a net that might cover them and keep the sadness from their backs.

'Like what?' she smiled, touched at the thought.

He opened the cupboard over the fridge. 'I know you always do pancakes for our birthdays, but I don't know how to make batter. But I *can* do you a bowl of Crunchy Nut? Or sugar-free muesli? Or . . .' He ran over to the bread bin and peered inside. '. . . half a toasted teacake?'

It wasn't quite her definition of 'special'. 'Actually, Mario, think I'll just stick to my toast and marmalade.' Her day wasn't right if

27

not started with a slice of toast and a zingy dollop of bitter marmalade with bits of shredded peel dotted about the toast. 'Just a
coffee'd be lovely.'

She peeled the cellophane from her new plant and let her fingers tickle the delicate silken-headed, bell-shaped flowers that were
so perfect and beautiful they looked like they might be fake. One
dropped as she touched it. Catching it, Bess scrunched it into her
palm and shoved it in her dressing-gown pocket.

'How about we do a chippy run tonight for your birthday?'
Mario said, adding milk to the black coffee and passing her the mug.

'Yes, it'll be nice not to have to cook. Why don't we do that?'
She sipped her drink, as Chutney scratched on the back door.
Mario let him in.

'Maybe the kids'll come over?' he asked.

'Maybe. I'm seeing Nats later; she said she'd pop in on the way
to work. I'm not sure if Jake'll be let out – it is a school night, after
all, and they'll be tired after travelling back from Scotland.' She
pulled a face to make her husband laugh.

'I hope they've had a nice time.' Mario sipped his tea. 'I thought
they might go further afield for their honeymoon. I'm sure Dan
gets money off flights, as he's with the airline.'

'Mmm.' It was apparently just one of the many, many perks of
her son-in-law's job as an air steward. 'Well, I shall look forward to
my fish and chips. I have a day of cleaning and laundry ahead, and
a quick lunch with Mum and Dad.'

'Not much of a day off, is it?' he said, making his way to the
bottom of the stairs.

'Day off? What does that mean?' she smiled.

'When that lottery win comes in, eh?'

'Yep.' She sat at the table and drank her coffee, reading her
birthday text from Natalie one more time. If she ever did win the
lottery, Bess wouldn't be fussed about the acquisition of gold and

diamonds, nor would she visit one of the flashy garages on the out-skirts of town and lay down bundles of cash for a shiny sports car or a massive four-by-four. No, all she wished for was the ability to wake naturally every day and for someone else to clean her house and do the laundry. Her fantasy lottery wishes, however, were varied and ever-changing. Some days, she pictured opening an orphanage in a hot country and feeding hundreds of kids who might be more grate-ful for her efforts as a dinner lady than the children of the Evergreen Academy. Not that her job wasn't without reward: she liked what she did, helping to prepare and dole out food, and she loved to cater for the pale, allergy-riddled kids who broke her heart, unable to imagine what it must be like to have to check and double-check against the real possibility of every single morsel they forked into their young mouths sending them into anaphylactic shock.

Once again, she thought about Leonard Bethelbrook, the boy in the year above her at school, who, with an undiagnosed pea-nut allergy, accepted a bite of his mate's sandwich and dropped to the ground. He died right there on the edge of the football pitch, where his peers were using jumpers as goalposts. She had only been eleven when it happened but remembered the day – the sound of the ambulance arriving at speed through the school gates, the blue light of the emergency vehicles bouncing around the walls of the classroom, casting everything and everyone in a lilac glow.

'Funny the things that stick in your mind, even after all these years,' she said to Chutney, who ignored her.

Bending down, Bess picked up a small blue piece of confetti in the shape of a heart, which had been hiding around the leg of the kitchen table despite her best efforts with the vacuum cleaner and feather duster. That darned wedding confetti hid in the folds of cushions, nestled on top of the laundry basket and even clung to the lounge curtains. It taunted her as it fell from the creases of clothes and dropped from light fittings. It wasn't only the irritating littering of her home that bothered her, but also what it represented. Not that she would tell a soul – how could she? Jake, twenty-eight, was now married to the love of his life – what was not to like? But the truth was, there was much she didn't like: the feeling that she had been supplanted in her son's affections, the way it aged her, having a son old enough to marry, despite this being the case for many a year, and the finality of it. *Are you jealous, Bess?* She silently asked herself the unpalatable question.

It wasn't that she *disliked* Daniel, exactly, but there were certain things about him that . . . he just . . . It was as if . . . he was a bit . . . It seemed like Mario wasn't the only one having trouble finding the right word this morning. Her son's hastily planned wedding and absolute joy at setting off on his new life adventure had made her realise that her adventure had ceased to be joyous some time ago now, and the lurking confetti, the untouched tier of wedding cake now taking up a disproportionate amount of space on the kitchen worktop and the stack of beribboned gifts piled high on the floor of Jake's old bedroom stoked something close to rage inside her. She couldn't help it.

Where Jake and his husband were concerned, she walked a delicate, winding path where rocks tumbled from a great height, the way ahead was obscure and all she could do was keep her head down and keep moving forward. Her son-in-law was a gate-keeper and it bothered her how every plan, every celebration, every thought had to be run past Daniel. She hated the way Jake deferred to him and privately had to admit that yes, this feeling was rooted in jealousy. *She* used to be the person he came to. She had secretly christened Daniel 'The Jake Whisperer', not that she would ever tell them, as that would be mean. And one thing she hated was mean.

She heard Mario whistling upstairs and looked at the orchid sitting in all its vibrant glory on the draining board.

'I hate orchids,' she whispered to the dog, who gazed up at her. 'Best not tell him, Chuts.'

CHAPTER THREE

August 20th 1984

Bessie pressed play on her tape recorder, then pulled down her cheek with one finger and closed her eye, the lid of which was already painted with bright metallic-blue eyeshadow. With her other hand she ran the creamy tip of the dark green kohl pencil over her upper eyelid, close to her lashes. She blinked and studied the effect in her little make-up mirror with the iridescent back. It felt important to look as fabulous as possible today. Whenever possible, she and Michelle liked to match outfits and make-up, so it was absolutely clear they were best friends.

They didn't look alike, not one bit. Michelle was dark-haired, petite yet curvy, whereas Bessie was mousy with a rather flat figure, more test tube than hourglass, but with the right clothes, colour scheme and attention to accessories, they could make themselves look passably similar or at the very least draw comment. They were not the most popular of girls and there was no gaggle of wannabes trotting after them down the corridors or circling them on the school field, flicking their hair and hanging on their every word, but that didn't matter because they were the most perfect gang of two. Together they were glorious! That said, it didn't mean Bessie wanted to look anything other than her best, should Melanie Hall or any of her cronies cast a look in her direction. After completing the other eye, she used the tip of her finger to dab a thick coat of concealer over Mount Etna's little sister, which had taken root on her chin.

Her bedroom door opened suddenly.

'Your dad let me in!'

Bessie's face broke into a smile at the sight of Michelle. She leapt up and threw her arms around her friend's neck as if it had been nineteen weeks and not nineteen hours since she had seen her last. The two settled back on the single bed with their backs against the wall.

'Ta dah! Happy birthday!' Michelle pulled two white disposable razors from the back pocket of her jeans.

'Thank you! I've got the Maltesers!' Bessie grabbed the box from her bedside table and shook it to make a pleasing rattle. Quickly she tore off the lid and the two scooped handfuls of malty chocolate into their fingers, before stuffing them into their mouths, laughing as they crunched and swallowed the sticky, sweet, melting treat. Michelle handed her a razor.

'How d'you do it, exactly?' Bessie asked through her mouthful, running her thumb over the hard plastic shield that sat over the double blade.

'I've seen my dad shave a million times – you just put the foam on and drag this up and down. How hard can it be? He even whistles while he does it!'

'Come on!' Bessie pulled her friend from the bed and they ran to the bathroom, locking the door behind them. She ran a shallow bath. Both whipped off their dungarees, discarding them in piles on the bath mat and perching now in their knickers and T-shirts on the flat corners of the tub opposite each other. Bessie grabbed her dad's shaving foam from the little shelf over the washbasin and squirted a sizeable puff into her friend's hand before doing the same

32

in her own. They each slathered it on to a leg and then carefully, hesitantly, pushed the guard from the blade.

'I guess it's like when we first plucked our eyebrows – remember how much it hurt?' Bessie laughed, thinking of how they had tweezed one hair and screamed! 'And now we're used to it,' she said, to reassure her friend.

'I guess so. I'm just worried that it'll grow back like whiskers, like my dad's beard.'

'No, I don't think it works like that. I think the hair on your legs is different.' Bessie went first, confidently sliding the razor along her shin, aware of the moment, the rite of passage. Michelle followed suit until they were twisting their legs at odd angles to reach them with the razor before rinsing the blades in the warm, ankle-deep bathwater to unclog them of suds and fine hairs.

'It's funny, isn't it?' Michelle said, holding her defuzzing weapon aloft. 'We've been at school all these years and in less than an hour we'll know if it was all worth it.'

Bessie laughed. 'Well, of course it was all worth it! First, I met you . . .'

'Your best friend in the whole wide world ever, ever, ever,' Michelle interjected.

'Yes, that. Plus, we've learned lots of stuff that'll be useful, and our grades are our ticket to the rest of our lives.'

'And by that you mean being an air hostess?'

'Yep.'

She looked at the toothpaste sitting in a little plastic beaker next to her mum's toothbrush by the sink. She wanted a more exciting life than her mum's, that was for sure.

'It's weird, but there's nothing else I can think of that I'd like to do. I want to go up in that aeroplane, Michelle. I want to put on that red uniform and I want to go to California. America!'

33

She, like everyone else at school, had a fascination for the place where big skies, big burgers, big cars and big hair were the order of the day. A country whose culture she soaked up via the medium of TV and her favourite programmes: *Dallas*, *Dynasty*, *Hart to Hart* and *Miami Vice*. The closest she could get to the US of A, however, was sitting in McDonald's.

'Urgh!' Michelle pulled a face. 'I've told you before, I can't think of anything worse – not the California bit, that sounds nice. I'd like to go somewhere sunny, but imagine having to give someone a sick bag while the plane darts all over the sky? I think *I'd* be sick!'

'I won't mind it too much.'

'Good job. "We have clearance, Clarence."'

Bessie giggled: '"Roger, Roger. What's our vector, Victor?"'

They both howled, having seen *Airplane!* three times at the Odeon.

Michelle sobered first. 'I'm happy you know what you want to do. I was worried for a minute back there, when you were thinking of becoming a nun! We wouldn't have been able to hang out.'

Bessie felt a twinge of guilt; keeping a secret from Michelle wasn't a nice feeling. 'They must get some time off. Plus, think of the advantages: they always wear a scarf and so I'd never have to worry about backcombing my hair.'

'True. You'd save a ton on hairspray,' Michelle piped up.

'I would. And I'd live in the convent, so no bills or decorating to worry about.'

'But you'd never get married or have babies, Bessie – wouldn't you miss that?'

'Yeah, I would. It's partly why I decided against it. I'd like to find someone who loved me, and we could just be happy, someone that I fancied forever. That'd be great.' She smiled as Lawrence's face came into focus in her mind.

'Someone like Simon Le Bon,' Michelle giggled.

'Exactly.'

Michelle paused from her shaving. 'Anyway, don't you have to be really religious to be a nun? I'm sure you have to believe in God.'

'Well, I do believe in God.' *I talk to him often enough . . .* 'Plus, I worry that if I *don't* believe and I die and it turns out all to be true, I could be in real trouble, and so the fact that I'm worried about that means I must believe, doesn't it?'

'I guess so.' Michelle seemed to follow her logic. 'I haven't a clue what I want to do after school. Mum says something will find me and I just have to keep my eyes open, ready to spot it. Or that I should marry money.' She scoffed. 'She says everyone who's married is miserable, and so you might as well be miserable and rich as miserable and poor.'

'Mmm.' Bessie thought it best not to disclose that *her* mum thought Michelle's mum was a bit 'relaxed' in her approach to parenting. 'Shit!' Bessie had momentarily lost her concentration and, while considering her friend's question, pressed down a little too firmly. She dropped the razor beneath the soap-scummed water and watched in horror as a neat row of dark beads of blood bloomed on her shin. She sloshed water on to them and watched as the beads very quickly grew into three large splats before forming a single persistent strawberry-coloured trickle.

'Urgh!' Michelle yelled, for the second time in so many minutes, seemingly finding nothing wrong in sharing suddy, hairy water with her friend, but the addition of blood was apparently quite repulsive to her. 'You've cut your leg!'

'Thanks, Cagney and Lacey, I can see that.' It stung.

There was a gentle knock on the door. 'You all right in there, lovey?' her mum asked. 'Thought I heard a kerfuffle?'

'No kerfuffle, Mum, all good. Just cut my leg a bit.' She pulled a face, worried that she might be in trouble and doubly worried about being scolded in front of her friend.

35

'What do you mean, you've cut your leg? How have you done that in the bathroom?' Her mum's tone carried the beginnings of frantic.

'It's okay, Mrs Worrall – it's not too bad,' Michelle said reassuringly.

The pair of them stifled their giggles and, with razors held aloft, threw their heads back to laugh silently towards the ceiling.

'Why are you in there with her, Michelle? What are you two up to? Can you open the door a sec, please, girls?' It was phrased as a question, but her stern manner and clipped tone left Bessie in no doubt that this was an instruction.

Michelle hitched her top lip and made a face towards the door. Bessie wanted to laugh again but felt the pull of loyalty. She grabbed the hand towel from the metal loop by the sink and held it to her shin before hobbling to the door and opening it.

'Hi, Mrs Worrall!' Still in her knickers, Michelle waved from her perch on the corner of the tub.

'Hello, dear. What *are* you doing, apart from ruining my hand towels?' She looked down. 'Have you been shaving your legs?' she asked a little curtly.

Bessie nodded and bit the inside of her cheek, embarrassed at her mum's tone.

'For the love of God, Bessie! I told you not to! You have fine down that's not noticeable and, once you've shaved it, it grows back thicker and then you *have* to get rid of it! Fancy doing that on your birthday, of all days,' she tutted.

Bessie couldn't figure out why it was worse to shave her legs on her birthday rather than on any other day.

'Remember your eyebrows?' Her mum glanced at Michelle, on whom Bessie knew her mother laid the blame for the whole famous eyebrow incident. 'You had lovely glossy brows, and now? Two thin little lines way up on your forehead, wispy spider's legs that you have to keep plucking and plucking – I wish you'd never started that! You'll regret it one day.'

She and Michelle exchanged a brief look; her mum clearly didn't understand fashion. They had both wanted the brows of Cyndi Lauper and not Brooke Shields.

'Stay there, don't drip blood on the carpet, and I'll go and see if we've got any plasters in the first-aid tin,' her mum sighed, and trotted off along the landing.

◆ ◆ ◆

The girls got dressed and made their way down the stairs. Michelle's shins, now enviably shiny and hairless, looked fabulous beneath her baggy rolled-up dungarees. Bessie's, on the other hand, not so much. She only gave her hems one roll, trying to hide the three round plasters that sat like traffic lights on her shin, permanently set to red from the seeping blood.

'We should wear jeans tonight with our new sweatshirts,' she declared, thinking that at least they might hide her injuries. Both she and Michelle had purchased hot-pink cropped sweatshirts from Chelsea Girl at the top of the high street only the day before, the result of months of saving, and vital to them matching for such an important social occasion as the party tonight.

'Yep. Good idea.'

After a big birthday squeeze from her dad and an excited smile of encouragement from her mum, the girls linked arms as they walked past the posh, newish estate off Branch Road and headed towards school.

'You nervous about seeing Lawrence tonight?'

'Nope.' This was the truth. 'I'm not, actually.'

Michelle looked at her with wide eyes. 'What, because you don't like him? Have you changed your mind?' she said quickly.

'Not exactly.' This felt easier than to confess that her nerves were minimal because she knew *exactly* what sex with Lawrence Paulson would be like.

The first time, it had been unplanned, spontaneous and fantastic. They had met by chance at the bus stop, both a little late finishing school, her because of volunteering to litter-pick, trying to curry favour with Miss Carter, who had organised it, and him because of football practice. It was only later that Bessie would swap the word *chance* for *fate*, thinking that this meeting had surely been written in the stars . . . They had sat on the bench chatting, the bus had come and gone, and they had flirted. He had kicked at her leg playfully, she had touched his hair with the excuse of restyling his fringe – and the next thing she knew, they were kissing frantically and he was pulling her body on to his. They had grabbed each other's hand and then, without too much planning or forethought, she had whispered into his ear, 'Come on!' and they had hurried to the alley that ran up the side of the school playing field, where she kicked off her pants and stood on the step to a garage, and they had done it. Quickly. And that was that. The virginity ship had sailed.

It wasn't romantic or chaste or gentle or loving or anything like she had imagined it might be. But then most of what she knew about sex was gleaned from reading *The Thorn Birds* under the covers with a torch or from the *Endless Love* video she and Michelle regularly rented from the petrol-station video shelf. In fact, it was *nothing* like she had imagined it might be. It had felt wonderful, exciting, exhilarating, and to see Lawrence's face in the throes of submission had made her feel nothing short of powerful. *Lawrence Paulson*, the good-looking boy who had made the football team, was a prize that made her feel less ordinary. He had chosen her – *her*! And she had chosen him. Familiar were the tales around the kitchen table of how her parents and grandparents had met, and their stories were truly non-eventful, and so why could her and Lawrence's love story not start at the bus stop? In the wee small hours, her mind leapt ahead and she saw him taking her little case from her hand after a trip and admiring her red suit – before welcoming her home with a cup of tea, open arms and a need for sex. The thought thrilled her.

What did make her nervous, however, was the fact that this was a secret from Michelle, the girl with whom she shared everything.

After leaving the alleyway, she and Lawrence had giggled and run back to the bus stop and she had felt changed in the subtlest of ways, having cast off the last vestige of childhood and taken control of a situation that she had at some level feared.

As the number seventy-two bus pulled into the stop, Lawrence had whispered in her ear, 'You're special, Bessie, and so cool. I think about you before I fall asleep.'

Bessie had thought her heart might burst through her chest. Her first thought was that she couldn't wait to tell Michelle. His wonderful admission had been almost as intoxicating as their physical act. Turning to him, she had beamed, and he had leant in with his end-of-day breath and the whiff of sweat clinging to his skin and said, 'We should keep this between ourselves. Let's not tell anyone.'

'No one?' she had questioned, wondering initially how she might keep such a thing from her friend.

'No one.' His eyes had bored into hers.

'Okay.'

They made a pact and it had given her the confidence to repeat the act eight more times over the coming months. And what was the harm, if no one was ever going to find out? She and Lawrence secretly passed notes; these too sent a frisson of joy through her core. The messages were always simple, scribbled in pencil on scraps of paper – *Tonight after school* or *Thursday at six*. No need to state a venue; Bessie knew where: the garage step in the alleyway, where they would meet, giggle, and she would hurriedly kick off her underwear. For the fleeting minutes of their union, nothing in the whole wide world existed . . . She could escape, free from all the small worries that sat in her mind like tiny thorns in her shoe: Would her mum drive her dad away with her nagging? Would Bessie ever feel as confident as a girl like Melanie Hall? Would an airline want to hire her? How could she make herself prettier?

She too now thought of him before she fell asleep each night, which meant actual sleep was delayed, as she tried in vain to tamp down the explosive bomb of excitement that bounced in her gut. To be liked in that way felt wonderful. A secret! That was what they had, and the fact it was a secret gave their liaisons a whole other heightened element of joy. It was a special thing indeed between the two of them.

Until she had experienced it, it was romance, not sex, that had filled her imaginings, but now she was hooked on its heady power. They kissed a lot, even though his breath was often a little eggy. She didn't care, not one bit! The kissing, which she used to think of as the end goal, was, she now realised, a mere stepping stone towards the main event, or an accompaniment like ketchup on chips. Sex – that fabulous, messy, hurried, clumsy contact – that was the real deal. Having sex with Lawrence had changed something inside her. She felt grown-up and confident. She felt . . . alive! And even though her mum had made her view on girls who had sex quite clear, and was even judgemental of her own sister, Bessie's Auntie Nerys, who had lots of boyfriends, who all looked remarkably similar and all seemed to work in the motor trade, she felt no shame – didn't understand even why she *should* feel shame! She looked up to Madonna, who oozed sex and was proud of it. The act between her and Lawrence was mutual and wonderful! Not that she quite felt confident or shameless enough to share the event with her mum, but if anything, she felt calm, knowing and liking the fact she had a glorious secret. After that first hurried coupling, Lawrence had treated her differently. They weren't going out, weren't official or anything like that, but she now noticed how instead of her trying to catch his eye across the playing field or at the bus stop, he sought her out, stared at her until she acknowledged him.

But the weight of withheld knowledge did not come without its price and it sat heavily upon her. It felt like a betrayal of her friendship with Michelle, but that was what she and Lawrence had agreed. It was like she was under a spell, intoxicated by the thought of him, and it was as surprising to her as it was scary that her loyalties could shift in this way.

'Well, I wouldn't mind if you had a change of heart,' Michelle now said, pulling her from her thoughts, 'and I don't want this to be weird.'

Bessie stopped walking and stared at her friend, swallowing the spike of guilt that was never far away and wondering what exactly Michelle might have found out. 'Don't be daft! Nothing could be weird – you're my best friend in the whole wide world ever, ever!'

Michelle twitched, as if not entirely reassured by her words. 'The thing is, Tony Dunlop told me something.' She paused and licked her top lip.

Bessie felt her heart leap. She didn't like Tony Dunlop, didn't like the way he looked at her and didn't like his little brown front tooth. She was particular about teeth. Tony was Lawrence's best friend and her gut flipped at the possibility that maybe Lawrence had told Tony about them meeting up for sex and maybe Tony had told Michelle! The very thought angered her on so many levels, namely that Lawrence had not kept his word of secrecy, but also that it was not Tony Dunlop's story to tell – it was hers.

'Well, I shouldn't believe a thing Tony says, he's full of shite.'

'Yeah, you're probably right.' Michelle linked arms with her as they walked slowly towards school.

41

'Well, you have to tell me now,' Bessie said with a nervous laugh. 'You can't start a conversation like that and not give me the punchline!'

'The thing is, I know Tony's full of shite, but . . .'

'But what?'

Michelle's voice changed, taking on a softness Bessie rarely heard from her friend. 'He . . . he told me that Lawrence fancied me.'

The words thumped Bessie's chest and smacked her in the face. She felt her heart jump and her face colour.

'Fancies *you*?' The quake of unease in her bones made her want to cry. *Why would Tony say something like that?* It wasn't true! It couldn't be!

'Yeah. Jesus, no need to sound so shocked – I'm not that unfanciable! Especially now I have such smooth shins.' Michelle's big eyes pleaded, and Bessie knew in that moment that her best friend wanted Tony's words to be the truth. It was one thing to joke around about both wanting to marry Simon Le Bon and each agreeing to be bridesmaid for whoever he asked first, but it was quite another when the boy in question was Lawrence. This was not in the least bit funny.

'I . . .' She didn't know where to begin, how to begin. 'I just . . .'

'I mean, don't worry! I haven't said anything to Lawrence, and I ignored Tony because I wanted to talk to you first, but there are things I want to say to you before anything happens . . .'

'What . . . what things?' Bessie was flustered and confused. Regardless of Michelle's doe-eyed response, the news from Tony was either bullshit and infuriating or true and upsetting, and until she knew which, her response was going to be measured, lest she give the game away.

Michelle squeezed her friend's arm so they were walking as close as could be, hip to hip. 'I wanted to say that I know we joke about Simon . . .'

Bessie laughed through her nose.

'And you know I would never do anything to hurt you, Bessie?' She nodded. This she did know. They were a team.

'But I kind of like him. In fact, more than kind of – I like him! I like Lawrence.' She bit her lip, clearly awaiting Bessie's response.

The words rang in her ears. How the hell was she supposed to answer that? What would Michelle say when she knew that her ship of dreams had sailed and that she, Bessie, and Lawrence were a couple in all but name and announcement – they had had sex nine times. *Nine times!*

'Here's the thing . . . we do need to talk,' Bessie said as the school building came into view. *I'll tell you the whole story on the way home. With more time and our results out of the way, I'll tell you the truth that Lawrence and I have been meeting for sex and it's fabulous. I really like sex! And the truth is, I really like him. I think we're very close to going official.* 'Can we pick up about it after we've got our results? It feels like too big a subject to rush here on the pavement.' She wanted more time, unsure of how to broach the subject or, more specifically, how to justify having kept it from her friend.

'Sure.'

A cloud of unease descended upon them. It was unknown, uncomfortable territory, this awkwardness with the girl she peed in front of, shared a bed with, chatted to until the early hours and did her darndest to look like. Such was the weight of the moment that she almost forgot they were about to walk into school and find out their exam results.

Michelle took her hand, and she was glad of it. A reminder that they as a duo were bigger than the fancying of any boy, stronger than the meddling words of Tony Dunlop.

'So what do you think, low hundreds?' Michelle asked.

'Fingers crossed.' Bessie chose not to divulge that she thought possibly inside a hundred – there were, after all, three hundred and

43

sixty-two pupils in the year and she figured she would likely make the top third. Good grades would mean a breeze for the next two years of school, acceptance into the sixth form, and her ticket, quite literally, to the skies . . .

'Let's do this!'

'Yes, let's do it!' She gave a small smile, tinged with relief. The two ran up the wide steps and into the old school hall, the room busy with all the drama she had anticipated. A couple of girls held each other's forearms in a fierce grip as they jumped and squealed, their side ponytails rising and sinking in unison. Monica and Verity – she might have guessed. Both were drama queens, the kind of girls who regularly cried hysterically and publicly as they stormed out of rooms and who were even now making way too much noise as they pogoed on the spot. Their antics only added to the already palpable tension. One or two of the nerdy kids, usually the ones in glasses, as if the world needed some outward sign to indicate their nerdiness, stood with their necks craned and spiral-bound notebooks resting on the wall as they scribbled down their grades. Standing behind him, Bessie glanced at the pad of Harrington Ainsworth – goodness only knew why he felt the need to write them down: Maths A, Advanced Maths A, Physics A, Chemistry A . . . and on it went until he had ripped through all thirteen of his subjects – *thirteen!* – and all with a shiny A grade. Harrington, with the best results in the year, had Oxford in his sights and, with this set of grades, within his grasp as well.

'You're here, Michelle!' Louise Berry called out, pointing, as she spotted Michelle's name just below hers. *Michelle Biggs.*

'Cheers!' Michelle smiled. Her hand slipped from Bessie's and she walked slowly up to the board, running her finger down the list.

How were she and Lawrence going to handle the situation? Bessie felt a little shiver of unease at the prospect.

'One hundred and seventy-two!' Michelle beamed back over her shoulder.

Not bad at all. Bessie gave her a double thumbs-up, pleased for her friend, who had come almost slap bang in the middle of the year in terms of results. She continued along the boards towards the W's, X's, Y's and Z's, with her heart beating louder with each step . . . This was it! Her eyes skimmed the list and she was drawn to the number three hundred and sixty-one. *Oh dear!* She cringed for whoever had done this badly.

There she was on the last page, as she had expected, thanks to her grandad's Yorkshire roots. 'Worrall,' she said aloud, knowing she was the only one in the year. Narrowing her gaze, her heart gave a little skip and her mouth felt dry.

'Well, that can't be right!' she whispered aloud.

She looked around to see clusters of pupils all studying the board. She stared at the line with her results and it was as if they became magnified. She had attained a handful of F's, a couple of U's, which meant 'ungraded', and the odd E, but it was the number that burned into her mind.

Three hundred and sixty-one.
Three hundred and sixty-one!!!!

'Are you actually fucking kidding me right now?' she yelled. 'No way!' All eyes turned to face her. She could feel their stares burning into her back, but it was too late to keep quiet now.

'Come on.' Michelle, suddenly by her side, put a hand on her lower back and steered her towards the exit.

'Bessie?' Louise Berry's shout echoed, and she turned slowly to see the smiling girl, staring at her with palms out and shoulders raised as if to say, *How did you do?* Louise was apparently the only person in the hall who had not heard the fiasco at the other end of the noticeboard.

Well . . . I won't be coming back to attend the sixth form. I won't be doing A levels . . . These facts lodged in her throat like sharp sticks. *I'm stupid! I'm as stupid as my teachers and brother think I am! How can I apply to airlines without a single decent grade? What am I supposed to do now?* She blinked at Louise and watched the girl's smile fade; Bessie's expression was apparently enough to convey all she was struggling to contain.

On shaking legs and with Michelle navigating through the crowds, steering her, they walked the length of the hall. The entrance seemed to move further away with every faltering step and the door got smaller and smaller.

'All right there, Bessie?'

She turned to see Melanie Hall and her crew all huddled with their hands in or around their mouths, chewing nails, stifling giggles or whispering. Her face burned hot with shame and she again felt the sting of tears at the back of her nose and throat.

'I heard MENSA were trying to get hold of you!' Melanie called, and her mates laughed, as Bessie picked up the pace and walked as quickly as she could with Michelle towards daylight and fresh air. They came to a stop in the foyer beyond the school hall.

'Are you okay?' her friend asked, bending to peer into her eyes, like a mum checking on a sick child.

'I don't . . . I thought . . .' she managed.

With whoops of joy and congratulatory chants ringing in their ears, Michelle led her down the shallow steps and out on to the parking apron at the front of the school. Even here, friends were hugging each other before running in the direction of home to share their success, while others jumped into waiting cars, where parents sat with engines ticking over before enveloping their offspring in tight hugs of delight. Everyone seemed to be screaming with happiness. The noise was loud in her ears and the air thick with an oppressive energy. She looked at the eager faces of her peers, all keen to announce the grades that would mean a ticket out of here – the first step towards making their dreams come true.

A ticket she did not possess because she was simply not as smart as she had thought.

Bessie's confidence was haemorrhaging from her. Of course, there might be a way to get the grades, resit the exams possibly, but it was more than that – Bessie had thought she was clever and capable of travelling the world . . . but her results had brought her to an abrupt halt and made her think otherwise.

Michelle put an arm around her shoulder. 'So come on, what did you get? It can't have been that bad, Bessie.'

Bessie shook her head, tears stuck like a plug of salt at the back of her nose and throat.

'I got . . .' She couldn't say it. 'I did crap . . . I messed up . . . I . . .'

I had a head full of Lawrence. I haven't studied properly for a couple of months – more interested in meeting him in the alleyway . . . I found it hard to concentrate . . .

'Whatever you got, it doesn't matter, not really. None of it does!' Michelle applied the same kindly logic that Bessie had earlier when her friend had asked about her birthday gifts.

Bessie gave a wry smile. 'And you did okay, one hundred and seventy-two?' She didn't really want to hear, knowing it would be another knife to swallow, but wanted to support her best friend.

'Good enough, yeah.' Michelle kept it vague, looking now at the grey paving slabs, warmed by the sun, anywhere but Bessie's face. The small smile at the corner of her mouth and the sparkle to her eyes told Bessie she had done more than good enough. And she guessed at a handful of B's and C's. One hundred and seventy-two . . . What wouldn't she give right now for one hundred and seventy-two?

'Come on.' Michelle tried to pick up the mood with her perky tone. 'Let's go via my house so I can tell my mum and dad, and then we'll go to yours and—'

'Actually, Michelle,' she interrupted her friend, 'I . . . I think I just want to go home on my own.'

'Oh . . .' Michelle nodded. This never, ever happened; they never *chose* to be apart. 'Okay, of course! Well, I'll come over later and we can get ready for the rugby club. I think the whole year's going! And I'll bring m—'

'Can I just meet you there?' Bessie knew at that moment that what she wanted – needed – was as much time alone today as she could manage, to try to think things through, wash away the sticky sense of failure and embarrassment that coated her skin, order her racing thoughts. She needed to clear her head, come up with Plan B.

'Oh, sure . . . If that's what you want.' There was a crease of confusion at the top of Michelle's nose, as if she were struggling to fathom quite what was happening. She stepped forward and wrapped Bessie in a loose hug that felt a little unfamiliar, as if someone had placed a thin veneer between them. Their touch was muted, a little cooler than they were used to and, for the first time ever, verging on awkward. It didn't feel nice at all and only added to the unease that suddenly enveloped them both.

The two girls went their separate ways at the school gates. Bessie looked back over her shoulder and watched her friend speed up, eager to get home, no doubt, to knock on the caravan door and shout, 'I did it!', while she did the opposite, slowing her pace, uncaring if it took all day before she had to tell her parents and her smart brother of her failure. Her tears came at last and she rubbed at her eyes.

Looking down, she saw bright smudges of eyeshadow and dark streaks of kohl on her fingertips; no doubt it was all over her face.

How stupid she felt, wanting to look nice when it was the last thing anyone would remember about her today. Gary Bradshaw, who lived at the bottom of her road, whizzed past her on his bike, heading in the direction of home. The sound of Melanie Hall snickering behind her rang in her ears and as Bessie came to the roadworks on the corner, she stared at the big hole the workmen had dug and thought for a minute how nice it might be to jump right in and never come out.

CHAPTER FOUR

August 20th 2021

It wasn't that Bess wanted birthday fireworks or anything of the sort, not at her age, but for Mario not to have a card ready was disappointing. Duck or not. When they were younger, he used to regularly leave cards and notes for her to find, sometimes just a postcard with a heart on it, others crammed with tiny writing: long, descriptive, effusive ramblings of what she meant to him and how very, very thankful he was that she was his wife. They had made her feel nice. Safe. It had been some years now since a card of that nature had been left under her pillow or propped up against the kettle. She sat on the sofa with her legs tucked beneath her and Chutney illegally by her side. Sipping at coffee that had cooled to the point of unpleasant – although at this hour, caffeine was caffeine – she felt a small bite of resentment that was hard to explain.

An irritatingly catchy tune came through the TV. How this advert grated on her nerves: '*For all your skip-hire needs, call P . . .*' She pressed mute and rubbed at the twitch beneath her left eye. The sound of her husband thudding around in the bathroom overhead caused her to look up and sigh. He was *so* noisy. The ceiling light in the lounge shook as he slammed the shower screen door, as he did every morning.

'For the love of God!' she whispered under her breath. She took in the empty mug, folded newspaper and discarded crisp packet down by the side of Mario's chair. There was a loud rap on the front door. She opened it to find Jim the postman standing on the step with his heavy bag slung across his body. It was unusual for him to knock. Ordinarily whatever he had to deliver was small enough and flat enough to plop through the letterbox without further interaction. She greeted him with a smile. Her mum liked to remind her that in an emergency it was good to be able to call out to someone like the postman. Although, in fairness, Bess was hard pushed to think of an emergency in which Jim would shine, plus the chances of him being at the end of the driveway in such an event seemed slim.

'Someone's popular!' the postman said cheerily, waving a fan of pastel envelopes in her direction.

'Morning, Jim. It's my birthday.' Bess rolled her eyes, hoping to convey how over the whole birthday thing she was and how it was more than a little embarrassing to be discussing it. She was conflicted, partly of the opinion that anyone over the age of twenty-one should simply and quietly acknowledge the day if they felt so inclined and move on without all the fuss, shenanigans and expense that a birthday incurred – save a decent card from their other half, which should at all costs exclude ducks. Nonetheless, she was keen to see all her lovely social media messages, which cost nothing, but showed the world that she was loved.

'Twenty-one again, is it?' Jim gave the throaty laugh that irritated her as much now as it had done for the last seventeen years. And yet, weirdly, she liked their interactions – it always broke up her day and made her feel part of the community.

Bess didn't mix too often with her eclectic bunch of neighbours. It wasn't their fault per se, but she just found it easier to keep herself to herself, uncertain of what she could possibly contribute to any gathering or whether she had anything of interest to say. Not that she was averse to peering at them through the haphazardly fitted slatted wooden blind at the bedroom window. These observations could brighten up the dullest of mornings, especially if she got a glimpse of the handsome Mr Andrew Maxwell, who was tanned, slim and had very good teeth.

The Maxwells' Christmas drinks party was an insufferable annual affair where neighbours who pretty much ignored each other all year round, save a nod and a wave on bin day, were herded together and fed morsels of food, while Mrs Helen Maxwell told you exactly what was in them and how she had made them, like anyone cared. To get through it, Bess either ate and ate or bit the inside of her cheek to stop from yelling, 'Sweet Lord above, woman! No one – and I mean *no one* – cares that you added a pinch of cayenne and let the pastry rest for forty-five minutes! Do what we do: go to Asda! Buy the bloody things!'

But, of course, she didn't. Instead she nodded and smiled through her mouthful, dreaming of getting home, when she could ping off her bra, which was cutting into her left shoulder, and kick off her silver sparkly-heeled sandals, snatched from the shelves of TK Maxx at such a ridiculously reduced price that the fact they didn't quite fit was secondary, even if it meant her little toes were alternately numb and then throbbing. And all the while, with Simon and Garfunkel duetting in the background, Mr Maxwell padded across the soft carpet, pouring wine, decanted into a carafe, while explaining the grape profile and soil mineral content, as the bewildered residents of Larkspur Close nodded and sipped the chilled white, as if they could discern any difference between the wine Mr Maxwell described with its heady bouquet and rich oaky notes and the cheap plonk they bought by the boxful from the petrol station up the road for a little under five quid. Mario detested the evening as much, if not more, than she did, and she had to stand and smile, trying to paint the affair with a happy gloss, just to make it bearable.

Last year had been particularly memorable because, as she was tapping her watch face across the room, an indicator to Mario that she was ready to jump ship, Mr Maxwell suddenly stood very close to her, so close that she could smell his grassy cologne. He breathed down her neck, whispering, 'Please call me Andrew.' That was weird in itself, as they weren't even talking, but what came next was even weirder. 'Tonight, Bess' – he paused, as if making sure he had her full attention – 'you look absolutely fanfuckingtastic!'

Her breath came quickly and her heart raced. She turned to face him, their eyes locking briefly while a smile played about his mouth, his lips parted to reveal his beautiful teeth. He leant closer to her and she thought for one horrific moment that he might kiss her! Right there in the lounge within feet of Mr Draper! When he pulled back, she felt a strange and intoxicating mixture of relief and disappointment.

'You know Helen and I have an open marriage?' He was barely audible.

This she did *not* know and said the first thing that popped into her head, which was, 'Well, it takes all sorts, I suppose!' before marching forward to grab Mario by the arm and quickly saying their goodbyes. The strange thing was, no matter that she thought of Mr Maxwell as a pompous dick, there was a power in his wine-scented admission that sent a frisson of something uncomfortably like desire through her very core. She had forgotten what that felt like.

She kept this to herself, of course. She and Mario had walked back to their house, arm in arm and giggling, chiming, 'Thank God that's it for another year!'

They had slipped into bed to make love without locking up properly, cleaning their teeth or even making a fuss of Chutney. It had felt illicit, spontaneous and lovely, yet today it seemed an age ago. Once more the lump rose in her throat, as she thought sadly how she and her husband seemed to have slipped off course, left clinging to the wreckage – caring little that they might be heading in different directions and just grateful that their heads were still somehow above water.

'I was saying, Mrs T – twenty-one again?' Jim enunciated, staring at her intently, and she wondered how long she had stood in front of him, daydreaming.

'Yep, something like that.' She gave a forced smile.

'Ah, many happy returns. How old are you?'

'Most people don't ask that.'

'Well, I think it's a lot like singing.'

'How d'you mean?' She shook her head, trying to keep up.

'You know, when you're a kid you sing loudly and wherever the fancy takes you because singing makes you feel good, opens your lungs, fills your heart, lifts your spirit!' He leant back, opened his eyes wide and gazed towards the heavens, and just for a minute she thought he might actually burst into song and was overly thankful when he didn't. His words had reminded her of that exact same feeling, the memory of waking with joy in her breast and energy in her limbs, ready to face the day and happy to be lying next to Mario.

Straightening, he smiled at her.

'Think about it, Mrs T. You see a baby or a child or a teenager, and you ask, "How old?" We shout from the rooftops, "Happy sixteenth! Happy twenty-first!" We celebrate how many months or years someone has been on the planet, announce it all over social media, write it on banners. And for the life of me, I can't figure out the age we're not supposed to ask any more. When does it go from being polite and showing interest and quite rightly a celebration to something shrouded in mystery as you approach the decaying years . . . ?'

'Fifty-three, Jim,' she said to cut him short. 'That age is fifty-three.'

'Well, blow me down! All this time I have wondered, and you had the answer all along. Fifty-three.' He shook his head and looked up again, as if she had enlightened him. 'You don't look too happy, considering it's your special day.'

She leant on the doorframe and ogled the envelopes in his hand. 'You know, I'm not too happy about it. I mean, I get feeling excited when you're six, if it means cake at school and a party, and when you're nine, of course, and about to go into double figures, but when you've got more years behind you than ahead' – she pulled a face – 'what is there to celebrate? Another couple of decades before I start properly losing my marbles, my remaining looks and my continence?'

I'm running out of time . . . I will never have the job of my dreams and take to the air like lucky Daniel . . . Gone is the prospect of great sex with someone who is yet to discover me and who in turn will help me discover myself . . . I'm running out of time to make amends . . . And with each year my kids slip further from my reach . . . falling into the arms of their life partners, who they put before me, and I know that's how it should be, but I find it hard to be happy about it . . . because it leaves Mario and me on our own.

'Wow, you're even starting to make me wonder what's to celebrate!' Jim kicked his steel-toe-capped regulation boot under the lip of the step in her porch.

'The thing is, Jim, everyone tells me that each year is a blessing, and sometimes I agree, but on other days I want to ask why. Why is getting older in an already over-populated world a blessing? Have you been to those old people's homes? Good God, they are bloody awful! Rows and rows of plastic-covered chairs, crammed

55

with people waiting for death. Wrinkly and stooped, supping on mashed food seasoned with regret. Gratefully drinking tepid milky tea with third-rate TV programmes on too loudly in the background and the smell of urine and lavender in the air – why would I look forward to that?' She was aware this was probably more analysis than her friendly postman had bargained for, but once she had started it was hard to stop.

'I don't . . . I don't know.' He let out a deep sigh, seemingly at a loss for a more satisfactory response.

'No, Jim, I don't know either. I read once about an artist who, when she felt her life was slipping from brilliant to rubbish, went to live in Florida in an out-of-town community for senior citizens, with a big gate to keep out the riff-raff. She lived in a pink bungalow behind a low fence, and if so much as a bulb blew, a little man in coveralls came along to fix it. Easy living. As if that wasn't fabulous enough, she drank wine with every meal, including breakfast, and had champagne on Saturday nights and gin on a Sunday. She sat in the sun crisping her skin and swam naked in the communal pool. I mean, I wouldn't mind getting old if I could be like her and live like that. But the thought of another thirty years in Larkspur Close?' She looked up and down the cul de sac, which was now coming to life, with curtains being drawn, car engines starting, and bikes being lifted from the back shed. Kids could be heard bickering and at least one dog was barking for its breakfast or commenting on Brexit – it was hard to tell from this distance.

'Well, I hope she's happy in her little bungalow,' Jim said, staring at her. 'I don't drink, so . . .'

'Probably not for you then, Jim.'

'Probably not.' He sniffed. 'D'you know, I felt quite happy until I knocked on your door.'

'Oh, that's my particular talent. My daughter calls me the funsucker, my husband the joy hoover and apparently I even upset the dog.' She gave a small laugh to counter the possibility of giving in to the tears gathering at the back of her throat. Bess did not want to be that person who pulled joy from the room.

Jim laughed. 'We're all allowed off days.'

'I guess.' She gave a wry smile, deciding not to share that she had more off days than on at the moment, and happy to have made him laugh and maybe restored a little of the ease with life he had felt before knocking on her door.

She wanted nothing more than to close the front door and make her third coffee of the day, but Jim stayed put, looking back down the street as if he wanted to say something. Embarrassment ticked in her veins.

'You know I think you *should* enjoy your birthday, Mrs T, and I think you should treasure every day. My wife . . .' He swallowed. 'My wife passed away at forty-two, and I swear—' He shook his head. 'I would give anything – anything – to be handing her a birthday card each year, marking the time that I got to spend with her, and if she had lived to be a hundred it wouldn't have been enough. She was my world, you see.'

'Oh, Jim . . .' There was a thump of guilt in her stomach – what right did she have to feel low? 'You always seem so . . .'

'Happy? Joyful?' he sniffed. 'What's the alternative, Mrs T?'

'I guess you're right.' The words were easy, but her sadness seemed to sneak up and catch her unawares.

'I *am* right, and if losing her has taught me one thing, it's that you need to value every single day.' He handed her the bundle of cards. 'Happy birthday.'

'Thank you.' Bess's gaze danced over the postmarks. 'I think she was very lucky, Jim, your wife, to have someone who felt that way about her and who misses her so.'

'Oh no.' Jim wiped his face and coughed. 'It was me that was the lucky one. She was absolutely smashing.'

His words, so sincerely offered, took her breath away, and she was almost jealous of this woman who had lost her life so young.

Out on the street again, Jim called out a cheery 'Morning, guv'nor!' to whichever neighbour he had spotted next. Closing the door, Bess felt a jolt of affection for this man, who seemingly made it his mission to brighten everyone's day.

Mario jogged down the stairs in his pants and long-sleeved T-shirt, with his zip-up top in his hand. 'Have you washed my work trousers?' he asked.

She looked up at him and blinked. 'Do you think I'm smashing, Mario?'

'What?'

'Do you think I'm smashing?'

'Smashing?' He narrowed his lips and seemed to consider this. 'I think we have a lot of smashing history. A lot of smashing memories.' He made his way to the kitchen and the back of the kitchen chair, where his washed and dried work trousers awaited.

'But it's not the same, is it?' She followed and watched him wrestle with the bulky bottoms with the padded knees that made plastering in cold empty houses a little kinder on his body.

'No, it's not the same, Bess.' He held her gaze briefly before looking away, a little embarrassed, as if aware of the impact of his response. And while not a surprise to hear, her heart nevertheless sank at the confirmation. 'But there we are. See you tonight. I'll go to the chip shop after work. Shall I call you when I get there to see who wants what?'

'No, Mario, it's easier if I text you with who's here and what everyone wants, surely?'

'Yep, surely.' He gave the hint of a smile, which disappeared as quickly as it had flashed. 'Enjoy your birthday, Bess.' He held her gaze for a moment before grabbing his flask and sandwich box from the kitchen table.

'I will, and maybe my card might turn up!'

'Maybe it will,' he said, without looking back.

'Do you have cash?' she asked. 'They don't take cards at the chippy.'

Mario shut the front door with a little more force than she thought seemed necessary.

'Well, Chuts, just you and me then.' She looked down at the dog and was sure she saw him sigh.

CHAPTER FIVE

August 20th 1984

Bessie stood at the end of the road, trying to plan what and how she would tell her parents about her dire performance. It sounded so alien in her head she couldn't even practise it. Fierce nerves raged inside her; she felt sick and her legs, plasters and all, were like jelly. The situation wasn't helped by the fact that Philip had done very well in his O levels only the year before, gaining a clutch of A grades and a very impressive forty-seven in the year ranking.

Three hundred and sixty-one.

Three hundred and sixty-bloody-one!

She walked past Gary Bradshaw's house, where his bike now lay abandoned on the front path, and heard his dad yelling, 'Bloody brilliant! Moira! Moira! He's only gone and done it! Wahey! That's my boy!'

The sound of Mr Bradshaw's celebrations only added to the sinking, hollow feeling in her stomach. She thought she might actually throw up.

Drawing close to home, she caught sight of the very large home-made banner strung across the front door:

Congratulaytions!

It was a funny thing, but pre-exam results, she would have asserted with self-assurance that this was not how you spelled CONGRATULATIONS, but now? With her confidence tank entirely drained, she wasn't sure she was right and would not say a word for fear of being wrong.

The banner was edged with crudely drawn hearts and flowers – no doubt the handiwork of Judith, Mrs Hicks's young granddaughter, who liked to hang around. The sight of it made her heart and spirits sink even further, if that was possible – with absolutely nothing to be congratulated on, and suddenly aware of just how many people she had let down. She wanted to tear it down and rip it into a million pieces.

Before she had the chance to fish for her key in the front pocket of her dungarees, the door was flung open and the smiling, expectant faces of her parents greeted her. Her dad had the harmonica in his hand.

Oh, please God, no!

Her prayer fell on deaf ears as her dad brought the instrument to his lips and began to toot out an almost passable version of Cliff Richard's Eurovision-winning ditty while her mum did her best to sing along, including a false start.

'Con . . . congratulations, and celebrations . . . doo-doo doo!' Stepping from foot to foot, her mum waved her hands in a crappy dance.

Bessie looked down and shook her head as her tears broke their banks.

Her mum stopped singing. 'Shut up, Eddie!' She elbowed her husband, who stopped playing abruptly, and stared at him as if he were all alone in his musical endeavours and she were not the driving force behind the whole welcome idea.

'You can't cry on your birthday!' Her mum's words only made Bessie cry harder. She had completely forgotten it was her birthday.

'What's the matter, love?'

For the love of God – what do you think might be the matter? I've just got my results and they're shit! But she pulled herself together enough to talk softly and slowly, with a veneer of calm, other than the odd gulping breath.

'I messed up, Mum,' she said, shaking her head. 'I messed up really badly.'

'Oh, come on inside, love. I bet you haven't! It'll all be okay. No need for tears.'

Bessie stepped over the threshold, and as she saw the three round plasters on her shin, they reminded her of Michelle's words earlier and another layer of worry now settled in her gut – Michelle liked Liquorice Popcorn? How had that happened? Michelle knew how she felt about him and now she would have to come clean about the whole sex thing *and* have to deal with the fallout of her friend's confession . . . on her birthday. It was all a bit much and she slumped down in one of the chairs at the kitchen table with her head in her hands. Her elbow stuck to a lurking residue of gluey lemon juice, a reminder of the pancake fiasco of earlier. No good day started with bad pancakes, not even a birthday.

Her dad sat opposite her, while her mum hovered awkwardly behind, leaning on the work surface.

'No one cares about exams, not really! There's plenty of people who've succeeded without exams,' her lovely dad piped up, 'and as your mum says, they can't have been that bad!'

'So come on, Bessie, just tell us what you got?' Her mum bit her bottom lip and gripped the sink behind her, as if bracing herself for the news.

Bessie coughed, her voice quiet, entirely different from when she had yelled upon waking to let everyone know it was her birthday.

'I failed nearly everything – I got ungraded on most subjects and then a couple of E's.' She folded her hands into her lap and her shoulders drooped.

Her parents stared at her with their mouths slightly open, seemingly at a loss as to what to say. She quite understood – *she* was at a loss as to what to say, what to do . . .

'What exactly does "ungraded" mean?' her mum asked, with her hand at her throat. Of course, she didn't know. Her only experience of O level exams to date was with Philip, who would never have used the word – why would he, with his clutch of A's and a shiny gold star for every piece of work he had ever handed in? Having to explain only added to Bessie's mortification, cloaking her in a veil of stupidity that her results only confirmed.

'It means I failed so badly they couldn't even give me an E or an F, so they gave me a U for no grade at all, which is worse than not turning up, because at least if I hadn't turned up I could use that as an excuse, but to have sat the exam and got U is . . . it's horrible.'

'What did you get for maths?' her dad asked, with a nervous twinkle in his eye.

'Ungraded.' She noted his efforts to keep his smile in place, but under duress and with his eyes watering a little, it looked more like a grimace.

'So how did you do in English?' Her mum held her breath.

'Ungraded.'

Her mum nodded and her mouth moved, as if she had plenty to say, although no actual words came out.

'Biology?' her dad ventured, his expression pained.

'Ungraded.'

She watched her parents exchange a hurried, horrified look before beaming back at her.

'Home Economics?' Her mum stared, wide-eyed and intense, as if her encouragement could nudge the grade up a place or two.

'I got a D.'

'Oh marvellous!' her mum smiled, exhaling with obvious relief.

'Well done! You love to cook!' her dad chimed.

She did?

'You could become a chef!' her mum said, clapping her hands. 'We need to celebrate – you could be the next Delia Smith!'

'Who could be the next Delia Smith?' Philip asked as he sauntered into the kitchen. His chest was still bare but he had put on pyjama bottoms. Thankfully.

'Your sister!' Her dad pointed at her, lest there be any doubt as to whom he was referring. 'She's a smashing little cook!'

Philip snorted his laughter and reached into the carousel cupboard in the corner to grab a mint Club from the Tupperware box where the snacks lived.

'Are you joking? She can just about manage beans on toast. I don't think Delia should be fearful for her crown,' Philip scoffed.

'You never know!' Her mum gave her brother a hard stare, to which he was oblivious as he peeled the foiled paper from his biscuit.

'So how did you do?' he asked, standing alongside their mum. 'Where did you come in the year? What's your number?'

All three stared at her as the dastardly digits danced on her tongue and gummed up her mouth.

'Philip, I am literally one of the most stupid people in the year!' she yelled.

'Surely not – come on, what's your number?'

'Three hundred and sixty-one,' she whispered, staring at the bitten fingernails on her stubby fingers, which had left a sweaty print on the tabletop.

'Ha!' Philip shook his head, so his long fringe fell over his face. He flicked it back and deposited the rest of the Club sideways in his mouth. Everyone was too distracted to comment that his biscuit was covered with a thin coating of chocolate made predominantly from cow juice. 'Good one! But really' – he straightened, lifting his chin and speaking through his mouthful – 'where did you come?'

This time she looked her brother straight in the eye.

'I came three hundred and sixty-first out of three hundred and sixty-two. I came second last in the whole year. That means only one person did worse than me. Happy now?' She felt the slip of fresh tears on her cheeks. She knew it didn't matter how many times she had to repeat the number; the shame of her ranking would not lessen. Not ever.

'Oh my God! You *literally* weren't joking.' He stared at her. 'How the fuck did that happen?' Philip, seemingly unmoved by her tears, asked the question that the lack of response from her parents at their son's swearing told her they were desperate to ask also.

She swallowed and took a deep breath, wiping her eyes with the back of her hand.

'I thought I'd revised enough. I did read all the books.' *But then I kind of got distracted. This boy I like fills my head!*

'Did you make notes?' he asked.

'Sometimes,' she confessed. 'I thought I could remember most of it.'

'And did you?' her mum joined in.

'I'd say not, Mother.' Philip rolled his eyes in his mum's direction and swallowed the last of his snack.

'I remembered *some* of it,' she explained, 'and if I didn't fully understand the question or felt flustered, I just wrote down all the things I did remember – quotes, anything! I wrote pages and pages and pages.' Her bottom lip quivered at the memory of her post-exam hand ache.

'But that's the thing, Bessie, you can write a whole essay on Greek mythology, reams and reams of it, word perfect, but if the subject is Chemistry, then it won't get you very far.' Her brother's tone was surprisingly conciliatory, and she was grateful for it. 'Being smart and passing exams are two completely different things.'

'There you go!' their dad smiled. 'Philip knows about these things!'

Of course, he does. Mr Forty-Seven.

She shook her head. 'I don't feel very smart.' She wiped her tears; her breath lost its rhythm and stuttered in her throat. 'They won't let me go into the sixth form; they have a minimum requirement and I am way off.'

'I'm sure we can sort something out – don't you worry about that,' her mum asserted, going into solution mode. 'Daddy or I will talk to Miss Carter.'

'Bessie's right, I'm afraid, Mum,' Philip said slowly and calmly. 'They don't have enough spaces in the sixth form for everyone, and it's how they weed out the numbers. Plus, the work at A level goes up such a gear that if you struggle at O level it might be too much to cope with, and that would just make Bessie's life miserable.'

'Miss Carter is calling me later,' Bessie sniffed.

'Well, see! All's not lost,' her dad chirped, as if he just wasn't listening.

'Michelle got in. Just.' The thought of her friend turning up in September for the first day of term without her only made her tears fall harder.

'You could go to college and repeat the year?' Philip suggested. 'The tech in town runs O level courses and you'd get to sit the exams again.'

Bessie shook her head. 'No way! I'm not going to the tech. I don't want to.' She raised her voice. The tech had a rubbish reputation and she couldn't stand the idea of joining their ranks, knowing the humour Melanie Hall and her gang would find in that. She would find a way, but not that way.

'It's okay, love,' her dad intervened, reaching across the table to take her sweaty hand into his. 'No one is going to make you do anything. You have a lot of options.'

'I do?' She so wanted to believe him.

'Sure you do.'

The telephone rang in the hallway and Philip sprinted to answer it. Bessie might be a proper thicko, but even she knew he was desperate as ever to hear from Carmen the vegan.

'Just a sec,' she heard him say before he raced back into the kitchen. 'Bessie! It's Miss Carter.'

'There now, what did I tell you?' her mum said, as if she were a baby, and it drove her crazy. She resisted the urge to snap at her mum – it wasn't her fault she'd messed up.

Miss Carter was her form tutor and head of year and had always been an ally. Bessie sniffed and went to take the call.

'Hello?' She gripped the receiver and closed her eyes, while her stomach flipped with nerves heaped with embarrassment.

'Hi, Bessie, it's Miss Carter here. I wanted to check in and see how you're doing.'

'Not great.' Her voice was no more than a squeak.

'I guessed as much. I spoke to Mr Watts, who told me you were upset in the hall, and Miss Bartram saw you leave and said you looked a little pale. I wanted to grab you before you left, but got caught up in an exam appeal for one of the other students.'

'Do you think *I* can appeal?' Was this why Miss Carter was calling? Bessie had a brief image of herself and Michelle walking into the sixth-form centre together – in matching outfits, natch.

'Oh! No, lovey, I'm afraid not.' Miss Carter gave the smallest titter, a scythe to Bessie's already failing optimism. 'Appeals are made when a student feels a particular grade is unfair or challenges a decision regarding a piece of work, but it's usually based on past performance and, as I say, is usually just for *one* subject, where that single grade might make a difference, but with you . . .' She heard her teacher take a deep, slow breath. 'It's all of your grades that are challenging, so they wouldn't entertain an appeal.'

'I see.' Fresh tears slid down Bessie's face, washing away the image of her and Michelle.

'Exams are not where you shine, Bessie! I think part of the problem is your handwriting. I know all of your reports across all subjects talk about the need for improved legibility and penmanship' – she paused – 'but I guess there's no point in going over that now or picking your performance to pieces. I was really only calling to see how you were feeling and to say that it might seem like the end of the world right now . . .'

'It does,' Bessie interjected.

'But it won't always feel that way. You will move on, find your path, and this will be no more than a footnote to a lovely and successful life. You mustn't let it hold you back, Bessie.'

'Thank you, Miss.' She didn't know what else to say but tried to picture the school year pared down to a select clever few, an elite group of which she would not be a part . . . Philip was right – this was how they weeded out the numbers for a much reduced sixth form.

'Take care of yourself, Bessie.'

'You too, Miss Carter.' She put the phone down and sat on the stairs with her head in her hands. Her legs were shaking and a sick feeling swirled in her gut. What was she going to do? She thought about going to the tech, a drab, square red-brick building with a flat roof, where students, mainly dum-dums and boys training to be mechanics, gathered noisily on the steps. She hated even walking past, always looking the other way with a cloak of self-consciousness about her shoulders. She shuddered at the very idea of walking up the steps and into a class at the start of a new term and into a building full of people who were also there to repeat the year. But the fact was, this was where she actually belonged. Her results confirmed it. She wrapped her arms around her torso and thought she might actually throw up. What she wanted was for things to remain exactly the same and to be able to walk to school with Michelle each morning, chatting about stupid things, laughing about the inane and using their special code to talk about boys.

This thought was immediately followed by the memory of her friend's face looking at her with eyes wide, excited at the mere mention of the boy she liked. *Her* boy! Her breath came in fast bursts that left her a little light-headed and with the start of something close to panic building in her chest. She gripped the banister and slowed her breathing.

Come on, Bessie! Get a grip!

Okay, so what was the alternative to the tech? Maybe she should write to the airlines straight away? See if she could work her way up? It felt like the beginnings of Plan B and gave her the smallest lift.

'What did Miss Carter say?' Her mum's voice made her jump.

'She said I would feel better in time, or something like that.'

'And she's right!' Her mum gripped the banister.

'The thing is, Mum, I knew I hadn't sailed through the exams, they were hard, but I filled pages with answers, and I thought they'd at least be able to pick out some stuff that was worthy of marking.' She shook her head at her own naivety. 'That's what I thought.'

'You mustn't dwell on it, love.'

'It's hard not to. I thought I'd go into sixth form and then up in the air! But now what?' She looked up at her mum, who looked a little lost for answers.

'I guess you regroup and rethink and make a new plan.' She ran her hand over her daughter's pineapple ponytail. 'And Miss Carter's right – it'll all come out in the wash. You have options. There'll be another way to achieve your dreams.'

Bessie stared at the letterbox, knowing that, any day now, her results would plop on to the coconut welcome mat, written proof along with a stamped certificate that she was the second from last most stupid person in the school year – a fact that loomed large in her thoughts. The phone rang on her lap. She shoved it towards her mum, who grabbed the receiver. Bessie was in no mood to chat right now.

'Oh hello, Michelle, love – how did you do?'

Bessie buried her face briefly in her hands and felt the pull of tears. She could hear her friend's excited tones, if not the actual words, as Michelle catalogued her middle-of-the-road success to Mrs Worrall – a middle-of-the-road success that was way beyond Bessie.

'Well, that's marvellous! Well done you. I'll just pop Bessie on. Here she is.' Her mum held the phone out at arm's length and she took it reluctantly.

'Hi,' she said, her voice low.

'Just thought I'd give you a ring to see how you're doing.'

Peachy!

'M'okay,' she lied.

'You know, you weren't the only one, Bessie – lots of people didn't do so well.'

'Just don't, Michelle!' She couldn't stand to hear the words of consolation, knowing that there was in fact only one person in the whole year who had actually done worse than her. 'There's not much to say about it really.'

There was silence for a beat.

'Do you want me to come and knock for you later? We can walk to the rugby club together, or I could come earlier and we could . . .'

'No,' Bessie said, shaking her head. 'I don't even know if I'm going to go tonight.' The thought occurred as the words left her mouth.

'You must go!' her mum enthused, while at the same time Michelle said, 'You have to go! Everyone's going – we've been talking about it for weeks!'

'I just don't know if I'm in the mood,' she said to her friend, while looking at her mum.

'We can have a dance and it'll cheer you up. We can dance all night! And I've got some cigarettes. My brother gave them to me.'

'Mmm,' was the only way she could respond with her mum standing within earshot. 'Can you give us a minute, Mum?'

'Oh,' her mum laughed, as if unaware of the intrusion, ''course!' She tiptoed in an exaggerated fashion back to the kitchen. Bessie turned her full attention back to the phone call.

'I'll see how I feel nearer the time. I just don't think I can face anyone.'

'No one cares!' Michelle yelled. 'They're all busy dealing with their own shit. Honestly, Bessie, everyone has so much going on, and it's only a piece of paper, at the end of the day. My mum says exams are overrated, and look at my dad! He has loads of exams but that's not what stops him working – good exams can't make up for poor health and a bad back, can they?' Michelle gabbled, as she did when she was nervous or lying, as if trying to fill the air and avoid either questions or comment.

Bessie was only half listening. 'Did you hear Melanie say something mean as we left the hall?'

'So, what's new? Melanie always says something mean. That's why she's ugly even though she's beautiful. Ignore her!'

'And . . .' Bessie said, closing her eyes, not really knowing where to begin.

'And what?'

'We need to talk about Lawrence.'

'I know. I wish I hadn't said anything, Bessie. I could kick myself, I really could. Can we just forget about it?'

'No, it's good you raised it. So, when you say you like him, is this a new thing or . . . ?' It felt easier to broach the topic over the phone, where her friend was unable to read her expression – fraught with tension over what she was going to have to reveal.

'Not really. I've liked him for a while . . .' Michelle let this linger, 'but you seemed quite keen and so I didn't say anything and then we've kind of been smiling at each other a bit . . .'

'You and Lawrence?'

'Yes.' The confirmation made her heart boom.

'And so, when Tony told me he liked me,' Michelle continued, 'I wasn't that surprised because we've been quite flirty and stuff, but obviously I didn't want to do anything with him or say anything about it until I'd spoken to you. I didn't want to hurt your feelings.'

Bessie's jaw tensed with irritation that this conversation seemed necessary, but also in anticipation of Michelle's own feelings getting hurt when she knew the full story.

'I would never stand in your way with anyone you liked, especially if they liked you back . . .' Bessie started cautiously.

'Thank you, Bessie! I really hoped you'd say that! I'm so relieved – thank you.'

'No, but . . .'

The doorbell rang and her mum ran up the hallway to open up, wiping her hands on her pinny as she went. Nanny Pat and Grandad Norm stood smiling at her from the front step with a large bunch of flowers and a big, brightly wrapped gift. Bessie gripped the receiver; there was so much more she wanted to say.

'There she is!' her nan yelled.

'I've got to go, Michelle; my nan and grandad are here. Look, I'll meet you there, if I decide to go, I'll meet you outside.' *And then I can tell you all the reasons why you can't start seeing Lawrence and all the reasons I think you might be mistaken about his feelings for you, all nine of them.*

'Okay, see you later then, Bessie. Love you!'

'Love you.'

Replacing the phone in its holder on the small telephone table by the front door, Bessie stood still to receive the inevitable hugs from her grandparents, which always went on a fraction longer than she was comfortable with.

'What a day for our girl!' said her nan, who, at a little under five foot, grinned up at her. 'These flowers are for you.' She presented her with the pretty pink bouquet. 'A *proper* bunch of flowers from the florist on the high street, none of that rubbish from your grandad's garden, tied with a bit of old string.' She gave her husband a withering look, suggesting the topic had been under discussion, and Bessie noticed for the first time how her nan treated Grandad Norm in exactly the same way her own mum spoke to her dad.

'They're to say congratulations, darling, on your results.' Her grandad reached for her hand and squeezed it. 'And this,' he said, handing over the large, flat, wrapped box, 'is an extra birthday present. What a day!'

Bessie stared at the gift in one hand and the flowers in the other. Her sweet, loving grandparents had showered her in kindness, as they always had, and it was almost more than she could stand. The looks of adoration they fixed her with were certainly more than she deserved. This and the echo of Michelle's words swirled in her head as hot tears of wretchedness trickled down her face, dripping from her chin and falling in fat droplets on to her birthday present.

'Oh lovey! Whatever is the matter?' Her nan gripped her arm and stared up at her.

73

'She's had a bit of a day, Mum,' her own mum said, pulling a face and putting a finger to her lips, trying to covertly ask her mother to be quiet, jerking with her head towards the kitchen, where no doubt she would give her the full low-down.

'Did you not get your grades?' Her grandad was clearly not paying attention.

Bessie shook her head. 'I didn't get any grades. They were all absolute rubbish.'

'Well, you can't trust them people who do the marking! I think you need to get them re-marked. What do teachers know? They're rubbish, all of them! You're the cleverest girl I know.'

His blind support, blinkered by his love for her, only made her tears fall harder.

'Now, now,' her nan said, pulling her into her arms, 'don't cry, baby girl – you'll make your Monopoly board all soggy.'

'Brilliant, Pat, now you've told her it's Monopoly before she's even opened it!' Grandad Norm shook his head, disappointed.

And strangely, this was the thing that made Bessie laugh. It was her sixteenth birthday and her grandparents had bought her a new Monopoly set. No doubt the same one they had bought her for Christmas and for her birthday the year before last. She resolved to put it with the others in the bottom of her wardrobe.

'Thank you,' she managed through a giggle verging on hysteria.

'Atta girl!' Her mum breathed a big sigh of relief and Bessie wished she could do the same.

CHAPTER SIX

August 20th 2021

Bess put away the breakfast things, sprayed the surfaces with an antibacterial cleaner and wiped them down with a damp dishcloth. She did this on her day off – cleaned, wiped, plumped, fluffed, vacuumed and laundered, until she fell into bed exhausted and ready to go back to work the next day for a rest and a change of scenery. This morning she decided to tackle the chores with more of a spring in her step. Jim was right: she should try to celebrate the day!

Pulling on her rubber gloves, she knelt on the floor with her face pushed up against the toilet bowl and wiped round the back with her sponge, soaked in hot water and bleach, still amazed after thirty-odd years of marriage just how much wee Mario had managed to splash there in seven days.

'Oh Mario! Can't you control your pee-pee?' she had once asked him over the tea table.

'Control my pee-pee?' he had asked, his fork midway to his mouth, held still, as the minced beef and onion gravy dripped through the tines back on to the plate. 'What am I, six?'

'I don't know, Mario. Can six-year-olds control where they pee-pee?'

He had thrown the fork down and gone out in a huff, angered apparently by her comment, which was just too bad – it was her, not him, that had to face this most unpleasant task each Friday. With the bathroom sparkling, the bed stripped of linen, and the duvet cover, sheets and pillowcases tumbling inside the machine on a hot wash, she hummed along with the radio to Cher's dark tones declaring what she would do if she could turn back time . . .

'Ooh, if I could turn back time . . .' Bess sat down at the kitchen table and took a sip of her third cup of coffee of the day and thought about it. 'I'd revise for those bloody exams, become an air hostess and marry a pilot. And I'd live in one of those executive mock-Tudor numbers up on the highway, and I'd have a firepit in the back garden and an ornamental fountain in the front.' She ran her tongue over the broken tooth at the back of her mouth. 'And he'd probably drive me home from my private dentist appointment in his sports car, before ripping the clothes off me and taking me on the kitchen table.' She patted the top of the table at which she was sitting and noted the slight wobble to one of the legs. This table would need levelling before it could withstand any hanky-panky, that was for sure. She could just see her suggesting such a thing to Mario, who would probably ferret around trying to find a playing card or two to fold over and make up the wobble on the short leg before they could commence. And by the time the table was steady, they would undoubtedly have gone off the boil and would settle for a cup of tea and a couple of digestives instead.

Chutney, she was sure, rolled his eyes at her.

'Actually . . . Chutney, if I *could* turn back time . . .' She closed her eyes briefly, inhaling the scent of sandalwood that filled her nostrils as she blinked away her tears. 'If I could turn back time, I'd be braver – I'd *be* brave,' she corrected, 'at least I like to think I would. And I might not be able to change my past, but I know I need to change my future, because feeling this way, with so much bottled up, it doesn't do me any good and it doesn't do Mario any good, does it? I know it, but how do I begin? How do I go back and reclaim the person I was? How do I get back to that?' She bit her lip and wiped her eyes. 'Come on, Bess, not today.'

Her phone rang and made her jump. 'It's me! It's Mum!' her mother called into her ear, as if she were calling long distance and had to yell.

'Yes, Mum, I've told you a million times: when you call, I see your number and name pop up on my phone, so I know it's you before you even say a word!'

'Righty-ho. Well, just a minute, love.' There was the sound of fumbling and then her mother yelled, 'Eddie, she's on the phone! Come on – and don't forget your harmonica!' She came back to the phone. 'Your dad's just coming, love. Hang on!'

'I'm hanging!' Bess breathed slowly, waiting for the commencement of the dire tradition. Her mother then began to whisper, and it sounded like water sloshing in her ear. Bess had to screw up her eyes and concentrate to hear.

'I promised I wouldn't say happy birthday until he got here, but happy birthday, Bessie.'

'Thanks, Mum,' she whispered back, although God knows why – there was only Chutney to hear her.

'Right, here he comes. Come on, Eddie, for the love of God – she's *waiting*!' her mum yelled, with a tut at the end of the sentence that she reserved solely for talking to her husband. As usual, she placed the blame for any impatience solely at her daughter's door, as if, while her dad rummaged in his sock drawer to find his instrument, Bess had been whispering, 'I haven't got all day . . . Tell Dad to get a move on!'

'Hello, darling, it's Dad!'

For the love of God! 'Yes, hi, Dad!' She rubbed her forehead with her fingers and took a deep breath.

'Right, here we go!' her dad chuckled. 'This is the fifty-third time we've done this – hold on to your hat.'

Her mum counted them in. 'And two, three, four – happy birthday, darling!' they chorused.

'Thank you, both!' Bess put the phone on loudspeaker and sat back in the chair, listening as her dad warmed up with a couple of squeaky blows before starting properly on something that was vaguely recognisable as 'Happy Birthday'. Her mum warbled the words slowly and her dad did his best to keep up. They played and sang for approximately half a minute, which warmed her heart and made her smile. She loved them, her funny mum and dad, who had their eccentricities but who loved her and always had. That, in truth, had been part of the problem. They loved her that little bit too much. A little bit too much for her to shatter the veneer of perfection in which she was coated, believing it would break their hearts. How do you look someone who holds you in such high regard in the eye and watch their expressions as you tell them they have been living a lie, worshipping a false idol, have backed the wrong horse?

'Oh, that's lovely. Thank you,' she smiled, touched, as ever, by their efforts.

'We are so looking forward to our lunch!' her mum yelled. 'Your dad got a voucher from Philip in the post. Hang on, I'll go and grab it.' Her dad, now silent, was no doubt creeping back up the stairs to restore his harmonica to the sock drawer until Philip's birthday in three months' time, when it would be called upon again.

'No, that's okay, Mum – I don't need you to fetch the voucher!' Bess called, but too late. Her mum was gone for what seemed an age, so that when she eventually came back on the phone, Bess jumped, having started to daydream about straightening her hair.

'Hello, Bess, are you there?'

'Yes, Mum, I'm still here.' She swallowed her sigh of irritation, knowing she should be grateful to still have both of her parents and that there would come a day when they were no longer around to sing to her. She remembered Jim's words of earlier and smiled at the fact that her parents had never been embarrassed to launch into song. *Good for them!*

'Right, your dad got a voucher from Philip.'

'Yes, you said.'

'It's for a two-for-one main course or get one free pudding or something like that. We can use it at the carvery, as it's part of a chain now.'

'Oh, lovely.' Philip, who now ran his own estate agency in Knutsford, was rich and largely absent in their parents' lives. He did, however, send generous gifts, as if this could somehow make up for not having him there in person: a gas barbecue that was still in the box, a fancy foot spa, a garden lamppost yet to be wired up, and 'his and hers' down-filled coats for hiking. Bless him, it was as if he was buying for strangers, guessing what they might like and how they might live, and to a degree this was true. Bess knew that if she had all of Philip's money, she'd send her mum and dad on a celebrity cruise. They spoke often of their neighbour's experience. Mr and Mrs Franklin had gone to Madeira on a big boat and in the evening were entertained by Tony Christie. *The* Tony Christie! She could tell by her dad's wistful stare off-centre that he had visions of joining Tony onstage to accompany him with his harmonica to a rousing rendition of 'Is This the Way to Amarillo?' Mario liked to remind her that her brother was rich because he was mean. She tutted, knowing this was far from the truth, keen to defend her brother always. Always. Bess knew it wasn't meanness that made him keep his distance, but something more like self-preservation.

Philip had put up walls to stop the words his parents wanted to say from reaching him, words like: *we miss you; we love you; what did we do wrong?* And walls, she knew, kept words in that he did not want to reach them, like: *this is what happened; this is what we did; this is what I know; this is the secret we keep* . . . She avoided talking about it and thinking about it most of the time: this was *her* act of self-preservation. Not that she would swap lives with Philip, no matter how well off he was. He was married to the lipless Nanette, who liked to follow whatever sentence was spoken to her with the words 'Oh dear . . .', leaving you wondering whether what you thought was good news was, in fact, just 'news', or whether she might have misheard. Nanette also knew more about being lactose-intolerant than anyone else on the planet and liked nothing more than to talk about it. It was in fact Nanette's second-favourite response to most things.

'I have a headache.'

'You're probably lactose-intolerant.'

'I can't sleep.'

'Lactose-intolerant.'

'I've lost my car keys.'

'Lactose-intolerant.'

'Global warming, eh?'

'Lactose-intolerant . . .'

'Yes,' her mum now said, drawing her from her thoughts, 'Philip sent Dad this voucher. I'm holding it now. Oh, wait a minute, I'll just fetch my glasses.'

'No, Mum, I tell you what . . .' but it was too late. She was gone again . . . Bess leant forward and banged her head on the tabletop.

Eventually she managed to get off the phone and at last grabbed the neat bundle of envelopes Jim had handed her from on top of the microwave. *Six.* She counted. That wasn't bad for someone as old as her, remembering being a kid, when popularity was directly proportionate to the number of birthday cards you received. This in part was the reason her parents always had and still insisted on sending her a card each.

Bess ran her finger under the gummed flap of each envelope and read words of love, congratulation and best wishes in various forms from Jake and Daniel. One from the girls at work, including Sushmita, with whom she shared a birthday – she had of course signed Sushmita's card. There was also one from Philip and Nanette, while Auntie Nerys had sent her a home-made card, which was a bit rubbish, but at least she had tried. One from Mario's sister, Bianca, who she was surprised had stayed off online bingo long enough to actually mail a birthday card, and one from 'Shimmer Me Beautiful', the beauty parlour on the high street where she went twice annually for a mani/pedi. Once at the start of the summer so she could go barefoot without shame in her flip-flops, and once around Christmas time so she could wear the sparkly silver heels that damaged her little toes. Her beloved silver shoes lived on the top shelf of her wardrobe in front of the old cardboard box; again she smelled sandalwood . . .

'Ah, lovely.' She studied the candy-pink cards studded with glitter and flowers. All, that was, apart from Bianca's card, which was nothing of the sort and had the words 'YOU'RE HOW F*CKING OLD????' emblazoned across the front. Bess tutted. It just wasn't funny! Who would think that a good choice of birthday card in this day and age? She decided to hide it behind Auntie Nerys's little creation on the mantelpiece, lest anyone should see it. Not that she wasn't grateful for any contact with Mario's family, whose parents had more or less disowned Jake when he came out as gay, declaring they would pray for him. Mario had been her hero on that day. She would never forget the way he had calmly put down his knife and fork and pushed his chair back from the table. Grabbing his parents' coats from the banister, he had literally shown them the door, and all before they had even finished their pudding.

'Jake doesn't need your prayers – he needs your support,' he had almost whispered.

'It's a sin, unnatural,' his mother had fired back, shuddering as she slipped her arms into her coat and his dad jangled the car keys, keen to get going.

'What I think is unnatural is not offering your grandchild unconditional love.'

Bess hadn't said a word, but had admired his quiet, calm conviction and *his* unconditional love. Her love for him had swelled that day and there had been many days like that, good days, where to be adrift with him on the tumultuous sea of life felt quite wonderful. But those days had grown fewer and fewer over the years and she had started to look back, wondering how far it was to swim to the shore and whether she could make it alone.

Settling back on the chair, and with three hours until she had agreed to meet her parents at the carvery, she opened Facebook and saw a banner crisscrossed with bunting and a message from the Facebook team wishing her a 'Happy Birthday!'

'Ah, that's nice,' she smiled, wondering how they knew.

Her eyes were drawn to a number of posts all cued up and awaiting her attention. Her heart soared and Bess realised in that second that she might not be six, but actually, popularity among her peers was still quite important.

'Look at that, Chutney – sixteen birthday messages!' she chortled. 'Not bad, eh?'

Bess clicked on one to open it and her face fell when she saw it was a message for Sushmita that she had been tagged in. This was in fact the case for over half of them, all with heartfelt 'love 'n' hugs' sent from her colleagues to Sushmita on her special day! It shouldn't have bothered her – she was a grown woman, after all – and yet it did, and pretty soon, she was plunged straight back into how she had felt in the school hall, like she just wasn't good enough.

She wondered if everyone had those moments from the past that stuck in the grooves of the brain and were there for perfect recall decades later. It might have been a surreptitious look you weren't supposed to see that pulled the plug on your confidence, or as in her case, a comment that took hold quickly, a tiny seed that germinated, taking root faster than she could reach for a mental scythe with which to fell it. A little moment that had shaped her in ways she hadn't realised until she was able to look back and see the track it left in her consciousness: a trail that grew deeper the more she mentally walked it, until it was carved for all eternity. And then something curious had happened – other thoughts, ideas and preconceptions became rooted in it until it filled her brain like a tree with branches and snaking, vine-covered tendrils over which all thought had to climb or navigate.

She drummed her fingers on the tabletop, deciding what to do. It was ridiculous to let a small thing like Sushmita's popularity spoil her birthday, but at the same time it smarted a little. She did a quick count in her mind, figuring she could ask her mum and dad to send her a birthday message on Facebook when they were at the carvery, and Natalie and Jake would do it anyway, most probably. Picking up her phone, she called Mario, who didn't answer. He was more than likely up a ladder or mixing plaster or had left his phone for safekeeping in the van or couldn't find it. Maybe it was stowed away with her elusive duck-themed birthday card? She decided not to leave him a message, a little embarrassed about leaving audio evidence of her neediness.

Craig always had his phone on him – Mario's boss had crossed the line from supervisor to friend some years ago. She could drop him a message to pass on to Mario.

Craig, could you please ask Mario to make contact ASAP. Thanks. Bess.

With that, she plugged her phone in to charge on the kitchen work surface, fed Chutney a dog biscuit and went upstairs to run a deep bath. Bess shaved her legs, whipping the little razor over her shins with expertise before reaching for the shampoo and then the conditioner, with which she was extravagant. Well, it was her birthday. Lying back in the bubbles, she thought of what she might eat at the carvery. Images of tender slices of pork with crispy crackling and soft cuts of lamb slathered with rich, dark gravy filled her mind, and both of course accompanied with golden, crispy roast potatoes on which she'd be generous with the salt. With the flat of her palm she ran her hand over the bulge of fat that sat on her tummy. 'Baby weight,' she used to say. It was starting to wear thin now that those babies were twenty-six and twenty-eight. She decided she would forgo pudding, especially as she and Mario were having fish and chips that night. That was, of course, unless it was apple pie and custard, as that could not be resisted and would definitely be the first choice for her last meal on the planet—

A bang sounded downstairs and, just before her heart actually exploded with fear, she heard Mario's voice.

'Bess!' His yell was urgent and sent another bolt of fear right through her gut. 'Bess?'

'Yes, up here in the bath!'

Oh my God, what's happened? What's happened? Jumping up, she sent a wave of soapy water over the back end of the tub, which would no doubt at some point find its way on to the kitchen ceiling. Mario sounded desperate, and terrible thoughts swirled in her mind: *Please not the kids! No, no, no! Please not Jake travelling home from Scotland, and please not Natalie, rushing from the gym to home, as she always does, with those bloody earphones in and her eyes on a phone screen . . . How many times have I told her: concentrate when you cross the road! Look up and listen!* She grabbed a towel and, with her pulse racing, flung open the bathroom door, her conditioner running in tiny, soapy rivulets down her back. Mario stood on the top stair, his eyes wide. The sight of him in a state of such high agitation only frightened her even more.

'I got . . .' He stopped talking and leant on the wall, struggling to catch his breath, 'I got here as quick as I could – what's wrong? What's happened?' He wiped the sweat from his brow with the flat of his fingers, his eyes searching hers, as if trying to figure out what was wrong.

'What's happened?' she repeated quizzically as her heart stuttered and she tried to figure out the weird situation that was making the air around them crackle. Could this be in response to her text to Craig? Had there been some misunderstanding? 'Nothing's happened!' She too was now leaning on the doorframe. 'I thought you'd come crashing in to tell *me* something.'

'What?' He narrowed his eyes at her, his breathing a little slower now. 'What are you talking about, Bess?'

She stared at him, noting he still had the little pencil behind his ear that he used at work for doing the maths for his mixes. He had told her once that he wrote on the walls of the houses he was about to plaster.

'Have you come home to give me bad news?' She swallowed.

'What? No! Me give *you* bad news? What do you mean?' Mario shook his head. 'What the fuck is going on? I was in a new-build on the far corner of the estate and one of the contractors came hammering up the stairs and told me I needed to get home, ASAP! Said Craig had sent him to fetch me.'

'Oh God, Mario.' An uncomfortable cold film crept over her skin. She was responsible for this whole horrible misunderstanding and she was going to have to come clean. She didn't relish the thought. Wrapped in embarrassment, her mouth ran dry and her tummy flipped. 'I sent Craig a text . . .'

'You sent Craig a text saying what?'

85

'I can't remember exactly, but nothing urgent, just asking if you'd give me a call.' Her voice was small.

Mario exhaled slowly. 'I saw a missed call from you and tried calling you all the way home, but you didn't pick up. It only made me panic more.'

'My phone's on charge in the kitchen and then I was in the bath.'

'What did you need me to call you about?' He looked at a loss, seemingly still trying to understand the nature of the emergency.

Bess tightened the towel around her body and licked her lips.

'I wanted to ask you to send me a birthday message on Facebook,' she said, looking in the general direction of his face, but quite unable to meet his gaze.

'Is this a joke?' He took a big breath and again wiped sweat from his brow. He stared at her, as if waiting for the punchline, his eyes narrow and his mouth open. 'I jumped in the van and Craig waved me out of the gate without saying a word, like he knew something I didn't. The lads stared after me with their heads down. I've driven all the way back with my heart in my mouth, gone through every red light. I broke the speed limit on the dual carriageway, and you *know* when I'm not on site I'm not earning money, and all that for a fucking Facebook message? Are you for real?'

'I didn't think, I—'

'No, you didn't, Bess! For the love of God, can you imagine what the last half an hour has been like for me?' He ran his hand over his face and flexed his fingers, before staggering to the bedroom, where he sat on the edge of the bed with his big, plaster-covered boots planted on the carpet, the ones he usually left by the front door. He slumped, as if weakened. 'I honestly don't know what to say to you.' He snorted through his nose, bovine and furious.

Bess felt her intestines shrink with remorse and unease.

'I'm sorry, Mario.'

The words felt thin. She sat behind him with her back against the headboard and the cold, slimy creep of wet, soggy hair on her shoulders. It was unpleasant, but this was not the time to mention that. 'It's Sushmita's birthday as well and I logged on to Facebook to see my messages and there were loads for her and it felt so unfair. I mean, it's my birthday too. I've worked in the school canteen much longer than her and—'

Mario raised his hand. 'Please, Bess, just listen to yourself!'

And to her distress and dismay, she heard the crack in his voice. Bess leant forward and put her hand on his shoulder, watching as her husband did what she had only seen him do a handful of times throughout their marriage – he cried.

'Mario, I'm so sorry!' She buried her own distress, desperate that she had caused this reaction. It was a shock to see him like this, but also strangely warming to know he cared enough to cry – a reminder of the old Mario, with whom she had laughed and loved every day of their newly married life. 'I never dreamt this would happen – I didn't give it any thought.'

'Clearly,' he managed.

'I *am* sorry,' she repeated. 'This isn't like you, love. I understand you being angry, but I can't remember the last time I saw you so upset.'

She watched as he anchored his palms on his thighs and let his tears fall.

'I thought,' he began with a croak to his voice, 'I thought something terrible had happened, and I remembered the last time I got called home, when you lost the baby.'

His words were a jolt. She would not have guessed that this would be at the front of his thoughts. It had been nearly two decades ago when she had called him at work and he'd rushed home to drive her to the hospital, where he'd sat on a green chair by the side of her bed, holding her hand and kissing her palm, repeating, 'It's all going to be okay . . . It's all going to be okay . . . We have so much to be thankful for, my Bessie . . .'

And she had heard his words and nodded, feeling guilty that a small part of her was enjoying the peace of the room, the quiet away from the kids and the fact that someone was giving her permission to lie in a bed and close her eyes in the middle of the day . . . No washing up to be done, no dirty laundry, no scrubbing of the bathroom, no preparing food – all she had to do was lie still and rest. While terrible, it was a welcome break. She had waited an age for the porter to come and wheel her into the operating theatre and all while the iron scent of her loss clung to her nostrils and tainted each breath. It had made her want to vomit, this repulsive smell of warm blood that was the sticky essence of life, but on her legs, her stomach and pooling on a plastic-backed pad over the mattress and not where it should have been, inside her womb, nurturing that little baby. It was a scent that was as distressing as it was familiar. It was when she got home that her unravelling had begun – that was when fun Bess had first left the building.

'Honestly, Bess, that was one of the worst days of my life.' Mario turned now to look at her briefly over his shoulder, his eyes red and puffy. This was news to her. She had wrongly assumed that, like her, he had put the whole sad episode to the back of his mind and moved on. It was shocking that he had carried this distress for all these years, tangled with concern for her and sadness at all he himself had lost. 'To see you curled up in the middle of that bed, gripping your stomach and crying – and me not being able to do anything to make it better . . . I remember Jake and Nats were downstairs playing and making so much noise I wanted to punch the wall!'

'Oh Mario!' She reached for him and he sidled back on the bed, coming to rest with his head on her chest and his hands clasped between his thighs, unintentionally mirroring the pose she had struck on this very bed. His large work boots sat neatly ankle to ankle on top of the duvet. She smoothed his hair, which smelled of lemons and sweat, holding him until his sobs subsided. It felt good to hold him close, a privilege she had forgotten. She wondered if it was only the baby he was crying over or whether he, like her, used it as a way to flush out all the things he found most distressing, knowing that once *she* started crying, other reasons for sadness would always tap her on the shoulder and add their voice to her tears. It was rare, this level of contact, rare and now therefore unnatural, making her realise just how far they had drifted. This thought she would keep to herself, along with the other secrets. He nestled into her in an act so trusting and authentic it gave a glimpse into the couple they once had been, where intimacy and honesty were the bywords. She missed it and kissed his scalp.

'Everyone told me it "just happens". Some even said it was "nothing" – that we'd get over it and all I had to do was look after you, and I did look after you, didn't I?'

'You did! You really did.' Bess felt a surge of love at the memory of just how much he had cared for her, his never-ending patience and his love.

'But it didn't seem nothing to me. It felt like something, a very important something, and I still think about it sometimes. He'd be nearly twenty, wouldn't he?'

She nodded. Twenty? God, that had gone fast, but yes, Mario must be right, twenty . . . She pictured Jake at the same age and, try as she might, could not imagine a different, younger version of Jake, brothers, which was odd, as she had no trouble picturing a different, older version of Natalie.

89

Mario took a breath. 'And I've always thought of him as a boy, because that was what I wanted – another son. I mean, God knows I love Nats, I do, but I wanted another boy, and I think about what he'd be doing. I think about him by my side in the van on a long journey. I think about all three of my fabulous kids together with me down the pub, and I talk to him and tell him I'm sorry he left us too soon . . .'

Bess felt her own tears gather at his words – *all three of my fabulous kids* . . . She'd had no idea this was how he felt and that he had kept it to himself for all these years, unaware of his desperate mourning for this child who had left them too soon. It made her feel closer to him, and she understood, more than understood.

'Mario, don't cry,' she whispered, humming quietly into his scalp, running the flat of her fingers over his neck and ears.

'And I find it hard to talk to you about the stuff that matters, Bess.'

'Do you?' She knew this was true. It was as if neither had the energy or inclination to unearth events that were wounding or painful. It felt somehow easier to let them simmer beneath a veneer of banality. Far safer to talk about that night's tea, the merits of a TV programme, whether either of them fancied dessert, Mario's day at work, the kids she'd served lunch to and Chutney's antics. Yes, these discussions were far easier than to mention their lack of sex life, how lonely she often felt sitting right next to her own husband on the sofa, how she often howled tears of remorse, and how she wondered sometimes if he felt the same. A little trapped, a little cheated by the life they lived, and a little as if they deserved something more.

'I do, Bess. I find it hard to mention certain stuff. Like when you lost the baby, I remember they gave us a leaflet at the hospital and it had a number you could call with details of a support group for mothers, but there was nothing for a fat plasterer who felt so

90

out of his depth. The lack of any phone number for the dads, the lack of a support group, made it hard for me to be open about my feelings, as though they simply didn't count. The lads on site asked after you and I was grateful, but no one, not one person, asked me how I was doing, and I wanted to yell, *It was my baby too!*'

'It was, my love. It was. And we *should* talk about it.' She knew the words were easy, but the practice was so much harder. Moved by his tenderness, she hoped that maybe this new-found openness was a beginning, the start of finding the words that would allow them both to unburden all they kept hidden. It was a thought as terrifying as it was welcome.

'You're always nagging me about peeing at the back of the toilet and slamming the shower door or losing my car keys, but just for once, I'd like you not to nag me about shit that doesn't really matter and I'd like us to sit down and talk, really talk, about all the difficult stuff.'

'It never seems to be the right time.' Her body stiffened. *My fear overwhelms me, Mario! It silences me! How do I break the habit of the quiet I have kept for nearly all my adult life?*

'I know. Like, right now, I have to get back to work.' He shuffled from her and sat up straight, wiping his face, his expression a little embarrassed, and she matched him, gripping the towel closed over her chest where it gaped and trying to pull it down over the bulge of fat on her knees. 'But I hope, Bess, the right time will come up and we can really chat.'

He reached out and ran his thumb over her newly shaved legs, letting his callus trip over the three little nubs, scars that reminded her of another time when conversations were just as hard to have, and she was carrying the same burden of distress at the secrets she was keeping. Secrets from a day when she had sported three round plasters soaked with blood – a day when how she viewed herself had changed forever.

'I'm sorry, Mario, about the text and for making you scared. I never meant for that to happen.'

'I'll see you later,' he said from the doorframe, where he lingered, his eyes searching, as if trying to place her.

'Yes, I'll see you later. And Mario?'

He paused on the landing and looked back at her.

'I just wanted to . . . I just wanted to say . . .' What did she want to say? *I still love you! I have always loved you! I want us to be close again, like our old love in our old life?* 'I . . . I am sorry.'

Her husband nodded slowly and ran down the stairs.

CHAPTER SEVEN

August 20th 1984

Bessie spent the afternoon lying on her stomach on her bed with her feet crossed at the ankles and kicked up behind her, listening to the slow, doleful, haunting tones of Simple Minds on her tape recorder, which suited her melancholy. She had only ventured out of her room once, and that was under duress, so her family could sing her 'Happy Birthday' while she blew out the candles on her cake. The soft, pale, buttery sponge, which only that very morning she had been looking forward to, had tasted vaguely metallic on her tongue.

''Course, I was married at sixteen,' her nan began, with a mouthful of sponge and buttercream dotting her top lip. Her mum and dad had exchanged a knowing look – the story was one her nan liked to share, and they had all heard it many, many times before, not that anyone had the heart to remind her of this.

'Sixteen? That's very young!' her dad said, playing his part, and Bessie loved him for it.

'Young, Eddie? I was a baby! Never been kissed! And there I was, being waltzed up the aisle.'

Bessie's mum mouthed the latter part of the sentence over her mother's shoulder, while Philip laughed softly.

'He was in the Scouts and I was a Girl Guide and we went on a charabanc to Margate. He kept larking around in front of me and I thought he was a right show-off!'

Bessie pictured the scene around a kitchen table of her own in the future . . . *We met properly at the bus stop. He was in the football team and I'd stayed late to pick litter* . . . She smiled at the thought, this one bright moment cutting through the grief of her dire grades, but as she imagined this, Michelle's words of earlier suddenly loomed large and her stomach churned at the thought of the conversation they needed to have.

'So why did you marry him if you thought he was a show-off?' Philip asked, as if Grandad Norm weren't sitting only feet away.

'Well,' her nan said, adjusting her bosom and sitting back in the chair, 'because he asked me! And it all happened quite quickly, and once I'd taken the plunge I quite liked him . . .' Grandad Norm rolled his eyes and lifted the side of his mouth in a half smile. 'Then the next thing I knew,' Bessie's nan continued, warming to her theme, 'bloody war broke out and I didn't think I'd see him again for years and it all felt very romantic, him going off to fight the Nazis in his uniform and me stuck at home with my sisters and none of them had a fella. I liked getting his letters. He made me feel special.'

'I hope I always have Patsy.' Bessie's grandad winked at her and bit into his slice of birthday cake.

'Oh, you have, love,' Nanny Pat said, studying the face of the man she loved, 'you have.'

Bessie watched the two older people lock eyes and wondered how you got to be half of a couple like that. A couple that were still together and had survived a long marriage, childbirth, loss, redundancy and a world bloody war. She thought of Lawrence Paulson and the fact that her nan had by all accounts never been kissed when she became a bride, whereas she had had sex nine times already, and most of that had been hurried and conducted within strolling distance of the bus stop. *What is wrong with me? Is it okay to like doing sex?* She didn't know who she could ask. Certainly not Michelle. Not now. Having done her duty by the cake and with a jumble of thoughts that needed sorting, she had been keen to get back to the safety of her bedroom.

'Knock knock!' her dad said as he pushed her door open, entering her bedroom slowly, giving her the opportunity, as he always did, to close a book, hide a letter, cover up – it made her feel comfortable in her own private space. Her dad might be a wally when it came to playing the harmonica and making klutzy jokes, but he was smart in other ways.

'Just came to see how you're doing, sweetheart?'

'I'm fine,' she lied, sitting up on the bed with her back against the wall and her shin plasters on full display.

'I can't stand the idea of you hiding up here on your birthday. You should be downstairs, celebrating with us.'

'I'm not hiding,' she lied again. 'I just don't feel much like celebrating.'

Her dad breathed through his nose, as if he understood this. 'We could have a game of Monopoly if you like, on the kitchen table? That is, if you *have* a game of Monopoly?' he winked, leaning on the doorframe.

This made her smile. She looked towards her wardrobe. 'I think I have five or six now.'

'And I believe your brother has about the same. So I guess the good news is, you never have to lose a game again.'

'How do you mean?'

'Well,' her dad said, lowering his voice, 'with all that cash, you can stash some about your person and, when no one's looking, like when Mum has to nip to the loo mid-game, you can produce a couple of spare five hundreds and buy Park Lane!'

'Dad, are you telling me to cheat?' She was mock aghast. One of his golden rules of parenting was, *'Always, always tell the truth, no matter what. A lie makes any situation a million times worse!'*

'No.' He gave a wry smile and walked forward, pulling the little pink velour pouffe with the buttoned top on which she liked to rest her feet while she did her homework from under the edge of her bed. He sat on it, looking comically large and having to plant his feet either side to keep his balance. 'But what I am saying is that you need to think of a way to overcome the obstacle that has been put in your path. I know you're upset about your exams. But life is about taking whatever you find in your pockets and making the very most out of it.'

Bessie's tears gathered as again she pictured life at school carrying on without her. She saw Michelle, and even Melanie Hall, gathered for the first day in the sixth form, laughing and excited, as if she had never been there, forgotten . . . The very idea hurt, leaving her adrift and empty. Everything – *everything* – hung on her grades: her social life, her plans, her happiness and, not least, her self-worth.

'I feel so stupid, Dad! And upset that I'm going to be left out.'

'You're not stupid, Bessie. Exam results don't make you clever. Just look at your brother – on paper, he's a genius, right?'

'I guess so.' She really did not want to talk about Philip's brilliance.

'Yet only yesterday I caught him in the garage, holding a lighter up with the flame flickering because the bulb had blown. He was looking for the jerrycan full of petrol – with a naked flame!' He made the sound of an explosion with his mouth, while at the same time touching together and then fanning out his fingertips. 'He could have blown himself up, along with the whole house, and probably taken Mrs Hicks next door and her cat with him!'

'Oh don't, Dad, I love that cat.'

They both laughed.

'The thing is,' she said, trying her best to swallow the lump of hurt lodged at the base of her throat, 'when Philip comes to fill out a form for university or a job, the person looking at it won't be interested in him nearly blowing up Mrs Hicks, they'll only look at his long list of good grades, and they'll look at my long list of bad ones.'

'You're probably right,' her dad said, pausing for a beat, 'so you need to be clever – think about what you're going to do next and how you'll do it. Draw a picture in your mind of what your future looks like and then figure out a way to make it happen.'

'I want to be an air hostess,' she said out loud, as a reminder to herself as much as her dad.

'I know, and you still can! You should go to the tech and resit your exams, if it means that much to you. Or why don't you write to all the airports, saying you'd like to do work experience – *any* work experience, whether it's filing paperwork, running the fax machine or scrubbing floors, but get inside the building and let them get to know you, and then ask about opportunities – make it happen, Bessieboo!'

His broad smile was almost enough for her to believe he was right and that it was possible, but there was one big issue that was a whole lot harder to overcome.

'I *could* do that, Dad, and I would have done it in a heartbeat if you'd suggested it to me last week, but now?' She picked at the edge of one of the plasters, working it loose with her fingernail. 'I know I don't have the minimum entry-level exams, but it's more than that. The truth is, I don't *feel* like I'm capable.'

'But you are!'

'Am I?'

'Of course you are, you're smart, and those results . . .'

She shook her head as she interrupted him. 'I thought I'd done okay; I thought I knew what I was doing – and *that's* the problem. Not the *actual* results, but the fact I had no idea how wide of the mark I was. *That's* what makes me feel stupid.'

He stared at her, and she could tell by the flicker of his eyes and his silence that he didn't know how to answer her.

'I think you need to not rush into any decision. Let things percolate and see how you feel when the dust has settled, okay, birthday girl?'

Bessie smiled at her dad with an enthusiasm she didn't feel. 'Okay, Dad.'

'And it's simple, really, Bessie – you either want it badly and will smash the obstacles in your way to make it happen, or you'll fall and give up. And you're not a falling-down kind of girl, are you?'

She looked at her refection in the mirror and sat up straight – he was right! Enough moping . . . She had to make it happen!

'I'm not, Dad.'

'As I suspected,' he smiled at her. 'I'm proud of you – proud of all you're going to do and all the places you're going to go.'

'Thank you!' She threw her arms around his neck and held him tightly. Her brilliant, brilliant daddy.

'Right,' he said with a cough. 'I'll leave you to it. You've got the rugby club social tonight, haven't you? I'll drive you both, pick Michelle up on the way if you like, or is she coming here first?'

'I'm meeting her there.'

'Oh well, that's good. I can put my Dire Straits tape on without you nagging, all embarrassed about me singing along in front of your friend.'

'Dad, I'm embarrassed for you whether Michelle is there or not. And thanks, but I think I'll walk. I fancy the fresh air.' *I want to clear my head and practise my conversation with Michelle . . .*

He stood and pushed the pouffe back from where he had taken it.

'We all have setbacks in life, love. The real test is how we get back up and how we go forward. Just remember, you are not a falling-down kind of girl.'

'I will,' she nodded, her spirits lifted and lightened by his words. He was right, this was just a setback – she would write to the airlines and see if they had any openings, and if that came to nothing, then it might just be that she would enrol at the tech.

I am not a falling-down kind of girl . . . I am not . . .

◆ ◆ ◆

Bessie wasn't aware she had fallen asleep, but clearly she had, as she was now waking up. Her bedroom door creaked open and Philip poked his head in.

'Fancy some Cinzano?'

'What?' She blinked at him – not only was she still half asleep and a little drowsy, but it was quite possibly one of the most random questions her brother had ever popped up with.

'For the party tonight?' He looked over his shoulder to check his parents weren't within hearing distance. 'I've got a bottle of Cinzano.' He might have been eighteen, but her parents still thought of him as a four-year-old.

'Oh.' She sat up and thought about having to walk into the rugby club to meet Michelle stone-cold sober. Nerves bunched in her gut – maybe a slug of Cinzano might take the edge off. 'Sure, thanks.'

'I'll put it in Mum's old thermos.'

'Okay, cheers, Philip.' She liked this version of her brother, who did nice things for her. 'How's Carmen?' She thought taking an interest in his girlfriend would be kind.

He twisted his mouth and looked into the middle distance. 'She's good, I think. I'll see her later.' He smiled at the thought.

'You really like her, don't you?'

'Yeah, I do. A bit too much, if anything.' He laughed nervously.

'How can you like someone a bit too much?' It was a curious concept.

Philip took his time forming a response. 'Because when you like someone more than they like you, it's almost a cast-iron guarantee that you're going to get hurt, but the trouble is, because you like them so much and because they hold all the cards, there's not a damn thing you can do about it.'

'That sounds crap.' She thought of Lawrence and felt the first flicker of excitement at the thought of seeing him and catching up after the party, where she hoped to take their tally to ten and in the process take her mind off the number three hundred and sixty-one.

'It *is* crap – completely crap,' he agreed, and closed the bedroom door behind him.

Philip's words and the thought of Lawrence galvanised her into action. She pulled her very large make-up bag from the top of the dressing table and sat on the pink pouffe, before laying out all the products she intended to use, neatly and in rows. She liked doing it this way, looking at the array of colours, creams, lotions, eyeshadows, lipsticks, glittery powders and pencils for lip, lid and brow and then all of her brushes, puffs and sponges, which sat in an old pencil pot. There was a strict routine to putting on her make-up, it was artistry almost, and she took her time, settling for nothing less than painted perfection. It felt especially important tonight. The sound of Imagination's 'Body Talk' filled the room as she prepared to transform from number three hundred and sixty-one into a goddess. Her dad was right: she needed to find out what she had in her pockets and make the very most out of it.

As she blotted her lipstick on a tissue from the box, her mum walked straight into her bedroom and took a seat on the edge of Bessie's bed. She never showed the same courtesy as her dad, as if she believed there was nothing going on inside that room regarding which her contribution would not be entirely welcome. Bessie had already decided that when she and Lawrence went official, if he ever came up to her room, they would shift the chest of drawers to block the door. Sex in her own bed would be a very good thing; the memory of it would keep her warm when she was alone or chilly. Just the thought of his head on her pillow, his long, dark eyelashes that grazed his cheek with every blink and his mouth that twisted at one side in a lopsided smile that was to her beautiful, was enough to send a jolt of longing right through her bones.

'I said, are you feeling better, love?'

'Yes, Mum, a bit, but . . .'

'Life goes on,' her mum cut in.

'I was going to say, I'm not going to let it stop me. There'll be a way for me to get back on track.'

'There absolutely will!' her mum said, squeezing her shoulder. 'You don't want to phone Michelle and get her to come over and get ready with you?'

Bessie shook her head. 'No.' *I need to think about what I want to say. I need to have the words straight in my head and I'll practise my speech as I walk to the rugby club.* 'I think it's best I meet her there.'

'You look very pretty.' Her mum studied her face.

'Thanks.' Bessie glanced in the mirror and yes, she did look pretty.

'I can't understand it.' Her mum shook her head now and stared out of the window.

'Can't understand what?'

'Well,' her mum said, adjusting her apron over her legs, 'I mean, your dad and I provided a good environment for you kids to flourish – look at Philip.' Bessie took the slight and folded it into a small seed that would sit in her gut. 'And I thought we did the same with you.'

Maybe it's me . . . Is that what you're saying?

'And then we've got Michelle, whose family are a bit . . .'

'A bit what?'

Her mum pulled a face. 'Well, for a start, they've got half the family living in a bloody caravan! I mean, how does someone in that environment do better than you?' she huffed.

Bessie faced her mother, aghast. Yes, it was true. Michelle's two brothers slept in a caravan on the driveway as there was no space inside the house for them, not since her nan, who suffered from Alzheimer's, had been widowed and had moved in. Michelle said they had briefly considered putting her nan in the caravan and letting the boys stay put in their bunk beds, but as she was prone to leaving the gas on and going a-wanderin' in the wee small hours, it wouldn't have worked. Her dad had suggested padlocking the door from the outside so she couldn't escape, but Michelle's mum thought that was a bit cruel and, besides, they might lose the key. Her dad had apparently smiled jokingly at the thought and her mum had cried.

'You mean because they're poorer than us?' she said.

'Well, no.' Her mum gave an awkward laugh. 'Although, in a way, yes.' She ran her tongue over her teeth.

'That's a terrible thing to say, Mum!'

'Why? It's true!'

'How is it true?' Bessie felt a hot flame of injustice in her breast. Michelle's family was lovely, money or not, and it wasn't lost on her that her own family lived in a very modest house where income was low. It bothered her that her mum took this view, enjoying the elevated position, whereas in reality, both families were in a leaky lifeboat, bailing hard month after month and always only one lost paycheck away from sinking. The only real difference was that Michelle's family had a caravan on the driveway, whereas her family couldn't afford a caravan.

'I just mean that people like Michelle's family don't seem to value education in the way that people like Dad and I do.'

'What do you mean, people like you and Dad? Who are *you* friends with – Lady Di?'

'Oh God, I wish! I would've loved you to have been a bridesmaid. We'd have had to pencil your eyebrows in, mind.'

Bessie looked at her thin brows in the mirror and felt some of her earlier confidence falter, not that Lawrence seemed too bothered about such detail when they were having sex.

'You can smirk, but it's good to have standards in life, Bessie.'

'Standards? Mum, I failed practically everything. What if Michelle's mum is saying, "I don't want you mixing with that Bessie Worrall – she's a right thicko!"'

'Well then, I'd have to go and have a word with her,' her mum said in a low voice, leaning forward with her eyes narrowed. Her attempt at menacing was so funny, Bessie laughed out loud.

'That's more like it. You should be laughing today, of all days. Promise me you'll have a lovely time tonight, won't you?'

'I will.' Bessie pulled down the hem of her cropped pink sweatshirt and felt her tummy flip at the prospect of the conversation she knew she was going to have with her very best friend in the whole world ever, ever, ever . . .

CHAPTER EIGHT

August 20th 2021

Bess pulled out the bath plug, letting some of the tepid water drain away, before replenishing it with hot and climbing back in. She lay back and watched the conditioner leach from her now glossy hair. Shaking her hands free of water, she reached for the packet of cigarettes and lighter that she had balanced on the side of the bath. With the filter in her mouth, she held the tip against the flame and inhaled deeply, enjoying the first hit of nicotine as the smoke rolled into her lungs. Smoking was her dirty secret and her guilty pleasure. It always had been. She wasn't addicted and had no need to puff away on a daily basis, but as and when the mood and opportunity arose, she loved to indulge and kept a secret packet of menthol cigarettes and a lighter secreted in an old Tampax box in the bottom of the airing cupboard. Closing her eyes briefly, she put her free hand on her tum, where that little baby had taken root, only to fly too soon. Her tears gathered, not for her loss but at the guilt that washed over her. Not only because Mario had felt forced to rush home, but also because she *would* never – *could* never – tell him that, when all was said and done, when she knew she was losing the baby the strongest feeling that had pierced her breast and sat in her throat was one of relief.

With two boisterous young children to look after, getting pregnant was the last thing on her mind, and the surprise of it had floored her. When the pee-soaked test had read positive, Bess, who was sitting on the loo with it in her hands as the kids caused mayhem in the hallway, had cried and asked her reflection in the mirror, 'What the hell am I supposed to do now?'

She had waited for Mario to come home and, at the end of a very long day, made the announcement in the most subdued way she could manage, with her back to him as she tackled the dirty dishes. She turned from the sink, with the plates stacked on the drainer, to tell her husband in no uncertain terms that she thought they had messed up, that the timing could not be worse, not with two small kids and her having recently started a new job at the school. But before she could utter another word, he was whooping with joy around the kitchen, skidding on the floor in his socks in a poor imitation of Elvis, dancing and beaming with joy.

'Yes, we did it, Bess – three babies! This is brilliant! How are you feeling? How far are you? My clever girl. God, I love you so much. What do you think the kids will say? When can we tell people?'

As she tried to figure out which question to answer first, she saw all her options disappear down the sink with the suds from the washing up. How could she tell him of her doubts, her *dismay*, when he was already coming up with names . . . ?

'I like Ryan for a boy and Misty for a girl.'

'Misty? She'd sound like a porn star!' She dug deep and found a smile.

'Okay then, you name the girl and me the boy.' He had grabbed her then around the waist and pulled her into him. 'God, I love you! I can't stop saying it.'

'And I love you.'

And she did, but that didn't stop her heart from jumping and her spirit from fluttering, trying to beat its wings and stay upright when all it wanted to do was slump a little and rest. Things were just starting to get easier for them as a family; Natalie and Jake at six and eight were a bit more independent, and financially, they were getting straight, now that she could work. It had made sense to take a job within school hours, fitting it around dropping them off and collecting them each day and in time to supervise homework and reading.

She was happy, managing finally to balance her guilt and sadness with the new and overwhelming sense of peace that being mum to Jake and Natalie and wife to Mario gave her. She had never, ever, wanted more children; her kids filled her life and her heart. Once Jake and Natalie had arrived, she thought it far better to be able to provide properly for the two she did have, rather than struggle to accommodate a third child they had never planned for or discussed. They lived in a three-bedroom house, which meant a bedroom each – what would happen with a third child? Would they have to move? Or God forbid, be forced to put a caravan on the driveway? Besides, moving was out of the question financially. That, and they were in the right catchment area for the primary school, at which the children were thriving.

Bess thought back to that time and sank lower in the bath, letting the water soothe her. Mario's reaction earlier had floored her – and saddened her, of course. Not only the depth of his distress, but the fact that he had felt unable to talk to her about it. It was hard to fathom that at no point over the last two decades had he managed to find a moment to broach the topic – not until today, when his grief had finally tumbled from him. Bess took a long draw on her cigarette and lay back with her eyes closed. It would seem that they both kept secrets. Mario's private sadness was surprising but also mirrored her own. Maybe *that* was the way in to the hardest of all conversations, one where she might begin to share her long-held secret, the thought of which was enough to send a shiver along her limbs.

'Least said, soonest mended,' she said aloud, her words spiralling up with the wisps of cigarette smoke. The only response was the drip drip of the tap into the bath.

The sound of footsteps on the stairs sent her into a small panic and her heart raced, until a voice called out, 'Mum? Mu-um?'

Jesus Christ, what was it with this family! How hard was it to get a bath in peace?

'In the bath, Nats! Just getting out now!' Natalie, of course, like Jake, had a door key. Bess jumped out of the bath for the second time that morning and lobbed the cigarette into the bath water. Grabbing the towel around her body, she opened the bathroom door a crack.

'Hello, sweetie.' She beamed at the sight of her beautiful girl, who in her blue suit and heels with her straight blonde hair tied into a ponytail managed to pull off professional and attractive in the way some women could. Bess always thought she would have made a wonderful air hostess.

'Happy birthday!' Natalie said, beaming at her. 'Your pressie's on the kitchen table – are you coming down? I've only got ten minutes. I'm on my way to work. A late start.'

'Yes, darling, just give me a minute to dry off.'

She watched as her daughter began to sniff the air, her nose lifted, and the corners of her mouth turned down in disgust.

'Are you smoking in the bathroom, Bess? I can smell cigarettes!'

Bess gave a derisory laugh, as her daughter used her name in the way she did when reprimanding her. 'Don't be ridiculous. I don't smoke! I hate smoking, you know that!'

'How very odd.' Natalie pursed her lips and turned on her heel. 'I'll see you downstairs.'

'Shan't be a sec.' Bess shut the door and whipped off her towel, wafting the air towards the crack in the dormer window. She grabbed Natalie's old dressing gown from the back of the door and picked up the lighter from the side of the bath, before hiding it inside the pocket. The packet of cigarettes she dropped in the wastepaper basket and covered it with her flannel, to retrieve later.

Bess raced down the stairs to find Natalie rubbing Chutney's ears and talking to him as though he were a baby,

'My little Chuts! My beautiful boy. Who do I love? You, that's who! I love you!'

It made Bess smile. She bent down to pat his back and her lighter fell from the pocket and on to the kitchen floor. Natalie was quicker than her and grabbed it, raising it to her face.

'Well, I don't know whose this is!'

'Me neither.' Bess stared at the lighter as Natalie rolled the flint with her thumb and flicked it on, blowing out the flame.

'Not to worry, Mum. I'll bin it. Don't want to leave it lying around – might give Dad the wrong impression.'

Bess looked at her nonchalantly. 'What, he might think someone in the house is a secret smoker?' She tried not to laugh.

Natalie fixed her with a stare, her voice teasing, 'No, Mum, he might think someone in the house is a not-so-secret liar.'

'Oh, for the love of God, Nats, it was one cigarette on my birthday! Give me a break!' She wrapped her daughter in a hug. 'You look beautiful, did I tell you that?'

'You didn't, and thank you.'

It impressed her how her daughter was able to take a compliment. On the rare occasions when someone said something nice to Bess about her appearance, she would instantly rebuff it, batting it away with her hand and making light of it as her tongue roamed the crevice of her crumbled tooth that had once been white and whole. The way Natalie accepted her words made her seem worldly and confident, two things Bess was not. She felt the smallest flicker of envy at the life her professional daughter led.

'But stop changing the subject,' Natalie said, breaking free and putting her hands on her hips. 'You can't be smoking – not at your age, in fact not at any age, but definitely not at yours.'

'I don't care, not really. The odd *one* doesn't count.' Bess had never wanted her kids to see her weaknesses, her failings, knowing they had already surpassed her in terms of achievement and prospects. She didn't want them to think any less of her than they might already when they got out into the world and realised she had done very little with her life, other than cook countless bland suppers and vacuum the hall carpet to within an inch of its life.

'Actually, it does count, but I'll let you off, as it's your birthday.' Natalie reached for the fancy cream bag with a black edge and black ribbon tied in a bow on top and handed it to her. 'Happy birthday, Mum.'

'Oh darling, you shouldn't have done that!' Bess took a seat at the kitchen table and took her time, undoing the grosgrain ribbon carefully, with the express intention of reusing it. She pulled apart the stiff paper bag, whose quality was evident to the touch, and reached in to grab the square box, which was swathed in delicate tissue; inside that sat a tightly packed glass candle. The sweet scent that wafted from the gift was intoxicating.

'Oh, Nats, this smells heavenly!'

'It's my favourite: lime, basil and mandarin – it's Jo Malone.'

'Ooh, well, I hope he doesn't want it back – it's amazing!' Bess held the glass votive to her nose and inhaled the stunning fresh scent. 'I shall save it for best and light it in the front room. Thank you, Nats, I love it.'

'You're welcome. What did Dad get you?'

'Oh, a lovely orchid.' She pointed to the potted plant sitting on the drainer, which had shed some of its blooms.

'I thought you hated orchids?'

'Yes, but Dad doesn't know that.'

'Evidently.'

'And a card with a duck on it, apparently, which he can't find.'

'Surprise surprise,' Natalie laughed.

'Yep, I know – most unlike him to misplace something. Anyway, I'm sure it'll turn up, and tonight we're getting a chippy tea, if you're around?'

'I'm not sure when I'll finish, but if I can I'll let you know nearer the time.'

Bess nodded, hating the vagueness of the response. She liked to text Mario in advance and to know exactly what everyone wanted to eat. She felt a ridiculous swell of anxiety over this smallest thing: who would be coming for fish and chips and who wanted large or small chips and who wanted their sausage battered or plain and whether their preference was for cod or haddock and were they all fans of salt and vinegar, did anyone have a yearning for curry sauce or the peas of mush? Despite knowing this was ridiculous, anxiety lurked in her gut nonetheless.

'Are Jake and Dan coming over – when are they home? Can't wait to see them!' Natalie asked brightly.

'Well, your guess is as good as mine!' Bess took another long, deep sniff of the candle. 'I'd like to see Jake, of course, being as it's my birthday.' She put the candle back in its box. 'What's that sigh for?'

Natalie shrugged and used the long nail of the index finger on her left hand to clean the nails on her right. 'I just hate the tension between you and Dan.'

'It's not my fault. I have tried.'

'Yeah, I know, you've said that before, but—'

'But what?'

'But it upsets him, Mum, and that upsets Jake, which isn't fair. Dan's not going anywhere, so you need to figure out a way to make things easier.'

'God, Nats! I welcomed him into my home. We paid for half of their wedding, sprung on us with zero notice. I've done nothing but try to make things easier.' Bess bit her bottom lip. Jake and Daniel had been a couple for a little over eighteen months, and Bess had found him hard to take to. His constant references to all the fabulous places he jetted to for work, the shimmering swimming-pool posts on his social media, the fancy hotels. She didn't like show-offs. And being excluded from their wedding planning and the whole thing being pulled together in a matter of weeks with none of the joyous build-up had been the final straw. 'I just find it hard to see Jake so controlled! He looks to Dan for approval on just about everything and now it's his diet, his clothes and he's even suggesting he change his career!'

'What did Dad do when you met him?'

'Dad? Oh, he was working in sales, but I told him what my dad had always said, that if you get a trade under your belt it can see you through feast and famine – there's always a need for good tradesmen, especially in the building industry.' She looked at her daughter, whose expression was judgemental. 'What?' She resented the silent suggestion that she was in any way like Daniel.

'Nothing, Mum. Look, I should probably get going,' Nat said, glancing at her watch, 'but I'll try and see you tonight if I can get away in time, okay?'

'Okay, darling, and thank you for my candle. It's beautiful.' She liked having something so fancy. Natalie was a good girl.

'You know, Mum,' her daughter said, pushing the chair back under the table and giving Chutney a final pat, 'Daniel's—'

The ringing of the front doorbell cut her off.

'Daniel is what?' Bess asked, folding her arms across her chest subconsciously to deflect the blows.

'Nothing. It doesn't matter. I'd better go.' Nat went to open the front door and smiled at the deliveryman standing there with a large cardboard box.

'Bye, Mum. Hopefully see you later!' Natalie waved, as she tripped down the driveway and into her shiny little Mini.

'Mrs Talbot?'

'Yes?'

He handed her the box and tapped into his little hand-held computer. 'First name?'

'Bess.'

'Cheers!' He too ran back down the driveway to his waiting van.

Bess caught sight of Mr Maxwell, keys in hand and about to jump into his gleaming Audi. He looked smart in his navy suit and burgundy tie against a white shirt, while she, in contrast, was still in Natalie's old dressing gown, her hair wet on her shoulders and the whiff of cigarette smoke on her breath. The two stared at each other for a second or two until she coughed, looked up and down the cul de sac and was about to close the front door when he suddenly set off down his driveway and made his way swiftly towards her. She felt a flicker of panic. *Don't be ridiculous!* she reminded herself. It wasn't as if anyone knew of their exchange at the Christmas drinks party, and no one other than she knew of her reaction to it.

'Good morning, Bess,' he said, raising his hand in a wave.

'Morning.' She held the neck of the dressing gown firmly together as her heart beat a little faster.

'What a lovely day!' he said, looking up at the sky.

She nodded. He lowered his gaze then, as if taking her in piece by piece. A flush of embarrassment spread across her face and chest.

'It's my birthday,' she said, lifting the box of flowers.

'Many happy returns.' Again that small hint of a sexy smile that was no more than a twitch to his lips.

Her heart fluttered and her cheeks flamed all the more. She wished she were wearing the fancy wrap dress he had so admired. *For the love of God, pull yourself together, Bess!*

'I hope you're doing something scrumptious later,' he said.

'Erm . . .' She pictured herself earlier, scrubbing Mario's pee from the back of the toilet. 'I don't know about scrumptious!' she giggled.

'I have the good fortune to not be in the office today, at least not all day.'

'Lucky old you.' She tried to punctuate his rambling, self-consciousness urging her to end their chat and disappear from view.

'I shall in fact be at the Glade Hotel this afternoon, with a view over the park and a bottle of bubbly on ice . . .'

'Oh well, that . . . that sounds nice,' she said, swallowing.

'Room 626 – that's room 6-2-6,' he enunciated, with a brief flash of his pearly-white teeth. 'I shall be there from one p.m. onwards and it would be delightful to have some company.' He stared at her and she stared at him, quite at a loss as to what to say. *Was he really suggesting she join him for sex? Had she got the wrong end of the stick?* She felt her face colour further and was simultaneously thrilled and horrified at the prospect.

'Well . . .' She swallowed. 'I'd best get these flowers in water.' She closed the front door and saw the shadow of his dark suit striding away through the frosted glass panel at the top of the door. Sinking on to the floor, Bess slid down until she was concealed from the outside world and laughed until she wheezed, putting her hand over her mouth and cringing with embarrassment.

'Well I never, Chuts, and the Glade Hotel – very fancy!' She giggled until her laughter exhausted itself and her cringe level dropped. He was so blatant, so confident! And she would have been lying if she didn't admit to finding the whole exchange more than a little exciting. There was something about him, something about being propositioned by a good-looking man who knew his wines . . .

'Don't be so bloody ridiculous, Bess!' She pulled herself together and scrambled up, then ripped the card from the top of the box and read the printed message:

Happy Birthday with love from Philip and Nanette. X

'Ah, how lovely.' Her brother always sent flowers on her birthday and she kept his printed cards in the drawer of her dressing table. She thought of her sixteenth birthday, when he had bought her stripy legwarmers and presented them to her in his pants. The memory of that moment, the smell of pancakes on the stove top, the dust of their childhood home, the morning smell of her dad as he enveloped her in a hug: it was almost more than she could bear. 'Actually, I think if I could turn back time, it would be to then . . .' she confessed into the ether. *That perfect moment. Before . . .*

Just as Bess was tugging open the stubborn cardboard flap of the delivery box, which was thoroughly glued down, the phone rang.

'It's a madhouse today, Chuts!' she said to the dog, who looked up at her briefly but said nothing.

'Hell-oo?' She fully expected to hear her mother's voice, confirming again the details of their lunch or some other small and irrelevant detail that Bess knew need not warrant a phone call. There was the briefest pause before the person on the other end of the phone spoke.

'Bessie?'

The one word and its intonation, the ever so slight accentuation of the 'S', was enough for her to feel the pull of memory. Her gut folded with something like relief, as her tears gathered and her heart boomed in her chest. The rush of emotion was a spike that lanced her heart and let longing flood her veins. It was a voice she had spent hours and hours talking to on the phone, giggling with over the funniest shared insights, and one she had not heard in the longest time. Funny, after all these years, it took no more than a microsecond for her to place it.

'Yes?'

'Oh, Bessie, this is weird but wonderful! Happy birthday! It's me – it's Michelle.'

I know! I know it's you!

'Goodness me! Michelle . . .' There was something joyful about saying out loud this word that had lived for so long in her mind. Bess caught her breath and realised her hands were shaking. Why was Michelle calling now? What had happened? The knife-edge of fear glistened in the sunlight pooled on the laminate flooring of her hallway.

Don't be ridiculous, Bess, keep calm . . . Just keep calm . . .

She felt a thick tangle of emotions, but primarily the jolt of loss, a wave of joy and a knot of shame, which all gathered in her brain and slipped down her throat, making speech tricky.

'I can't believe it – it's been a long time.' Her mouth was sticky with nerves, and with trembling limbs she took up her favourite seat on the stairs, about a third of the way up.

'It has – a lifetime.' Her friend gave a small humph of laughter. 'Do you know, it's . . . it's the weirdest thing . . .' Michelle started to chat like it was yesterday and not over thirty years since they had last spoken. 'I was on my morning walk and the date came up on my phone and it was nagging me for a couple of miles: August the twentieth, August the twentieth . . . I kept repeating it, couldn't think why it was important, and then I rounded the bend in the road and remembered: Bessie's birthday! I knew you were now a Talbot and did a quick search, and hey presto! Your number popped up and here we are!'

Bess recognised the nervous babble as her friend remembered this about her.

'And it was yours last month.' *The last gift I bought you: bubble-gum-flavoured lip gloss . . .*

'Yep. Fifty-three. How on earth did that happen?'

'I don't know!' Bess laughed, and her old friend joined in. It was like a warm, rounded pebble cast into water, breaking the surface, sending out ripples to ease the tension and uniting them. They could always make each other laugh. Bess knew she hadn't laughed as hard or as carelessly since she'd done so with this woman by her side, as they gripped their stomachs and, with tears sprouting, made a desperate dash to the bathroom.

'Trouble is, Bessie, I still think I'm sixteen until I look in the mirror and think, Jesus, my nan's come to visit! But no, it's me.'

'Ah, your lovely nan . . .' Bess remembered the old lady who had commandeered her grandsons' bedroom and sent them to sleep in a caravan. The old lady who used to try to escape at any and every opportunity. Bess pictured her with her rolled-up swimming towel under her arm and in borrowed wellington boots.

'I still miss her,' Michelle whispered. 'It's not very often I speak to anyone who knew her. Mum too, she passed away a few years ago now.'

'I did hear that, Michelle, and I was sorry.'

'Oh, it happens, right? The one certainty, but she had a lovely life – she was always with us, used to joke she was a lady of leisure, and she bloody was. Dad's in a great flat with help on hand and he's doing well, considering.'

Bess smiled at the thought of Michelle's dad, who had been at death's door for over five decades, still going strong, and her mum living the high life. No wonder she had wanted her daughter to marry money . . . The irony of how things had turned out was not lost on her. She looked at her narrow hallway and the chipped paint on her front door and wondered how close she herself had come to having a very different life.

'And your mum and dad . . . are they still . . . ?' Michelle's tone was hesitant.

'Both still very much around.'

'But not still playing the harmonica on your birthday, surely?'

'They've done that this very morning over the phone.'

'That's hilarious!'

Their laughter was familiar and emotional and was followed by a beat of silence. Bess held the phone close to her face. Both were seemingly at a loss as to how to continue. Silence wrapped them, as words too fragile to voice lay flat on her tongue: *How I have missed you, my friend . . . How I wish sometimes to go back to those days when we sat on the sofa, eating sweets, singing songs, pondering our glittering futures, dreaming of pop stars and all that lay ahead for us . . . My dearest, dearest friend . . .*

'Where . . . where are you?' Bess had picked up on the smallest delay and the slightest echo on the line, nothing obvious, but subtle enough to tell her that this call was not being made from a house within the same postcode.

'Portugal,' Michelle said.

'Oh lovely,' Bess supposed, having never been. 'Are you on holiday?'

'No, no, we, erm . . . It's . . . We live here a lot of the time. It's okay.'

Bess recognised a reticence that smacked of pity and insight.

'So whaddya get for your birthday?'

'Can't remember . . . not much . . . Some Maltesers . . .'

She knew, of course, about her friend's wealth – there were many from school she still bumped into who were, if anything,

117

a little obsessed with it. Melanie Brooks, née Hall, for one, who liked nothing more than to fill Bess in with whatever she had seen on Facebook about the Paulsons' glamorous life – who would have thought a skip-hire business could have given them that kind of cash? But it had. '*The Paulsons*' – a couple. Official. Michelle and Lawrence. Lawrence and Michelle. It didn't matter that decades had passed since they tied the knot, the fact still had the power to knock the wind from her sails and brought back memories too painful to voice. And Bess certainly didn't need Melanie's bright-eyed commentary in the shopping aisle, gushed across their trolleys, as if they had always been mates. Advertisements for 'Paulson's Skips' were on billboards, on the radio, on TV and in every newspaper she picked up; the jingle had seen her reach for the mute button that very morning. Melanie had seemed agitated in her desire to share what she knew.

'I think it was her youngest who posted it, but they were on a massive boat, like a yacht thing – massive! And she had this whopping great Rolex on her wrist, and he still looks really good, like *really* good, and she was tanned and in a white bikini and Gucci shades and he was sitting there with a fat cigar and a gold bracelet! And you didn't hear it from me' – she leant in and spoke out of the side of her mouth – 'but I'm sure Michelle has had work done, I mean, if not work then definitely Botox – she looks about thirty and her teeth are perfect, too perfect, if you know what I mean, so white and straight. She looked like a flippin' Bee Gee!'

This was typical of Melanie – everything was undercut with a little meanness. It wasn't pleasant. Bess had barely raised an eyebrow, didn't want to give Melanie the satisfaction in the retelling of how she had looked crestfallen, regretful, envious . . .

'We're in Vale do Lobo – do you know it?' Michelle asked now. *How would I know it? I'm lucky if we get a week in Clacton!*

118

'No, I don't. Is it lovely weather? Must be hot this time of year?' She pictured the two of them sunbathing with baby oil slathered on their skin, burning to a crisp – oh, the damage! The wrinkles, the carelessness! *I remember our tanning hours when the little square of garden at my mum and dad's house used to get the sun . . . and we'd sit, staring at its crisping rays . . .* Bess didn't feel confident enough to mention this; it seemed a bit pathetic now that Michelle lived in warmth and splendour – their childish imitation of living the high life a little embarrassing now her friend had the real thing.

'Yeah, it's lovely most of the time, bit too hot for me right now, hence my morning walk along the coast road, where there's a bit of a breeze. I'm never missed – this is when Lawrie plays his golf.'

Michelle had done it. Mentioned his name – her husband. She had brought the man who had driven the wedge between them into the conversation, the boy who had tossed a grenade into the heart of their fantastic relationship and who was now the elephant in the room.

'And he's . . . you're . . . you're both well?' Bess cringed and screwed her eyes tight shut. Her mind faltering, she struggled to find words that were safe and not incriminating, trying to act normally while her stomach churned with something that felt a lot like fear.

I'm scared, Philip, I'm scared . . .

'Yeah, we're great. Getting on a bit, but still like a couple of old bookends!'

'I . . . I like a nice walk too.' Bess changed the topic, picturing the grey jaunt she sometimes took up the shops and back when they had run out of milk or to get a sliced loaf for Mario's sandwiches. It was about as far from a coastal view with the Portuguese sun on her back as you could get. Bess felt hollow, a little inadequate and terribly left behind as she listened.

'Even winter is bearable. I remember you were always such a sun-worshipper. You didn't go and live in California then?' Her friend laughed softly, and this shared memory was enough to make her stomach fold with loss. They had been so close, and Bess knew she had never had a mate like Michelle before or since, thinking how hard it had been to reach out the hand of friendship, knowing when she met new people that her reputation might have preceded her. As she looked through the frosted glass in the front door out over the cul de sac and watched Mr Draper watering the carnations in his plastic tub, she knew that her sixteen-year-old self would have described the place in which she lived as a bit 'Ronnie'.

'No, not quite,' she said in the end. 'But you did – you followed the sun.'

'Yes, quite unplanned, Bessie. We used to come out for holidays when the kids were little, but since Lawrie retired and our oldest, Brandon, took over the business, we're here more and more. Funnily enough, when we bought the house, I thought of you – we always said, didn't we, that we wanted a balcony with a fantastic view?'

'We did.' Bess felt suddenly a pang of longing for that sunset view as much as for the company of her old friend.

'We've still got a place in London, though. I couldn't bear to be away from my grandchildren for too long.'

'Michelle, you're a nanna! How wonderful!' She meant it – funny that this was the thing that caused a flare of pure envy, not so much the second home in the Vale de doo dah or whatever it was called and not a place in London, but grandchildren . . . Little ones she could love unconditionally and who she hoped would love her in return, and she could immerse herself back in family life. She pictured Natalie rushing off to work and wished her daughter had someone nice to support her in both her career and in her desire to become a mum.

120

'I know you have a boy and a girl. My mum used to chat to your mum when they bumped into each other.'

'Yes, Jake and Natalie, both lovely.'

'Of course they are.' Michelle was smiling kindly, she could tell.

There was another pause, as if, when they weren't discussing the rudimentary, they faltered. Maybe Michelle was also fearful of opening old wounds, reliving past hurts or of souring this rare contact that, so far, was going well.

'I often think about you, Bessie,' she said.

'And I you.' Bess swallowed: it was the truth. Many were the moments in her life big and small when her instinct was to call Michelle, to make her laugh, share her joy, get her take on things or to fall into her arms when the world felt a bit too much. Her wedding day, the births of Jake and Natalie, her miscarriage, her cancer scare, her sad days and her angry ones, all had a Michelle-shaped hole in them.

'It's funny, isn't it, how you have great mates throughout your life, but those teenage years, that closeness' – Michelle paused – 'it was a special time, wasn't it?'

'It really was.' Bess hated the emotion that threatened.

'Can you imagine now wanting to wear the exact same clothes as someone and have the same hair and same accessories?'

Bess chuckled. It *was* funny, and yet every sentence seemed to veer dangerously close to the topic she knew they would both be keen to avoid.

'We were kids,' Bess reminded herself.

Michelle took a deep breath. '. . . In some ways.'

Bess felt uncomfortable and looked down at the welcome mat by the front door, covered in clumps of plaster from Mario's boots.

'Anyway . . .' her friend whispered. There was an awkward pause. 'I just wanted to wish you a happy, happy birthday, Bessie, and I hope you're doing something nice to celebrate?'

'Actually, I'm going out for lunch with Mum and Dad.'

'Oh smashing. Do you remember they used to love going to that grotty carvery on the London Road?'

'I do.' Bess closed her eyes and felt her face colour, wondering what lunch would be like where Michelle was. She pictured cocktails and sun-drenched terraces, comfortable loungers placed around crystal-clear pools and fancy kitchens, a bit like the ones she had always so admired in *Knots Landing*.

'Well, half your luck. I'm playing tennis and quite frankly I could do without it today, it's far too hot.'

Bess opened her mouth and did not know what to say – what was the correct thing to say to someone about to play tennis? *Hope you win? Break a leg?* She didn't know anyone who played tennis or golf – apart from Lawrie and Michelle that was, the girl whose brothers used to sleep in a caravan on the driveway. Sitting on the stairs in Natalie's old dressing gown, Bess thought of how their lives could not be more different, and those differences erased their past closeness and nullified their shared experience.

'If you're ever in Portugal, it would be so lovely to . . .' Michelle went quiet and they both listened to the tick of awkwardness across the miles. What was she suggesting? Lunch? A catch-up? A game of mixed doubles? It all felt a little ridiculous in the face of thirty-odd years with no contact.

'I'd better let you get on, Michelle.'

'I hope it was okay to call?'

'Of course it was, it was lovely.' She meant it, crying now, cursing the crack in her voice and feeling a stab of loss at how their wonderful friendship had ended, so abruptly and so painfully. And knowing the call was coming to an end with so much left unsaid.

'I always wondered . . .' Michelle began hesitantly, coughing to clear her throat. 'I always wondered what I'd done wrong. I still think about it sometimes, less now than I used to, but . . . We were so close, Bessie, and then just . . . nothing.'

She could tell that Michelle was crying too. Bess held the phone more tightly to her face.

'It felt . . .' she tried, closing her eyes and trying to find the right word, '. . . easier.'

'Easier?' Michelle's voice broke and Bess could sense her distress across the miles. 'God, well, I would hate to have experienced the tougher option. It wasn't easier for me. It was like you'd died. I grieved for you, if that makes any sense.'

It made perfect sense. Bess recalled the lingering dull ache of loss in her chest, lying in her childhood bed as the summer wound on and on, waiting for her life to begin, waiting to make new friends, but always, always, keeping them at arm's length and avoiding boys altogether because that was where danger lurked. She had remained closed down entirely until Mario had walked into the staffroom at the back of the supermarket some three years later and smiled at her.

'I don't suppose you're Mr Roger Hamilton?' he had asked, and they had both laughed.

'I'm not,' she had smiled.

'Well, that's a pity, because then I'd get to spend the afternoon with you, as that's who I'm here to see.' He had held her gaze a fraction longer than was polite and it had woken something inside her, something that had lain dormant for the longest time. 'So, if you're not Roger Hamilton, who are you?'

'I'm Bessie, Bessie Worrall.'

'Bessie Worrall,' he had repeated. Her name left his lips like music, calling her to him with a soft, slow symphony that would help her mend.

'You know, Michelle . . .' Bess liked the novelty of saying the name; she tried to speak, tried to find the honest words of both justification and apology, but found it almost impossible, so instead she took a sharp breath and closed her eyes. '. . . it really has been so lovely to hear from you.' She was aware of the closing nature of her sentence and of her clipped tone. Not for the first time in her life, this felt easier.

'Well . . .' Michelle too sounded like she wanted to say more. 'Happy birthday, Bessie. And goodbye.'

'Bye.'

Bessie put the phone back on to the charging station and let her head fall heavy on her chest. Leaning on the box the flowers had come in, her cry was a long, deep howl of heartbreak.

CHAPTER NINE

August 20th 1984

Bessie sat at her dressing table with a new sense of optimism that had been missing all day. There *would* be a way for her to achieve her dreams! She just had to figure it out. This change in mind-set alone gave her hope of getting into the sky and landing in California. Shaking her head, she closed out images of Michelle walking into the sixth-form building and the allocated common room and sitting on the top deck of the bus, where only those in the final two years of school dared to venture.

'Okay, enough!' she said, staring at her reflection in the mirror. 'Just get over it, Bessie! It's not going to happen. Mum and Dad are right – you have to make a new plan, find a new way. Are you going to let a lack of grades keep you on the ground, stuck here? Of course you're not! You are going to ignore the fact that the world thinks you're stupider than Nicola Pie or Sean Thornton or even Ronnie Booker!' The thought of any of them studying their dire results and sighing with relief, thinking, *Well, it could be worse! I could be Bessie Worrall!* was as embarrassing as it was unthinkable. 'And you're going to go for it!' She smiled, admiring her fabulous teeth.

'Knock knock!' Her dad walked in slowly, and she smiled. 'Well, don't you look like a proper bobby-dazzler!'

'Thanks, Dad, I think.' She had no idea who or what a bobby-dazzler was, but figured it was something good.

'I just wanted to say, don't worry about anything, my love. Put your results out of your head and have a nice time tonight. This is the kind of evening you'll remember – the one where everyone lets their hair down.'

'I'm a bit embarrassed, Dad, but I will have a nice time. I'm going to dance and laugh, and tomorrow is a brand-new day where anything can happen, right?'

'That's the spirit! And being embarrassed isn't going to change anything, but it just might hold you back, and that would be a damn shame.' He reached into his pocket and pulled out the harmonica. 'Would you like me to play you a little something before you go out?'

'Oh God, please no!' Bessie jumped up and pressed play on her tape recorder. 'I really wouldn't.'

She heard him chuckling as he left the room. Before the door closed, Philip appeared, keeping his distance, as if the girly vibe within the four walls might be contagious.

'This music is shit!' he sneered. She ignored him. He said this no matter what she listened to, trying to prove he was cooler than her with his Joy Division cassette on a constant loop.

'I found these – cherry brandy!' He held out a flat box of chocolate liqueurs that she vaguely remembered arriving one Christmas, a gift from their tarty Auntie Nerys.

'They look disgusting! Dark chocolate, yuk!' she said, wrinkling her nose.

'Yes, but they're still booze. They were at the back of the sideboard. I think Mum and Dad have forgotten they're there – look,' he said, flipping the box over to read the back. 'It says not to be sold to anyone under eighteen! They're out of date.'

'By how much?'

'A year or two, but alcohol's a preservative, right?'

'I guess so.' She shrugged; Philip knew about these things. He wasn't the one who had failed his exams. 'I might have one or two,' she conceded.

His face lit up, as if delighted that she was on board.

'And this, as promised.'

From under his shirt he pulled out the old green-and-blue-checked thermos that their mum filled with tea for long journeys and picnics. Or more specifically, picnic, as they had only ever been on one and that had ended in disaster, with the car stuck in sand and a blazing row between her parents over whose job it was to take notice of 'DANGER DO NOT PARK' signs, followed by a two-hour wait for the vehicle recovery man in the rain. No wonder they had needed a thermos of hot tea.

'I tipped half the bottle in. It's not too bad – I had a swig. Try it!'

Philip watched as she unscrewed the top and tentatively brought it to her mouth, the fumes of the sweet liquor dancing up her nose before she had even taken a sip. It tasted warm and sharp, zingy and fruity, like wine but stronger, and yes, her brother was right – not too bad at all.

'I'll leave you to it.'

'Thanks, Philip,' she smiled at him.

'That's okay. I know you've had a rubbish birthday, but it's not over yet, eh?'

'No, it's not!' She beamed with the thrill of what the evening ahead might hold. First, she had to tell Michelle about Lawrence, but then she would get to *be* with Lawrence.

It was nice to be conspiring with her brother and not arguing or competing with him.

Bessie wielded her blusher brush as Yazoo sang to her from *Upstairs at Eric's*, and even though she hummed along, her stomach flipped with nerves at the prospect of walking into the party alone. The thought of it was enough to make her puff her cheeks out and exhale sharply like an athlete pre-event and to reach for another swig of booze.

She had the evening mapped out in her mind. Her plan was to arrive a little late, as the only prospect worse than walking in alone was walking in alone and her friend not being there. If she couldn't see Michelle upon arrival, she'd ask someone to go and find her while she waited outside. Her mission then would be to speak confidently and plainly, holding her friend by the shoulders, looking her in the eye and setting out all the reasons why Lawrence Paulson was off limits. Bessie didn't want to hurt Michelle's feelings, of course she didn't, she loved her! But what Bessie and Lawrence shared was no mere fling, and the sooner she spoke out, the less awkward it would be for them all. She truly wanted the three of them to be friends and saw no reason they couldn't hang out together once the news was out. Bessie practised her speech in the mirror, swigging again from the thermos before speaking as earnestly as her self-consciousness surrounding the topic would allow.

'I never want a boy to come between us – we agree on that – but this is a bit more than just any old boy, Michelle. This is Lawrence Paulson. And the truth is, he and I have a thing going on.' She took a breath and held up her hand. 'Please don't be mad at me for keeping it a secret. I didn't want to tell you because I didn't know how you'd react, plus we agreed to keep it between the two of us.' She liked how that sounded, conspiratorial and coupley. 'But the fact is, we've had sex, Michelle, and not just the once, but *nine* times . . . Yes, nine times. And I like it – I mean, I *really* like it, and I want more of it. It's all I can think about – it fills my thoughts. It's one of the reasons I didn't do well in my exams: I couldn't stop thinking about him. I have wanted to share it with you, and the good news is, now I can. I know we've spoken about what sex might feel like, and I can tell you honestly that it doesn't hurt, not after the first little bit and, oh Michelle! It feels amazing and it's addictive and the look on his face . . . It makes me feel alive! And I know what Tony said to you, but Lawrence told *me* I was special and cool and that he thought about me before he fell asleep – those were his *actual* words. I mean, how sweet is that? And that's the reason you have to ignore what Tony said because, and I know this sounds ridiculous, I think Lawrence and I have a future . . . A very sexy future.'

Bessie smiled into the mirror. Okay, her speech needed a bit of work, but it was almost there. She studied her face, looking at her smile from all angles, liking what she saw. As her mum said, *pretty*. After cleaning her teeth to wash away the nasty tang of Cinzano that lingered on her tongue, she rubbed strawberry-scented body lotion on her flat stomach, which was just visible if she reached up or bent over, liking the tan she had cultivated over the last few weeks. She and Michelle had spent hours lying in the park or on the small square of patio in her parents' back garden, which caught the sun during what they had christened 'the tanning hours', between one thirty and three thirty in the afternoon, when they would slather their face, neck and shoulders with baby oil and stare at the bright, bright rays. They had burned fairly quickly, which was standard to achieve the best tan, and having gone through the burn and peel phase, were now blessed with stay-put, long-lasting tans that left them with skin the colour of burnished caramel. It also gave them the look of worldly-wise women who had travelled, possibly to Los Angeles, somewhere Bessie could not pinpoint on a map and yet was at the top of her list of places where she would like to live, should she ever decide to move out of St Albans. She gave her armpits a double slick of deodorant. The three grubby round plasters, she replaced with fresh ones that sat on top of the nasty red cuts on her shin. It was important that she looked perfect tonight. The Cinzano felt nice, warming her from the inside out and adding a hazy glow to her world.

With one final look in her narrow full-length mirror and having blown a kiss to Simon and the rest of the boys on the wall, she raced down the stairs, keen to get out of the house with minimal fuss and, more important, before her mum noticed her glassy eyes or the heady whiff of booze.

'Let's have a look at you then!' her mum called out from the sofa, where she sat with her legs tucked beneath her. A mug of coffee and three 'Shortie' biscuits rested on her thigh, as canned laughter from *Terry and June* filled the room. Her dad was in his chair in his slippers, legs stretched out and crossed at the ankle. Bessie walked in and gave a little twirl to show off her new sweatshirt.

'You look gorgeous!' her mum beamed. 'Really lovely, Bessie – your make-up is so clever.'

'Thanks, Mum.' She felt properly boosted by the words of compliment. Her dad nodded in agreement and went back to his programme.

'Now what can I get you to eat before you leave?' Her mum sat forward, piling her biscuits in a little tower and resting them on the larger of the tile-topped nest of tables by the side of the sofa, placing her mug next to them, as if they could wait.

'I'm just leaving now, actually.' Bessie pointed at the front door. 'Plus, I'm not hungry.'

'What do you mean, you're not hungry? You haven't had any tea and it's your birthday!'

Bessie exchanged a look with her dad, who pulled a face, indicating that he too had no idea why her birthday might be a relevant factor with regard to her hunger levels.

'I'm just not. I can always get a sandwich when I get in,' she insisted.

'I suppose so.' Her mum seemed to consider this. 'Shall I make you one and leave it in the fridge? I'll cling-film it for you?'

'That'd be lovely. Thanks, Mum.' Bessie had no intention of eating the sandwich, but this was the easiest and quickest way to get her mother to drop the subject.

Her mum visibly perked up. 'So what do you fancy, chicken and mayonnaise? Tuna and sweetcorn? Corned beef and pickle?'

'Urgh!' Philip called from the bottom of the stairs.

'Oh, that's right, you're a vegan now, aren't you, mate?' their dad chuckled. 'He'll have a lentil sandwich! Or another chocolate Club!' He looked again at his son and his laughter fell away. 'Are you wearing make-up, boy?'

'A little bit,' Philip said sheepishly.

Bessie admired her brother's eyeliner, which was, she noted, rather artfully applied.

'Well, I never thought I'd see the day!' her dad sighed. 'Socks without feet and now my son in make-up!'

'Leave him alone, Eddie. It's all the rage,' her mum said, batting at him with her hand.

Bessie smiled at Philip, pleased that he was this confident in his skin.

'Or cheese and tomato?' her mum continued, as if the previous twenty seconds had never occurred.

'Yes, cheese and tomato would be lovely.' Bessie couldn't care less about the sandwich but wanted her mum to stop with the sandwich choices – it felt like an added pressure all on its own.

'Smashing.' Her mum, clearly satisfied, popped a whole biscuit in her mouth before picking up her knitting and click-clacking the needles together with a small smile on her face, happy that she could prepare a sandwich for her daughter who might or might not be hungry later.

'You look . . .' Her dad now lowered his paper and stared suspiciously at her with narrowed eyes. '. . . a bit rosy-cheeked?'

'Blusher,' said Bessie, slurring a little and glad she was far enough away from him not to smell the Cinzano fumes she was sure wafted from her.

'Have a lovely time, darling, and be careful,' her mum said through her mouthful.

'I will. See you later, guys!' Bessie lifted her hand in a little wave and left the house, closely followed by Philip, who was off to meet Carmen. She wondered if the next social might see her and Lawrence arriving as a couple. A small squeal of excitement left her mouth as she ran her hand over her flat stomach, confident that she looked great, sexy even. She strode confidently down the pavement, flicking her hair over her shoulder; Philip had to jog to catch up.

'Are you drunk?' He looked a little worried.

'Maybe just a little bit.' She held her thumb and forefinger together. 'I reckon it was those horrible cherry brandy chocolates,' she laughed.

'Yeah, that'll be it, and not the Cinzano you necked. Did you drink it all?'

'Uh-huh,' she nodded.

'God, Bessie! You were supposed to sip it and make it last all evening!'

'Oh yeah! I can just see me on the dance floor with Mum's old thermos in my hand. That wouldn't look weird at all!' She giggled again, quite sure he had not given her the specific instruction to sip it.

They came to the end of the road, where Philip had to branch off to make his way to Carmen's house.

'Are you sure you're going to be okay? Do you want to come with me to Carmen's and then we can all walk together? Or you can wait here, and we'll come back this way and collect you?'

'No! God, no!' Bessie waved her hand in his direction. 'I don't want to be a gooseberry, plus I need to get to the rugby club.' She could only picture Lawrence's face and recall the feeling of his hands on her skin; she ran her fingertips lightly over her stomach.

'Well . . .' Philip looked up and down the street, as if making a judgement call, before flicking his long fringe. 'We won't be far behind you. I'll see you there.'

'Cool, and Philip?' she called over her shoulder as he walked away.

'What?' he asked, turning towards her and walking backwards.

'Nice eyeliner.'

He beamed and jogged out of sight.

Bessie liked being a little sloshed, liked the way it took the edge off her upset, although the aftertaste of dark chocolate and the sting of cherry brandy at the back of her throat, not so much. She might have been a little wobbly on her feet, but she was energised and ready to dance! She and Michelle had standard moves that they performed for every song, speeding it up or slowing it down accordingly. They largely copied the sideward arm across body movement of Marc Almond singing 'Tainted Love', alternately tapping each foot, with a little finger click thrown in occasionally.

From side streets and driveways, students from her school began to emerge, clusters of friends, duos and lone travellers like herself, but all heading towards the rugby club, from where, even at this distance, the unmistakeable sound of Bronski Beat's 'Smalltown Boy' drifted over the rooftops. The powerful blend of distant music and summer air thick with hormones, cheap scent, chewing gum and teenage sweat wrapped the party-goers in a hypnotic trance as they trundled along the grey-slabbed pavement to the social event that held such promise, sparkling in their finery and in anticipation of the magic that lay in wait.

Bessie hated the feeling that she and Michelle were not okay – an unwelcome shift in her world, impossible to fathom. She needed to speak with her first thing. After that, she would take Lawrence by the hand, and so what if people saw? What better way to shout to the world, *I may have fluffed my exams, but look at my consolation prize!* Her heart squeezed with excitement – this felt like a whole new beginning.

She could see the disco lights flashing through the steamed-up windows of the rugby club, as the gravelled car park crunched beneath the soles of her boat shoes. Scanning the crowd, her eyes searched the generous amount of neon on display, trying to locate a pink cropped sweatshirt like the one she was wearing, but without any luck. Standing still, she pulled the birthday lip gloss from her jeans pocket and applied another sticky coat, sliding her lips together and knowing how good it would look against her white teeth. She felt a little tipsy and with the first stirring of nausea in her gut, and put this down to nerves as she continued to look for Michelle in the crowd.

Monica and Verity, the pogoing drama queens, squealed past her quite suddenly like fireworks fizzing into the night sky as they ran to the main doors and disappeared inside.

A loud peal of laughter caught her attention. She turned in time to see Melanie Hall and her gaggle all bent double and laughing at some snarky comment, no doubt.

'Oh my God! No waaaaaay!' one of her gang shrieked in an earsplitting scream. 'That's disgusting!'

It surprised her how little she cared what they might be laughing at. Someone grabbed her arm and yanked her towards them. It was Tony Dunlop, who had, she noted, slicked his hair back in a poor imitation of the Fonz.

'Bessie!' He grinned at her and, despite being a little drunk herself, she recognised the slur of someone who had necked more than their fair share of booze.

'Let go of my arm!' She pulled away from him, not liking the way he handled her, and began to search the crowd in earnest. It was funny how that little moment of alertness had sent a shock of sobriety through her veins.

'Oh come on, don't be like that.' He leant in, and with his hand half hidden by their close proximity, stroked her bottom.

Bessie's gut jumped in fear and revulsion. 'Get off me, Tony, you creep!'

'What's the matter? I thought you liked it "up the alley" – if you get my meaning?' Tony chortled.

A hot poker of shame lanced her gut as she stared at this pig of a boy, his one brown tooth at the front quite repulsive, his words even more so.

'I don't know what you're talking about,' she spat. Surely . . . surely Lawrence hadn't broken his word . . . He wouldn't do that to her . . . He wouldn't. He was the boy who thought about her before he fell asleep. The boy she had trusted with her body.

'Oh, I think you do,' he grinned. 'I'm talking about the fact that you didn't seem quite so choosy when Lawrie was at the bus stop. "Gagging for it," he said you was. And I just wondered, why him and not me?' He stared at her, unblinking.

'Go away and leave me alone!' She folded her arms across her chest to stop them from shaking. Cornered, she spun round, her heart racing and her throat tight. *He had told Tony! He had told Tony!* Her arms fell to her sides, as if she no longer had the strength to keep them up. She felt more than a little sick.

'To be honest, I didn't realise you were that picky, Bessie,' Tony smirked.

'I told you, I don't know what you're talking about!' The trembling spread from her arms to her legs at his words and the way in which he delivered them. She prayed that her denial might smother his intentions.

'Yes, you do. So you're a liar too? Me and the lads, you see, we're all hoping to become part of the BBC . . .' He let this hang.

'The TV station? What are you talking about?' Half a bottle of Cinzano sloshing in her veins did nothing to aid her lucidity.

Tony laughed hard, again showing his little brown tooth. 'No, you silly cow, the Bang Bessie Club – who would have thought a plain girl like you would be such a goer?'

Bessie's mouth fell open and her knees felt weak. She was shocked and deeply offended at his foul suggestion, and thought she might vomit as a cold film of sweat crept over her skin.

Tony tutted and shook his head. 'And the thing is, the alleyway is not that private, Bessie.' He reached out and ran a thumb over her cheek.

She recoiled, slapping his hand away from her face.

'People might have been watching. In fact' – he paused and smiled again – 'people were most definitely watching.' He winked. 'You should be more careful.'

Bessie gagged and swallowed the wave of sick rising in her mouth. She clapped her hands over her ears. 'Stop talking to me! Just fuck off and leave me alone!' Outwardly she raged, but inside it was as if her very fabric was dissolving, rendering down into nothing more than mush in the acid of his words. She closed her eyes for a second, wishing she could literally disappear.

'I see how it is, and that's a shame.' Tony pulled out a packet of cigarettes and lit one, drawing on it between his thumb and forefinger, trying and failing to look like a T-Bird in his plastic leather jacket. 'You're a slut, Bessie Worrall.' His words were weapons and they wounded her so distinctly she could feel the pain of them in her chest. He exhaled and his second-hand smoke hit her in the face. 'I know it, Lawrie knows it and *you* know it, and by tomorrow, everyone in that rugby club will know it.' He pointed with his cigarette towards the low building where the music pulsed and the lights flashed, before removing a small fleck of tobacco from his tongue.

'I am not!' she croaked, her tears rising and with something close to panic in her throat. His threat was horrific, laced with venom, and worst of all from Bessie's perspective, it was rooted in truth.

'But you *are*! Having sex with someone you don't even know – nine times?' He tutted loudly. 'That's sluttish, you dirty girl.'

'I want to talk to Lawrence.' Bessie wanted to face the boy who had been as keen as her to get physical and had apparently done the worst thing he could: turn on her, lie to her, ridicule and use her! She needed to look him in the eye to confirm he had really done this because there was a chance, the smallest chance, that he had told Tony in confidence and was unaware of his friend's behaviour. Maybe he would leap to her defence, take her hand and tell her it was all going to be okay . . . She wished with every fibre of her being that this might be so, still unable to think that the boy who had lived in her mind, stolen her daydreams, and by doing so helped mess up her exams and re-route her future, would be capable of such shitty behaviour.

Tony laughed out loud. 'I bet you do, but he doesn't want to talk to you.'

'Yes, he does,' she managed, her limbs quaking. 'You don't know what we share!'

'Oh, you saddo – that's priceless!' He took a step closer. 'And *you* don't know what I do.' He came closer still and she could smell the cigarette smoke on his breath. 'You see, there's this girl he likes, I mean *really* likes – not just a hole, but someone he wants to go out with, someone he respects.'

Bessie cried hard at hearing this and hated herself for it. Instinctively, she shoved him as hard as she was able in the chest. It might have been his slippery soles on the gravel of the car park or his drunken state that made him lose his balance, but either way, Tony toppled backwards, hitting the deck with a thud.

'Waaaaaaagh!' went the roar of all those close enough to bear witness, as they pointed and chuckled, nudging the next person to make sure they didn't miss the sight of Tony Full-of-Shite Dunlop on his back, scrabbling in the stones to stand up and rubbing dust and gravel from the arms of his jacket. Bessie felt her heart race, wary of his revenge. Tony stood eventually, before calmly raising his hands to all those laughing. He then took a bow and the crowd laughed some more; the odd one or two even clapped. From a certain distance it was all very jolly, but Bessie was close enough to see the froth of spit at the corners of his mouth, the red stamp of embarrassment on his neck and his eyes, the pupils of which were mere pinpricks. He came at her again, closer now, too close. Her fear was real and her limbs shook.

'How dare you push me over!' he spat through gritted teeth.

'Well, don't touch me! Don't say such horrible things to me!' she replied. She scanned the crowd, looking for Michelle, the girl who was like family, comfort and solidarity to her, a safe harbour.

'Do you know what?' Tony laughed, 'I'm going to really enjoy telling everyone. You won't be able to set foot outside of your house without someone giving you a certain look, and they won't even have to say a thing, but you'll know what they're thinking. You'll know what we're all thinking – that you're fucking dumb and a fucking slut!' From the floor he retrieved his cigarette, which had miraculously survived the tumble, and drew on it sharply. 'Why are you crying?' he asked sarcastically.

Bessie swiped the tears from her cheeks and struggled to find words of retaliation, wary of angering Tony more and of him wreaking worse havoc with her reputation. She laid her arm over her stomach, hiding her skin, wanting to cover up so as not to look like a girl who'd had sex in an alleyway.

'Just leave me alone!' Her voice cracked as disappointment and self-recrimination poked at her – was this the best she could come up with?

'Don't cry, Bessie, you should be proud!' he goaded her. 'I mean, nine is a respectable number, far better than three hundred and sixty-one.'

Something inside of Bessie snapped, and all the buds of confidence that had started to bloom shrivelled away. All her wonderful thoughts of becoming an air hostess became entangled in Tony's disgusting words – is that what she was? *A hole? A slut? Fucking dumb?* Her breath came in starts. She pulled the hem of her sweat-shirt down, wishing she wasn't wearing it as the cool evening air grazed the bare skin of her midriff. It made her feel exposed, *dirty*. She watched Tony walk away with a spring in his step. The crowds around her seemed to have swelled and the loud beat coming from inside the hall was now deafening.

All her earlier bravado fled. She felt alone, anxious, sick and full to the brim with hot shame.

'Bessie!' Louise Berry called out and waved.

Bessie turned away. *Did Louise know? Did everyone know? I thought it was just between the two of us. Tony's right: I am so stupid – so stupid! I trusted Lawrence!*

She looked beyond Louise and saw Philip and Carmen walking along the pavement, hand in hand. She knew it was only a matter of time before Philip heard what Tony had to say, and the thought of that was almost more than she could bear.

'Louise!' she called out, wanting to talk to someone – anyone.

'Hey, Bessie!' Louise walked over, her expression excited, eager. 'They're playing "Oops Upside Your Head!" Come and sit in the boat!' This was a reference to the dance performed by every teenager in the land, where they sat on the floor in long lines, each close behind the other with legs splayed in a V, clapping in time and leaning side to side or from front to back until the music finished.

'I don't . . . I don't feel like it, Louise,' Bessie sniffed.

'Oh no, have you been crying? Are you okay?' Louise put her hand on Bessie's shoulder. She was a sweet girl.

'I'm . . . I'm fine,' Bessie lied. 'Have you seen Michelle?'

'Yes, erm . . .' Louise patted her finger on her lips as if this might help her think. 'I know, I saw her going out towards the benches!'

'Thanks, Lou.' Bessie headed around the side of the building to where the benches sat in a strip along the side of the football pitch. She stumbled in the dirt as dusk pulled its blind on the day, almost doubled over with relief as her eyes were drawn to a flash of neon pink.

Michelle! She wanted to reach the safety of her friend, but as she quickened her pace and drew closer, she noticed she was not alone. She was in fact frantically kissing a boy with his hands up her sweatshirt, while her fingers roamed his hair.

Bessie stared, and felt her knees sway. That boy was Lawrence Paulson. Of course it was.

My Michelle . . .

CHAPTER TEN

August 20th 2021

It had shaken Bessie, talking to the woman who used to be her very, very best friend in the whole world. Hearing her voice had been enough to take her back to a time and place she'd rather forget, the memory of her physical and emotional trauma only ever one thought, one scent, one memory away. Pulling down the sun visor, she looked in the little mirror and ran the tip of her index finger over her top lip to remove the small lines of lipstick from the tiny tributaries around her mouth. With her usual dull feeling of regret, she stared also at her teeth, her pride and joy in times gone past.

Pulling into the car park a little late, Bess looked up through the windscreen of her ancient little Nissan at the dated exterior of the pub. The blue-grey paint was peeling on the wooden fascia, the word *carvery* was missing its second 'r' and, yes, Michelle was right, it was grotty. She pictured the grand facade of the Glade Hotel and felt a roll of hunger in her gut that had nothing to do with food. It was the same feeling she had carried as a teenager – wanting something more, but without understanding how to grab it or even what it was she wanted exactly. A low hum of dissatisfaction that made her ask over and over, *Is this it?* Bess recalled the way her neighbour had looked at her ravenously. It was flattering and stitched a small patch on the tatters of her self-confidence. She shook her head; a nice lunch with her parents and a catch-up on her birthday was the whole point. They didn't need fancy-pants surroundings, no room with a view of the park and champagne, and they didn't need the sparkling sea and a gold bloody Rolex on their wrists to have a nice time, did they?

With her bag over her shoulder, Bess pushed open the swing door and inhaled the stale scent of neglect: damp mixed with fried food and sweet sloshes of syrupy booze that had no doubt permeated the luridly patterned carpet. She spotted her parents immediately, sitting side by side at a table in the corner in front of a flashing quiz machine. Apart from a few men propping up the bar, they were at one of only two occupied tables in the place. She knew midday was a little early for lunch and hoped the pub might fill up a bit, knowing it could only add to the atmosphere, which was sadly lacking.

'Here she is!' her mum called out, clapping her hands to attract her daughter's attention. Her dad sat up straight and adjusted his tie, worn, she knew, especially for the occasion. The sight of them and the way they greeted her made her heart flicker with love. She wondered what they saw when they looked at her: no doubt the same young girl full of promise who had ripped off her birthday-present wrapping and spent the afternoon getting ready for her big night out.

The lone drinkers at the bar stared at her, their expressions a little disappointed, as if the fanfare from her mum had led them to expect more.

'Happy birthday, darling!' Her mum stood and kissed her warmly on the cheek.

'Thanks, Mum.'

'Happy birthday, Bessie.'

'Thank you, Dad.'

She took a seat opposite her mother at the table and laid her arm on the wooden tabletop, which was a little sticky, placing her bag on the empty seat alongside her.

'Fifty-three, baby girl, how did that happen? It doesn't seem possible,' her mum said.

'Do you feel fifty-three?' her dad asked, as he always did.

'Do you know, Dad, today I bloody do! And a whole lot more.' Her dad laughed, while she thought of Mario's face, contorted, crying, and Natalie holding up her lighter – '*Someone in the house is a not-so-secret liar.*' Her daughter's words had been whips that cracked the air around her, sending shivers of discomfort down her spine. The veiled accusation had left her feeling uneasy.

'Mind you,' her mum cut in, lassoing her dad's happy laughter from the room as her dour tone wiped the smile from his face, 'the day I had you was not exactly the happiest for me – my goodness, no! – and it certainly wasn't what you might call an easy birth . . .'

'Really, Mum? Why have you never mentioned this?' Bess held her mum's gaze while her dad chortled.

'Hello, early birds!' The waiter arrived at the table with the slightly sarcastic air of someone who had been hoping for a few more minutes to prepare for customers and yet there they were!

'We have a voucher!' Her mum whipped the shiny piece of paper from her pocket and held it up like a winning ticket. Bess felt her stomach shrink with self-consciousness.

'Very good. Well, I can take a look at that when it comes to settling the bill.' The waiter's condescension wasn't lost on Bess and she disliked him for talking in this way to her parents, for whom this was a big day out.

'I think we know what we want – three carvery plates, please!' Her dad banged his hands on the table and spoke assuredly, and this before they had been presented with a menu.

'Ah, I'm afraid we're not running the carvery today, sir. Being lunchtime and a weekday, we find that demand is low and, in these uncertain times, it's not economic to offer the carvery every day, so . . .' The waiter made a clicking noise with the side of his mouth.

'Can we still use our voucher?' Bess's mum asked desperately.

'I'm sure you can, and we do have a lovely selection of hot meals and sandwiches. Let me fetch some menus.' He disappeared around the corner and her parents looked at each other.

'No carvery?' Her dad's mouth fell open a little.

'I can't believe it.' Her mum shook her head like it was the end of the world.

Bess painted on a happy face. 'You know, it's just lovely to be out having my lunch. I'm usually the one serving lunch and so, carvery or not, it's still a treat for me.'

'Here you are, darling.' Her mum gave her a card, which had a ten-pound note nestling inside.

'And one from me!' her dad said, handing over his card, which she knew in advance would also contain ten pounds. This was how they kept the birthday excitement rolling.

'Thank you both!'

'You can treat yourself,' her mum pointed out helpfully.

'I will!' Bess made the silent snap decision to put twenty quid's worth of petrol in the car on the way home.

'Here we go.' The waiter reappeared and handed out wipe-clean menus that were decidedly dog-eared on the corners.

'We'll take some bread and butter to start,' her dad announced. 'And a white wine for the wife, a pint of bitter for me and a Coke for the daughter – unless you fancy a Cinzano, Bess?' her dad said with a big wink.

'Ooooof.' Just the word was enough to make her feel properly ill. She hadn't touched a drop of the stuff since the day she had got

144

drunk on it, and as for the smell . . . Her stomach heaved at the memory. 'I'll stick to Coke, thanks.'

'Certainly. We do a bread basket with various breads and olives, so one of those?' the waiter suggested.

'Yes, lovely,' her dad smiled.

'I don't like olives and she won't be eating bread,' her mum said, pointing at Bessie.

'Why won't I be eating bread?' Bess waited for her mother's standard response.

'Because you need to watch your weight, darling. You've got the Worrall genes, and just look at how Nanny Gloria bloated post-fifty. She was huge – absolutely huge.'

'I think we've got the message,' Bess chided her mother.

'Massive!' Her mum clearly wanted one last word on the matter, opening her hands wide like a fisherman trying to relay the size of the one that got away.

The waiter looked about as uncomfortable as Bess and made his escape to fetch the bread basket and drinks. In the moment of ensuing quiet, someone at the bar belched loudly. Bess and her parents stared at each other, their silence speaking volumes. What on earth had happened to the place? Michelle was right, it had always been grotty, but today it was both grotty and sad. Not the best combination for a birthday lunch and certainly not scrumptious. The three of them studied their menus.

'I quite fancy the scampi,' her mum said aloud with enthusiasm.

'I'm thinking steak and ale pie with mash,' her dad replied. 'What about you, Bessie?'

'Maybe a chicken salad?' She couldn't deny her mum's comments had gone some way towards influencing her decision.

'Don't be daft, you can't have a salad – it's your birthday! Don't worry about your weight on your birthday!' her mum tutted.

'But . . .' The fact was, she hadn't been worrying about her weight until her mother's comment, not at all.

'Plus, pub salads are sometimes bland and a bit too cold and tasteless. Why don't you have the scampi too?'

The waiter delivered their bread and drinks and took their order. He was speedy and smiley and redeemed himself a little in Bess's eyes. Her mum turned her nose up at the olives. Bess ate seven, straight off.

'Just nipping to the little boys' room.' Her dad ambled off.

'I hate it when he says that – it makes him sound like a paedophile,' Bess said aloud.

Her mum put her buttered bread down sharply. 'Honestly, what a terrible thing to say about your dad!'

'No . . . I'm not saying he *is* a paedophile, I'm just saying that phrase, "nipping to the little boys' room" – it's a bit, eeuuw!' She shuddered.

'Right, I'll put it on the list of all the things that we collectively do that are either wrong or irritate you, but I might just need another piece of paper.'

'What are you talking about? You don't do anything that irritates me,' Bess lied.

'Yes, I do. Like asking the waiter about using my voucher. I saw you shrink and blink. It's always those little looks, the sighs, the biting of the lip.' Bess bit her lip. 'I irritate you.'

'No, you don't.' Bess stabbed another olive with a cocktail stick.

'Yes, I do.'

'No, you don't,' Bess said, holding her ground. She didn't want to argue with her mum, not today of all days, but the volcano was bubbling inside her with lava-frothed images of Sushmita and all her birthday messages; the orchid she detested, withering on the draining board at home; and even Natalie, who had interrupted and denied her a cigarette. She pictured Michelle and the lovely life she led, and looked down at the tabletop, smeared with what looked to be the remnants of last night's gravy. She pictured Daniel, jetting off with his little case dragging behind him, heading off to work in the skies in a job she could only dream of, and she pictured Mario, who felt so far away from her even when they were close, and thought the best birthday card to buy her was one with a bloody duck on the front!

'I'm irritating you right now, I can tell.' Her mum took a sip of her wine.

'God, okay – yes! You win, Mum – you drive me absolutely batshit crazy!' Bess said, more loudly than she'd intended, and with a mouthful of olive. 'But don't worry, you're not the only one, and sometimes I wish I could run away! Mario's furious at me for calling him away from work, Natalie judges me for secretly smoking and my house is covered in bloody confetti!' Again, she imagined the glamour of the Glade Hotel: *Room 626 . . . Bubbles and a view of the park . . .* and she thought about running there right now, away from the stress of lunch with her parents. Her birthday treat.

She noticed that the couple on the other table had stopped eating and were staring at them, and she smiled at them apologetically. Bess was silent for a beat while her mum sat forward in her chair and stared at her, but in a way that was kindly, concerned, and it caused a lump of emotion to gather in her throat.

'What *is* wrong with you, Bessie?'

'God, isn't that the million-dollar question? We'd all like to know the answer to that one!' she scoffed, breathing hard to control the tears that threatened.

Her mum laced her fingers together on her chest for a moment and then rested her hands on the table, like she did when she was waiting for an answer.

'You're not yourself, love, and you haven't been for a while. You seem . . .'

'I seem what?' *Tell me, Mum! Tell me what you see – open the floodgate and let me pour out my heart. Let me try and explain my unhappiness, my state of anxiety about what it's like to live with a gut shredded through with the constant churning of the knives of inadequacy and guilt . . .*

Her mum drew breath. 'You're on edge, judgemental, unhappy, snappy, distant – and it baffles me because you have so much to feel happy about. It's your *birthday*, and Dan and Jake are happy and coming home today! And Nats is doing so well, and you have a lovely little house and a job you like . . .'

'I know all that. It's just . . .' Bess cursed the thickening at the back of her nose, not wanting to cry. And as much as she was driven to speak, it was truly far harder to open up than she had realised. She knew that no matter what she said it would only ever be half of the truth and would bring no comfort at all. 'I feel like . . .'

'You feel like what, love?' Her mum's tone was soft now, the crease at the top of her nose evidence of her concern.

'I'm fifty-three, and sometimes I can't help but wonder if this is it, Mum?'

'You think you might be dying?'

Bess questioned her mother's calm demeanour at this possibility. 'No, you silly moo! I mean all the things I thought I'd do, the way I thought I'd live. I thought I'd become someone – see the world, or at least some of it. I thought I'd feel different, be happier. I thought being happy was a given.'

'Being happy is never a given. You need to take risks. I *told* you to enter "Miss Frinton-on-Sea" when we were there on holiday.'

'This is not about "Miss Frinton-on-Sea".' Bess pinched the top of her nose, the back of her nostrils stinging with frustration. 'It's about being sixteen, and then twenty-four, and then thirty-five – and then fifty-bloody-three! And every other birthday you can think of: planning my life in my head as I get older and older, thinking about the house I might live in, the car I might drive, the sex I might have, the places I'd like to see on the planet before they're either underwater or burnt to the ground! And yet knowing deep down that I would never achieve any of it because I was too stupid and too trusting and too . . . not enough! I'm just not enough. I was never going to be pretty like Melanie Hall or rich like Michelle. And it didn't matter, not really, because above all else, I was being the best mum I could be to Jake and Nats, doing everything I could for them. It was all about my little family.'

Bess knew that every penny, every thought, every opportunity and every experience she had managed to catch in her hands had all been balled, neatly wrapped and handed to her two kids and, even now, despite them being grown-up, she was still, every single day, watching their backs. Seeing Jake married and waltzing out of the door with Daniel and the way Nats had to fit her in around her gym visits and her busy job made her question for the first time whether she had been right to put herself last, to let the fire of her marriage dwindle until the roaring flames of love and desire were no more than glowing embers. Had she been right to pour all of her energies into her kids, while Mario kept quiet and for decades had struggled to find the right moment in which to tell her how much he mourned the baby they had lost? Her thoughts spun and she felt the beginnings of a headache.

Her mum took her time in responding. 'You went on that holiday to Ibiza with Mario before you were married, and I'm pretty sure you had sex there!'

'I did, Mum, yes, you're right,' she said sharply, frustrated.

Her mum opened her mouth to speak, but the look Bess shot her encouraged her to stay quiet.

'And I look at Mario,' Bess continued, 'who works and sleeps and then works and sleeps some more, and I wonder when we're going to get going. It's like we've lost our way. We've stalled. It's like we're stuck on this bloody treadmill, and the years slip by . . . Sometimes I want to get in the car, take the holiday money out of the tin and drive as far as I can – which, knowing my luck, would be Frinton. Not that there's anything wrong with Frinton.'

'Your Auntie Nerys lived in Frinton.'

'I know she did.' There was a pause while both considered how to proceed. It was obviously not quite the birthday lunch either of them had envisaged.

'Mario's a good man.' Her mum's voice was steady.

'I know this too.' This apparently was now her stock response and all she could draw from the well of despair. It didn't feel good to be reminded of how wonderful Mario was and what a burden she must be.

'He looks after you, he looks after the kids and he's very good to us. He takes care of everything.'

'Yes, and he always has; he has always taken care of everything – he's a saint.' Bess was aware of her sarcastic tone, but it was too late to retract. She didn't mean it. The truth was, she had always felt that Mario could do so much better than a screw-up like her and it didn't make her feel good.

'You're lucky to have a man like Mario who puts up with you – he's a wonder!' her mum said, gazing out of the window.

Bess stared at her mum, distracted from her train of thought in that moment, as she wrestled with the idea that even her own mother knew she was lucky to have Mario. She wondered with a feeling of dread if that luck might run out. And what then? Alone again, an outcast *again* . . .

'I suppose the thing is, I don't remember having time to make different choices, Mum. Everything has always moved so quickly, too quickly, like someone shoving the menu in front of you and saying, *Salad or scampi?* When you don't want either, you might not even want to eat at all! But instead you point at one because you don't have the confidence to say, *Neither, thanks.*'

'You want me to call the waiter? You can change your order.'

'No, Mum. It was just an example.' Bess rubbed her forehead. 'I just don't remember thinking, *Oh! I know what I want: a dormer bungalow and a shitty job in a school canteen, where Sushmita is more valued and better liked and gets more Facebook birthday messages than me.* And then when it comes to it, the kids only pop in when it's convenient for them, and meanwhile, I'm left at home wondering where my life went! It's like I went from being sixteen with plans of how I wanted to live, to working in a supermarket, before being put on a path that I've walked in a straight line, and all because I lost faith in myself. Lost belief that I could be anything more . . .' She shook her head, thinking of how she had gone from being a teenager with the whole world at her feet to feeling like a failure, not quite up to the mark, mired in self-doubt. And it had happened in a blink. And recently it was like she had fallen so far from that straight path and into a ravine filled with rocks fashioned of shame and guilt and she spent every day scrabbling on them to try and climb her way out. And at fifty-three, Bess was sick of scrabbling.

'So what is it you actually *want?*' her mum asked.

'I want to feel valued, appreciated, *needed*, like I did when I had my family around me – my whole family. I want someone to love coming home to me and I want to love coming home to them. I want to feel like I'm enough – desirable!' She thought again of Room 626 . . . 'The house is so quiet now, and no one needs me, not really. That's it, Mum. It's so quiet I can hear myself think, and that's the problem. I have managed to avoid thinking for decades.' *It's like I can't hold it all in much longer . . .* 'I want cards left on my pillow or propped up by the kettle. I want to know where I fit in and I want to feel excited about my future.' She raised her voice and kicked the table leg. The bread and olive basket jumped and the whole place suddenly seemed very quiet.

Her mum leant forward. 'Do you think *I* had choices, Bessie? Do you think most people do? It's not like you fill out a form and your life gets delivered! It's not on Amazon! You can't order it up and wait for it to arrive, swathed in brown paper and in a box that's too big, and if you don't like it you can send it back! That's not how it works . . .'

'I *know* that.'

Her mum ignored her.

'*You* have to make the changes and take control. Or you can carry on doing what you do – what you have always done – sit at home, feeling envious, anxious and hard done by, and telling yourself that it's because you ticked the wrong box! Is that the life you want, Bess?'

She gave a wry laugh. 'It's not the life I want, but it's the life I got, Mum. I love my family, but what if I did tick the wrong box?'

Bess remembered at sixteen, watching Philip stop outside the window of her digs, and she had the words lined up on her tongue – '*I've changed my mind, Philip! I've changed my mind – take me home!*' – but was not then brave enough to let them leave her mouth. He had turned and waved and she had thought her heart might burst. Placing her palms on the glass, she had cried, '*Don't leave me here, Philip! Please don't leave me!*'

'There you go again,' her mum said firmly. 'Nothing has been given to you, nothing has been foisted upon you. You're the captain of your own ship, the pilot of your own plane!'

'It's not that easy. I wish . . .' Looking at her reflection in the window, Bess studied her face and superimposed it on that of the sixteen-year-old who had woken up on her birthday and admired her teeth, who had pictured herself flying all over the world. 'I don't know what I wish.'

Her mum tutted in irritation. 'Here's the thing: I *like* my life, Bessie, and you need to like yours.' She took another bite of her bread and butter. 'I have always liked my life. I like your dad. I like my house. I like the city I live in and I love you and Philip. And it makes me happy – all of it. It's enough. But if I didn't like it, I would change it.'

'You make it sound easy.' Bess looked her mum in the eye. *I can't go back and change things, it's too late.*

'It *is* easy – you just need that magic thing beginning with "C" and you can go anywhere you choose.'

'A car?'

Her mum closed her eyes. 'For the love of bloody God! No, not a car! Courage, Bessie! Courage!'

Courage – she saw the word scrawled on the window frame of a speeding train, remembered the Tupperware box with the piccalilli stain in the corner, nestling on the table, filled with sandwiches she did not want to eat, and the sound of the conductor, calling out, '*Tickets, please! All tickets, please!*'

The waiter waltzed up to their table and deposited her dad's pie and mash, her mother's scampi and chips and her own rather disappointing salad. She took one look at the fat golden chips on her mother's plate and knew she had misfired. It was an ailment that dogged her: 'post-order regret syndrome', where she always, always, preferred the look of what someone else had chosen.

'Thank you,' her mum beamed.

Bess forked a piece of sorry-looking lettuce into her mouth. It was indeed too cold and a little tasteless.

'Sorry, ladies, thought it'd be a tinkle – turned out to be a package.' Her dad arrived back at the table, interrupting with his graphic update, and both Bess and her mother winced in disgust.

'For the love of God!' Bess said, pushing her plate away. The image of her dad on the loo was enough to put her right off her food.

'What's the matter? I used code as it's your birthday,' her dad chuckled, and holding his tie flat to his chest, sat back down. 'Besides, I think it's good to have a dump mid-meal – means I've made room for pudding!' He winked at his wife, who laughed.

'Ignore Bess, she's feeling a bit sensitive. She has a lot on her mind,' her mum said out of the side of her mouth, loading up her fork with a glorious-looking chip, glistening with salt flakes glued on with vinegar.

'Is that right? You have a lot on your mind, love?' her dad asked loudly, shoving gravy-laden pastry into his mouth. Her mum could put that on her list if she liked – the way her dad ate; it irritated the shit out of her. 'Like what?'

Bess toyed with her salad.

'I think her and Mario might be having marital problems,' her mum whispered loudly from behind her raised fork. Her mouth was now half hidden by a curl of scampi.

'I *can* hear you, Mum! I'm sitting right opposite and you're not whispering, even if you think you are!' Bess took a breath. 'And we're not having marital problems, not at all, and I can't believe you just told Dad that!' Her mum's summation had in fact struck a chord, but to hear it put so plainly was frightening.

'We don't have secrets, your father and I, never have.' Her mum pursed her lips as if delivering another salient lesson in life.

'No, but I thought you and I did.' Bess stared at her. *Secrets . . . bloody secrets . . . Secrets are ticking time bombs, and the longer I carry them, the louder they tick, until I have to strain to hear ordinary life above the din – and the weight of them, so heavy, pulls at my limbs*

154

from the moment I wake until the moment I fall asleep, heavy and draining and too much . . . Just too much, all of it. She placed her fingers under her nose, certain she could smell sandalwood.

'Are you menopausal, d'you think?' her mum asked, reaching for her wine.

'Jesus Christ!' Bess sighed desolately. 'Why is that if a woman shows any emotion or expresses a desire for change or says she's unhappy, the first thing anyone says is that it must be the sodding menopause! Or it's her hormones! Why can't she just be a little pissed off?'

'Please stop shouting that language!' her dad said, pulling a face.

'Sorry, Dad, I didn't mean to swear.'

'No, I don't mind the swearing, Bess, it's the word "meno-doodah" I struggle with. Always have.'

'Menopause?' Bess asked, aghast.

'That's the one.' He pointed his fork at her, his expression full of distaste – and this from the man who had announced his dump at her birthday lunch . . . 'You went off the rails a bit, didn't you, love, when you were afflicted?' he said, now jabbing his fork at his wife.

'Yes, I did a bit.' Her mum took another large glug of plonk.

'A bit? She painted the whole kitchen blue! And I mean every-thing – walls, cabinets, ceiling, the cat . . .' He chortled. 'We had to get a brand-new kitchen! Only way to get rid of the gloss everywhere.'

Bess smiled at her mum, remembering when she had confessed that the only way to get a new kitchen was to spoil the one they had.

'Yep, no secrets, Mum, isn't that right?' Bess pursed her lips, wide-eyed, while her mum studiously looked the other way.

'Anyway, happy birthday, love,' her dad said, clinking his pint glass with Bess's Coke as they both said cheers.

'Yes, happy birthday, darling.' Her mum lifted her now empty wine glass in one hand, while simultaneously beckoning the waiter with the other. 'Not that it was the happiest day for me when you were born.'

Here we go . . . Bess steeled herself, pushing her feet into the sticky carpet underfoot and hoping the other patrons of the pub were not about to be regaled with the worst aspects of her mother's birthing experience.

'Nine pounds you were, arse first, and split me like an over-ripe pumpkin from nose to tail. I had to sit on a rubber ring for weeks! Your dad had to blow it up for me just so I could sit and watch *Crossroads*, didn't you, Eddie?'

'I did,' he nodded, 'but thank goodness I was younger then – had a lot more puff.' He tapped his chest.

'How is your meal?' the waiter smiled weakly. Bess wasn't sure how long he'd been lurking behind her but felt her face colour accordingly.

'Lovely,' Bess beamed, pulling the plate of dead salad back towards her.

'Delicious,' her mum smiled, handing him her empty wine glass.

'Smashing!' her dad said, shoving another wedge of pie into his gob, as if proof were needed.

'I think she might be vying for a new car – is that what all this is about, Bess?' her mum asked, running her tongue over her gums to free up trapped shreds of scampi, as if the waiter were not standing right there at the table.

'Yes, that's exactly it, Mum – I'm vying for a new bloody car.' Bess pointed at her mother's glass and then at herself, deciding to go for a glass of wine after all.

'Red or white, madam?'

'Both?' she laughed, half joking.

'When you come back, young man,' her mum said to the waiter, 'remind me to give you this.'

Bess didn't know whether to laugh or cry as her mum reached into her pocket and whipped out the bloody voucher.

CHAPTER ELEVEN

August 20th 1984

Having run blindly from the rugby pitch, dodging the crowds and elbowing her way against the flow through the entrance gate, Bessie walked home in the shadows, partly to hide from anyone who might know her and partly to keep her tear-soaked face out of view. Her heart felt cleft in two.

Michelle and Lawrence! Lawrence and Michelle! The words were like knives that cut at her throat. They hadn't known she was there. Watching from behind the bins, she had seen them locked together, holding each other tightly, oblivious, lost in the moment, and she knew only too well what that felt like. She knew what it was to stand so close to Lawrence and to feel the whole world reduced to the single point beneath his fingers where they touched her skin. And she knew that in those moments she would have followed him anywhere, this boy she hardly knew. This boy she had trusted with her body and her heart. The thought immediately led her back to Tony's words: *That alleyway is not that private, Bessie. People might have been watching. In fact, people were most definitely watching.*

His nasty snipes were enough to summon a fresh batch of tears. *What am I going to do? What am I going to do? Everyone will know, and they'll all think the same as Tony! I don't want to go outside; I don't want to go outside ever again! And what if it gets back to Mum and Dad – how could I ever look them in the eye? And Michelle – what will she think when she hears it from someone other than me, and how can we be friends after her and Lawrence . . . ?* Bessie stopped to lean briefly against the wall of one of the Georgian houses opposite the petrol station at the bottom of Verulam Road. Fighting to catch her breath, she felt sick and the ground wobbled. Three boys in a gold Austin Montego crawled towards the pedestrian crossing alongside her.

'Hey babe, need a lift?' called one of them from the passenger seat, half hanging out of the window. There was raucous laughter from his two mates. Bessie looked away and let go of the wall. Keeping her gaze in the middle distance, she sped up, just wanting to get home. *Did they think she was a slut? Easy? Could they tell by looking at her? Could everybody?*

The car roared away towards Redbourn, and the moment her feet hit the Batchwood Estate she ran across the grass and along the pavement, feeling simultaneously relieved and anxious to be walking the path to her front door. With alcohol still sloshing in her veins, she wasn't quite sure how she was going to explain her early return, her obvious distress or her desire to go straight to bed, early as it was, on her sixteenth birthday. She hoped her parents might be in the front room with the door closed so she could sneak in and shout her hellos before rushing up the stairs and into bed in one swift action.

Fishing in her jeans pocket for her key, Bessie found it hard to look down at the ground and remain upright. With her feet fixed to the floor, the top of her body lurched forward and her forehead met the front door with a thump loud enough to alert her parents, who were suddenly both standing there, staring at her.

'What on earth?' her mum asked, her mouth open, her eyes darting over her face.

'She's drunk,' her dad noted, in a tone that sounded a lot like disappointment.

'Get her in!' her mum snapped, as if once again her dad was in some way responsible, while looking up and down the street to check none of the neighbours were watching.

Not entirely lost to the alcohol slurring her speech and sending her gaze off centre, Bessie made the quick and smart decision to let them think she was smashed to avoid having to explain the most horrendous of evenings.

Her mum rushed into the small kitchen at the back of the house and filled the kettle.

Her dad took a step outside and smiled weakly at her. 'Come on, poppet, let's get you inside.' His tone was warm and loving, almost more than she could bear.

Part of her wanted to run up the stairs and hide until this horrible sense of being out of control had passed and her sadness had ratcheted down a level, while the other part of her wanted to fall into his arms and let him tell her everything was going to be okay. She stumbled into the hallway and looked at the small round mirror above the radiator. It seemed almost impossible that only an hour or so ago she had admired herself in the same mirror, in the same clothes. Her hair had now fallen flat and her make-up was grotesque. Bright colours were smeared all the way up to the thin arch of her eyebrows, while a streak of lip gloss glistened across her cheek. How could it be that she had left the house thinking she was in control, smart and grown-up? She now knew the truth: she was young and scared and she had been reckless. Her behaviour, her choices, her desires had damaged her, damaged her in ways she could not possibly understand, not yet. All she wanted was to curl up in a warm spot and cry.

'Go and wash your face, love, and get your jimmy jams on.'

'Thanks, Dad.' The way he treated her was something to cling to through the Cinzano-muddied swamp through which her thoughts had to crawl – a kindly lifeline when she needed it most. To him she was still whole, unbroken and worthy of his love. At that moment and in his eyes, she was no more than his little girl who had messed up. Bessie wondered how long it would be before he looked at her differently. Her tears came at the very thought.

'What are you crying for?' her mum snapped over her dad's shoulder. 'Honestly, Bessie, I expected more from you . . . Look at the state of you! Where did you get alcohol?'

'Someone at school,' she said. This wasn't entirely a lie. Philip did go to her school. Or rather the school she used to go to. *Three hundred and sixty-one!* She cried again.

'Up you go, Bessie. This is certainly not the sixteenth birthday I would have planned for you.' Her mum's words dripped with disapproval.

'Really?' Bessie shot back at her. 'Well, that's funny, because it's *exactly* what I wanted – to be home within the hour looking like I fell down a well! While everyone else on the planet is having a party and thinking about the sixth form!'

'Now I know you're upset, but don't shout at your mother.' Her dad took his place by his wife's side.

'I think you should go up to your room this very minute, Bessie.' Her mum kept her tone level.

'Well, where else am I going to go? The library in the east wing? For a dip in our pool? Or maybe a sobering stroll around the grounds? Or how about I take the bloody Monopoly money and use it to buy my plane ticket?' Her anger and sarcasm were closely bound and sadly misdirected. Gripping the banister, she made her way slowly up the stairs. Before she had reached the landing, her mum's voice called after her.

'Do you . . . do you want that sandwich?'

161

Bessie shook her head and laughed. That sandwich was the very last thing she wanted. Her mouth filled with water at the thought. Opening her bedroom door, she was met with the clutter of make-up brushes, tins of hairspray, pyjama bottoms, old crisp packets and a half-drunk bottle of cherry Panda Pops on every surface – the washed-up detritus of her earlier preparations. She remembered how great she had felt in the moments before her life had been pulled apart by Tony's words, and what she had seen from her covert spot behind the bins. Jumping up on to the bed, she ripped at her Duran Duran poster.

'I fucking hate you, Simon!'

Instantly she regretted destroying the poster she held so dear. Her tears were exhausting. She collapsed on to her mattress and lay staring at the ceiling. The walls seemed to spin and again she thought she might be sick. Closing her eyes, she wondered if Michelle was wondering where she was and if Tony had filled her in on the details yet. How? How had her whole life been dismantled in just one day? It was bad enough that she had done so badly in her exams, but to be so humiliated by Tony, let down by Lawrence . . . It seemed ridiculous that such a small thing as sex had become such a big, big thing. A few minutes of intoxicating joy had led to this? And again, her tears fell. Bessie flipped on to her stomach and buried her face in the soft pillow. She tried to quieten her noisy and destructive thoughts, hoping for the sweet escape of sleep. Her door opened slowly, and she was aware of her mum, standing on the landing but with her head in the room, checking on her. Seemingly satisfied, she quietly closed the door, and Bessie was glad, not wanting any more interaction with her parents this evening.

My whole life is ruined . . . My whole life is totally ruined . . . I'm plain! I didn't know that – I thought I might be pretty. I felt pretty . . . but I'm not . . . I'm nothing.

◆ ◆ ◆

Evidently she had fallen asleep, as she was now being woken by a sound that was unfamiliar. The first thing she noticed when she lifted her head from the pillow was that she was still a little sozzled, and she gripped the mattress to stop the room from turning. This did little to allay the leap of nausea in her gut. Jumping out of bed, she ran to her bedroom window, which was where, coincidentally, the sound was coming from. As she levered open the sash, vomit rose in her throat. She saw Michelle in the front garden with a handful of gravel, which explained the harsh pitter-patter that had woken her, as the small stones hit the glass. With desperate sweeps of her arm, Bessie managed to shoo her friend away from standing directly beneath, before shoving her head out and throwing up. Fortunately, Michelle was not in the firing line. The front of her parents' house, however, was not quite so fortunate and she scored a direct hit. The painted pebbledash now sported a dark red-brown stain that sat like a giant ink splat, if that ink had been made of dark chocolate cherry brandy liqueurs and Cinzano.

'God, Bessie!' her friend gasped.

'M'sorry.' She wiped her mouth and was relieved to note that she felt almost instantly better.

'Come down!' Michelle beckoned quietly.

A quick glance at the bedside clock told her it was eleven o'clock. It was doubtful Philip would be home yet; he liked to sneak in in the early hours and then lie to their parents the following morning that he had arrived just as they were turning in their toes. She knew differently and would listen to his slow and painful progress along the landing as he tried and often failed to avoid the creaky floorboards and piles of laundry, discarded towels or abandoned shoes that might litter his path. Her mum and dad would be asleep in bed at this time of night. She had never gone outside this late without them knowing, but this was no ordinary night and she figured therefore that ordinary rules did not apply. Her body hurt physically, as if the toxic bruises from the mental pounding she had taken had seeped into her muscles. Fear lined her gut, unsure of how things stood now between herself and Michelle. And her desire to howl in distress was as strong as it had been when she walked home earlier. She wanted to tell the world how very broken she felt. Pulling on her slippers and still in her crumpled finery, she crept down the stairs and opened the front door as quietly as she was able.

Bessie stood opposite her friend on the tiny patch of lawn. In these dire circumstances, she felt a little daft wearing an outfit that matched Michelle's, which, despite much planning and expense, neither had been able to celebrate – there was little point in matching if you weren't together. The temptation was to fall into her friend's arms and say she was sorry and that nothing was as important as having her as a best friend and that, no matter what, they would find a way past this. But this was not about temptation – this was about what she had seen.

'It's late.' Bessie looked up at the violet sky of the summer night. The moon lit their encounter. It was beautiful.

'I waited for you, Bessie, but you never came,' Michelle said.

So this was how it started, and her challenge set the tone. Bessie felt the thump of her friend's words in her throat; it killed her to hear the sorrow in Michelle's voice, amplified by the fact that she was undoubtedly partly responsible. Her hurt, however, was tempered by the image rolling on endless loop in her mind's eye: Lawrence and Michelle, clinging together as if their lives depended on it. Her fingers twitched and her feet shifted on the grass; she was undecided as to whether she should walk forward and hug her friend or turn away and fold her arms. Her heart was breaking and she could feel waves of sadness roll from her. To feel estranged from Michelle was painful, wounding, and filled her entirely with distress. Glad of the low light surrounding them, Bessie wondered if her expression was as tortured as she felt. 'Uh-huh' was all she could manage, as she ran her fingers through her ratty hair and remembered her ruined make-up.

'I kept looking out for you,' Michelle said.

'Did you?' snorted Bessie.

'Why are you saying it like that? 'Course I did!'

'I'm saying it like that because I hung around outside for ages.' Bessie recalled the touch of Tony's hand on her skin and shuddered. 'I asked if anyone had seen you around and it didn't seem like you were waiting for me then.' *I needed you, but you were preoccupied . . .*

'What are you talking about? I went inside when I arrived because I thought you might be in there, and I danced and hung out, but I *kept* going outside to see if I could see you. I did!' Michelle's desire and keenness to make her point suggested she might feel as guilty as Bessie did. She looked at the floor and Michelle continued, her tone agitated. 'There were so many people around, and then I was getting worried because I didn't know where you were, and I wondered if you'd decided not to come after all, and then someone said they'd seen you talking to Louise, and then it was like you'd just disappeared . . .' Michelle reached down to fold the backs of her boat shoes under her heels. Bessie knew they rubbed with no socks after a while.

'Yeah, and you were so bothered it's taken you four hours to come and see if I'm okay!' Bessie didn't know why she said this. She knew it wasn't Michelle's job to come after her, aware that it was her who had left the party, run away. It just came out, and her voice cracked at how terrible it felt to talk to the girl she loved in this way.

'Well . . .' Michelle looked over her head, 'firstly, I couldn't come sooner cos we've been out looking for my nan for the last hour, so . . .'

Bessie wondered if by 'we', Michelle meant her and her family or, crushingly, her and Lawrence, meaning he had already been introduced to her mum, dad and brothers. This would represent a major step and another reason for her to feel sidelined and envious.

'She'd done a runner again. Mum was going frantic and Dad was a minute away from calling the police, but she turned up, thank God! They found her walking through the park with a rolled-up towel under her arm in her nightdress and wearing my brother's wellington boots – said she was hot and off to Westminster Lodge for a swim.'

Despite the myriad of emotions that fought for space in Bessie's mind, it saddened her to think of the old lady in the darkness, heading off to the municipal swimming pool all alone.

'And before that, I didn't know what to do! I wanted you to be there, Bessie, of course I did – I always want you there. We'd made plans and I was looking forward to it! But when you didn't show up immediately, I thought you'd stuck to your guns and weren't coming. I nearly left myself. I felt like a right wally standing there in the car park on my own, but then Lawrie came over and spoke to me and we danced and . . .' Michelle swallowed. 'I was having a really nice time with him and I stopped missing you so much.'

There was something about the way she used the shortened version of his name, which spoke of such intimacy, such familiarity, that it was simultaneously like a match to kindling and a punch. Bessie waited to see if Michelle had any more to say, knowing the two had shared a bit more than 'a dance and a really nice time'. Michelle kicked her boat shoes into the grass and said no more. Bessie felt a flare of jealousy spiked through with grief. Her friend was not going to say any more – she was lying to her, lying through omission: another first. And having come clean about the fact that Michelle had stopped missing her, Bessie found herself replaced in every sense by Lawrence. It really hurt. Her tears pooled as the sense of betrayal reverberated in her chest.

'Chatted to him?' she said, raising her voice. 'I fucking saw you!' It was the first time she had ever sworn at her friend in anger.

Michelle took a step backwards on the short brown summer-dried lawn. 'Saw me what?' Her voice shook.

'With Lawrence! I saw you with Lawrence! It looked like more than chatting to me!'

'So?'

'*So?* Jesus Christ, Michelle!'

'What, am I not allowed to have a boyfriend? That's ridiculous!' Michelle's eyes were wide, and her bottom lip quivered, her words assertive but her stance not so much.

Boyfriend? Boyfriend! Bessie put her hand over her mouth, in part to stop all the unfair and judgemental words rooted in jealousy from spewing out of her mouth, but also because she feared she might throw up again. *Boyfriend . . .* She had hoped that tonight would be the night she and Lawrence went official, had visualised the moment, made mental plans, leaping ahead towards a future that had felt within reach. She had imagined introducing him to Nanny Pat and Grandad Norm.

Michelle's expression was one of confusion. 'I don't understand, Bessie! We agreed earlier we'd never let a boy come between us, just this morning! And you said you needed to think about what to say next, that was all! The whole discussion.' Her palms were upturned, beseeching.

'Yes! Because I had stuff I wanted to say on top of that, and I needed time to figure out how to say it,' Bessie sighed.

'What, am I psychic? So go on then, say it now.' Michelle folded her arms, her stance resolute.

'Well, not now! There's no point. There's no bloody point.'

They stood in silence, only metres apart, both quiet as the air cleared a little and the warm summer-night breeze whipped over them. Bessie didn't have the first clue how to navigate this situation. Her brain was still a little addled by alcohol and her emotions were bruised. She was hurt, angry, upset, humiliated, but this girl was as close to her as family. Her stomach felt sore with the agony of the interaction and her head ached; she wished she could rewind time and start over. This was Michelle, her Michelle – how in the world had it come to this?

'Are you going to let a boy come between us?' her friend asked, with the suggestion of a sob to her words.

'No, Michelle, you are.'

'How can you say that to me?' Her friend wiped her eyes. 'I've always, always, put you first, Bessie. You have been my very best friend in the whole wide world ever, ever.' Her voice was small. 'And you can't punish me because I've fallen in love with someone. It doesn't work like that! It's mean.'

'In love?' This was the part of the conversation that stuck. The final blow. Bessie found it hard to form words in her head that were not wrapped in despair. 'You've only known him five minutes!' she shouted, hiding her desire to scream.

'Keep the noise down, please!' Mrs Hicks, who lived next door, leant out of her bedroom window.

'Fuck off, Mrs Hicks!' Bessie instinctively spat the words in the old woman's direction – she, Bessie, who had been raised to always say hello and goodbye and please and thank you and to do so with a smile. It was uncharacteristic, thrilling and devastating all at the same time. She felt sick.

'Really, Bessie Worrall – there is no need for that language! You should be ashamed of yourself.' Mrs Hicks slammed shut her bedroom window.

Michelle stared at Bessie like she was a stranger. She looked down the road, as if planning to leave, and Bessie's heart lurched with all it struggled to contain.

'I'm sad if you feel that way.' Michelle took a deep breath, as if what she had to say next required courage. 'But as I told you earlier, I really like him, Bessie – and he really likes me.'

'Did he say that to you?' Bessie felt the sting of distress at the back of her nose and throat, but wanted the details, knowing she would chew over them, prolonging the hurt for the longest time. Her voice trembled and her eyes narrowed as she prepared to hear the confirmation that she knew would hit her like a nail in her heart.

Michelle nodded and a wide smile split her face, as if even the memory of his words lit joy within her. Bessie looked away – the sight of it was almost more than she could stand.

'He made me a mixtape.' Michelle put her hand on her jeans pocket and Bessie could see the outline of a cassette. Her arms fell to her sides, as if she had lost her core strength and was unable to hold them up. The gift of a mixtape spoke volumes. It was code. Giving someone a mixtape was a very big deal, a gesture of magnificent proportions. Proof that you wanted to share something precious: your music, your identity. It linked you, not only in thought, but while you lay on your bed and they lay on theirs, you were together, joined by the lyrics and poetry of the songs . . . A mixtape took a long time to make, especially if you were recording it off the Top Forty and had to keep pausing and recording to make sure you cut out all the talking. It was the most thoughtful, loving and intimate of gifts. Bessie had quietly longed for a mixtape and knew that while Lawrence made that tape, his thoughts would have been of Michelle . . . Making a mixtape for Michelle . . . and who knows when he did that? Maybe on a day he passed her a scrappy note and met her in the alleyway for sex?

Michelle smiled again, a seemingly visceral reaction in consideration of what she was about to say. Her demeanour was that of someone who wanted to share the joy of her new-found love with her very best friend, knowing that before this terrible encounter that friend would have pulled her into her arms, and they would have whooped with shared excitement. 'He said I was special and not like anyone else he had been out with and that we have a connection. He thinks about me before he falls asleep, Bessie – that's what he said! And we do have a connection, a wonderful one. I just want you to be happy for me because he makes me happy and I won't give him up – why would I?'

Bessie recalled almost the exact same words uttered in her own ear as she kicked off her knickers. The words that she had thought were special and had filled her with pleasure and delight now made her feel stupid and grubby, no more than bait, and she had swallowed it whole.

'Do you think you're the first person he's said that to, Michelle?' she asked defiantly.

Her friend shook her head slowly, her response calm and drawn from a point of confidence. 'No, no, I don't, but I think it's probably the first time he's meant it.'

Bessie's head jerked as if to shake off these words, which hurt as much as any physical blow. 'Well, I hope you'll both be very happy together.'

'Yeah, you say that, but in such a nasty way that I know you don't mean it. Who are you right now? I don't even recognise you!'

I don't recognise myself! I thought I knew who I was. I thought I was clever, I thought I was pretty, I thought Lawrence liked me and I thought you would put me first because we're best friends . . . Bessie felt hollow, sucked out by loss, envy and the uncomfortable landslide of her confidence. The boy she loved and trusted had chosen another girl – and not just another girl, but her best friend.

'You think I care?' she continued. 'Why don't you fuck off back to Lawrence and the fucking sixth form and your fucking mixtape and your whole fucking life!'

'I will, Bessie, I will.'

Michelle's calmness would bother her every time she looked back on this awful exchange in the future. The way she hadn't fallen into the bitter accusatory trap that held Bessie fast was something Bessie envied. She knew she had gone too far and Michelle's expression of shock and horror offered ample confirmation. Bessie knew she would never forget it. Seconds later, her Michelle walked stiffly away from her down the street. Horribly sick with shame and regret at her actions, Bessie was left standing in her small front garden, shouting after her friend in her mind.

I'm sorry – please don't go! I'm sorry . . .

CHAPTER TWELVE

August 20th 2021

'Drive safely!' her dad called out, as he always did, like she was some teenager who had newly passed her driving test. 'There are idiots on these roads!' This too he liked to point out, regardless of how many idiots were getting into or alighting from vehicles in the now busy car park of the pub in which they said their goodbyes.

'Text us when you get home!' This was one of the rules set by her parents whenever she drove away from them, no matter the journey: miles or yards. Her mum had once explained that she could not 'settle' until she knew Bess was home safely. There had been several occasions when Bess had forgotten to send the text, only to receive a barrage of near frantic messages along the lines of:

Are you in a ditch?

Have you hit a tree?

Have you been arrested?

Kidnapped?

Should we call an ambulance?

The police?

Or the fire brigade?

Her reply was always similarly mundane:

Sorry. Nipped to the garage for milk. Forgot to text. No need to call emergency services. All good.

On one occasion, however, this had invited the response:

That's exactly what a kidnapper would say who had got hold of your phone! What was the name of our next-door neighbour who you had to write an apology to because of your drunken antics? I doubt a kidnapper would know this!

Jesus Christ! All Bess wanted to do was have a wee and a cup of coffee.

Mrs Hicks. Her name was Mrs Hicks . . .

Did the kidnapper force that information from you or is that actually you, Bess?

And on it went . . . It used to annoy her, until her own children started to drive and then she understood completely, her mind able to conjure the most terrible outcomes, all involving other idiots on the road. And God forbid she should hear an emergency vehicle siren before they had texted their safe arrival – this could send her into a right old spin. Yes, when her own kids started to drive, she finally understood the value of those texts and the power of a phone call.

'Thanks for a lovely lunch!' she called, and waved from her window before indicating and pulling out of the car park, watching her parents standing side by side like a couple of white-haired sentries, getting smaller and smaller as she drove away.

She liked being in the bubble of her little car, one of the only places where she found peace, where no one could get to her. The familiarity of the interior comforted her: the fruity-scented air fresheners that swung from the back of her mirror; the splash of green and bright turquoise from a broken necklace in the cup holder. It was a far more daring decor than she would have in her house, where everything was safe and biscuit-toned, lifted with a splash of bright colour from the odd flowery cushion and her fancy-pants three-arm bedroom chandelier picked out in gold. She liked sitting in the driver's seat at the end of the working day or when she'd finished her shop at the supermarket. It was her tiny rusting haven on wheels.

Her mum's question loomed large in her mind.

'What *is* wrong with you, Bess?' she said aloud into the rear-view mirror, gazing at her reflection. The plain, dough-faced woman who stared back was apparently just as fresh out of answers. The car behind beeped and she realised she had slowed to a dangerous speed as her concentration wandered. She put her foot down, holding up a hand in apology.

Her mum was right – she did need to find a way to like her life, and she used to, remembering how happy she had been when Mario came home and the kids ran to greet their dad at the door. But what if she was incapable now of liking the life she had? What if she was too laden with guilt, regret and the web of deceit she had spun to truly be happy? These thoughts had bubbled to the surface before. Standing on the front step to wave Jake and Daniel off on their Scottish honeymoon, she had watched the car disappear from the cul de sac and realised that with her kids gone and setting out on their own life adventures, she was left with a gaping hole in her thoughts, filled with memories of a train journey taken with her brother, and all that came after. Gripping the steering wheel, she felt a tight belt of dissatisfaction around her waist. She *should* like her life! They lived in a nice enough house, had two nice enough children and she went off quite happily to her nice enough job at the Evergreen Academy to prepare and serve lunch, and yet the sum of all these parts was not, as she might have hoped, a life that was enough. Not even close. The sum of these parts was for her in fact a life that was nothing short of disappointing. Any small bursts of happiness were a welcome distraction from the disappointment of the daily grind and frequent enough for her to stay put.

The small red-ringed events on the calendar that hung on the fridge were in fact stepping stones that helped her navigate from one month to the next, each one offering a tiny rainbow on the grey horizon, something to look forward to on the dullest or most trying of days.

Natalie's birthday . . . Jake's am dram night . . . School staff bingo . . . Mario's five-a-side BBQ . . . Mum's 80th . . . Little red circles that took no more than a second to draw and yet would provide days and days of glorious anticipation . . . *twenty days until . . . ten days until . . . tomorrow . . .* counting down her life. That's what she did. Counted down her life until what – death? The thought was as sobering as it was distressing.

Again she looked in the mirror, wondering if she was happy or unhappy or just *not* happy right now, and were they the only three choices? Was there a fourth category of 'happy-ish', with an underlying sadness that could at times overwhelm her?

This might be as good as it gets for the rest of my days . . . a half-life, a hidden life, because I don't have the courage. Courage . . .

She had done such a good job at hiding that she was now actually invisible. Mario didn't see her, not any more. He was happy to fart or scratch his groin while he watched TV, as if her presence was of no consequence, giving her no more consideration than the remote control, his footstool or the lamp in the corner, sometimes changing the channel without asking if she was watching. Maybe he would notice her if she was younger, prettier and cleverer.

There was a time in her early teens when she had been all of those things. And yet, back then, all she had wanted was for her life to fly faster and faster to get over the hump, ride the wave, move on.

What might her life have been like if she had made one different small decision on one seemingly insignificant day? That's all it would have taken. One moment when she might not have volunteered to pick litter after school, or she could have gone to the bathroom, cadged a lift, visited the library, stopped to tie her shoelaces, any number of permutations, but all meaning she would not have been at the bus stop at the same time as Lawrence Paulson. She would therefore not have initiated sex with him and her whole life might not have fallen apart in the way that it had. And just like that, her tears came: hot, salty tears that were all-consuming. It still had the power to do that to her, the memories vivid and so sharp they cut as deep as they always had.

I was only a little girl, just a little girl . . . Sixteen, but so naive . . .

Her mum was right – she needed to take risks, be braver. Bess looked at the junction at which she needed to turn left to head for home. Her fingers hovered over the indicator stalk, but driven by something other than duty and thirsting for a red-ringed day, she chose to drive straight on – unsure of where she was heading but knowing with certainty that she did not want to go home and sit among the biscuit-coloured surroundings and check Facebook to see if she had caught up with Sushmita. She didn't want to park in her usual spot on the driveway, fumble around in her bag for her door keys, reach into the fridge for milk to splash into her umpteenth cup of coffee of the day, which sometimes she only drank to break up the monotony. No. It was her birthday and she wanted to do something for herself – go somewhere she wanted to go. Somewhere glamorous where she might not be invisible, and wanting so desperately to shake off the belt of dissatisfaction cinched so tightly around her waist, she was finding it hard to take a full breath.

Bess drove as if on autopilot, paying heed to the law and stopping at red lights, until suddenly there it was – the sign that read 'The Glade Hotel'. She drove into the car park and pulled up among the fancy shiny motors. It was a far cry from the grotty carvery, and just to be among it all was a thrill. Pulling on the handbrake, she stared up at the imposing building. It was busy. There was no surreptitious hiding of her face or creeping like a robber in the shadows. She sat up straight and didn't worry about being seen – why would she, when she was mostly invisible? Smartly dressed people crisscrossed the car park, entering and leaving the adjacent grounds, while others strolled in and out of the entrance. Families, couples, mates having afternoon tea, and solitary businessmen with solemn expressions, wearing formal clothes too restrictive for the weather – and one such man was waiting for her in Room 626.

Bess could hear the sound of her blood rushing in her ears as her heart raced and something like excitement jumped in her gut. Studying her face in the small mirror, she spat on her finger and wiped it beneath her lower lashes to remove stray flecks of mascara. Next she opened her handbag and grabbed the half-tube of slightly softened Polos, from which she peeled the two nearest the top and popped them in her mouth, doing her best to disguise the tang of chicken salad and deceit. She texted her mum with the message 'Home x', deleting it immediately, knowing it would arrive and allow her mum to settle, but also knowing she would be quite unable to face the lie later. That was how lies worked – easy to put out into the world, but very hard to live with long term.

She set off with sudden confidence and pushed open the door. The place was gleaming! Marble floors, white pillars and gold-edged round tables on which sat vast, stunning displays of flowers in gold urns. Not a wilting orchid in sight. Bess had never actually craved wealth, not truly, but she could certainly see the attraction of having money if it bought you access to places like this. The girl on reception lifted her hand in a wave and smiled enthusiastically. Bess gave a curt but polite nod and walked to the lift. She was in no mood to engage with anyone and strode forward before calling the lift, as if she had been here a million times before, as if this were any other day and there was nothing untoward going on, as if her heart were not clattering inside her ribcage, while nerves made her feel as if it might jump out of her chest altogether and bounce over the tiled floor. As if she were used to this kind of life, this glamour! Standing now in the lift, facing the melee of the reception, she prayed no one else would get in, jabbing the button for the sixth floor with her finger as surreptitiously as she was able, while smiling into the top corner of the lift, as if this were not the case. The thought of making small talk about the weather while heading up to meet Mr Maxwell – *'Please call me Andrew'* – was almost more than she could stand. The lift doors seemed to take an age to close and the moment they did, she breathed out, steadying herself against the wall as if she might fall. She felt quite light-headed. The lift shuddered to a halt on the sixth floor.

'What are you doing, Bess?' she asked out loud, whispering into the depths of the subtly lit corridor lined with identical white doors displaying shiny brass numbers. The striped russet and gold carpet beneath her feet was vertigo-inducing and the temperature a little too warm. She realised there were no windows and the air was stale. It smelled of dust and the residual scent of food, thick with

178

particles breathed in and out while countless people like her made their way to the bedrooms. Well, maybe not people like her with dual hammers of guilt and excitement thumping away in her chest, but it was almost too late to consider that. Here she was.

620 . . . 622 . . . 624 . . .

This was it. Bess raised her hand to knock, but it took a split second for her to find the courage, and when she did, she immediately looked back along the corridor, wondering if she had time to run back to the lift before Mr Maxwell – *Andrew* – opened the door.

Suddenly, the door opened and there he was.

She stared at him and the look of absolute delight he gave her was encouraging, warming and made her feel very much like a woman to be desired. The exact opposite of invisible.

'I can't tell you how very, very glad I am to see you,' he said softly, his smile wide as he opened the door.

Her feet moved slowly, aware this was no mere step over the little brass strip between the hallway and the bedroom but in fact a canyon across which she was about to leap. On this side was safety, monotony and the life she knew she should like and on the other was something new and thrilling, the very idea of which sent a jolt of rousing electricity through her bones.

Bess stepped inside.

Her initial feeling was one of disappointment and her stomach sank as reality burst her bubble. It turned out that the Glade Hotel was one of those establishments where the communal areas were a darn sight fancier than the rooms, and where its reputation and assumed elegance was apparently far more important than the comfort of the actual paying guests.

Andrew displayed none of the nerves she felt. He was eager, smiling and relaxed. She, on the other hand, stood by the door, scanning the room, looking for small details that might occupy her mind, to distract her, almost, from the reality of the situation in which she found herself, albeit a reality which she alone had created. She felt like an observer, thinking how she would tell Mario about the general shoddiness of the interior, before remembering she would not be telling Mario, she would not be telling anyone.

Another secret . . .

A plastic tray sat on top of a faux wooden chest of drawers, and on it two old-fashioned floral cups with teaspoons resting on the saucers. Next to these were two small plastic-wrapped packets of oaty biscuits. Bess turned to look at the door and stared at the handle, trying to think of her exit phrase, wanting to leave, when Andrew spoke.

'I believe I promised you bubbles!' He walked to a small table in front of the window and picked up a bottle from an aluminium bucket. She noticed he had taken off his socks and shoes, and it sent a quiver of discomfort along her limbs. She could see his feet! Their neighbour who she nodded to across the cul de sac as he pulled the wheelie bin in and out of the road on a Wednesday night and on a Thursday morning – she could see his feet! The man whose drinks party they attended each Christmas, as he offered advice on wines, and nearly always wearing a cherry-red, V-necked sweater over a white shirt. She could see his feet! Feet and toes were such an intimate thing, reserved for family, very close friends, babies, lovers and fellow swimmers. And just the sight of them padding across the carpet was enough to break the seal on any deeper-lying anxieties. She felt the first stirring of fear – no one knew she was here and the fact that she was in a bedroom, alone with Mr Maxwell, was ridiculous, almost comical. She pictured Mario lying in her arms earlier, crying over their lost little one and wondered how comical he would find it. Sickness and regret swirled in her gut, and again she looked at the door.

Whatever are you doing here, Bess?

'Actually, Andrew, thanks, but I don't want a drink – driving,' she explained.

'Not even one?' He waved the bottle back and forth at her as if this boozy pendulum might hypnotise her into changing her mind.

'No, but a glass of water would be nice.' Her mouth was dry and she felt ridiculously that it was the polite thing to ask for.

'Righto. They forgot to bring glasses, the bloody idiots.' He shook his head and she took the slight personally. She was someone who served food and drink for a living and knew how easy it was to slip up on one small detail when her mind was overloaded, doing three things at once with one ear out for timers, the system often chaotic and unpredictable, with tasks building until she was running just to stand still and always with one eye on the clock, waiting for the moment she could get into her rusting little car and head home, tired, desperate for a cup of tea and wondering why she wasn't as popular as Sushmita.

Andrew reached for the cups from the tray and she saw that one had something welded to the inside, which looked like a small piece of cabbage or lettuce. She guessed it was either the handiwork of a belligerent former guest or the result of an inefficient dishwasher. Either way, she didn't want to raise it, not when his reaction over forgotten glasses had been so acute – God only knows what the man might have to say over a rogue bit of green veg.

His jacket, she saw, had been placed over the back of the chair in front of the desk/dressing table, the finely hemmed edges brushing the floor. It left her with a dilemma: she wanted to sit, but didn't want to crush his jacket or take a place on the bed, not yet, maybe not at all. She began to realise the situation more fully and was certain she had neither the desire nor the daring to go through with whatever it was he might have planned. Sex, certainly, but then what? Regular meet-ups for more sex? Falling in love? She gave a quiet snort of laughter. That would never happen. He really was not the kind of person she could ever love, but was he the kind of person who might make her feel good? Was she really about to say no to the only offer she had had in over three decades? Was *that* courageous? Would she regret it? The air was heavy with his scent, suggesting he might have sprayed his aftershave shortly before her arrival, and again she was flattered.

She watched him through the open door of the en suite. This really was the weirdest thing. She was in a bedroom with Mr Maxwell, who was fetching her a glass of water from the bathroom tap, his long bare toes gripping the pale grey tiles.

'I want you to know,' she called out, 'that I don't make a habit of this. I've never done anything like it before.'

'Well . . .' He came into the room and handed her the cup. Bess took a sip and only when she pulled away did she see the water was a little cloudy with whitish particles floating in it, while a little green curl of vegetable matter still clung to the inside of the cup, hidden, lurking and disgusting. Mr Maxwell hopped on to the bed, his manner boyish, overly exuberant as he lay on his side with his head resting on his elbow. He was a handsome man, tanned and toned with thick hair and eyes that looked at you rather than around you. There was power in that: the feeling of being seen. It felt nice.

'I can't claim to be an expert, but let's just say this is not my first time at the rodeo.' He laughed then, the laugh that she and Mario had mocked, slightly nasal, considered.

'Does . . . ?' Bess paused. To mention his wife, even to say her name, felt disloyal, abhorrent, and that was before she had taken her place next to him on the bed with the shiny counterpane and the micro-evidence of a thousand encounters like this. The thought left her a little nauseous. 'Does Helen know how often you attend the rodeo?' she asked. The self-conscious turn of phrase, her hesitancy and tension all added to the weight of awkwardness now pushing down on her shoulders.

'We have a kind of don't ask and don't tell policy,' he beamed, raising his eyebrows.

'I guess it's her who doesn't ask and you who doesn't tell,' Bess said, speaking her thoughts aloud.

'I guess.' Mr Maxwell sat up and leant against the headboard, as if a little chastised, her awkwardness contagious. 'Why don't you come and sit down?' He patted the space on the bed next to him and Bess tried to imagine what she might look like, standing there with her bag over her shoulder, holding her cup of water with a shred of cabbage in it. It was hardly *Fifty Shades* . . . She didn't feel sexy or willing, just embarrassed and again unsure of how she could leave without causing a scene or incurring the ire of the man she had seen shouting up at his wife from the lawn a few years ago now: *You're a fucking joke, Helen! A fucking joke!*

She sat, but not next to him, preferring to take a spot on the edge of the bed with both her feet resting on the floor, her toes pointing towards the door and her back to him, like an awkward encounter on a hospital visit when they had run out of chairs. A half-hearted seat, really, neither engaged nor distant, keeping her options open.

'I didn't really plan to come here, Andrew,' she said, glancing briefly at him over her shoulder.

'So you're here by accident? You stumbled into the wrong building and then the wrong lift and then pressed the wrong button?' He laughed – *that laugh* . . . and she felt stupid.

'Not exactly. I was having lunch, and then I got in my little car.' She chose not to mention her parents, not wanting to bring them into this.

'Which, I hope you don't mind me mentioning, is losing quite a lot of oil. I noticed it the other day when you were parked in the road – might want to get that looked at, not to mention the stain it leaves on the tarmac.'

'Oh yes, I will. Thank you.' She again briefly met his gaze. 'Anyway, I was going to head home and went on autopilot and—'

'I have to be honest, Bess,' he interrupted, 'but I don't think that would hold up in a court of law: "Please, yer 'onour, I never meant to drive five miles out of me way and get in a lift and knock on a door."'

It sounded like he was impersonating her and she didn't like it one bit.

'Are you being funny?' she asked directly.

'No.' He pulled his knees up and hugged them to his chest, blinking slowly. 'Sorry, Bess, I'm just a bit nervous – that's why I thought the champagne might, you know . . .' He nodded over at the bottle, its neck emerging from the metal bucket on the table by the window, warming in the sunshine. 'So, you were telling me about your route here. Please carry on. Mine was a pig of a journey too. There's a sewage pipe broken in Duke Street; traffic was gridlocked.'

'That'll be murder come the school run.' She sipped gingerly at her murky water. 'It's sort of a crossroads between the St Bede's primary and secondary and the new academy.'

They fell silent for a moment or two and she wondered if he, like her, was thinking how this was exactly the kind of conversation they might conduct if they bumped into each other in the cul de sac. Only weirder.

'I lost my job.'

'You what, sorry?' She thought she might have misheard, so random was the admission.

'I lost my job. My company, they downsized and kept the junior roles – cheaper salaries, you see, and so easier to manage financially. But I was let go. Twenty-three years I worked for them.'

He swallowed. 'Man and boy, as my old dad would have said, but actually it was just man. I was twenty-nine when I started there. Only took the job because I failed my accountancy exams. Helen laughed when I told her I was going to work there: "Roller blinds!" she said. "You're going to sell roller blinds?"' He looked at Bess, his expression thoughtful. 'But it wasn't just roller blinds – we sold Roman blinds, venetian blinds and ready-made curtains. In over three hundred and seventy-four choices of fabric. Three hundred and seventy-four!'

His words were shot through with emotion. The whole thing made her feel incredibly sad. It was about as far from sexy as she could imagine.

'I'm sorry to hear that. So how are you spending your time?'

'Well, I've been here all day waiting, hoping that you might show up, and you did.' He smiled weakly.

'So where does Helen think you are?'

'At work.' He rolled his eyes.

'But you've lost your—'

'Yes,' he said, pinching the bridge of his nose, 'but I just haven't been able to tell her yet.'

Bess swivelled on the bed to face him. His words were familiar and yet bizarre. She understood only too well what it was like to keep something historic from the person you loved, but to not be able to tell your partner you had lost your *job*? She was curious but not judgemental, knowing what it felt like to withhold parts of your life that were too difficult to share.

'Why haven't you told her?'

'Because, shitty as it is,' he said, taking a deep breath, 'she judges people by how much money they earn and the car they drive and the holidays they take.' He swallowed.

'Blimey! She can't rate me very highly – eight pound ninety-one an hour, my old banger and a week in Clacton if I'm lucky!'

She had hoped her breezy tone might cheer him up, but noted he didn't reply or correct her assumption. 'So how long are you going to make out that you're off to work every day?'

'Until I get another job,' he said.

'Can't you just tell her?' It made her think how, from the outside looking in, the Maxwells appeared to have a lovely life, a happy and lavish life of wine and trips to Crete. She pictured her own husband and knew that what she and Mario shared might not be dressed in ribbon or doused in expensive plonk but was special in comparison. She felt a swell of affection for her man and an increasing sense of discomfort that she was here at all. It was neither glamorous nor fancy here in this room with a view of the park, actually just rather sordid and cringe-inducing, and she wanted to go home.

'I might have been able to tell her once, back at the beginning, when she seemed to give me a bit more grace, but failure now is really not an option.'

This seemed to her at once unbearably sad and uncomfortably familiar. She saw the man in a new light with his laughter and bravado . . . 'It's funny, isn't it, the things that change in a marriage?' she said. 'They happen so subtly you don't notice, like a tanker a little bit off course and it only comes to light when it arrives in the wrong port. And there's a captain scratching his head on deck, trying to figure out how it happened.'

'Yes, it's exactly like that,' he said with a cough.

'So why did you ask me to come here?' she asked, looking him right in the eye.

'Because I wanted the thrill of making the plan. I wanted to see if I had the backbone to act instead of just thinking about it. I wanted to spend time with someone with whom I didn't have to pretend. I've always found you very easy to talk to, Bess, and I wanted to have sex with you. I've always wanted to have sex with you.' His words were forthright and shocking, but the thrill she had felt when he made the pass at her at the Christmas party? The electric current of longing that had shivered along her limbs? Both were absent. There was no thrill and no current, nothing bar an uncomfortable film of awkwardness over her skin that made her itch.

'But that's not going to happen, is it?' he asked quietly.

Bess shook her head and stared into her cup at the cloudy water, anything other than meet his gaze. 'No, it's not. I thought it might for a minute back there, but—' She bit her lip and wanted in that instance to be anywhere other than here. In fact, that wasn't strictly true. She knew exactly where she wanted to be – on the sofa with Chutney and a cup of tea, waiting for Mario to come home with the chips. Mario, who was a good man, a man who put up with her, and the man she loved. The man she had *always* loved, even when she didn't love herself, and thank God she had realised it before she had done something really stupid.

'Why did you come here, Bess?' he asked with a slight quaver to his voice.

'I thought . . .' It sounded stupid to say how she thought that maybe if someone wanted her and made her feel wanted, it might stick, and Mario might want her. She thought she might stride from the room changed, daring, able to forget the dark underbelly of deceit that fogged her thoughts and be ready to go and *like* the life she lived! 'But I guess life doesn't work like that,' she said aloud, as if she had shared her thoughts, leaving Andrew looking a little lost.

'I thought for a horrible moment you were going to say, *It's not you, it's me*, and whatever comes after that . . .' He gestured with his hand. His voice, she noted, was back to sounding almost pompous.

'But that's true, Andrew. It *is* me, not you. This was a bad idea for a million reasons, not least of which because I love my husband

187

and I know Helen and we're neighbours in a cul de sac where Jane Harris at number thirty-six keeps tabs on our every move.'

She looked up at the man, who to her horror looked very close to tears.

'I'd better go.' She stood, not wanting to be his shoulder to cry on, not wanting to get that close to his desperation, desperate herself to get home to Mario.

'I think I'll stay and drink that bottle of champagne. Helen thinks I'm away on business so I have the whole night.' He snorted. 'Might even order up a snack!'

'You should take the time to think about your life. You need to live a life you like.' She gave out her mother's sage advice and it loomed large in her mind like a neon sign, bright, illuminating and concentrating her thoughts. Her mum was right – Bess needed to take what she found in her pockets and make the very best out of it. And the very best was life in her modest home with her lovely hound and the man who had bought her a crappy orchid.

'Sure you don't want to join me for a glass of champers and whatever might come next?' he said, jumping up off the bed and grabbing the bottle. 'I mean, come on, Bess, it's just sex! It's nothing!' he laughed, trying and failing in one final attempt to convince her.

'It's never just sex.' She picked up her handbag and put the cup back on the tray. 'Sex is powerful and damaging and, yes, exciting and wonderful when it's with the right person, but it's not nothing. Even if it's casual, it's not nothing. It can make or break relationships.' *And it can make and break reputations. It can make and break lives . . .* 'I forgot that for a minute when I failed to turn left.'

'But no harm done, eh? We'll keep this between ourselves?' He looked nervous.

She nodded, remembering when she was sixteen and intoxicated by the physical act of sex performed in an alleyway. The smell of Lawrence, his less than fragrant breath and the whiff of sweat clinging to his skin. *We should keep this between ourselves. Let's not tell anyone . . .* The shame of duplicity was as familiar now as it had been when she was a teenager.

'No harm done,' she whispered, as she made her way out of the room. Closing the door behind her, she ran the length of the corridor and jabbed the call button for the lift, almost frantic in her desire to get out of the building and back home.

'Come on! Come on!' She pressed the button again and again with urgency. 'I just want to get home!' She closed her eyes, trying to ignore the quake of unease that filled her gut. Finally the lift arrived and carried her to the ground floor, where she looked down, unable to meet her own gaze in the mirrored walls. As the doors opened, she didn't stop to admire the white marble or the ornate blooms, but instead ran as fast as she could and with trembling fingers found her car keys in the bottom of her bag before letting herself into her rusting little haven. It was a relief to be alone and her sobs came in great gulps that left her breathless.

'What were you thinking, you stupid, stupid cow? You nearly blew it all – you nearly blew your whole fucking life!' She hit the steering wheel with the heel of her hand and inadvertently beeped the horn. A couple strolling in front of the car jumped and the man put his arm around the woman, fixing Bess with an angry stare in a move that was so protective, so caring, it made her cry even harder.

'I'm coming home, Mario! I'm coming home, my darling!' she managed through her tears.

CHAPTER THIRTEEN

August 20th 1984

Bessie stood and watched Michelle walk away down the road without looking back. She felt consumed with sadness, overwhelmed with loss, and utterly clueless as to how they might put this right. As she turned to walk back into the house, she caught the swish of Mrs Hicks's net curtain and cringed with regret, recalling the way she had spoken to their neighbour. Quietly closing the front door behind her, she flopped down at the kitchen table with her head on her arms, and finally gave in to the sobs that had been building. It had been the worst possible day and she struggled to understand how things had gone so very wrong. Was it only that morning that she had sat at the same table with excited anticipation and a sense of hope, as she ribbed her brother and opened her gifts?

'What on earth is the matter, Bessie? What are you doing down here in the kitchen all alone at this time of night?' Her mum's voice took her by surprise, as she flicked on the overhead strip light and put her arm round her, palming circles on her back and cooing, just as she had done when Bessie was a little girl and had tripped over. Bessie wished in that moment that she *was* still a little girl and that she could rewind to a time when things were less complicated and the touch of her mum's hand on her back was enough to make everything feel that little bit better.

She looked up, knowing her face would be a teary, snotty mess.

'Stay where you are – let me grab a cloth.' Her mum reached for the tea towel, which lived folded in half and dangling from the oven handle, and proceeded to wipe her daughter's face. Bessie could smell the fumes from bacon fat lurking in its cotton fibres and again fought the desire to vomit. She pushed her mum's hand away.

'Now, Bessie, this will never do! Not on your birthday.'

'Everything's gone wrong, Mum. Everything.'

'No, it hasn't! This is just a little bump in the road, a hiccup. So what? Who cares where you came in the school year?' She pulled out the chair opposite and sat down. Bessie noticed that her arms looked fat in her sleeveless cotton nightie and wondered if she too would have fat arms when she was older.

'*I* care, Mum,' she whispered. Her exam results were at that moment the very last reason for her tears, not that she could say so.

'Well, you won't over time, because much bigger and much worse things will come along for you to worry about.'

'Jesus! How is that supposed to make me feel better?' Bessie closed her eyes. How could things possibly get any worse?

The two sat in silence for what felt like an eternity. Bessie was glad of her mum's company, but really didn't want to talk about what had happened, not without incriminating herself or exposing her shameful behaviour. Ridiculously, she was grateful for her terrible exam results as a foil for all her sadness.

'I always find that, in a situation where I'm upset, eating something makes me feel a whole lot better,' her mum said at last.

Are you for real? Bessie didn't have the answers to the terrible mess in which she found herself, but one thing she knew for certain – food was the very last thing on her mind.

'I could get you that sandwich?'

'I don't think I could eat, Mum. It's a bit late.' She looked at the clock on top of the cooker. It was nearly half past eleven. She then remembered the stain of sick down the front of the house and wondered if it might rain heavily between now and the morning, when her parents would surely notice it. *Please, please, God, make it rain!*

'It's all made and ready in the fridge in case you change your mind. Cheese and tomato . . .'

'Yes, Mum, okay! Go and get the sandwich!' If she didn't take the bloody sandwich, her mum would go on and on about it until she did.

Her mum jumped up eagerly and bustled to the fridge, where she peeled the cling film from a small hexagonal side plate edged in her favoured eternal bow pattern, which Bessie disliked. She stared at the flat slices of greyish-white bread in front of her. From the biscuit tin, her mum grabbed three Garibaldi biscuits and crammed the first into her mouth.

'Tomorrow is another day, lovey.' Her mum sat back down. 'You could write your thank-you notelets to everyone to say how much you like your gifts to help take your mind off things. You know it's the highlight of Nanny Pat's life when she gets something from you in the post – she's still got all your paintings from play-school on the kitchen wall!' She chuckled at the truth.

'Okay. I'll write my thank-you notelets tomorrow,' Bessie said. More words designed to placate, and shut her mother up.

'Good girl,' her mum beamed, satisfied.

'I should probably write one to Mrs Hicks as well,' Bessie added, thinking out loud.

'Mrs Hicks next door? *Our* Mrs Hicks? Why, did she get you a birthday present?' her mum asked in a tone that suggested she was slightly miffed to be out of the loop.

'No, she didn't. It's more of an apology card.' Bessie's jaw was tense, hating what she was going to have to confess and hating even more that she had done it at all.

'Why would you need to say sorry to Mrs Hicks?' Her mum looked confused.

'I might just have told her to fuck off.'

Her mum dropped the biscuits on the tabletop and her mouth fell open. 'Bessie! You never did!' Her tone managed to convey both disappointment and anger. It was a neat trick. 'I honestly don't know what to say to you right now!'

'Well, hello!' Her dad's jolly tone distracted them both. 'And I thought we'd had all the parties we were going to have today – what am I missing out on? Your sandwich looks nice, Bessieboo. In fact, I quite fancy a snack meself with a large glass of orange squash! Or maybe milk . . .' he announced, as if this information was newsworthy. She pushed the plate with the sandwich in his direction. His smiley face, his sweetness and his affectionate nickname caused a fresh flare of shame and distress in her gut. The temptation to run into her dad's arms and hear him tell her it was all going to be fine was strong, but not even her lovely dad's words of comfort could fix this pickle.

'I've told her, Eddie, she shouldn't be crying, not on her birthday.'

'Your mum's right.' He took a bite of her sandwich.

'Are you okay, Bessie?' No one had heard Philip come in and all three stared as he stood in the hallway, leaning in, clinging to the doorframe as if out of puff, and with his eyeliner a little smudged. His tone was urgent, his chest heaving, his long fringe stuck to his forehead with sweat. Bessie's heart skipped a beat. Breaking into a sweat, she stared at her brother, terrified he might blurt out what he had been told or what he had overheard.

'She's fine, Pippin,' her mum smiled. 'Just a bit upset about her results, which we have told her not to be, not today, on her birthday.'

'And it's still her birthday for another half an hour or so – she can't officially be upset until gone midnight!' her dad mumbled through his mouthful.

'Oh.' Philip stared at her. 'I just thought . . . I didn't know if . . . I thought you might be upset because . . . I've just spoken to Louise Berry, who told me—'

Bessie shot up straight with her heart beating a little too fast. '. . . *that* I was upset because of my exam results!' she interjected, over-enunciating to make her point absolutely clear. Her blood felt thick in her veins as she recalled Philip and Carmen saying good-night in the garden below her window, him suggesting they might have sex and Carmen flatly putting him off. And now he would know what she had done and how and where she had done it, and no doubt the whole thing would have been embellished, if Tony had had anything to do with it. She felt dirty and ashamed and stared at her brother, her expression as guilty as it was pleading.

'Oh right. Yes. Your crap number – three six one.' He held her gaze, blinking quickly, cottoning on to the message she was sending. His expression was soft, his lips pressed together, curving into a slight smile of support that was a balm to her brain in turmoil. 'Well, Mum's right. Don't worry about anything.'

It was easier said than done, but she gave a subtle nod, her heart bursting with gratitude and relief.

'I think I might go up to bed,' she said.

She slipped from the table and tramped up to her room with the weight of her family's stares on her back.

'Sleep well and have good dreams, sweet one!' her dad called out. Bessie felt like a fraud – there was nothing sweet about her; she was dirty, sluttish, easy. She clamped her teeth down over her lips to stop from yelling this to her dad.

Michelle's words played over and over in her mind. *He said I was special and not like anyone else he had been out with and that we have a connection. We really do and I just want you to be happy for me!*

The tears fell down Bessie's cheeks from eyes that were now puffy and sore. Looking over to her dressing table, she spied the pile of notelets her mum had left along with two pens. She would write to Lawrence! It might not change anything but it would at the very least help clear her muddled thoughts to tell him just how she felt and how much of a shit she thought he had been.

Trying to ignore the strips of her torn Duran Duran poster that hung forlornly on her wall, she slumped down on the chair at which she had sat only hours earlier to put on her make-up and picked up a pen. She opened the packet of notelets and, caring less about legibility and penmanship, she wrote to the boy who had taken her heart, her virginity and her reputation, leaving all three in tatters.

> *So, Lawrence,*
> *I don't know what to write to you. I don't even know what to say to you. My mind is racing and I feel so sick. I trusted you! We had an agreement and you lied – you broke your promise and you told Tony we'd had sex and he will tell everyone, EVERYONE! And my life is ruined. My life is fucking ruined because of you! And now you like Michelle? The one person I could rely on, my person! She was the one I could tell anything to, but now? I've got no one and you said the same shit to her that you said to me and I fell for it. I don't need rubbish exam results to tell me I'm stupid – you've already proved that because I fell for it all. I hate you and I love you. That's the truth – I hate you and I love you . . .*

She stopped writing and put her head in her hands. Her tears continued to fall. Her thoughts were conflicting and confused. The ache of distress sat deep in her gut. How was it possible for her to feel such dislike for the boy who only hours ago she had contemplated a future with? But it was the truth – she hated him and she loved him, yet neither mattered now because he was with Michelle. Bessie was sobering fast and one quick read through of her letter made her realise two things: first, she would never have the confidence to send it to Lawrence, and second, it was proof of her deeds that needed to be destroyed. She cringed to think of accidentally mailing this to Nanny Pat. Fumbling in the drawer of her dressing table, she dug out the lighter hidden at the back, which she and Michelle had used to light the cigarettes Michelle stole from her dad's packet when he was napping. The memory of their shared adventures was enough to summon another bout of snotty tears. Rolling the flint until the flame leapt, she held the notelet at an angle, carefully positioning it so the fire licked the paper, picturing a soft flutter of fire that would destroy her words. Dramatic, but necessary.

Bessie gave a loud scream as an almighty whoosh was followed by a flash of bright light.

Far from the gentle and symbolic smouldering of her words that she had envisaged, worthy of a Roxy Music video, the coating on the cheap notelets her mother had bought set it flaming, scorching her fingers. She dropped it on to her dressing table amid a sickening acrid smell.

The door flew open and her parents burst in at the exact moment Bessie recognised the smell as burning hair. At the sight of the orange flash in the mirror, she began to panic, screaming again, as she patted her head. Her dad yelled, adding to the melee, and threw his pint of orange squash over her head, thus dousing the flames and meaning that only half of her very hairsprayed 'do' was burnt to a crisp. Levering open her bedroom window, her dad flapped at the air before gripping the windowsill, as if overwhelmed by this latest development in his daughter's day. Bessie more than understood, as she wiped the squash from her eyes and sat very still in the chair, unsure with so much that had gone wrong of exactly what she was crying for right this minute. Philip called from the landing as her mum ran from the room and Bessie heard the taps in the bathroom running at full force. The next thing she felt was a wet towel being placed over her head. She wasn't sure why, as there were no flames left to smother. The soggy, cold weight pushing down on her somehow felt apt and Bessie was glad of it. Hidden beneath the sodden cotton, she cried great, gulping sobs for the day that could not possibly get any worse.

'Thank God!' she heard her mum sigh and then the sound of her dad kissing his wife.

'No damage, love. Just a bit of burnt hair and a scorch on her dressing table.' He let out a long breath. 'My heart is going boom! What were you thinking, Bessie? Lighting a fire in your bedroom?'

'I didn't mean to!' came her muffled reply. Or maybe she did mean to . . . Maybe burning down the whole fucking house might actually be preferable than the life looming large in her mind – a life with no school, no Lawrence, no sex and, worst of all, no Michelle.

Her mum tutted. 'We'll talk about this tomorrow, young lady!'

Bessie came out from under the wet towel to find her parents staring at her as their breathing calmed. They looked sorrowful and concerned and it ate at her – *she* was the cause of this, of all of it. Confident the drama was over, her mum and dad left her room, pausing only to stroke her face and kiss her damp head. She stared at her rather bedraggled reflection. The right side of her hair was frazzled, melted and a good four inches shorter than the left. Her face, hair and new hot-pink cropped sweatshirt were sopping with orange squash and sticky to the touch. The sight only caused more tears to spring. She now looked more Phil Oakey than Madonna, and that had never been the plan. Her fingers stroked the blackened edges of the abandoned notelet: a charred, damp and unsatisfactory farewell to her love.

'I hate my life! It's my birthday and I hate my life!' she whispered into the ether.

CHAPTER FOURTEEN

August 20th 2021

Bess drove home cautiously, with the roll of relief in her stomach and a pulse that raced, shaking her head at what had nearly been her undoing and beyond relieved that nothing had happened. Sitting at the red traffic light, waiting to turn right, she twisted the wedding band on the third finger of her left hand.

She tried to pay attention to the rules of the road while her limbs shook. She kept picturing Mr Maxwell's feet: bare, hairy toes and a high instep, facts she should not know about her neighbour but now did.

As she pulled into the cul de sac, her heart sank. Helen Maxwell was unloading groceries from the boot of her shiny car, her keys dangling from her mouth as she juggled large, overstuffed paper bags from which poked glossy packets, a glass jar of coffee and most tantalising, the spiky top of a pineapple. Helen Maxwell, whom she now knew judged people by the money they earned, the car they drove and the holidays they took. Again Bess wished she didn't know this. It was another small puff of wind with which to further blow away the fine dust of her self-confidence. She should be old enough not to care how others judged her, but it was the judgement of others that had damaged her, had provided the thread that, when pulled, saw her whole life unravel. She decided to park on the driveway and pretend to take a phone call or to root in the glove compartment for an elusive item, anything to distract her until Helen had gone inside. She would do whatever was needed to avoid contact with the woman whose husband she had spent the best part of forty regrettable minutes with, listening to how unhappy he was. It wasn't a pleasant feeling and it reeked of duplicity. She should also not know that he had lost his job, something the judgemental Helen did not, as she unloaded the grocery bags which no doubt hid olives and several varieties of hummus. Bess wiped the nervous lick of sweat from her top lip and took a deep breath. Finally – *finally* – Helen kicked the front door shut with her foot and it was Bess's cue to move.

Slamming her own front door shut, she sat on the stairs and took a minute to catch her breath. Her fingers trembled, knowing she needed to be in control and less jumpy when Mario came home. Her eyes roved over her neat little home. *Home.* The place where she had raised her kids, cooked endless meals, slept for thousands of nights, nursed her family when they were sick and helped them celebrate so many milestones. A small blue confetti heart clung to the wainscot beneath the radiator, trying to evade detection. Bess bent down and plucked it from its hiding place, but instead of scrunching it in her fingertips, she laid it on the thigh of her jeans and smoothed it, deciding to pop it in her purse as a good-luck charm. She recalled Jake's face when Natalie launched the confetti cannon, beaming and happy on his special day, and her heart soared . . . It was Daniel who had made him smile like that, Daniel who she should be thanking, not judging.

'You stupid woman, Bess.'

She let her head hang down and closed her eyes, recalling the feel of Mario, the weight of him warm and trusting as he lay against her earlier. She wanted more of that contact, more of that intimacy.

Placing her hands on her chest, she felt a surge of something close to hope. She raised her eyes to the heavens and then closed them briefly, beyond relieved that she had not made the costliest of mistakes.

Jumping up, she decided to make herself look nice for when he got home and to put a bottle of plonk in the fridge to chill. She might even suggest an early night, with Chutney scooted from the bottom of the bed.

It was unusual for her loyal dog not to come and herald her arrival. Having dumped her bag on the hall table, she went to find him in his basket, where he sat with his head on his paws and his eyes following her every move. Bending down, she rubbed his ears and kissed his sweet head.

'I'm sorry, Chuts; I know I left you longer than I said I would, but I'm home now. Did you miss me? Are you mad with me? Is that it – are you sulking? And I know I've been a bit of a grump, but I promise you, happy mummy is coming back. I need to fix it, don't I? I have so much – I do, I have so much.' Only as she stood to go upstairs and clean her teeth did she notice the large pool of dark yellow pee on the floor by the back door. This caused her tears to spring as guilt, her old friend, came knocking.

'Oh, Chuts! That's my fault.' Again she dropped to her knees and held him close. 'I'm sorry I wasn't here to let you out, boy. I'm sorry.' He lifted his muzzle and grazed her cheek. She went to grab the mop and noticed that nearly all the blooms from Mario's orchid had dropped and now sat like dead butterflies scattered across the drainer next to the sink – small, delicate crumples of wilting purple that she had known wouldn't stand a chance in her inexpert care. A fleeting image of the ornate display at the Glade saddened her that she had knowledge of the place and also that the life of her orchid had ended.

'What do you think, Chuts? Stick them back on? Would Mario notice?' She was just considering how this might be possible when the front doorbell rang. Her heart skipped a beat at the thought of it being Helen. It was not.

'Mrs Talbot?'

'Yes?'

'Flowers!' The woman shoved a wide and weighty bouquet into her arms and made her retreat. Bess waved her thanks and closed the front door. The place was starting to look like Kew Gardens, if you ignored the state of her orchid. There was no need for her to guess – she knew instantly who they were from: Jake. Or more specifically, Jake and Daniel. She was determined to make an extra effort with Daniel from now on. Natalie was right – he wasn't going anywhere.

The phone rang and she grabbed it, jostling the bouquet into the crook of her arm.

'Hey, Mum! Happy birthday!'

'Oh, Jake, I just got your flowers! They are so beautiful – thank you!'

'Yep, I got notification of delivery on my app so I knew it was a good time to call.'

'How clever is that?'

'Very. Are they lovely?'

'They really are.' He always sent her yellow roses, and here she was, with armfuls of them – just stunning. They left her feeling like one lucky mum. Her eyes roved the tightly bound yellow buds that she knew would be glorious at every stage. 'You shouldn't have done that, darling, but thank you, and please say thank you to Dan too.' Her words were both conciliatory and heartfelt. Bess propped the flowers against the bottom step and took up her favourite stair, about a third of the way up. She gripped the phone and held it close to her face. 'It's lovely to hear from you. How was Scotland? Did you have a great time?'

'Oh, Mum, the best. When people found out we were on our honeymoon they were just so kind, the sun shone, the scenery was stunning and just to have time to be together, to breathe . . . It's been everything we hoped for.'

'I am so glad!' she said, and she was. 'I'm still finding bits of confetti all over the house – that was some party!'

'It was. And you can blame Nats for that – she brought the confetti and started lobbing it everywhere! There was even a bomb thing, I seem to remember!'

'There was!' Bess laughed.

'I've told her to be on standby for her wedding day. Plans are already afoot and I intend to create absolute havoc.'

'*If* she gets married. Do you think she'll ever find anyone to put up with her?' she joked, remembering her mum's words earlier and how Mario was 'a wonder', and she felt a surge of love for the man who had been by her side for most of her life.

'Someone will, Mum, and he'll be one heck of a lucky chap.'

The way Jake spoke about his sister made Bess realise that this relationship between her kids was one of her greatest achievements. She thought again of Philip and smarted at how much she missed him. *Her* big brother. There were days that stuck in her mind, days she treasured, like reading books in a caravan together with the rain bashing the roof while eating sweets from little paper bags as their mum and dad snoozed, collapsed together on the narrow sofa. Their dad had farted, and she and Philip had been helpless with laughter . . .

'I was explaining to Dan why they had to be yellow roses, your favourites.'

She could tell he was smiling and loved how she and her son had this little thing they shared. 'Yours too,' she pointed out.

'Yep. It drives Dan mad. I put them on the dining-room table without saying a word, but when he spots them, I hear him sigh with disappointment. He hates yellow flowers.'

'Well, there we are. Does he know why they're my favourites?'

'I'm not sure – you should tell him. He's next to me here in the car.'

And before she had a chance to think, Jake had handed the phone to Daniel.

'Hey, happy birthday, Bess!'

'Thank you, Dan. I hear you've had a wonderful time.' *I'm sorry . . . I'm sorry for not being more open with you . . . for not letting you in . . . You are Jake's choice and that is good enough . . .*

'Oh, the best! We've eaten far too much and laughed non-stop.'

'Well, that sounds about right.' She smiled.

'So come on, what's the deal with the yellow roses, apart from the fact they clash with our very expensive dining-room wallpaper?'

'Well, the day I brought Jake home from the hospital was the first time in as long as I could remember when everything felt perfect and possible. We used to have a rose bush in the front garden before it was all dug up to make the driveway, and when I went into hospital, there hadn't been a bloom on it, but as I stepped out of the car, it was a mass of yellow. Jake was so tiny. I held him in my arms and walked up the path like a queen. I can't remember everything about the way he looked, but I can remember everything about the way he felt, lying like a satisfied little lump in my arms. I sat on the sofa with him in a white babygrow, his little arms and legs splayed out, trusting and fragile and with all of his weight in my hands. It was all he knew – that tiny world right there with me holding him. He slept like he could have stayed there forever quite happily, and I felt complete. I looked out of the window and the roses were swaying, as if bowing their delicate heads. I thought they'd bloomed just for me. That's how special I felt, how lucky. I think about that moment a lot.' *It wiped away all my sadness. It restored my faith in the world. It made me feel invincible, and this is what I need to get back to, celebrating all I have rather than all I have lost!*

'Oh . . . Oh . . . Bess . . .' Daniel's sobbing prevented coherent speech. 'That's . . . that's so beautiful!'

'It's me, Mum. He's lost it – crying hard here.' Jake sounded a little amused. 'I heard what you said. Weren't you even a little bit scared about becoming a mum? I mean, babies don't come with a manual.'

'Oh, I was,' she smiled. 'I was really scared. I don't think I fully realised what I was getting into when I got pregnant. Not properly. I mean, I wanted you, planned you, spoke about you, pictured you, bought you clothes and stuff, but that's all superficial.' She shook her head, thinking back to that time when she would flop on the sofa, rub her bump and read a baby magazine, picking up top tips and letting her excitement grow along with her stomach. 'I mean, I knew I was going to get a baby – I saw the scans – but it wasn't until that moment at home, away from the protection of the maternity unit where I was looked after, and there were visitors, bustle and noise. It wasn't real in the hospital. I was a bit dazed – euphoric, but dazed – recovering from giving birth and a million other things. It was busy, but as I say, not real. No, for me it was that moment when I arrived home and kicked off my shoes and sat quietly on the sofa with you in my arms.' She smiled, remembering the feel of him. *It was real then. I had come home from the hospital with you, my baby, and I treasure you now as much as I did then.* 'Your dad came into the room and put my slippers on for me – it was the kindest act.' She swallowed, thinking of closing the door of the hotel room that afternoon, running down the corridor and watching Helen Maxwell in her driveway. 'He went to make me a cup of tea, and when he came back in the room, I couldn't figure out how to hold the tea, let alone drink it with you in my arms, and we laughed.

He stood there, holding both cups, his and mine, as if he couldn't figure out what to do either, how to help. And I laughed because I knew how much my life had changed, so I couldn't just grab a cup and take a sip of tea, but mainly I laughed because of how happy I was, how very, very happy – despite being scared and clueless. Because I had my family, and that was all I had ever wanted.'

And it's all I want . . . my family . . . I do like my life . . . I love my life! It's time to remember how much. I need to tell my husband my secret. I need to tell that man who held my foot so tenderly and placed a slipper on it . . . I owe him the whole story, the truth, and I owe it to myself. They say the truth will set you free and I want to be free of all that tethers me to my past. I want it so badly . . .

'Well, I take that as the highest compliment. I know how much you love your tea,' Jake said softly.

'Yeah, I do, but I love you a whole lot more. And just when I thought life couldn't get any better, when I was knee-deep in the running of the house, the preparing of food and the laundering of clothes, I fell pregnant with Natalie, the confetti-flinger!'

'I know the one,' he laughed.

Natalie, her beautiful girl, who had provided another burst of unimaginable starlight, another pocketful of magic to sew beneath her breast and into which her heart would dip whenever she saw her.

'I'm so lucky, Jake, so very lucky!' She felt the slip of tears over her cheek, overcome with love for those who loved her.

'You are, Mum, and I hope you've had a lovely day so far.'

'I have. I had lunch with Nanny and Grandad.' She sniffed.

'Oh? Pub carvery?' She heard the affectionate laughter in his tone and knew that, long after her parents had died, they would laugh about the dire carvery and their love of a good gravy.

'Of course.' They both laughed. Bess hoped she hadn't been too sharp with her mum about the voucher, making a promise

206

to be extra nice to her when she saw her next, aware that she had taken out her frustration on her lovely mum, the last person who deserved it. 'Dad's going to the chippy tonight if you fancy it? A treat for my birthday. I told him I'd text him who's coming and what you want to eat. About sixish? Can you and Dan make it?'

'Well, we're not quite home yet, Mum, so . . .' He paused, and she knew he was working out the timing, doing the maths. 'Can we let you know?'

''Course you can. That's fine, lovey, but the sooner the better! You know what your dad's like – I need to get the order off to him before he hits the chippy.'

'Yes, Mum, I know what Dad's like!' he laughed, as if in on the ruse, knowing that Mario wouldn't give a fig about the order or over-ordering or under-ordering or people turning up or not – she was the one who had been known to get in a tizz. 'But be sure we'll be there as and when we can, if not tonight then certainly tomorrow. We're excited to see you both!'

'Smashing. And don't worry if you didn't have time to do a Facebook birthday message.'

'A what?'

'You know, a message saying, "Happy Birthday, Mum!" or whatever on Facebook.'

'Oh right.' There was an awkward second of silence. 'Would you *like* me to do a Facebook birthday message?'

'Oh Jake, how lovely, thank you,' she said, as if he had raised the topic. 'Only if you have the time, and if you don't' – she thought of how different she felt now, compared with earlier: calmer – 'it doesn't matter, does it?'

'It really doesn't. I'm glad you like your flowers.'

'Thank you, darling, I do, and I love you, Jake.'

'Yep, love you too. Dan's waving goodbye. Still crying, but waving too.'

'Oh, bless him! And Jake?'

'Yes, Mum?' His speech was faster now, trying to get off the phone.

'I just wanted to ask, do you like your life?'

'Do I like my life?' He answered without hesitation. 'No, Mum, I absolutely love my life! I love Dan more than I ever knew was possible. I love our home, I love our friends and I love all that is coming our way. I have never been happier than I am right now, and I didn't know I *could* be this happy.'

She caught the euphoria in his tone and smiled. Despite her earlier reservations about Daniel, this was all she had ever wanted for her son, all she wanted for Natalie too and all she had ever wanted for herself. She was determined to get back on that path, the straight one that led, she was certain, to a place called happiness.

CHAPTER FIFTEEN

August 20th 1984

Standing in the bathroom, Bessie took her time, slowly peeling off her sticky clothes, still damp with orange squash, and piling them on the floor next to the laundry basket. She ran the cold tap and doused her flannel to wipe down her equally tacky body. Her movements were laboured, as if this was one final task that felt like too much at the end of the shittiest day. She was exhausted, but before, any tiredness had usually been tempered with thoughts of Lawrence, the next party or even the prospect of shaving her legs . . . All of these mental escape hatches were, however, now closed and her fatigue was bone-deep. With a clean, fresh-scented nightie over her head, all she wanted was to sleep and wake tomorrow at the dawn of a new day with less nausea and a clearer head. Or better still to wake in a little while and discover that the whole horrible day had been nothing more than a nightmare. She closed her eyes briefly, confused as to what to worry about next: her rubbish results? Her lack of confidence now in being able to achieve her dreams? Her crappy future now she was barred from the sixth form? The fact that the whole school would know she had had lots of sex? The fact that Lawrence had lied to her? Or that she and her beloved Michelle had fallen out? Bessie's head pounded and again her tears sprung from eyes red raw from crying.

Looking at her reflection in the mirror, she made a solemn vow. 'I am never, ever drinking ever again! Never.'

There was a quiet knock at the door. She closed her eyes, praying that at this late hour it was not her mum with the offer of a sandwich, and still terrified that at some point her parents would find out, hear the rumour, share her shame . . .

'Bessie?'

Relieved to hear her brother's voice, she opened the bathroom door. Philip came in and sat on the edge of the bath, while Bessie took up a place on the floor, using her discarded sticky clothes as a floor cushion. They each looked forward, avoiding eye contact. She scrunched the hem of her nightie between her fingers, fidgeting and embarrassed.

'I just wanted to say that Lawrence Paulson is a fucking jerk,' he whispered. Bessie's head dropped on to her knees and she cried. The fact that he was being kind and supportive was almost more than she could stand and certainly more than she felt she deserved.

'Who . . . who told you?' she managed.

'Gary Bradshaw.'

Of course, he and Lawrence played football together . . .

'Then Sean Thornton, Nicola Pie, Tony Dunlop, those two irritating girls – what's their names?' He clicked his fingers. 'Verity and Monica, and a couple of others whose names I don't know.'

'Oh my God, Philip!' Bessie's shame was complete, and she struggled to take a full breath. It felt like the walls were closing in. She remembered how when Leonard Bethelbrook, a boy in the year above, had died, and when Georgina Martin had gone to live with her nan in Cumbria when her parents got divorced and she went off the rails, they were all anyone could talk about. Information, opinion or an extra juicy fact was valuable collateral and she had become that very thing! *She* was the latest Leonard Bethelbrook or Georgina Martin, the person under discussion! Bessie wrapped her arms around her scraped shins and felt light, removed from the world and yet at the same time weighted down by the burden of this terrible, terrible event.

'I don't know what to do . . . I just don't know what to do, Philip!'

'Don't worry. Most people think it's utter bollocks. They'll stop talking about you in a week or so and then it'll be someone else's turn.'

'Lucky them,' she sniffed. 'Do *you* think it's utter bollocks?' She looked up at him now and saw the double blink and the way he looked towards the window.

'I think it doesn't matter if it's true or not. I think it's your business and all that matters is where you go from here.'

'I want to go to bed and never get up, that's where I want to go.'

'Well, that can't happen and so you need to be strong and tough it out.'

'I don't know if I can.' Bessie looked again at her brother.

'You have no choice.' His tone was kind yet calm, assertive. He let this sink in, and it helped, a clear directive offered without the emotion that clouded her every thought. 'If you go to the tech to do your resits, then that's a whole fresh start for you – new friends, new class, new everything.' He tried sweetly to lift her mood, and it did, a little.

'I am so ashamed.'

Philip stared at her, his face pained. Seemingly there were no words of comfort for that – she had as good as admitted that the rumours were in fact true.

'And Lawrence is now with Michelle and she was one of the best things in my life,' she whispered. To say the awful truth out

211

loud did not make it seem any more real. The fact hit her again with full force, like running into a brick wall.

'Well, if she wants to be with someone like him, then you're actually better off without her. You need to find a different best thing.'

Bessie gave a small smile but found no solace in his words.

'I mean it,' he said. 'Lawrence is a dick. He's got that smarmy look about him. You can do far, far better, Bessie.'

He sat next to her on the bathroom floor and wrapped her in the kindest hug she had had for a very long time. The warmth of it eased her and her limbs stopped shaking.

'I feel empty and full at the same time. It's like everything's whirling inside of me like a gas. I feel hollow and angry. This is my *life*, Philip, my life laid bare, and everyone's talking about me: my sex life, my exam results, how stupid I am, how easy I am . . . and it's too much! It's too much for me to hold in!' She broke free from her brother's hold and, with a sudden urgent and surprising need, lowered her head into the bath to throw up. With her head bent into the tub, she breathed slowly to try and stem the nausea with a line of spit joining her bottom lip to a small chunk of dark chocolate. Her brother handed her a small towel, dotted with blood from her shin. She mopped her face, upset that he had seen her in this state. Sitting back against the wall, she took more deep breaths. It helped a little. 'I can't stop being sick and I'm so confused, and a million other things are going round and round and round in my head. Everything's such a mess.'

'Bessie?'

'What?' she sniffed.

'Nothing.'

'No, go on, Philip, you can't say that and then not tell me! What were you going to say?' She braced herself for more

212

unpleasant revelations – did he know something about Lawrence and Michelle?

'I don't know if I should. It doesn't matter. It can wait.' He gave his fake smile, the one she had seen a million times when he was placating their mum or listening for the umpteenth time to one of Nanny Pat's stories.

'For fuck's sake, it does matter! Just say it! How much worse could things be for me right now?'

'Is there any chance . . . I mean, I feel awkward saying this, but—' He swallowed, and she saw him trying to draw moisture into his mouth, as if nerves had left him dry.

'For the love of God, Philip, either say it or leave!' Her reaction came, she knew, from a combination of tiredness and pure distress and, like most things about her day, was instantly regrettable.

He took a deep breath and clenched his fists, as if it took all of his strength to say the words out loud. 'Do you think you might . . . I mean, is there any chance' – he paused – 'that you could be pregnant?'

Bessie actually laughed, a rounded snort of laughter at the absolute absurdity of his suggestion. His words were like a fist to the gut. She sat back on the floor and racked her brains, trying to remember when she had had her last period. She pictured walking into the office at the back of the changing rooms at Westminster Lodge and explaining to Mrs Brown that she couldn't go swimming . . . When *was* that? And had she had a period since? She couldn't remember! And the harder she tried, the sicker she felt and the more terrified – *When was my period? When was it?* She placed a hand on her forehead. It was this one small detail that might have put her mind at rest, and yet it evaded her. Her spine seemed to go soft. *Please, God, please do not let me be pregnant. I would rather die!*

A crack of lightning made her and Philip jump.

'Thunder,' he smiled, as if trying to reassure her, as a low, rumbling groan came from the heavens. He walked over to the window, where the driving rain had begun to hit the glass, larruping the side of the house at a fierce angle. Bessie started to laugh, her giggle quickly turning closer to hysteria, as she realised that the rain would wash away the splat of vomit down the front of the house. She wished with every fibre of her being that she had not sent that prayer out into the universe, beyond petrified that prayers might be rationed and it had been her one request used up. She knew her parents would be a lot less bothered by a streak of Cinzano vomit on their brickwork than they would by an illegitimate baby. Lawrence Paulson's illegitimate baby. Lawrence Paulson, who was apparently in love with Michelle, the girl for whom he had made a mixtape.

'Philip.' Her voice was tiny. 'I am really, really scared.'

Again he sat next to her and put his arm around her shoulders. 'Don't be. It's only a storm, and I'm right here, Bessie. I'm right here.'

CHAPTER SIXTEEN

August 20th 2021

Her legs tucked beneath her, Bess sat on the sofa with Chutney by her side. Her eyes were drawn to the stunning display of yellow roses, now sitting in pride of place on the windowsill next to Philip and Nanette's bouquet and Natalie's lovely candle, which gave off the most glorious scent. She couldn't help but glance occasionally at the Maxwells' house with a sharp jolt of remorse lancing her with every glimpse. She reached for Chutney, the feel of him warm, anchoring, soothing and familiar. Quite what she expected to see over there she wasn't sure. Helen stomping up the driveway with a meat cleaver? Andrew arriving home with his feet nicely hidden inside socks? The image of the plastic tray in the hotel room with its grubby cup and the admissions about his less than perfect life made her stomach flip.

'Why did you go?' Bess asked herself aloud. 'Why did you *do* that?' Biting her lip, she wished she could rewind the day and turn left at the lights. That was all she had had to do – turn left at the lights! Closing her eyes, she took a deep breath, calming her flustered pulse. No one would ever know – not that she had done anything, much to her relief – but explaining her intentions in tandem with her actions would be hard. But enough! Instead she focused on seeing Mario, excited about their chippy tea and the bottle of wine that now sat chilling in the fridge, looking forward to feeling her husband's arms around her, holding her close, taking her hand as they climbed the stairs. She wanted to say she was sorry, wanted to tell him just how much she loved him and that she was going to prove it to him every day, and that closeness had to start with the truth. She owed him an explanation of where fun Bess had gone – the Bess he had married. Without warning, a great gulp of tears tumbled from her that made her catch her breath. It still had the power to do that to her, the memory of the day she had bumped into Melanie Brooks, who to her would always be Melanie Hall.

Melanie had been with her son, a quiet, sweet pale boy called Neil. It wasn't long after Bess's miscarriage and Jake and Natalie were larking around, in and out of the kerb, tapping each other in an irritatingly raucous game of tag and then coming to rest behind her legs until the other reached around to make contact – all this while she tried to listen to Melanie going into great detail about her planned extension and the paint scheme she had chosen. Natalie had jumped on to Neil's back and laughed loudly, and Melanie had stared at Bess's daughter, flicked her hair over her shoulder and said something that pulled the plug on Bess's fragile self-confidence, something that fired a bolt of shame through her very core, as all the self-belief instilled in her by Mario's love washed away,

'Well, there's no doubt who she takes after.' Melanie had smiled, a mean smile that didn't reach her eyes. 'Like mother, like daughter, eh? Seems she likes the company of the boys too . . .' And she had winked. Bess had looked at her beautiful girl and felt her insides shrink and, just like that, she was the girl outside the rugby club, the girl who felt exposed, vulnerable, and her biggest fear was that this kind of talk might reach the ears of her kids. It was a reminder that in their town, these rumours, these hurtful words and snippets of gossip still lived and while she might be able to hide in a school canteen or supermarket staffroom, she couldn't outrun them. She had walked home in silence, while Jake and Natalie laughed and ran around her in circles. Smiling at them meekly, her throat had almost closed with all the grief she struggled to contain.

Wiping her eyes with her sleeve, Bess knew that the future depended on her being open with Mario, no matter how terrified she was at the prospect. She needed to find the courage to restore them to happiness. The Maxwells, she could now see, had jack shit compared to her. Even Michelle with her high-end life, Bess didn't envy – how could she, when she had her husband, kids and Chutney by her side . . . ?

Her phone rang.

'Happy birthday, Bessie.'

Bess swallowed the last of her tears. It was typical of her brother to cut to the chase. He was never interested in chit-chat, chewing the fat or catching up. It always made her feel that to make contact at all was a chore, perhaps it was, and that fact alone pawed at her heart.

'Thanks, Philip. I got your card and flowers, thank you. They're really lovely.' She glanced over at the mantelpiece, where his and Nanette's card sat in front of the one from her sister-in-law, Bianca, the word 'F*CKING' just visible. She'd have to rearrange them when she got off the phone.

'I always feel old when it's your birthday, because if my little sister is notching up the years . . .'

'I get it.' She nodded. 'How's Nanette?'

'She's okay – heading off to a retreat in Thailand where they treat people who are . . .'

Lactose intolerant! Bess mouthed the words along with her brother.

'. . . lactose intolerant. Hopefully, it'll help.'

'Fingers crossed.' Decades ago, he would have recognised her sarcasm and laughed along, and then she would make some vegan-related quip, but those days were sadly long gone.

'How are M— Mum and Dad?'

'Great, good, you know, same old.' Nothing would give them greater pleasure than to see their son, but this she was unable to say, as she was the reason Philip was more or less estranged from them. The shame she felt at having been outed in the cruellest way, labelled 'a slut, easy, a tart', and worse still, knowing that these words had been delivered straight into her brother's ear while his friends snickered into their palms, was enough to cause a sudden silence, where Bess sensed the crackle of awkwardness down the line. Her shoulders hunched and her stomach seized with a guilt that was as familiar as it was unwelcome. Philip, it seemed, had found it easier to stay away over the years. She understood and could not pretend that his absence wasn't tinged with some small degree of relief, but this too she knew needed to be rectified, and it all started with being open with Mario.

'Did you get a harmonica rendition today?' he asked, a little more jovially.

'I did indeed.' A wave of sadness lapped at her memories, picturing Philip on his birthdays, his long fringe hanging over his eyes and his reluctant attendance in the kitchen as their dad belted out his best version of 'Happy Birthday' and their mum danced in little circles in her nightie while beating the pancake batter.

'Anyway, I'd better let you get on,' he said.

Bess gave a wry smile, knowing that what he meant was, *I'd* better get on, *I* want to end the call, having used something similar herself with Michelle earlier.

'Thanks for calling, Philip. Give my love to Nanette and tell her thank you for the flowers and good luck in Thailand.'

'I will.' And just like that he was gone.

Bess stared at the phone in her lap, feeling now, as she always did, the loss of her one and only sibling. It hadn't been instant, but rather a slow thing: where first he moved away and next declined an invitation to Christmas. He then sent gifts instead of tearing down the motorway to see her newborn babies and his phone calls became sporadic, their conversations stilted, until they arrived at the point where for him to pitch up or show more interest in her life would have seemed odd. It hurt and made her feel lonely, the lack of his presence – the one person who knew as much about her childhood as she did . . . She missed him as much now as she always had.

She looked out of the window as she ended the call, in time to see Mario walking up the driveway. Even if she hadn't been expecting him, couldn't see his face, she would have known him by his walk, the shape of him and the way he reached into his pocket for his keys. Her husband. The man she knew inside and out. Her heart jumped. They had a lot to talk about, a lot to do, but this felt very much like a beginning. Butterflies of nerves and excitement fluttered in her gut.

Mario swung his empty flask and lunch box in one hand and a small towel in the other, an old one that he used to wipe his mucky hands. She noticed the lack of chip bags and her stomach grumbled, not that she was hungry, not really, but the thought of chips was enough to override that minor factor. Plus, she wanted the distraction of unpacking the food, fetching the plates, cutlery and the ketchup bottle, props, anything, in fact, to occupy her hands, while she told him how much she loved him and how this was the start of a new dawn, deciding it would be easier to begin the hardest of conversations if she was busying about as usual. Her mind might be set on putting things right, but old ghosts still pawed at her confidence, confirming what they had established earlier, that they weren't the kind to sit down and analyse things, but more the 'chat as they went' kind of couple.

A quick glance at the clock told her it was five o'clock, probably a tad too early for supper and, besides, she hadn't heard back from the kids yet. She heard his key in the door, followed by the thud, thud of his heavy, sweaty boots, proof of a hard day's graft, hitting the laminate floor. Later, she would pair them and place them in the cupboard under the stairs, like she did every night, and he would retrieve them in the morning, and she would be happy for this life lived in sync – in glorious sync!

'In here, love!' she called out, settling back into the corner of the sofa as he walked in. She wanted him to see her the way she wanted to be again: not as an atmosphere hoover or a mood magnet, but someone instead who was optimistic about her future, happy for all she had, grateful that the fog of melancholy was lifting.

'Cup of tea?' She unfurled her legs, ready to move if he wanted a drink.

'No, I'm okay.' He raised his hand, almost a subconscious command for her to stay put, and sat on the chair by the side of the fireplace, leaning forward with his arms on his legs, as he often did, so the smallest possible area of his grubby end-of-day body and plaster-spattered clothes came in contact with the almond-coloured upholstery. Bess appreciated the consideration, but then that was Mario all over – considerate.

'No chips?' she said to make conversation, stating the obvious.

'No, no chips.' He ran his palm over his stubbled chin. 'I thought it was a bit early, plus I wanted to talk to you.'

His tone was a little cool. Her smile faltered – she understood. He was still smarting from the misunderstanding this morning.

'Well, I want to talk to you too.' *I really do, and I'm plucking up the courage . . . Courage . . .*

He nodded. 'So how was your day?' His expression was drawn, as if he were figuring how to get to the point, and it unnerved her.

'Okay. You know . . .' She shrugged.

'Your mum and dad on good form?'

I think her and Mario might be having marital problems . . . Her mum's whispers rang inside her head. *Not any more, Mum. I'm going to set things right.*

'Yep. Food was ropey and Mum was obsessed with a bloody voucher Philip had sent, as you can imagine.'

'Saint Philip of Knutsford?' he smiled weakly.

'The very same.' It felt mean, but it was easier to go with the flow, letting her husband assume Philip was an aloof stuck-up shit who considered himself a cut above, unwilling to come and visit or overly engage, but she knew differently and hoped that when Mario knew the full story he might feel differently too. 'That was him on the phone, actually, just before you arrived, wishing me a happy birthday. And you'll never guess, my old schoolfriend called me today, Michelle – you've heard me talk about her?'

Again he nodded.

'It was so out of the blue and yet so normal to be chatting to her. I realised how much I've missed her, Mario, and I want to call her back. I want to get to know her again.' *And I want to tell her as much as I can, because I have missed her, how very much I have missed her!* 'She was a big part of my life. What do you think?' She raised her eyebrows, wanting him to engage, to smile, to give her permission to start the dialogue that she had been practising in her head. His coolness sent shivers of inadequacy along her limbs. She folded her shaking hands into her lap, wanting to feel his love.

'I think do what you've got to do.' He held her gaze.

'Yes, I'll give that some thought.' She took a deep breath and sat forward a little in the chair, her heart racing. 'Today's been interesting for me – it's really made me think about things.'

Mario nodded, as if only half listening. He tapped his fingers together nervously and she decided now was not the time for her great revelation of love, nor the time to come clean about everything, while he seemed so distant, so preoccupied, so angry.

'So, how . . . how was your day?' She smiled. He didn't.

'Interesting,' he fired back, holding her stare.

Again her gut jumped. She didn't like this atmosphere; it felt like punishment. 'Oh well, interesting is good – better than boring! Why was it?'

Mario sat back in the chair, the slump to his shoulders suggesting that fatigue now overrode any desire to please her or to maintain pristine chair fabric.

'First, I nearly killed meself driving like a loon to get here this morning, thinking the sky must be falling down.'

Guilt again lanced her chest. 'I am sorry, Mario. I don't know how it all got out of hand – one little text, eh?'

'Yep, one little text.' Still he studied her face and she felt the colour rise on her chest and neck. 'Then I worked through my lunch break to try to make up the time I lost in coming home.'

'I am sorry, Mar—'

'Yes, so you've said. I worked my arse off all day, took a couple of painkillers to try to stop the throbbing in my left shoulder making me want to drop to the floor.' He rolled the shoulder now and grimaced. Plastering was a job that made no allowance for the wear and tear on ageing joints. 'A young man's game,' Mario called it. 'And then, just before I left, I stopped by the site office to put my hours in for the week and I chatted to Julie, who does the timesheets – you remember her from the five-a-side barbecue?

Her boy, Leon, is our goalie – nice lad, bit slow on the uptake, but massive hands and no fear of hitting the ground.'

'Yes, yes, I do remember him and her.'

Mario sat up straight again. 'Well, Julie has two kids: a boy and a girl.'

'Like us.' Bess was a little bewildered by this turn in the conversation, especially given his demeanour – it didn't match this sudden desire for small talk.

'Yes, just like us. Anyway, her daughter—'

The sound of the doorbell stopped him mid-sentence.

'I'll go, you can tell me later,' she said softly over her shoulder, as she rose from the sofa with Chutney following behind, barking just in case. It was actually a relief to be out of his line of sight. His stare was making her feel uncomfortable.

'Quiet, Chuts!' she shouted. She saw Jake's outline behind the glazed panel of the front door, Daniel standing to the left of his husband, holding a large blue balloon with a blue ribbon tied to it. 'Oh, it's Jake and Dan!' she yelled back to the lounge. The sight of them lifted her mood and the atmosphere and she was grateful for both.

'Oh, what a lovely surprise!' She greeted them both warmly. If proof were needed that she was part of a wonderful loving family who cared about her, there they were – and they had brought her a balloon! 'I wasn't sure you'd be able to make it! I am so pleased to see you both!' She accepted a kiss on the cheek from Daniel and smiled at him.

'I told him we'd make it, but he was fussing,' her son-in-law said, raising his eyebrows at her.

'Anyway, when you two have finished trashing me . . .' Jake laughed, rubbing his palms. 'Where's Dad?'

'In the lounge,' she said, pointing.

'Come on!' He grabbed her hand and pulled her along the hallway, drawing her into this exuberant balloon-trailing moment.

'Hey! Hello, son!' Mario smiled and stood with his arms open wide. Jake did as he always had and took his place inside them, where his dad wrapped him in the tightest hug. Daniel hung back, allowing for the interaction and holding his balloon in his right hand like a kid at the zoo. 'Come on, Dan,' Mario called over Jake's head, 'there's plenty of room!'

Daniel went to stand next to his husband, and Bess watched the two men, arms across each other's backs, a safe unit held tightly now by Mario, while the balloon, for her birthday no doubt, floated abandoned towards the ceiling. While delighted to see their closeness, Bess felt a little excluded and grabbed the ribbon.

'I can't remember the last time I had a balloon!' she laughed.

'Ah, actually,' Jake said, almost snatching it from her, 'I need you both to sit on the sofa.'

'Oh, should I be worried?' She did as she was asked, sitting in her preferred corner, with Mario next to her now. She reached out to take his hand, but he curled his fingers against his thigh, and she pulled her arm back, mortified, wounded and worried by his reaction, but with her smile in place so as not to alert Jake or Daniel. Her heart, however, stuttered with rejection that was familiar.

'This isn't a balloon for you, Mum,' Jake said. He and Daniel took up position in front of the fireplace, a handsome couple holding hands, a couple very much in love. The sight of this bolstered Bess's determination to get closer to Daniel and highlighted quite how far she and Mario had slipped off course.

'It's a balloon for Mario Jack,' Daniel announced, his voice a little faltering.

'Who's Mario Jack?' Bess asked the obvious question. And before she could speak again, Daniel stepped forward and placed a grainy black-and-white picture in the palm of her hand. She could see instantly what it was. She held it out so Mario could see it too. Emotion stoppered the words in her throat.

Mario leaped up. 'How? Who is—? I mean, is this—?' He was as lost for words as she was.

'It's our baby boy!' Jake cried. 'It's your grandson.'

Bess felt her stomach leap and her blood race with joy – a baby! A grandchild! It was the most wonderful news. She recalled Michelle's words earlier, and Mario's too, and how he had longed for the baby they lost. Her tears sprang as she pictured holding the child, marvelling at how dearly she loved it already.

'Oh, Jake! Dan!' Jumping up, she crushed her son to her and then reached for the man who had made her boy happier than he had ever known was possible. 'Who's the mum?' she asked.

'Well, the *surrogate*,' Daniel corrected, 'is a very dear friend of ours, Gigi, who already has three children and has agreed to do this selfless, incredible thing for us.'

'Oh my goodness!' Just the thought of holding the little baby and all the glorious moments that would come their way was enough for her excitement to bubble. 'This has to be the best birthday present ever! I can't believe it!' Using her sleeve, Bess blotted the tears from her cheeks.

'Oh yes, happy birthday, Bess.' Daniel held her hand and the two exchanged a long look. It was time for her to build a bridge with this man who was now her family, the father of her grandchild.

'Gigi lives in Glasgow,' Jake explained, 'hence the Scottish honeymoon. She also fell pregnant a lot sooner than we had all anticipated. We thought it might take months.'

'And hence our sudden decision to marry,' Daniel said, filling in the gaps. 'We wanted our baby to share our surname.'

'I see,' she beamed, the facts still sinking in, finally understand-ing the rush to organise a wedding and why she had felt left out, a little excluded from her son's big day. It had *not* been his big day – that would be when he became a dad to this little boy who was still no more than a slightly smudged photograph in her hand. These two fine men were building a family, just as she and Mario had done all those years ago and just as they would continue to do in the future with this new generation.

'This is the most amazing news. Do you want to help me in the kitchen, Dan?' she asked. 'I'm going to make a cuppa and we can get the plates out for tea. Mario's getting the chips in.'

Her husband doffed an imaginary cap. 'And everyone can go large if they want and get a pickled egg, no expense spared. I'm going to be a grandad!' He wiped his eyes.

'Hi!' Natalie called from the hallway. Bess felt a sense of satisfaction – both her kids were home, just the way she liked it.

'In here!' Jake called.

Nat stood in the doorway and surveyed the scene in front of her. 'I guess they've told you then?'

'You *knew*?' Bess asked, happy that her kids were so close they would share this precious journey together; she knew how important it was to have a sibling who had your back. It broke her heart to think of Philip placing his arm around her. *'It's only a storm, and I'm right here, Bessie. I'm right here.'* And this thought only settled her decision to make amends, to bring her brother back into the fold, to put things right.

'Mum, it's killed me not to tell you, but they made me promise!' Natalie kissed her mum's cheek.

'We didn't want to get everyone's hopes up before everything was in place. We needed to get the legal paperwork drawn up and wanted to get the first scan out of the way, so we knew the baby was healthy and that Gigi was happy and that her kids and husband all knew and were on board,' Daniel rambled, caught up in emotion.

'We wanted everything to be as guaranteed as it can be before we broke the news, and that time is now!' Jake took the scan picture and held it up to his face, as if seeing it for the first time. 'I can't believe it – we are so excited.' He handed it back to Bess. 'You can keep this.'

'I can? I'm putting it on the fridge,' she announced, and marched off with Daniel following to do just that. He took a seat at the kitchen table, watching as she fixed on the fridge the photograph of Mario Jack, a combination of the two grandfathers' names.

'I think Jake is going to be a wonderful dad,' he smiled.

'I think you both will be. I'm so proud of you. Have you told your parents, Dan?'

'No, heading over there at the weekend. I'm a bit nervous, actually.'

'Why? It's such wonderful news!' She put her hand to her throat. 'It hasn't fully sunk in yet. A baby . . .'

'Yeah, it is wonderful news.' Daniel drew invisible loops on the tabletop with his finger. 'But you've met my parents . . .' He paused. 'It takes them a while to get their head around stuff – first me being gay, then me getting married, and now a baby.'

'It might take them a while, Dan, but that's okay, so long as they get there in the end – and just you wait until they meet him. It'll be a scrum, all of us trying to hold him. I can't wait!'

'I'm nervous too about being a dad.' He licked his lips.

'Of course you are – it's a big deal, a big change, but a wonderful change. It was for Mario and me, certainly. It made us, becoming parents, and it's the thing I'm proudest of, Dan, even if I don't always get it right.' She rubbed her palms together; the skin still smarted from where Mario had rejected her hand. She would ask him why later – use it to pave the way for the conversation that would make amends.

'Oh, I think you've done a pretty good job.'

She liked the way he spoke to her, saw how much he valued Jake, who had stolen both their hearts.

'And I know it's going to be a wonderful change, but—' He hesitated.

'What?' She sat down at the table opposite him.

'I adore Jake.' He smiled at the mention of his name. 'But he can be—' Again he paused, as if reminded that she was his mum. 'How can I put it . . . ? I worry how he'll cope with the disruption of a baby in our lives. I mean, we both want him, of course we do – we've spoken about nothing else since the day we met!' This was news to her, delightful news that split her face with a smile. 'But I think out of the two of us, I'm more practical and Jake sometimes has his head so deep in a work project it's like nothing else exists!' He raised his palms. 'God knows I love him, but I worry about it – how he'll adapt.'

'It's as I was saying earlier, Dan, you can never be fully prepared for parenthood. You can read all the books, take all the advice, but you kind of have to live it to learn it. Does that make sense?'

'It does.' He smiled at her. 'And I guess all that matters is that I really love him.'

'You do, don't you?'

'Yes,' he laughed. 'I really, really do love him.'

She found his admission heartfelt and moving. 'Becoming a dad will, I think, be the best thing that could happen to him and the best thing that can happen to you as a couple.'

'You and Mario – you two are like couple goals, right there! We want to be like you guys. It's hard to think of one of you without the other.'

Bess felt a tightening in her throat, wanting so badly to get back on track with Mario, never, ever wanting him to shrug off her hand when she tried to hold it. It had made her feel worthless and put her straight back in the body of her sixteen-year-old self, when she wanted to disappear. She hoped that when he knew her full story he might understand, and she needed to tell him sooner rather than later.

'Thank you, lovey,' she said gently.

Daniel looked to her, welling up. She grabbed the kitchen roll and threw him a square.

'I was so worried about what you might say, Bess. I know you haven't always . . .' He wiped his nose. '. . . haven't always thought I was good enough for Jake.'

Bess let out a long breath and her head hung forward, her words laced with remorse. 'That was true at first, and nothing to do with you. I wouldn't have thought anyone was good enough for Jake, but you are – of course you are, more than . . . You make him happy, and that's all anyone can ask for their kids. He's lucky to have you. You're lucky to have each other. And I want to say I'm sorry, Dan.' She swallowed the lump of emotion in her throat. 'I'm sorry if I was a little closed off. I'll make it up to you. I want us to get to know each other properly.'

'I'd like that. I thought it might have been the whole gay thing and that you were holding out for a miraculous conversion.' He held her gaze and it broke her heart a little. This could not be further from the truth.

Bess shook her head. 'The only thing that concerned me when Jake came out as a young teenager was that, as a gay man, he might experience prejudice or hatred because of his sexuality – that bothered me more than anything. I didn't want my child to go through that – who does? I didn't want him to experience something that was so unjust and that I couldn't shield him from. That, and I suppose a little bit of me selfishly thought I would miss out on becoming a granny.' She recalled her earlier flash of envy on learning Michelle was a nanna – and now it was her turn! 'Things were very different when I was growing up – it was unusual for gay men to become parents as a couple, and look how that's turned out.' She twisted her neck to look at the scan picture. 'When's he due?'

'January the twenty-ninth.'

'Wow! Will you be at the birth – how does it work?'

Daniel nodded. 'We'll both be in the room with Gigi. She's coming down here to have the baby and she'll stay at the hospital for as long as they need her to – could be a day or a week, depending on the kind of birth she has and her recovery – and then we'll take him home, just like any other couple leaving hospital with our baby boy.'

'Oh, Dan!' The tears came then as Bess pictured the day, picturing also the moments her own babies had been lifted from her body . . . That euphoria, that pure floating moment of joy. A time in her life when she had felt valued, good enough and excited about her future with Mario by her side and her babies sleeping soundly under her roof. This was the state to which she wanted to return, when she had felt invincible!

'I feel like we need to start over a bit, Bess, you and me. I'm going to need your support,' Dan said.

'Yes.' She held his hand across the tabletop. 'I would really like that.'

'Dan!' Mario called from the hallway. 'What you having, son – fish and chips?'

'Lovely.'

'Usual for you, Grandma?' Mario was trying out the word for the first time, and her heart swelled, not only at hearing it out loud, but recognising it as an olive branch, which she eagerly grasped and held close to her heart.

'Oh don't! You'll set me off again!' And just like that her tears returned, happy tears this time.

'I've called your mum and dad – they're on their way,' Mario informed her as he grabbed the keys to the van.

'Marvellous. Thank you, love.' She couldn't wait to see them receive the news of their great-grandson. She hoped her dad might have his harmonica on him. If ever there was the need for a rendition of 'Congratulations', it was now!

CHAPTER SEVENTEEN

August 20th 1984

Bessie watched the hands of the clock tick until they passed the number twelve. That was it. Her birthday was over. It was a brand-new day. She placed her hand on her stomach and knew that nothing would ever be the same for her again. How could it be that she had woken up this morning feeling like one person and then gone to bed seeing herself as someone else entirely? She stared up at her ripped poster and ran her hand over the burnt ends of her hair.

'What am I going to do?' Her words drifted out into the dark night sky through her open bedroom window and she hoped an answer might come back to her. It didn't. She lay back on her mountain of soft pillows and thought about what to do next. She would take a pregnancy test, but there was something about the way she felt that told her the truth in advance – it would only confirm what she already suspected and what Philip suspected too. Hot tears dripped down the side of her face and soaked into the pillowcase.

One thing was for sure: she would not tell a soul, no one, because that would be the end of her life as she knew it. She would keep it secret. The thought of admitting to her parents not only that she had had sex, but that she was pregnant too! The thought of their desperate disappointment, hidden behind smiles, tunes on the harmonica and the offer of sandwiches while their hearts broke was more than she could stand.

There was a gentle knock on her bedroom door.

'Come in.'

Philip entered slowly. 'I can't sleep.'

'Me neither.'

'I thought I'd better just check you weren't burning the other half of your hair off.'

She shook her head, totally disinterested in the state of her hair now she had something much bigger and much worse to worry about.

He sat on the floor by the side of her bed. 'Don't cry, Bessie. It'll all be okay.'

'It won't, Philip!' Tears strangled her words. 'I think I know already that I'm pregnant. As soon as you said it, it made sense. I can . . . I can feel it.' It sounded impossible but she knew it was the truth.

'You do have options, you know.'

'Like what?' She propped her head on her hand and stared at him. Fear stoked her from within and yet she rallied enough to hear these options, desperate for direction that might help sort her scrambled thoughts.

'You can tell Mum and Dad . . .'

'No, no way! Can you imagine? Mum quietly sobbing and Dad not knowing what to do, and the two of them hiding from the neighbours and dying with shame as they tell Nanny Pat and Grandad Norm? I'm their little girl, Philip – I'm their little girl . . .'

'You are,' he acknowledged.

'And you mustn't tell them – please promise me, Philip! Promise me you won't tell them, please!' she begged, her tone verging on hysteria. The thought of looking her parents in the eye if they knew

233

this about her was enough to again invite the rise of nausea as her stomach gripped with fear.

'All right, forget it – don't tell Mum and Dad then. But honestly,' he said, holding up his hands, 'you need to try and stay calm or they're going to want to know what all the fuss is about. I promise you I won't tell them. I won't tell anyone.'

Bessie's heart rate settled a little at his words, knowing that, unlike Lawrence, her brother would keep his word.

'You could have an abortion,' he said matter-of-factly, the word so awful and alien to her sixteen-year-old ears.

How might she be judged for this? Did it hurt? And could she actually bring herself to end the life of this baby? It would, however, make the problem go away . . . Her conflicting thoughts raged and were more than she could wrestle with right now.

She shook her head. 'I don't think I could do that.'

'Or you can have the baby and get it adopted. There are so many people desperate for babies.'

Her breath came in shallow pants. Every single one of the options he had laid out sounded ludicrous to her ears – how – *how* – was she having to face this? She felt winded as again the reality of her situation landed hard.

'Are there any other choices?' Her voice was small.

'Not that I can think of right now. You know Carmen is adopted?'

'I didn't.'

'Yeah. There are places you can go and have the baby and they sort it all out. I think it might have been done through the Church.'

'I considered becoming a nun once.' A reminder that she had been pure with a rosy future . . .

Philip laughed and, in spite of her terrible situation, she laughed too.

'I think, Bessie, that ship has definitely sailed.'

'I don't think I could have an abortion. I don't think I could go through with it.'

'First, you need to have your pregnancy confirmed – this might all be a whole lot of worry for nothing. And second, if you are, don't try to figure out what to do immediately – take your time and be certain.'

'I'm so scared, Philip,' she whispered.

'Well, if it's any consolation, I'm scared too.' He swallowed, and she welcomed this moment of warmth between them. It made her feel less alone. 'But I'll help you however I can, I promise. You won't have to go through anything on your own.'

'I think you're the best brother in the whole wide world.' She meant it, instantly and hugely relieved to hear his words of support, unsure she could get through it without him. Her vision was once again clouded by tears as her head hit the pillow. Her heart and eyelids were heavy.

'Today is a brand-new day,' her brother said, stroking her hair as exhaustion claimed her. His whispers were kind and reassuring. 'Today is a brand-new day . . .'

Bessie closed her eyes. Her last thought before floating off to sleep was that she wasn't sure her dad was right – maybe she was a falling-down kind of girl after all . . .

CHAPTER EIGHTEEN

August 20th 2021

Bess felt a bubble of joy in her stomach, the kind she got when something exciting and wonderful lurked on the horizon. This was the start of a brand-new chapter. She scraped the leftover chips, of which there were plenty, into the little plastic food recycling bin and folded the greasy vinegar-stained wrappings, crunchy with salt, into a soggy bundle. Grabbing the red pen from the pot on the windowsill, she flipped the pages of the calendar and chose a love heart instead of a red ring with which to encircle the twenty-ninth of January the following year.

'I'll pop these in the wheelie bin.' Mario grabbed the waste and went out of the back door.

Bess was pleased the visitors had left, enjoying the peace after the hubbub but still buoyed up by Jake and Dan's news. All she wanted to do now was make things right with Mario and tell him everything. The celebrations had been loud, tearful and memorable in their beloved family home. It might not have fancy balconies or a view of the sea, but it was jam-packed with love and there was nowhere else she wanted to be. As the clock nudged ten o'clock, Jake, Dan and Natalie had, like her, been keen to get to their beds in preparation for work tomorrow. Her parents, however, without any sign of tiredness, had congaed down the drive and were apparently planning on hitting the cooking sherry when they got home.

'A great-grandad!' her dad had beamed with tears in his eyes. 'Can you believe it?'

She looked at the scan picture on the fridge for the hundredth time. How happy she felt! *Happy!* She decided to make a supreme effort for bedtime, to really clean her teeth: floss, mouthwash, the lot, and to shower before applying a little of her precious scent, usually saved for special occasions. And in truth, if this wasn't a special occasion, she didn't know what was. Maybe she'd put on her fancy lacy nightie before she told Mario exactly how she felt about him and opened the dialogue that meant she could finally tell him of the things she had kept hidden, the secrets that burdened her every waking moment. The thought of it didn't faze her now, quite the opposite.

The outline of the little one on the scan was quite distinct, the shape of the back of his head and a little nose standing proud, the curve of a tummy. Gigi was a woman she couldn't picture, had not met and yet she was hosting this precious child. Bess sent love to her out across the darkness, looking forward to the day she could look her in the eye and tell her how remarkable she thought she was, giving the whole family, but especially Jake and Daniel, this most incredible of gifts. She closed her eyes and took a moment.

The greatest gift . . .

'Mario Jack, of all the crazy families you could pick . . . You will be so loved, little one. So very much loved.'

'Who are you talking to?' came a voice beside her.

'The baby. It's such a wonderful thing Gigi's doing.' She turned to smile at her husband, only for her face to fall at the sight of the newly bare orchid in his hands. Guilt filled her stomach, washing away the joy, as she and Mario stared together at the plant, no more than stalks now, sticking up from the fuchsia-coloured pot.

'I found this in the bin.'

She heard the bite of recrimination in his tone and her response sounded weak and apologetic, flustered as she was at the sight of the sorry-looking plant in his hands.

'Oh, all the flowers dropped off. One came away in my hand when I unwrapped it this morning and by the time I got to it this afternoon it was just stalks. I didn't know what to do with it.'

'Shoddy goods.' He almost threw it in the sink where it landed loudly, spilling dry soil on top of a couple of ketchup-smeared plates and a mug still holding the last dregs of tea in the bottom. She heard the distinct crack of china, unsure whether it was her crockery or the pot that had smashed. The action was most unlike her gentle Mario and in stark contrast to the jollity of the evening just spent. He was clearly hurt and she knew she was the cause. Her mind whirred with how best to approach him, what to say next. His resolute stance told her she had to tread gently.

'I wasn't saying that.' She kept her tone level. Ordinarily she knew the expression, the words and the action to defuse a situation because she knew every inch of the man, every nuance, every sigh. This presentation of Mario, however, was new and unnerving. He reminded her of someone swaying on the pavement at closing time, spoiling for a fight. She didn't like it one bit. 'I am sorry, love, I just didn't want you to think I couldn't take care of it.'

'So you put it in the bin?' His expression was confused, his tone sarcastic.

'I . . .' She couldn't get the right words out fast enough, wishing she could say that it hadn't been done with hate but with thoughtlessness.

'Have you had a nice birthday?' he said, cutting her off.

Have I had a nice birthday? She considered his lost card, the lack of birthday messages on Facebook and the grotty lunch with her parents. But all of that, however, was tempered by the wondrous realisation that her mum was right, that her happiness lay in her hands – she had so much to appreciate and to feel thankful for. Close insight into Andrew Maxwell and his shallow marriage had also played its part, and now the magical idea that she was going to become a grandma. So how to reply? She plumped for the truth.

'Actually, Mario, if I'm being honest, the start of it was a bit shaky, but right now, I think it's the best birthday I've ever had.'

'And *are* you being honest?' He held her gaze, challenging.

'Yes!' She hated the implication. She felt sick. 'What do you mean by that?' She wanted to unpick his question, for him to say his piece, moan about being called home and having to leave work and the fact he had paid good money for the dying orchid, so they could clear the air, fight and move forward. She wanted to tell him all she had kept bottled up for so long and knew that when she did, the state of the orchid would not matter a jot. Bess wanted to work hard to make their life whole again, so that without hesitation he would tell anyone who asked that his wife was indeed smashing.

Mario said nothing but looked into the middle distance.

'Mario?'

'Give me a second. I'm thinking of how to start.' His voice was low now, slow and deliberate, yet also with a tone that was unfamiliar.

She gave him her full attention, her eyes never leaving his as she sat at the kitchen table, strangled by the fear of what might leave his mouth next. 'Start what?'

Her husband sat opposite her, his expression serious, his brow knitted and his top teeth biting over his bottom lip in the way he did when nervous. It did nothing to allay her alarm.

'Why did you have such a rubbish start to your birthday?' he asked quietly, his voice faltering, as he did what she had wished for and gave her his full attention.

She took a deep breath and let her hands rise and fall on the tabletop. 'I guess . . . I suppose it started when you got me a card with a duck on it – a card that you lost!' She shook her head. 'Not that it matters – not now, not a jot. It really doesn't. But just for once, I wanted you to be one of those husbands who spends half an hour in Clintons choosing me something with a rose on it or an overly sentimental message that you don't really read but would fill me with all kinds of warm feelings when I find it in the drawer over the coming year. You know, words like "you are my darling, my one, my gorgeous wife", like you used to, and I'm *not* having a go at you – I know I need to be the kind of wife who buys her husband a card like that too. But a duck, Mario?' She tried out a laugh and shook her head. 'And then Mum and Dad, who I know try, bless them—'

'I'm not happy, Bess.' Cold, icy blocks of fear filled her as he paused and took a breath, as if getting the words out was a struggle. 'I'm not happy, and I haven't been for a while. I think . . . I think this might be the end of the road for us.'

His announcement cut through her words and severed her train of thought. She laughed, a nervous, short, sharp giggle this time, and felt the stab of a pain in her chest. She put her hand to her throat, fingers shaking, and struggled to stay calm.

'That's not funny.'

'It wasn't meant to be.' He used a voice she rarely heard. A voice saved for altercations with other road users, anyone who criticised his kids, door-knocking types selling Jesus when he was trying to watch the rugby or cricket, and now her.

'I don't . . . I don't know if you're joking?' There was a flutter in her chest of something that felt a lot like panic. All traces of fatigue disappeared and her mind was wired, on high alert, as if she knew she needed to take in every detail, make a case, or at the very least respond. The end of the road? She swallowed the temptation to say, *Don't be so ridiculous!*

'I think you do know.' He held her gaze and for the first time in their entire marriage she felt self-conscious, closing her blouse at the neck and wishing she'd left her shoes on. Shoes gave any situation a certain formality that might have helped keep her emotions at bay, plus when you were wearing shoes it was easier to bolt, should the need arise.

'Are you being serious right now?' The concept was too preposterous. They were a long-standing couple of nearly three decades. What was it Daniel had said? '*It's hard to think of one of you without the other!*' Mario and Bess. Bess and Mario. The Talbots. Three decades meant they had made it, got over the teething problems, most of life's hurdles, and had come out the other side, and now they had a whole new chapter ahead of them, as grandparents. The road ahead was clear and filled with love: a new beginning, not an ending!

He nodded, his eyes fixed, his jaw tense.

'I don't know what to say . . .' There was a loud and uncomfortable silence. 'Where has this come from all of a sudden?' She felt a little dizzy.

Mario rubbed his hand over his face and sat back in the chair with his arms hanging by his sides and his legs splayed, like a middle-aged rag doll that had lost every ounce of energy in its body. 'It's not all of a sudden,' he said. 'It's just taken me a while to find the right moment.'

'And today, my birthday, that's the right moment? When we have just waved off our son, who is about to become a father, and we have raised a glass of plonk to toast this new phase in our life?

241

Now is the right moment?' Anger edged her words, rooted in naked fear.

'Yes.'

'And when you say it's taken you a while, Mario, how long are we talking? How long have you had this thought rattling around in your head and the words on your tongue, waiting?'

'Three years.'

'Three years?' Her voice was high and unnatural. She hadn't expected something so specific. Mentally she quickly scanned three Christmases, three summers, three of Natalie's birthdays, three of Jake's. Their silver wedding anniversary. Jake and Dan's wedding. One week in a rainy caravan. Countless Saturday nights in front of the TV . . .

He nodded.

'Mario' – she sat forward and tried to stay calm – 'is this you being funny?' Despite the sharp suggestion of pain in her throat and the tightening of her chest, she hoped it was somehow all a joke, hoped she could in the next few minutes explode with relief and then laughter, which would be uncomfortable, but preferable, because if he was being serious . . . well, that was . . . that was unthinkable.

He stood and walked out to the hallway, where she heard him rummage in his lunch box, dumped on the floor by the front door. He came back into the kitchen with an envelope in his hand. He held it up and she read the word 'Bessie' in handwriting that she had always thought was way too elegant, wasted, in fact, on a man of his trade.

'You found it.'

He nodded and again took up his seat. 'It was in my lunchbox. You see, I *did* go into Clintons and I searched high and low for over half an hour, maybe more. But I found it hard to pick one.

242

I read all the cards with roses on the front, but they weren't quite what I was looking for – they were a bit over the top and mushy. And so I went to two more shops and, about an hour or so later, I found this.' Sticking his finger under the flap of the envelope, he slit through the gum and pulled out the card, denying her the chance to open it herself, as if she didn't deserve it – her birthday card, which was beautiful. It featured a Monet-like garden scene, full of wisteria and lilac-shaded blooms, weeping into an inky-toned lake where a beautiful mallard swam serenely with a trail of ducklings following in her wake. It made her weep. It was as far from cartoon and comical as was possible, a stunning card worthy of framing. She had got it wrong – so wrong.

'You don't remember, do you?' He held the card and banged the corner against the tabletop as he spoke. She watched the corner flatten and a crease appear. It bothered her, this destruction, this denting of such a beautiful image before she had had the chance to hold it in her palms and look inside.

'Don't remember what?' She shook her head.

He gave a derisory snort. 'Just after we got engaged, I picked you up from your parents' house and we went for a walk in Verulamium Park.' She pictured the day: they had laughed for hours and it had left her feeling restored, invincible, like she could take on the world and win if she was in partnership with him. He turned the card over in his hand and studied the image, this apparently being easier than having to look her in the eye. 'We saw a duck like this one' – he raised the card – 'paddling on the lake with about six little ducklings who were swimming in all directions, and the duck was quacking orders trying to get them to follow her, and you said' – he paused – 'you said, "That's what I want, Mario, to be a happy mummy duck like that with all my little ducklings close by and a daddy duck keeping an eye on us all and a safe little nest to return to."'

Bess nodded, her eyes brimming with tears. 'I do remember that,' she said, recalling her happiness, strolling along the sloping path of the lake, hand in hand with this man who had arrived in her life and offered her a future she had thought would be out of her reach. He was kind, reliable and he loved her, and that love had changed the way she had thought about herself. She wasn't soiled goods – she was worthy! But the truth was, she had forgotten about that day until he mentioned it, and probably many others.

'And there was me, a bit mad because I thought you'd got me a cartoon fluffy duck or something . . .' She let this trail, more than a little embarrassed by her dire summing up of her pathetic expectation and how it diminished all he had tried to do. She felt the stick of self-recrimination poke her gut.

'No.' He shook the card. 'I got you *this* card, thoughtful and symbolic. I *was* trying, like one of those husbands who spends half an hour in Clintons.'

'I'm sorry, Mario.' She meant it, wondering now, as they chatted so freely, if despite his mention of unhappiness and dramatic phrasing, this might in fact just be the forerunner to one of those nights where they would fight but in the process reset things, when all the worries, concerns and irritations that simmered, they could bring to a head. Sort things out. There had been one or two like this over the years – rows and discussions that were as draining as they were cathartic, but they had come out the other side, they always did. Because no matter what irked them, at the end of the day they were a family, and this was what she desperately wanted to return to: the safety of their nest, her haven.

He ignored her apology. 'That date in the park, Bess, I remember every detail. You brought a blanket. I thought you were either very fancy or very keen.'

'I was very fancy and keen.' She smiled. 'I remember we lay back on the grass and it was like . . .' She thought how best to phrase it. 'It was like I was awake for the first time – like I could really *see* things, *feel* things. The sky was the most perfect shade of blue. In fact, all the colours were brighter and the air seemed pure and clean, and the lake' – she sat up straight – 'the lake was so still, and I had this crazy thought that time had stopped just for us and that we could lie there on that blanket for as long as we wanted and we wouldn't be missed. Like the universe had given us that perfect window of time to get to know each other. It was our moment and it restored my faith in love, in sex and in trust.'

'Trust,' he repeated, with a look of pure sorrow as he again tapped the card on the surface.

The two sat silently. Bess remembered the warmth of the sun on her skin and how desolate she had been to say goodbye at the end of the day, a feeling mirrored right at this moment – she did not want to say goodbye.

'We had to leave in the end because you needed a pee.' Mario's words brought her back to the present.

'Yes, that's right. Two cans of Heineken will do that to you.'

'I thought you were fabulous because you drank two cans.' He smiled and she matched him; it was a fond memory of another time that warmed her.

'I was showing off. I wanted you to like me.'

'I guessed as much, as I've never seen you so much as sip a beer since, and definitely not out of a can in the street.' He ran his thumb across his mouth. 'How times have changed . . .' And just like that, his smile was gone and his tone was again verging on hostile. Her gut folded accordingly.

'Yes.' She studied him, this man she had felt held the answers to all her questions right there in the palm of his hand. This man she had trusted with her future and her happiness, as he had her. And this man she now knew she must trust with her past, although at this moment, he looked like a stranger. The thought left her cold.

'I think about that day in the park a lot. When I get a quiet moment at work, particularly over the last couple of weeks when you've said or done something that I've found hard to swallow' – he looked up briefly, another micro-admission slotted in – 'I think about your face. You were beautiful to me then and you're beautiful to me now.' This one phrase was enough to cause a bloom of pure joy. She was not invisible.

She smiled and allowed herself to breathe, the tight band of fear across her chest loosening a little.

'Yes, beautiful.' He gazed towards the heavens as if pinpointing her face all those years ago. 'But there was something else . . . You . . . you were beautiful inside. You smiled as if you were only ever a second away from laughing, and often you were.' He smiled in spite of himself at the memory. 'Your kindness, your positivity, your excited planning for the small things, like getting your own iron.'

She nodded. It was lovely to be taken back to that time and to hear him talk with such warmth about her, about them. It was both hopeful and welcome. She thought about the trip to Argos where they had stood close together and she had struggled with the little blue plastic pen and the fiddly paper sheet on which she had to tick in the appropriate boxes and write a catalogue reference, before handing it to a cashier who gave her a numbered ticket. And when her number was called out, she had jumped up as if she'd won the lottery, and actually she felt like she had. There she was, plain old Bessie Worrall, going up to the big counter to collect her boxed iron that would sit in a cupboard of the home she would share with her husband – yes, *her husband*, because someone wanted her! She was not to be laughed at, pointed at, whispered about.

Slut . . . hole . . . gagging for it . . .

She was going to be Mario's wife because they had chosen each other – he had picked her! And she would use the iron to press his clothes, like her mum had always done for her dad, and they would live happily ever after . . . So yes, it might have been just an iron, but it was so much more than that to her. And she knew it would be enough, and that she wouldn't mind not flying in an aeroplane around the world serving food and drinks at high altitude, stopping over in various hotels and larking around with her equally cosmopolitan mates on the deserted beaches that lapped paradise. And yet here she was, having a conversation because Mario had raised it. *He* was the one who was questioning whether a marriage that was 'enough' was in fact enough.

'I remember when we first got married and we lived in that little flat on Lemsford Road and it was like I'd woken up in a brand-new world.' She paused and looked over at the man she had fallen in love with – it was as if she had seen life anew and this was the state she wanted to go back to, this was where she wanted to pick up. 'I was so excited all the time and my happiness was at a hundred per cent.' She smiled at the memory, the thought alone enough to lift her spirits. 'You'd say, "Ooh, we've got to get the bins out", and I'd think, yes! Putting the bins out with Mario – brilliant! A chance to chat, hold hands, have a laugh. Everything, everything was brilliant.'

Mario, his lips pursed, nodded, as if recognising this.

'I didn't want to be apart from you, not for a second.' Bess remembered the desperate pull of unhappiness in her gut when he had to leave her to go to work and she, sitting on the doorstep, would watch and beam as he loaded up the van for the day, dreading any physical separation, and then the flare of joy at knowing he'd be coming home to her later . . .

'You used to make me sit in the bathroom and chat to you when you had a bath,' he said, looking up.

'I did. I wanted your company all the time and I wanted all of your attention.' She looked down, a little embarrassed not only at how demanding she had been, but also how comfortable she had been to be naked in front of him, confident that he would like what he saw, dimples and all, because he had taught her how to love herself again, had made her feel worthy of love, simply by loving her! And she prayed that once she had told him everything, this would be how they might live again. She nudged the small fold of her stomach resting over her knicker line.

'I was worried when we first moved here and you had Jake,' Mario said, 'worried how you'd react to me loving someone else, spending time with someone else, because things were so intense between us, we lived in a bubble.'

This was the first time she had heard this and the spike of discomfort that would usually trigger a robust vocal denial from her or an aggressive defence was today tempered by a beat of understanding and a quiet response. She knew enough to understand that with Mario leading the discussion, his words casting the first stone, she needed to listen and not leap.

'I didn't know that,' she began, 'and I can see why you might have thought it, but' – tears gathered at the back of her throat – 'the truth is, the thought of seeing you hold our child' – she looked up and met his stare – 'was the most truly wonderful thing. The thought of us sitting on that saggy old sofa with him between us . . . I remember the day we brought him home. I was in the kitchen putting the flowers from Mum and Dad in a vase and I heard you talking to him in the lounge. I turned the tap off and listened, and you were saying, "This is our little house and one day you will be running around the rooms and you might break stuff or make a noise and I will remember this moment, sitting here with you on my lap and how I feel. You are the bee's knees, Jakey, the best thing ever. I think you might play for Arsenal with those legs.'"

'I thought he might.'

'And I have never, ever felt a flicker of jealousy, just more love for you at the way you love our kids. Nothing is ever too much trouble for you where they are concerned. You'd drive to the ends of the earth if they phoned and asked you to. You'd give them our last penny – often have!' He humphed at this truth. 'And the way you support all of their choices, all of their tantrums, all of their dreams . . . You're a really great dad, Mario; I probably don't tell you that often enough.'

'You never tell me that.'

She acknowledged this with a pang of remorse that was unsettling. 'You're right, but I should, because you are. And there's lots more I need to tell you.' *I want to tell you of the trauma of Tony Dunlop's verbal assault, the damage he did to me. And then, as an adult, to meet Melanie in the street . . . Jake and Natalie were within hearing distance, and just when I was doing so well, her words dragged me back down! Words that were judgemental and cruel.*

'Thank you.'

The way the furrows on his forehead eased sent another shiver of regret through her veins. How had they come to this? *Mario is a good man . . .* Her mum's words came to her now.

'And I knew right from the off that you were going to be special for me. That we were going to be special.'

'We were special, Bess, because of that happiness.' He rubbed his eyes, a little red with tiredness. 'I used to look at everyone we knew, even strangers in the street, and think, they have no idea what it feels like to be this happy.'

'Like we were the winners,' she added.

'Like we were the winners,' he confirmed, his mouth turned down at the corners in a pre-crying pose which tore at her heart.

Wanting to speak plainly and heal this rift, she said, 'I was thinking earlier about how you used to arrive at the front door fresh off the building site and not be able to settle until you'd kissed me – before you'd even had a cup of tea or washed your hands or headed to the fridge, you'd kiss me and run your hands over my arms, as if confirming I was real. It made me feel special.'

'I always wanted to make you feel special. And I remembered what the word was I couldn't place this morning – yes, you're nice to me, but you used to be interested in me. *Interested*: that was the word I couldn't place. But then as time went on, I noticed you'd flinch if I touched you and ignored any compliment. You stopped caring what I thought and started pointing out all the things I did wrong.' He took a breath. 'And that sweetness you had, that kindness and positivity, your excited planning for the small things, it trickled away. All of it. It slowly trickled away and I didn't notice it so much at first, but now, it's who you are and it's how you are and . . .' He paused, running his palms over the thighs of his work trousers, steeling himself. She held her breath. Even Chutney stared at him from his basket, waiting . . . 'I honestly don't think I would pick you now, Bess. Not this version of you.' The crack to his voice told her it was as hard to say as it was to hear. 'That's the truth – I wouldn't pick you and I doubt you'd pick me.'

His words were like a knife in her heart and the blood drained from her face.

'Mario,' she began, struggling to find the words that would help her deny the facts. The consequences of accepting his words were too frightening to envisage. *The end of the road . . .* She struggled to keep her voice clear and not give in to the sob that threatened, knowing this would not help. 'I can see this is where we have been, but no, Mario, I have a plan, we need to move forward, we need to . . . We need to . . .'

He shook his head. She faltered and he sat forward.

'"No, Mario. No, Mario – no!" D'you know how many times you've said that to me in our marriage?'

She shrank back in her chair.

'"No, Mario, knives go the other way up in the dishwasher! No, Mario, not white bread, you wally, brown! No, Mario, not magnolia, white for the bathroom! No, Mario, not Wednesday, go back and tell them it'll have to be Tuesday! No, Mario, they don't take cards at the chippy, you need cash. No, Mario, fucking no!" I'm sick of it! Bloody sick of it! I've put up with it for years because I thought that no matter how negative you sounded or how many little things I did that irritated the shit out of you, I thought we were solid and that, when it came to it, we would bumble along because we shared a history, shared Jake and Nats, and that was enough.'

'It is enough,' she whispered.

'Is it?' He bit the inside of his cheek. 'It's like you have this whole world inside your head, a secret world that you escape to when you wash the dishes or do the hoovering. I see you deep in thought, in a bloody trance, and sometimes I speak to you, but you don't hear, lost to wherever it is you'd rather be than in our home with me and Chuts.'

She shook her head, thinking of the hours she spent replaying the words of Tony Dunlop and the consequences of her sexual adventures that had erased the future she had imagined and the woman she had thought she might be. She had fallen pregnant, pregnant at sixteen, and it had nearly destroyed her, or rather the weight of keeping it a secret – one that had spread throughout her whole body, deep in her intestines and riddled through her limbs, the root from which all other thoughts, dreams and intentions started. Her secret was part of her make-up, part of her fabric, and it shaped her as much as she shaped it. It was an energy-sapping symbiotic stranglehold that had indeed taken all her sweetness, her positivity and her excited planning. Just as her husband suggested, they had all trickled away, and this was how she was left . . . Sad, judgemental and sharp. Her tears came now as she saw this image of herself. It wasn't pleasant for her and it wasn't pleasant for those who loved her, especially Mario. She was wrestling with this thought when he delivered the final hammer blow.

'I started to tell you earlier, about Julie who does the timesheets, Leon's mum. I saw her today . . .'

'Yes?' She nodded, wondering what on earth Julie in the office might have to do with anything right now.

'Her daughter' – he coughed to clear his throat – 'her daughter is a receptionist. She works at the Glade.'

As the word *Glade* left his mouth, Bess felt her intestines shrink. Her tongue felt large and dry and she thought she might vomit. Her hands were now trembling violently, so she sat on them. She pictured the smiley girl who had waved – *of course* . . .

'M— Mario,' she began, but he quickly cut her off.

'No, Bess!' He held up his hand, and she saw the pulse of tension in his lower jaw. 'Just for once, you will let me speak!' he said firmly, not shouting exactly, though in a way she might have preferred it. His tone was menacing and the quake of fear through her bones was something she had never, ever experienced or been able to imagine with reference to her husband.

'She called Julie to say she'd seen you, recognised you from the five-a-side barbecue, and wanted to know if it was a special occasion for us. She was going to send a complimentary bottle of champagne to the room, which I thought was nice.' He gave a short, sharp snort of laughter. 'Julie told me when I went in to hand in my timesheet.'

'Mario . . .'

He gave her a second, a small window of opportunity in which to speak, to say the magic words that would explain her presence

252

at the Glade, but not only did such words not exist, there wasn't enough time. She couldn't form a sentence, couldn't think what to say or how to say it. Questions screamed inside her skull: *Why did you go? Why did you do that? Look what you've done!*

'I laughed. I laughed at Julie and told her to tell her nosey daughter to be sure of her facts in future, because that kind of talk and that kind of suggestion could be damaging. And she apologised. She's a sweet lady, quiet, and I thought she was going to cry. I'll have to apologise to her tomorrow.'

'Mario,' she tried for the third time, and again he silenced her with his words.

'I got in the van – thought I'd come home early as it was your birthday, get spruced up for our fish and chip night, make the effort.' He touched his plaster-dotted T-shirt. 'I put the key in the ignition and there was this' – he tapped his index finger on his temple – 'there was this little nagging doubt, this tiny voice I couldn't ignore. I drove along the main road and I was saying to myself, "You're such an idiot, Mario – why are you going to the Glade? Why are you listening to what some kid on reception has said? She's obviously made a mistake. I mean, why would Bess be at that fancy hotel when she's supposed to be out with her mum and dad? It's nuts!" I laughed at how nuts it was, and I vowed never to tell you that I'd listened to that little voice. I felt ashamed, and yet listen to it I did.'

His tears gathered and trickled down his face and she matched him tear for tear, the acidity of her fear breaking down all hope, all joy and optimism.

His voice now came as a husky croak. 'It's only fifteen minutes from the site. I pulled into the car park and your car . . . your car was the only thing I could see. It was like one of those fancy gold-covered Lamborghinis you see cruising the streets – the ones that make every other car disappear. There it was: your car that I service, clean, top up with washer fluid and oil. The car I put in extra shifts to help buy. It was right there, and I knew that Julie's girl wasn't lying. She was telling the truth. You, my wife, were in that hotel and you were up in a room with someone who wasn't me.'

Bess pictured her husband in the car park while she was sat in that horrible room with Andrew. She felt disgusting. Her breathing came in short, shallow bursts and she felt sick and broken.

Mario swiped at his tears and swallowed. 'I was going to go inside and ask which room. I wanted to know which fucker you were spending time with.' His top lip curled. 'I was looking around for a parking space and I saw . . .' He shook his head and looked towards the window as if still unable to process or believe what he was about to say. 'I saw Maxwell's Audi.' He started to laugh, while his tears fell again. He laughed and rubbed his hands over his face. 'Andrew Maxwell! The bloke I nod to in the morning, wondering how you get to be a bloke like that who drives a fancy car and goes off to a warm office in a suit while I have to haul my sorry arse out of the house and go to plaster houses with my joints on fire, racing every week to make my bonus so we can afford to live in a house opposite a man like that.'

'I don't know what to say. I don't know how to explain.' Her words squeaked through her distress as her heart raced and her legs shook beneath the table.

'I bet you don't.' He held her stare. 'How long has it been going on?'

Bess sat forward and shook her head. 'There's nothing going on – nothing happened! I swear it, Mario, I swear!'

Again he looked into the middle distance. 'Now there's a surprise! Who'd have thought you might say that? Give me some credit. You've been found out. The game's up!'

'No, Mario, I swear to you! I swear on the kids' lives! Nothing happened!' Her voice rose another octave, a clue to the frantic wave of panic that had consumed her.

'So what happened – you met him in a hotel room and had a chat, a cup of tea and came home? You think I'm stupid?'

'No, I don't think you're stupid, but we did just talk . . .' Desperation hit her and it was like running into a wall – how could she make him understand, believe her?

'Oh, for fuck's sake, Bess! Stop lying to me!'

'I'm not lying to you! I went to meet him and I know I shouldn't have – it was stupid of me, really stupid. I don't really know why I did, and if I could turn back time . . .' Bess realised she had come full circle: from wanting to change the life she had to desperately wanting to save it. It would have been funny if it weren't so tragic.

'Oh, Bess, if we could turn back time,' he said, rising to his feet, 'if we could turn back time, I'd have had the balls to have this conversation with you years ago when you first started looking inwards instead of out, when you gave up on me, on us, on life! So we might have a chance of salvaging things, of making a good life!'

'We . . . we do have a good life!' she stuttered.

'We *had* a good life,' he corrected, 'but we can't turn back time. We are where we are: fucking stuck with the fact that I gave you some of the best years of my life and you reward me by meeting that wanker over the road for some sordid shag!'

'That didn't happen! Nothing happened!' she shouted, beating her palms on the table. She thought she might faint and wrestled to stay upright. Chutney barked. There was weight to the air that even Chutney sensed, his head now raised, ears alert, eyes fixed.

'It's all right, Chuts,' she called, to soothe her beloved hound.

'Except it's not all right, Bess.' Mario sounded calmer now. 'And it hasn't been all right for a while.' He drew breath and she knew what he was going to say. Her heart lurched in anticipation and her mouth went dry. 'I want a divorce.' The hammer of his words fell hard, leaving her hollowed out, bruised and rejected. 'I want us to get a divorce.'

Rooted to the spot, she was stunned. 'No, Mario, please don't say that! Nothing happened, Mario, nothing,' she whispered, fear seeping into her blood.

'Truth is, Bess, it doesn't really matter if something happened or not, not now. My mind's made up. I want a divorce.'

This time she crumpled, her head inches from the tabletop as she struggled to take a breath.

He opened her birthday card and stood it on the table. 'How you're feeling right now – like someone's punched you in the throat at the same time as kicking you in the stomach, while panic flashes through you as the world as you know it spins out of control and everything you thought you could rely on drains away . . . ?' It was scary how accurately he had described her state. 'Well, that's how I felt when I saw your car in that car park today.'

'I'm sorry, I am, Mario. I'm sorry.'

He laughed bitterly and shook his head. 'Please don't.'

'But I am! I am sorry! My head is spinning.' She briefly buried her face in her hands and felt the rise of something close to hysteria in her chest.

The clock on the wall gave its customary ping at the stroke of midnight.

That was it.

Her birthday was over.

CHAPTER NINETEEN

August 21st 1984

Bessie sat up in her bed as Philip knocked on her bedroom door and entered quickly. He pulled the clear glass bottle from under his T-shirt. His face was puce, and she suspected it might have been this way since making his purchase of booze at the corner shop and then cycling home with it tucked inside the waistband of his jeans, embarrassed, as he knew the reason for acquiring the alcohol.

'Here you are,' he said, avoiding eye contact with her.

'Thank you, Philip. I couldn't have gone.'

The truth was, she was not only reluctant to attempt to buy alcohol illegally, but also she did not want to bump into Mrs Hicks or any member of the chattering club where she was the main topic, if Tony Dunlop had been as good as his word.

'What does it do?' She held the cool glass in the flat of her palm and looked up at her clever brother.

'I think it makes you miscarry. I read it once. You sit in a hot bath and drink gin, and that can be enough.'

'Will it hurt?'

He shrugged. 'I don't know.'

'What will happen to me?' She felt the first quake of fear.

'I don't know, Bessie,' he said, sounding a little agonised.

'I'm going to do it this morning.' She bit her lip.

He nodded. 'Mum and Dad'll think you're having a long bath to deal with your hangover. I'll do my best to distract them.'

'Thank you, Philip.' It seemed like this was all she could say to him.

'Are you sure you want to do this?'

Bessie nodded. 'I've been awake on and off all night thinking about my options, and this feels best for me, while it's still early days, and no one else need know.' Her tears fell at her decision, which she knew was at once brave and cowardly, a pre-emptive strike.

'Okay.' He opened her bedroom door and paused, looking back at her. 'I'll come and check on you later. If you need anything . . .'

At the sound of him clicking the door shut, she rose slowly and put the gin on her dressing table, the scorch mark a vivid reminder of the worst day of her life. Standing sideways in front of her full-length mirror, she lifted up her nightie to gaze at her tender breasts and flat stomach. She ran her fingertips over her navel, wondering what was going on inside there.

Hey God, she began, as her tears fell, *I've let you down; I've let my mum and dad down; I've let myself down. Is this your plan? I am so scared, so very scared . . . I know what I'm going to do is a sin, but I think I might die if I have to have a baby. I really do. I was going to ask for your help, but I guess this is not the kind of thing you help with, and I understand. I just don't know what to do and I don't have anyone else to talk to . . . Please forgive me and tell this little baby that I'm sorry. I'm sorry and I think I always will be. And not only sorry, but a part of me will always love it, this little thing that I'm going to say goodbye to. It's me, by the way, Bessie Worrall.*

Checking the coast was clear, she scampered from her bedroom to the bathroom, where only twenty-four hours earlier she had sat with Michelle and shaved her legs. She turned on the hot tap and watched the steam rise, adding only the smallest amount of cold water so the temperature was hot, but bearable. Steam fogged up the mirror. Bessie slipped her nightie over her head and placed the bottle of gin on the side of the bath. Gingerly she stepped in, sinking down into the water and feeling the flash of heat on her skin as it touched everywhere sensitive. Holding her breath, her discomfort eased as she got used to the temperature and the water cooled a little.

Reaching for the bottle, she unscrewed the lid and inhaled the slightly floral scent of gin, something she had never drunk before. It smelled disgusting. Her stomach heaved, and this was before she had taken a sip. Holding the bottle to her mouth, she was about to take her first swig when a sharp knock on the door made her lower it, checking the bolt was across. It was – thankfully.

'Bessie?' her mum called through the door.

'Just having a bath, Mum,' she sighed, laying her head back and wishing her mum would leave her alone to finish her task.

'Righto, lovey. I just . . .' Bessie heard the squeak down the paintwork of the door as her mum took a seat on the floor of the hallway. Bessie could see her shadow through the small gap at the bottom of the door. 'I just wanted to say that I'm worried about you and I hope you're feeling a bit better today. Your hair will grow – it's only hair.'

Bessie touched her fingers to the short-haired, stubbly side of her head, not caring a fig about it, not with so much else to occupy her thoughts.

259

'I know things got a bit out of hand last night and it can't have been pleasant for you, getting drunk like that and missing the party. And I know you'll feel awful about the way you spoke to Mrs Hicks . . .'

Bessie felt the slip of tears on her cheeks; she did feel awful about so many things.

'But you're a good girl, Bessie. You're my little girl, and your hangover will pass and Mrs Hicks will get over it and everything will be okay. I'm sad it happened on your birthday – those are our special days, aren't they? Or at least they are to me.'

There was a moment of silence. Bessie listened hard, wishing she could run into her mum's arms, but also knowing she was changed and that she had to keep her secret, preserve the way her mum felt about her.

'The harmonica-playing, the pancakes, the celebrations . . . They're important, Bessie, because until I had you, I was waiting to begin, waiting to feel truly happy, waiting to feel complete, and becoming a mum to Philip and you . . . it was like someone had given me the greatest gift.'

The greatest gift.

This phrase above all others rang loud in her ears.

'Anyway, darling, I just wanted to say, don't go pruney and don't feel down. Have a good soak and then come downstairs. I've made you a little pod on the sofa and you can watch TV and I'll make you a sandwich. Cheese and tomato?'

Bessie nodded through her tears. 'Yes, Mum. Cheese and tomato.'

She saw the shadow rise and heard the soft pad of her mum's footsteps on the stairs and then slowly climbed from the bath. Lifting the lid of the toilet, she twisted the cap from the gin and watched the clear contents glug down into the bowl. The bottle she hid in the bin under her flannel, ready to retrieve later. Wrapping

260

herself in her towel, Bessie rolled the top over to secure it over her chest, and then, wiping the steam from the mirror, she remembered Philip's words of last night: . . . *or you can have the baby and get it adopted. There are so many people desperate for babies.*

'The greatest gift, little one.' She placed her hand on her stomach. 'That is what you shall be. The greatest gift.'

CHAPTER TWENTY

August 21st 2021

At just gone midnight, Bess stood in front of the bathroom mirror and stared at her reflection, her movements slow and heavy, her thoughts stuttering. With a shaking hand she removed the residue of make-up she had not already cried off and cleaned her teeth. It was a strange thing to have woken up feeling like one person and then be going to bed seeing herself as someone else entirely. Gripping the side of the washbasin, she felt the strength leave her knees and swayed a little, before heaving herself up to stare at the face that stared back at her.

'It's time, Bess. The right time to sit down and talk – really talk – about all the difficult stuff. You need to tell him everything. *Everything.*' Knowing she had absolutely nothing to lose now, she reached out and touched the outline of her face reflected in the mirror. 'A whole secret world inside my head.' His words were as painful as they were accurate. Driven by a power she did not know she possessed, she stood tall before pulling her hair into a ponytail and grabbing a bundle of loo roll, which she shoved in her dressing-gown pocket, knowing without a doubt she would be needing it later. She had planned to sleep in Natalie's old room, putting as much separation between her and Mario as was possible, but right now she knew that separation was the last thing they needed. She had to talk to her husband.

Mario was in his pyjama bottoms and a clean T-shirt, leaning back against the headboard. He was quiet, reflective. At the sight of her, he leant over and clicked off the bedside lamp. Bess walked over and switched it back on.

'I've had a very long day,' he growled, 'and I have an early start tomorrow.'

'I know. We both have.' She was grateful for her steady voice; it helped her believe she could get through this. Closing her eyes tight shut, she sat down on the floor at his side of the bed, her head level with the mattress, as she leant on the bedroom wall. This position was vital to enable her to get the words out; she couldn't have looked her husband in the eye if she had wanted to. Doing her best to ignore the rumble in her gut, hollow with fear, Bess crossed her legs.

'You're right,' she said.

'So you did have sex with him?' he fired.

'No, not about that.' She was glad of the lamplight; it muted the emotion that threatened. 'It's what you said earlier – I *do* have a secret world that I escape to when I wash the dishes or do the hoovering, and it is exactly like being in a trance.'

'Well, I hope that wherever it is you escape to is worth it because it's damaged us.' His voice was hoarse, shot through with anger.

'I know. I know it has. And I have tried, Mario. I tried for years and years because I knew how much I had and that I should be grateful: our lovely house, our incredible kids and you. You're a wonderful man, a wonderful dad and husband.'

'Gee, thanks!'

She ignored his sarcasm. 'I had hopes and dreams for my life once . . .'

'Here's a newsflash – we all had those,' he spat.

'But as I got older, things overtook me, until I found myself living a life that was unthinkable to me in my youth.'

'Well, I'm sorry that everything has been such a crushing disappointment, sorry I couldn't give you more. What's Maxwell promising? Diamonds and a spin in his Audi?'

Bess shook her head, deciding not to respond to that directly; she had to stay on-message or she feared she might just lose her nerve. 'No, that's not what I'm saying. I meant it positively. I never thought I would have so much. You *gave* me so much. But this isn't about stuff or things, about how many bedrooms, the trappings, not that . . .' She took a deep breath, hoping it would fuel her speech. 'You never expect something to come along that'll change your life in ways you can't possibly imagine, do you? Or that you might have to keep it secret.'

'What are you talking about?' he hissed, as if he had no time for the discussion.

'I've never had an affair, Mario, but I have thought about it in that trance-like moment when I wanted escape. I've thought about a lot of things but never done any of it.'

'You want my thanks?'

'No,' she said, shaking her head, 'but I am trying to explain. I do love you, Mario, and I always will, but I know you're right: we have come to the end of the road. We can't go on like this, can we?' Her words came out on a torrent of sadness, as if saying it out loud made it real. Her admission changed the mood of the room and she saw his shoulders soften, as if relieved that he wasn't going to have to fight to make his position understood. He shifted until he was facing her. She could feel his stare and he took his time.

'I don't want us to fall out,' he sighed. 'Despite everything and whatever might come next, I don't want us to be bad friends. That would make everything harder than it's going to be already, especially for the kids, and that's the last thing I want. Especially with Jake and Dan, who have so much going on right now.'

His good sense and kindness made her ache with loss, further proof of the make-up of the man.

'I agree, but I need to tell you something,' she said.

'Tell me what, Bess?' His anger had calmed.

'I have . . . I have a secret,' she said, her voice shaking. To say this out loud felt like prising the top off a volcano and her heart raced.

'What d'you mean, "a secret"? What kind of secret?'

'I mean, it's something I've kept to myself for the longest time – the reason I keep things hidden and why I'm sometimes shut off, and the reason Philip doesn't come here very often and keeps his distance from my parents, and also the reason I try so hard to be a good mum to Jake and Nats.' She cursed her tears. 'It's the reason for this deep, deep throb of sadness that's in my bones, but I kept it at bay. I did. I buried it all until I miscarried our baby, but that triggered something inside of me, made me think about my loss and then, in the throes of my sadness, someone from my past, a girl from school, said some wicked things to me, reminded me of a time in my life I have tried to forget . . . and I started to unravel.'

He sighed, as if willing her to get to the point.

'And on and off in the years since, my secret sadness has risen to the top of my throat and threatens to choke me, and it's all I can do not to topple over with the force of keeping it down. That first decade of marriage with you, it was golden' – she smiled at the truth – 'and I thought I was over my sadness, or as much as I could be. But it's become an overwhelming and persistent thought that I can't shake: the memory of another time when I was pregnant, but, but . . . I didn't get a baby at the end of it.' To say the words out loud felt scary and liberating, like jumping from a great height, liking the feel of the wind in her face and the joy of the fall, while at the same time knowing she was going to hit the bottom soon.

'I don't actually know what you're talking about,' he said gently, sitting forward now to stroke Chutney, who had placed his head on Mario's lap. 'But . . . I suspect it's something to do with the box of letters at the top of your wardrobe?'

'Oh!' she yelled. 'Ohhhhhh!' She closed her eyes and let out a sound that was animal-like, almost a howl. Taking a deep breath, she looked up at his profile in the half-light. 'You . . . you saw them?' The thought of him reading her innermost thoughts stashed in a cardboard box, hidden behind her sparkling silver shoes, and worse still, not telling her he had – it was unthinkable. She felt exposed and completely floored.

'Calm down, Bess! I never opened them.' He leant forward and patted her in the way he might Chutney. 'I wouldn't do that. I held them, marvelled at them, all those envelopes addressed to "E" with a kiss by the initial and a kiss on the envelope.'

Bess stuttered her tears, trying to calm her distress and catch her breath. It was a relief to know the envelopes were still intact.

'I figured it was some past or imaginary love. I discounted it being a current love, or you would have posted them, right? Many is the night in recent years when you didn't want to kiss me good-night or went cold if I came in for a cuddle. I wondered if you were thinking of "E" and I'd lie awake long after you'd fallen asleep, trying to guess his name – Edward or Eddie like your dad, Ernest, Emlyn, Elvis?' He gave a dry laugh. 'I figured that if dreaming of him gave you a bit of a lift on the days when your mood was good or helped you through the dark days, then did it really matter? So I said nothing. I figured he must have meant a lot to you, because how many envelopes are there – twenty?'

'Thirty-six,' she whispered. 'There are thirty-six.' With her breath now more even, she took in his words.

'Well, there we go – a very precise figure,' he snorted.

'It's . . . It's a she, not a he.'

'A *she*?' He sounded incredulous.

'Yes,' Bess sniffed.

'Well, I didn't see that coming!' he said, blowing a sudden gust of surprise. 'So are you gay or bi? Have you . . . ?' He let this trail.

'No, Mario, how would I keep that from you?'

'I don't know, Bess. You tell me. It seems you're pretty good at keeping things from me.'

She took that.

'So, if she's not a love interest . . .'

Bess could hear her blood rushing in her ears. She had often thought what it would be like to hear this news from Mario if it were his secret, and she was no closer, all these years later, in fathoming how she might get through it.

'I had . . .' She coughed to clear her throat. 'I had a baby.'

'You . . . you what? What do you mean?' he asked, in the manner of someone who had misheard, misunderstood or both.

'I . . . I had a baby. She's . . . she's my daughter.'

Mario seemed to slump in the bed. Bess could feel the pulse beating fast in her neck. She shrank back against the wall, clutching her knees, weakened by having said the words out loud. It was as if a large boulder had slipped from her gut, leaving her spent and exhausted.

'I don't understand!'

'I had a baby. Before I met you.' She stared at the man she had married, the man she had tried to build a life with, but a life built on lies because nearly all of her thoughts and all of her sadness were hidden away and withheld. Mario had fallen in love with someone he had only ever seen half of, and the half she had shared was not mired in shame but a loving, devoted mum to Jake and Natalie, the half that on occasion in the early years had shone. But as the years passed, that shine had been dulled by the guilt of all she contained, making it harder and harder for her to pretend.

'When did you have her?' He was a little breathless.

'When I was sixteen.' She pictured herself at sixteen, lying in bed and running her hand over the swell of her stomach, knowing she had done this terrible thing for which she would be judged, and knowing that her heart would forever break as she judged herself. Lawrence never knew – it would have made everything infinitely worse – and of course she had refused to tell Michelle, who she knew was lost to her, watching as her friend spent time with her Lawrie, held hands with her Lawrie, got engaged to her Lawrie . . . Her sweet friend. Her best friend.

'So now she must be . . .'

Bess didn't need to do the maths. 'She's thirty-six.'

'Jesus!'

'I was only a little girl, really.' She picked at the loose, long twists of the shag pile rug by the side of the bed, remembering how she had felt when her pregnancy was confirmed, like she was floating, like she might lose her reason, like she was broken – soiled, damaged, and shaken by a fear so powerful that she knew she would rather die than have to face her mum and dad.

'What did your parents say?'

Bess shook her head. 'They never knew. I couldn't tell them.' Her tears came again, as she remembered going away on a fictitious course to learn how to be an air hostess. They had been so proud, sending her off with her suitcase packed and a Tupperware box full of cheese and tomato sandwiches and a stack of shortbread biscuits and the thermos that had once been half full of Cinzano now awash with stewed tea. Six months later, Bess had returned home to her parents, quiet, withdrawn and a little broken, explaining to them how she had failed the course and would not therefore be taking to the skies. They had ushered her up to her bedroom and showered her with reassuring platitudes, ruffling her hair as they hugged her better, telling her it didn't matter, nothing did! Loving her so deeply and so completely that she knew the last thing she could do was tell them she had had sex with a relative stranger in an alleyway and then given birth to a little girl – how could she, when she was *their* little girl? How could she shatter not only their perception of her but also the safe warm nest in which they lived – her haven, untainted by the sordid reality of what she had endured? Bess had lain on her bed with the walls closing in. The longing in her womb was the very worst kind of pain and the inability to mention her baby girl the very worst kind of torture.

She had withdrawn, and the once chirpy girl went quiet and took a cleaning job in a supermarket, letting the world rush by. Nervous to say anything for fear of letting her thoughts escape through her mouth, she kept her head down and, by not looking up, minimised the risk of catching the eye of someone who might look at her in the same way Tony had outside the rugby club that night. She also avoided making friends or falling in love, because without friends or lovers she never had to worry about letting her guard down, would never be tempted to tell or confess that she had done the most terrible thing. How would she have ever been able to say, 'I got pregnant at sixteen and handed my baby girl over as if she was a wrapped gift. I only saw her for a few hours and then they took her from me, and I lay on the bed, leaking milk and blood, and I wanted to die . . .'?

That was until Mario walked into the staffroom, smiling, kindly and interested in her.

Michelle had never called until earlier today. Their lovely friendship became collateral damage of the choices Bess had made, yet even now when an advert came on the radio for Paulson's Skips, Bess wanted to cry, and often did.

'So how did you manage? How did it all happen? You were just a kid!'

She guessed that Mario, like her, was probably thinking of Natalie at the same age, and the thought was heartbreaking.

'Philip knew.' She paused, thinking of her brother, who had been there in her hour of need, who as a newly minted adult had made all the arrangements, located the place, sat with her on the train, held her tight as she cried and then waved her goodbye as she got settled in the small room close to the hospital where she was to be confined. He had then met her on the day she was released. She had washed with sandalwood soap in the communal bathroom before leaving and the scent had clung to her skin for weeks. Even now, the merest whiff would transport her back to that place and time, about to put on the clothes she had arrived in. Her big brother had then walked with her slowly and in silence, all the way to the train station, with her suitcase in his hand, escorting her home to their dad's daft jokes and their mum's good-natured fussing. He hadn't pressed her, hadn't asked for details, but had simply let her be, as if he knew that the scooped-out shell of his little sister could not cope with any questioning at all.

Sworn to secrecy and with the weight of their shared experience crushing the closeness they had shared, they had slowly and steadily grown apart. Philip had stayed out longer, talked to her less and made plans without her knowledge. The two of them had harboured this biggest secret, which had sat between them like a wall of fire that neither was willing to step through. He had quietly but eagerly left home, moving further and further away, before coming to rest in Cheshire, where he and his wife had built a successful life. He had then chosen not to come back to the place where maybe the risk for him too of letting the secret bubble to his lips was a chance he was not willing to take.

'Philip was the only one who knew. He helped me. I honestly don't know what I would have done without him,' Bess said. 'I managed to keep the pregnancy secret for a few months and then I went away on an air hostess course, or so my parents thought – they gave me money for it, which paid for my B&B, and Philip came and saw me when he could. And then I went into hospital in Slough and I left the baby there.' Her tears gushed at this simplified version of her tortured experience. The memory of that day, that moment, walking through the electric doors and out into the fresh air without her baby was one she would never, ever forget. A pocket of emptiness had lodged in her breast which had grown over the years. 'I said I didn't want her. I signed a form to say I didn't want her.' Her speech was hard to understand through her tears. 'But that wasn't true – I did want her, but I knew I couldn't keep her. She was adopted by a couple who had been told about the baby when I was only a few months gone. It was an arrangement made through the Church.'

'I don't . . . I don't know what to say . . .'

'I don't know what to say, Mario, and it was me it happened to. I have never known what to say.'

'Did you meet the couple?' His voice was soft, reverential.

She nodded. 'Once, briefly. They came to the hospital when she was brand new and I was still holding her.' The words slid down her throat like glass. 'They were nice to me. They told me they had two boys already and had always wanted a girl, but she couldn't have any more children . . . and so I gave her mine.' She felt the sob build in her chest.

'Did you name her?' His voice cracked, and she nodded.

'Her name is Ellory – "E" for Ellory.' It was the first time Bess had said her name out loud to another human being since the day she had given birth to her. The sudden rush of emotion left her a little dizzy. 'The nurse told me the couple liked the name and would keep it.' Her head sank on to her chest and she fought for breath. Mario slipped down from the mattress and joined her on the floor, holding her fast against him as her tears fell. The solidity and proximity of him warmed her, as it always had. 'It's a big deal for me,' she sniffed. 'She doesn't know who I am, and I don't know anything about her, but I gave her that name and it's like she carries a little bit of me around with her every day because of it.'

'And you haven't seen her since you had her?'

'No.'

'Does she know about you?'

'I don't know.' The truth made her sob.

'And not once, in the whole of our marriage, did you think to tell me?' He looked hurt, his eyes brimming.

'I was so used to not telling anyone that I didn't know how to break that cycle. It made me so ashamed, Mario — at first because I had had her at all and then later because I had kept her secret, and the longer I kept her a secret, the harder it felt to tell a soul, especially you. How could I, after all the time that had passed? I couldn't tell anyone.'

'Apart from Philip?'

'I had no one else, but we paid the price for keeping the secret, Philip and me. That's why he stays away — it's too big a thing to know and keep swallowed. It put a wedge between us. It put a wedge between him and our parents. And it's all my fault.'

'Christ, Bess, what a bloody mess.'

'It is a bloody mess!' She cried into the front of his T-shirt, the scent of him warm and familiar. They sat locked together until their breathing found its rhythm and tiredness pawed at them.

'Come on.' Mario eased her from his arms and pulled back the duvet, gently shoving Chutney to his spot at the bottom of the bed.

'I was going to sleep in Natalie's bed tonight.'

'Not tonight. You shouldn't be on your own tonight.' He lay down in the spot that had been his for the whole of their marriage. Bess walked around to her side of the bed. Glancing briefly up to the gap at the left-hand side of the blind, she saw the bedroom light go off in Helen Maxwell's bedroom and her jaw tensed, thinking of Andrew in that grotty hotel room, hiding.

Pulling back her side of the duvet, she slid into the familiar dip where her hip nestled and felt the creep of Mario's hand across the mattress until he found hers, and then there they lay, staring up at the three-arm chandelier, which had cost more money than they had had, their arms forming a bridge across the bed.

'Thank you for telling me, Bess. I know that wasn't easy.'

She nodded.

'We have a lot to think about and a lot to talk about,' he confirmed.

'Yes, we do.'

'I can't take it in. I've got so many questions . . .'

'I'll answer them as well as I can, but not tonight.'

'No, not tonight,' he agreed.

There was a pulse of silence.

'We are very different people, aren't we, to the ones who waltzed up the aisle together all those years ago?'

'We are. I'm sorry, Mario.'

'I'm sorry too.'

The two of them lay silent and she felt the pull of sleep. Mario let go of her hand and wriggled on to his side, and as he got comfortable she heard the familiar knock of the headboard on the wall, which had worked its way loose over the years. Chutney pushed his head against her legs and got comfy in his own spot at the bottom of the bed, anchoring her foot.

'We got lost, Bess, didn't we? We got lost along the way. I feel like I never really knew you, not all of you, and that's a lot for me to take in. I feel like you didn't give me the chance. You could have told me about Ellory and that barrier would never have been there.'

She nodded through a fresh batch of tears, but knowing that tonight would be her first sleep unburdened by the secret that had weighted her dreams since she was sixteen years of age.

'We're going to break up our little family, Bess, aren't we?' His words were thick through his tears and her heart broke. She saw his broad shoulders shake as he cried.

'I think we are,' she managed, 'but it'll be okay, Mario. We'll put it back together in a different shape. We'll both start over.'

'I think you've been waiting to start over, Bess, waiting to begin . . .'

He clicked off the lamp and she nodded into the darkness, knowing this to be true, but also aching with some of the fear that had dogged her life. Yes, they would both start over, but they would be okay, they would take what they had in their pockets and make the best out of it, and they would be okay . . .

CHAPTER
TWENTY-ONE

August 24th 2021

Bess had spent the last couple of days like a shadow in the house, a stranger within these walls she knew so well, lurking in the corners and trying to sort her flustered thoughts in this new version of the world in which she found herself, albeit a world of her own making. She and Mario were in a state of shock, grief-stricken and a little bewildered. Even Chutney was quiet, head low. Time was skewed as she and Mario crept from room to room like bruised things, rubbing their arms and heads as if the damage were physical and howling in pain behind the locked bathroom door or in the early hours when the world slept, because this felt like the safest place and time to do so. There were brief moments of normality, false dawns, when they woke and met on the landing, coming out of the separate rooms in which they slept, before trailing downstairs to let Chutney out into the garden, where the sun was shining. And yet despite the warm weather, they huddled inside fleece tops and dressing gowns, the chill in their bones nothing to do with temperature. They made cups of tea, and as the kettle whistled and they reached into the creaking fridge for milk, it was as if it were any other day. They would then sit quietly on opposite sides of the lounge in their pyjamas, where the weight of what they were going through bore down on them and they stared at the floor, their mugs, the dog, the TV: anywhere but at each other. Mario didn't go to work and she phoned in sick. Sushmita took the call and was sweet, sending love and asking if there was anything Bess needed.

'We need to tell the kids.' His voice was a little unused and raspy.

'Yes.' She tried to picture the scenario and her face fell at the prospect.

'We'll do it together. That'll be easier for everyone.'

'Thank you.' She meant it, but even these two words felt insincere when spoken in the shadow of the news she had shared.

This state of affairs was not what she had expected. Over the years, Bess's daydreams had seen her tell Mario the full story, and with the burden of secrecy lifted, the two would find a way through, hand in hand. But this felt nothing like that. She felt just as hollow as before, adrift and alone, having hoped that opening up to Mario might bring instant relief. Now, however, the atmosphere was replaced with something close to confusion, and oh so many questions. How could they survive as a couple with so much to come to terms with? And was he judging her too? Her low self-esteem held her in its grasp and whispered in her ear, stoking the familiar fires of guilt.

'I'm sorry,' she repeated, until he got up and walked to the door, as if he couldn't stand to hear her apology one more time.

'You don't have to keep saying it, and it doesn't mean much,' he said. 'No words can atone for decades of deceit, Bess. You must know that?'

'I just don't know what else to say,' she admitted.

'Then don't say anything,' he said bluntly, before leaving her alone.

As she let Chutney out into the back garden, Bess spied the birthday card Mario had sent her, discarded on the floor by the bin. Gathering it into her hands, she took it inside and wiped the residue of dirt from the beautiful picture. Leaning against the sink, she read the words aloud: 'To my smashing wife on her birthday.'

Oh! Tears fogged her vision. It was more than she could bear, to see the words written to her in the days before she had pulled the plug on their life raft and sunk them both. She looked up at the sound of him in the hallway. He stared at the card in her hands.

'You don't have to keep that,' he said.

'I want to keep it!' she shot back at him.

Wringing his hands, he drew in a sharp breath. 'I'm . . . I'm going, Bess.'

'Going where?' Her voice faltered as she noticed the sleeping bag in a heap on the hall floor, his keys, his black folder with all his important numbers and notes, and his toiletry bag lying on top. He would shortly gather up and throw on to the passenger seat of his van all these things he needed to live without her . . . Scarcely able to breathe, her knees wobbled beneath her. She shrank against the sink to stop herself from falling, desperately not wanting him to go and yet knowing she had no right to ask him to stay.

'I could ask Nat if I could go and stay with her for a bit, but if you'd rather I found somewhere else . . . ?'

'No, no, of course, go to Nat's – not that I want you to go anywhere,' she managed, knowing that Natalie would keep an eye on her dad. The temptation was to run at him and throw her arms around his legs, anchor him to this place, this moment and to her, but she knew it would be futile and could not stand the thought of his rejection. The memory of him pulling his hand away from hers as they sat on the sofa was fresh in her mind.

'It's for the best, Bess.' He looked down as Chutney sniffed around his feet. Mario bent and nuzzled the dog, his buddy, nose to nose while stroking his ears.

'Should we perhaps' – she didn't know what she was asking – 'talk maybe in the week or . . . ?' This was a brand-new situation for which there was no blueprint. How was she supposed to behave with this man with whom she had shared every aspect of her life for the last few decades? Well, nearly every aspect. And here they were. 'It feels weird you leaving like you do when you go to work but not coming home to me.' Her voice cracked.

He stood and nodded briefly. 'It's weird for me too, but I'm not disappearing, only going to Nat's. We need the space, don't we? To try and work out what comes next.'

'Yes, I guess we do.' She imagined their bed with a Mario-shaped gap on the left-hand side and her tears came.

He took a step forward and she thought for a moment he might hold her, closing her eyes briefly and welcoming the thought of his arms around her, but instead he turned on his heel and walked away. Bess held the birthday card to her chest and, at the sound of the front door closing, slid down until she was sitting on the linoleum with Chutney pawing at her leg.

Her phone rang. She considered ignoring it.

'Hi, Mum.'

'Bess, it's me, it's Mum!'

'Yes, I know your number,' she sighed and pinched her nose. There was no point in explaining yet again how the phone worked, even if she'd been in the mood to do so.

'Are you crying?'

Bess nodded and tried to contain her sobs.

'For the love of God, Bess! What's this all about?'

'I'm okay.'

'You don't sound okay! Do you want me and your dad to come over?'

Bess shook her head. 'No, no, Mum,' she managed, 'I'll . . . I'll come to you . . . Be there in a bit.'

She put the phone down and composed herself as best she could, feeling just the same as when she had walked home from school with her dire exam results fresh in her mind – knowing this conversation was going to be a whole lot harder to have, but also entirely necessary and long overdue.

◆ ◆ ◆

Perching opposite Jeannie and Eddie on the little stool in front of the fireplace, she stared at her parents as they sat side by side on the sofa. With her leg jumping and her nerves jangling, she tried to begin. They looked worried and Bess knew she had to speak quickly, both to end their worry and to get the words out before she lost her nerve.

'Come on, Bessieboo, the suspense is killing us! What is it you need to say?' her dad prompted. 'Have you won the lottery? Has Mario been made redundant? Is Nats gay too?'

Their various guesses were at once endearing and scary to Bess, knowing they were thinking of the most outlandish things they could and yet still were not even close to predicting what she had come to say.

'Mario has moved out for a bit.' As her words landed, her parents stared at her with shock on their faces, their shoulders slumped.

'Oh no,' her mum whispered. 'Surely not!'

'Yes,' she sniffed, understanding the tone of disbelief – it was still unbelievable to her and she was living it. 'And I need to tell you how we got to this point.' She coughed to clear her throat. This was it. 'What I have to tell you is not easy. If it were easy' – she paused – 'I would have told you a long, long time ago. When I was sixteen, to be precise . . .'

They then listened silently, without the interjection or commentary she might otherwise have expected. She spoke slowly, the words having to swim around the boulder of emotion gathered at the base of her throat. Bess might have been fifty-three, but as she spoke, she felt like her sixteen-year-old self, even looking down at her shins and seeing three round plasters, dotted red with her blood. Speaking as calmly as she was able and at a pace to allow the words to sink in, she finished her desperate tale.

'So that's what happened to me, and it has made me so sad. Firstly, to have given her up, and secondly, to have kept her a secret, and also not being able to tell you or talk about her. I have this great sense of shame' – she put a hand to her throat – 'and it's shaped my whole life.' Nodding at this truth, she looked up at her parents sitting opposite. Both were silent, staring, trying to process the enormous news that they had another grandchild, and that during the time when they had thought she was anxious and upset over her less than adequate exam results, their sixteen-year-old daughter had in fact been pregnant and given birth to a baby. A baby girl. And she had done so without their help or knowledge.

'So you weren't on an air hostess course?' her mum whispered, her expression confused.

'No, I was in Slough, having a baby.' Bess's voice quaked.

'But all them postcards! I've still got them somewhere.' Jeannie shook her head.

'I wrote them on the train there and from my little room.' Bess remembered the searing pain of loneliness and the unease of deceit, as she popped a stamp on each card and shoved them in the letterbox.

'Were you scared of us? Is that it?' her dad asked, his voice altered by emotion. It tore at her heart. 'I don't think we ever shouted or punished you – we never needed to.'

'No, Dad, I've never been scared of you.' She reached across the rug to squeeze his hand. 'But I was a little girl and sex was part of a grown-up world and one I didn't want to talk about, much less admit that I had been part of. I wasn't scared of you, not ever, but I couldn't face disappointing you. Somehow the thought of that was worse than the thought of you being angry. I didn't want you to look at me differently. I didn't want you to stop loving me.'

Her mum looked into her lap, her bottom lip shaking before fat tears turned her eyes bloodshot and she cried in a way that was rare for her. Bess looked away; it was hard for her to witness.

'We have always loved you so much – nothing could change that,' her mum felt the need to clarify.

'I know, Mum. I know you have, always.' Her love for her mum flared and she smiled, hating that she was putting her parents through this.

'I think . . .' Her mum reached for a tissue from her bag to wipe her eyes and dab her nose. 'I think I would have been devastated, yes – I can't pretend I wouldn't have been.' She briefly met Bess's gaze. 'But I would've got past that because you're my daughter and you were my little girl, and the thought of you going through all that on your own . . .' Her voice broke away.

'It's so easy to look back and think of all the things I could have done or should have done, and it's impossible to do that without adding my grown-up experiences and my adult thoughts. But the truth is, I was absolutely petrified, and thought it was the end of the world. I thought I might die. A part of me did, I think.' Bess remembered the endless hours lying on the bed in her childhood room, rubbing her stomach where her child had taken root and trying not to think of what lay ahead. Torn between relishing the

281

feeling of being pregnant, the miracle of it, and battling the blanket of shame that threatened to suffocate her. She knew she had never felt so lonely or so alone.

'It breaks my heart to think of it,' her dad confessed, and her mum nodded her agreement, and there they sat, unified in heart-break, 'but a small part of me looks at the lovely woman you've become, the great kids you have in Jakey and Nats, and I feel proud that you came out the other side. It must have been the hardest thing in the whole wide world.'

Bess smiled at her lovely dad through her tears. *It was.*

'I suppose this is why Mario has moved out?' he asked plainly.

'One of the reasons, yes,' she answered sadly. She pictured her husband bundling the sleeping bag under his arm and the sound of his van door closing. 'But mainly, Dad, he's moved out because we both need space to figure out what comes next, no matter how much I hate the idea of him not being around.'

'It'll all work out if it's meant to, lovey,' he offered sagely. 'Am I allowed to call him and see how he's doing?'

''Course you are, Dad!' She loved that he had asked, as much as she loved his concern for his son-in-law.

'Do you think we can meet her then, your little girl?' her mum asked, with such hope it made Bess's heart flex. 'I'd make her very welcome: cook a nice dinner. I could do lamb and make one of my lemon meringue pies.'

'There's not a soul on the planet who would not love your lemon meringue pie,' Bess said. She watched as her dad took his wife's hand and kissed the back of it. A moment so tender it felt wrong to witness it, especially as she and Mario had never been so apart in every sense.

'What's her name?' her mum asked.

'Ellory.' Again the joy of saying her name out loud split her face in two.

'Celery?' Her dad looked at her quizzically.

'*Celery?* Who in the world would call their child Celery, Dad?' she laughed, his question enough to defuse the situation.

'Well, you never know nowadays. People call their kids all sorts!' her mum added.

'Ellory,' Bess repeated.

'Ellory,' her dad smiled. 'Our oldest grandchild . . .'

'And Pippin' – her mother's voice caught – 'he did the right thing by you, Bess. He looked after you.'

'He really did, but it's been hard for him to be near me and now you know why.'

Her parents looked at each other with relief and for the first time she realised that they must have wondered what they had done wrong. Mario was right – *a bloody mess.*

'I'm going to call him.' Her mum reached for her phone.

'Please don't, Mum!' Bess said, sitting forward. 'Not straight away – let me go and talk to him first.'

'Face to face?'

'Yes, face to face. It's long overdue,' Bess said as she made the decision.

'Cheshire is a heck of a long way.' Her mum put the phone back on the side table as she stood. 'I'll make you some snacks for the journey.'

Bess again felt the rise of tears.

'Cheese and tomato?' her mum asked from the doorway.

'Please, Mum.' She nodded. 'Cheese and tomato would be lovely.'

◆ ◆ ◆

The very next day, Bess climbed into her little car and tootled up the motorway with a racing heart but a lightness of spirit, knowing it was time to make amends. She arrived as the sun was setting and pulled into her brother's posh driveway, where his shiny car made hers look even crappier in comparison. Philip opened the wide front door in his jeans and polo shirt and did a double-take. He had put on a little weight, lost a little hair, but despite his look of concern, his kindness was unchanged.

'Oh my God, Bessie! What a lovely surprise! Come in! Are Mum and Dad okay?'

This was of course his first thought, with his sister turning up unannounced after all this time.

'They're fine, absolutely fine.'

She saw his body relax, as if he had been holding his breath.

'I'm sorry to just pitch up like this, Philip!'

'Don't be daft, come in. You look well.' His tone was a little formal, his movements a little stiff.

Bess followed him into the grand hallway and took in the wide sweep of the staircase with its half-turn. It felt odd to see her brother in such an established home in which she had never set foot.

'Nanette's at Zumba; she'll be home soon. She'll be so pleased to see you!'

Bess thought of how much it had meant when Mario's sister had made the effort with a card for her birthday, and wondered for the first time if her sister-in-law might feel abandoned by her. Another wrong that needed righting.

'Can I . . . can I get you a cuppa?' he stuttered, as if unsure of the convention after all this time. He turned to walk into the kitchen, she assumed, but she grabbed his arm.

'I've told them, Philip!' she blurted, desperate to get the words out that had lain snared in a steel cage of her own making for the longest time. It felt like freeing a trapped thing and letting it out to fly. She realised that she had been waiting to say this to her brother for decades.

He turned slowly to face her, his skin a little pale, his expression concerned. 'You told . . . ?' Even now she could see the words were too difficult for him to voice, and she understood.

'I told Mum and Dad about Ellory, about everything – just last night, in fact. They wanted to call you, but I made them promise to hold fire until I'd seen you myself. I wanted to be the one to tell you.'

'Wow!' His stance faltered and he sat down hard on the bottom step of the stairs. Bess took the spot next to him.

'Yes, wow.'

'Why? How? I mean, I'm glad you have, really I am, but why now, after all this time?'

'It's been like a pressure building up inside of me. For years I managed to keep it at bay, but it started to eat away at me, started to damage Mario and me. It *has* damaged Mario and me,' she corrected. 'We're living apart while we try to get our heads straight.' This single fact still had the power to bring her to tears. 'Things had to change – I had to change or sink. The secret was pulling me under.'

'I'm sorry to hear about you and Mario. And how did Mum and Dad . . . ?' He rubbed his stubbled chin. 'What did they say?'

Bess looked at her big brother, enjoying the proximity of him. 'They were wonderful, really wonderful.'

Philip was quiet and she was thankful he didn't feel the need to fill the air with platitudes. It was as if the realisation was sinking in – the fact that this was no longer a secret. His hands lay limply in his lap, his relief evident, and this she could feel without him saying a word. The air and silence between them was different, lighter and less fraught.

'I didn't know what to say to you, Bessie, not from that day to this. We went through so much and I never knew if I'd done the right thing in helping you.'

'Philip,' she interrupted, reaching for his hand, 'thank you for everything you did for me. Your support meant the whole world – you were the only help I had. I can't imagine what I might have done if you'd not been there. You were incredible.' Her voice broke away in sobs. 'I am and always will be so very thankful.'

He put his arms around her and held her close.

'I think about it a lot, you know. You were braver than anyone I've encountered, before or since. Your face on the train journey home . . . You looked so fragile, so empty, I feared you might break.'

'I feared I might break too,' she whispered. 'And you never told Carmen?'

'God! Carmen . . .' He took a beat and laughed out loud, throwing his head back, which snapped any lingering tension. 'Even hearing her name after all this time . . . That girl properly broke my heart.'

'Because you liked her a bit too much?'

He laughed softly. 'Exactly, because I liked her a bit too much.'

'It's my fault, isn't it, that you've stayed away?' Bess felt the familiar pull of sadness, fringed with guilt, but this was how to make amends, straight-talking, no matter how hard.

'No, not your fault entirely. It was a terrible situation and I had no idea how to be around you or around Mum and Dad without it spilling from me. It felt like lying every time I spoke to them and didn't mention it.'

'I understand that.'

'But this changes everything, Bessie. Thank you.'

His thanks were all it took for her tears to break their banks.

'Jesus, you're going to set me off!' He stood. 'And that would never do – might smudge my eyeliner!'

Bess laughed.

'Forget tea, I think we need a *drink* drink. What'll you have?'

'I don't mind,' she shrugged. 'Anything but Cinzano.'

'Good idea. If you were sick on the front of this house, Nanette would literally kill me.' He pulled a face.

'Literally?'

'Literally,' he asserted.

She jumped up and dusted the seat of her jeans, before following her big brother into his big, big kitchen.

EPILOGUE

Six Months Later

'They're taking their time,' her mother sighed, tapping her finger-tips on the wooden arm of the less than comfortable chair. Her dad looked close to nodding off. Natalie, meanwhile, was tip-tapping away on her phone, working, always working, no matter that she was out of the office. Philip re-read his broadsheet, shaking it from time to time to remove invisible creases.

Bess nodded. Yes, they *were* taking their time. The general hub-bub of conversation had dried up an hour or so ago, along with any initial excitement. The five of them had played several rounds of 'I Spy', which had ended in bickering, and now the atmosphere was a little strained. The family was getting edgy and uncomfortable. The air was a little thick and the temperature too warm. Bess felt the beginnings of a headache.

'I mean, we've been here since eleven o'clock this morning. Your dad's missed the lunchtime news!' Jeannie nudged him and he rallied, snorting a little and looking in that second as if he had no idea where he was. 'And his afternoon programmes – I've missed *Pointless*, and we're still no closer!'

'I guess that's the thing with having a baby, Mum. No matter how keen you are for them to arrive or what you might be missing on the telly, you can't really hurry them. He'll be here when he's good and ready.' Bess grinned at the prospect.

'I wish I'd brought some sandwiches,' her mum huffed.

'Did you bring sandwiches – is that what you said?' her dad chirped. 'Cos I'm proper famished. I could just go for a corned beef and pickle on white!'

'No, Eddie! No sandwiches, and it's not five minutes since you polished off your fruitcake, but I might have a Fox's Glacier in the bottom of my bag – hang on a mo.' Her mum opened her handbag and began to rummage inside.

Natalie caught Bess's eye across the small waiting room and smiled. 'Would you like me to go and get you a sandwich, Grandad – there's a Costa down the road? I'm happy to go,' she said, jumping up from her chair.

Bess was, as ever, touched by the way she treated her grandad.

'No, thanks, love, that's very kind, but I won't pay those prices for a couple of slices of bread and a lick of butter. They can shove as many fancy stickers on it as they like, but a sandwich is a sandwich and I can't bring meself to pay more for one than it costs for a whole loaf of bread. It's not right.'

'I'll treat you?' Nat offered.

'No, it's not who pays that's the problem, it's the amount, but thank you, sweetheart.'

'Okay, well, if you change your mind.' Natalie let this trail and settled down back into the seat next to her Uncle Philip.

Bess smiled at her. She was a lovely person – both her kids were, and the way these humans had turned out was her greatest achievement. Being in their company made her happy.

'How much was that scone we had in Knutsford, Jeannie?' her dad said, breaking into her thoughts.

Natalie looked up from her phone. 'Oh, for the love of God, Grandad, not the scone story again!'

'Well, it's all right for you, Nats, you have a marvellous job, but just you wait until you're a pensioner,' her nan said in her husband's defence. 'Four pounds seventy-five. *Four pounds seventy-five* for a scone, which was light on cream and jam – a bloody rip-off! And I told your grandad when we got in the car, I thought it was shop-bought.'

'Anyway, I thought I paid for it?' Philip lowered his paper and winked at his sister, happy, oh so happy, to be back in the fold.

Bess relished getting to know her brother all over again, and seeing him interact so easily with their parents and her kids brought nothing but joy. She smiled now at the thought of having been warmly embraced by sweet Nanette, who, post-Zumba class, had welcomed her with open arms and was at that very moment at home in Cheshire, kindly keeping an eye on the business and no doubt preparing lactose-free treats for her husband's return. Having taken the time to get to know her, Bess could see how she adored Philip and that they were happy – what more could a sister want?

'You *did* pay for the scone, Pippin, but that's not the point!' Her mum turned to Natalie. 'Your Uncle Philip is doing *very* well.' She spoke as if he wasn't sitting opposite. 'Such a lovely home – big pillars up the front, four bedrooms, mock-Georgian, a corner bath with little holders on the side of the tub you can rest your drink in.' She dipped her chin, her eyes wide, knowing this information couldn't fail to impress. Bess caught her daughter's eye and smiled.

'And don't forget the underfloor heating and outdoor water feature!' Philip joined in, chuckling.

Their parents were, Bess knew, remarkable, elderly, set in their ways and, like everyone, had their own set of eccentricities, but they had taken everything that had been thrown at them over the last year and handled it with grace.

'A baby? Jake and Dan? But how will they . . . Who will be the . . . ?' her dad had asked, scratching his head, before settling on, 'A baby will be a marvellous gift for us all!'

'Ooh, I've just remembered – it's also got a little remote control that opens the doors to the double garage!' Her mum had seemingly forgotten this very important detail.

Bess and Philip laughed.

'And solar lights all the way up their driveway,' her mum continued.

'Flippin' 'eck – enough, Nan!' Natalie scoffed. 'Uncle Philip will be giving you a job at this rate. Are you telling me about the house or trying to sell it? Not that I could afford it, not with all them cup holders in the bath.'

The door of the waiting room swung open at that point, interrupting their laughter, and they all whipped their head round in time to see Mario stroll in, wearing his work clothes. His heavy boots clumped across the floor and his hair was dusty. Bess's heart quickened and she smiled at the sight of him.

'How are we all doing?' He nodded and smiled, greeting everyone in the room. 'Still no news?' He had been there at the very beginning, diverted from his journey to work in anticipation of becoming a grandad, but then after a couple of hours and no action had returned to the site, and now here he was again.

'Not yet, Dad.' The corners of Natalie's mouth turned down, as if to say, *More's the pity.*

'I thought things would definitely be shifting by now.'

'You and me both, love. They're taking their time, I'll say that much.' Bess's mother sighed, tapping her fingertips on the arm of the chair.

Mario caught Bess's eye and walked over. She rose and stepped into his arms, breathing in the scent of him as he kissed the top of her head. Pulling away, he beamed at her. And that look, the one he

291

now gave her at the end of a long day when he came home, or when they sat and held hands on the sofa, or woke in the morning, or sometimes just because, told her how far they had come in the last six months. Her heart soared with gratitude and love for her man.

There had over the last few months been emotional hurdles, hard to get over – discussions and admissions over the phone that took them into the early hours when, with tears running, they spoke without reservation, politeness or reticence. Gloves-off conversations where the only rule was to be honest and to listen. The themes were well worn and recurring, but had with time lost traction.

'You didn't trust me enough to tell me,' he had cried, 'and that hurts. I thought we were partners, pals.'

'I didn't trust myself, Mario, to tell anyone. I thought if I let it out, I might fall apart, thought it might split me in two! My shame was so much part of my fabric that I didn't always think about *why* I was ashamed – it was just there. Ellory's existence has sat like a dark thing, hidden for so long, and it filled me up entirely. It was hard to admit to what I'd done, but also to the fact that I lived with deceit, and the secret of her became a burden in itself. It made me a liar and I lived in fear of discovery of both. And because I didn't tell you in the beginning, that meant there was never a moment when I could say, "Fancy a cup of tea, love? Oh, and by the way, I meant to say . . ."'

He calmed. 'It split you in two, right down the middle, and it was hard to watch, like you were slipping away, and I held your hand as tight as I could but I had to let go, Bess, I had to.'

She could only nod, her face twisted in distress.

'But we're not done, Bess, you and me, not yet. You're working hard to put yourself back together, I know you are, and I want to help you. Me and the kids, all of us who love you – and Dr

Meredith, of course, who I doubt loves you but seems to know her onions.'

'She does – know her onions that is, not love me.'

And it was true. Her therapist was the first person she had told about her whole experience of being sixteen: the impact of the attack by Tony Dunlop and his words, which had damaged her, and the shame that had cloaked her ever since, rearing its ugly head when any aspect of her life threatened to veer out of control. And all that before they tackled the loss of her daughter and the acute ache for her which haunted her still. Dr Meredith took a tiny pick-axe to her guilt and slowly, at every session, seemed to tap gently at it so that bits fell away. And Bess would gather those fragments into her palms and take them home, thinking of how far she had come and the person she wanted to be, moulding them into something new and positive.

'You know it's not your fault, don't you?' Dr Meredith had said to her straight out. 'A young man, who I think it's safe to assume had his own issues, wrongly judged you. It's most unusual for a stranger to want to make someone else feel so terrible. It makes me wonder what he was venting and why – he picked on you, Bess, but you probably weren't the only one he did this to. You were young, naive and open, and those three factors alone influenced your choices. They influence all of our choices at that vulnerable age, and he exploited every aspect of that. Plus, you don't know that what he said was true. I doubt it was. Think about it – what are the chances of being seen at every encounter? It's highly unlikely. Far *more* likely, he was acting on gossip fed to him by Lawrence, because he knew how to wound you, and the fact that he wanted to do so at all speaks volumes. He may have been a bit in love with you himself, jealous and angry? I'm *not* justifying or condoning his behaviour in any way, and you can't either, but it might help if we can understand it a bit. It wasn't your fault – you didn't do anything wrong.'

Bess had climbed into her little rusting car after the session with a clearer head and lighter shoulders than in decades. *I didn't do anything wrong . . . I didn't do anything wrong . . .* Dr Meredith's words had cut her free from the net she dragged behind her, and slowly, slowly, helped restore some of her self-worth. Bess knew this was a vital step in her new beginning. She called Mario from the car park outside Dr Meredith's office.

'I want . . .' She closed her eyes, turning her words simultaneously into a prayer. 'I want you to come home. I love you, Mario. I love you completely. I'm getting better, feeling better, and I pick you. I will always pick you and I want you to pick me, I really do.'

'Jesus, Bess! I'm stood in the middle of the site crying,' he half laughed. 'All the lads are looking. I will always pick you – you know that. I'm coming home, baby. I'll come home . . .'

Bess knew it would be much to Natalie's relief that her dad had packed up his belongings, lying scattered all over her apartment. She and Mario had lived apart for three horrible months and the first night they climbed together back into their slightly dilapidated bed, Chutney snuggled them both, delighted for the return to the status quo.

It hadn't been easy for her and Mario to talk so freely. Dismantling years of secrecy meant they were a different couple now, different individuals, stripped back and exposed, but what was left was genuine, raw and honest. Reminiscent of the young couple who had first lain on a blanket together in the park: a couple with the whole world at their feet.

Jake, Daniel and Natalie, aware of how she and Mario had been so totally floored, offered support without interference, checking in when they could, enveloping their parents in warm hugs of reassurance, like their very own flag-wavers at the end of a race, cheering them on. *Come on, Mum and Dad! You can do it!*

And she believed them: yes, they could.

Bess had also learned to let go of her guilt about Michelle. With Dr Meredith's help, she understood that because of the circumstances of their estrangement, heavily linked to her pregnancy, her old friend held a disproportionate amount of space in her head, but to continue to *think* about her every day, to *worry* about how their relationship had ended and even to hold on to misplaced resentment or envy, served nothing positive. It only kept her rooted in a dark time in her life. Bess had left her therapy session after the discussion, keen to get home. Sitting at the kitchen table, she pulled the pad from her bag on which she scribbled shopping lists and notes to herself and twisted the top off her ballpoint.

> *So, my lovely Michelle,*
> *I don't know what to write to you. I don't even know what to say to you. My mind is racing and I feel so sick. So I'm just going to get it out, write it down. You were right: I grieved too when our friendship ended. But here's the thing: I had a relationship with Lawrence, your Lawrence. Actually not a relationship . . . sex. We had sex.*
>
> *We had an agreement to keep our meet-ups secret and, as much as I hated it, I kept it from you, true to my word. Tony Dunlop ambushed me at the rugby club. It's not easy for me to recall that night, even after all this time. He said the most hurtful things and promised to tell everyone what he knew. I was so scared, so broken and ashamed. I don't know if he told you or if someone else did – I suspect they may have.*

But what no one knows is that I got pregnant. Strangely, I had not considered this might be a consequence – naive and stupid, I know. But that's what happened. I had a baby, Michelle, a little girl, and Lawrence is her dad. That little girl is now thirty-six. I named her Ellory.

Not that anyone could have told you about the baby, as no one knew, not Lawrence, not anyone.

One of the biggest tragedies for me is that I lost you, my very best friend. How I have missed you! You were the one person I could rely on, my person! The loss of you still sits like a sharp thing in my throat . . .

Bess picked up the sheet and held it close to her face, read it back slowly. The words were heartfelt and yet gave no indication as to how the incidents had chewed her up, spat her out and set her on a different path. She imagined her friend, possibly standing on her balcony with a fantastic view, maybe just in from playing tennis with the sun on her skin and her family in the house, opening the mail to find her letter. And in that instant, she knew she loved Michelle far too much to let these words fall into her hands, to lodge in her brain and infiltrate her happy marriage. Bess crumpled the sheet of paper into a ball between her palms. There was, she figured, no letter that could easily explain what had happened and what she had gone through, no letter that could glue her and Michelle back together or could ever now repair the chasm that yawned between them.

Grabbing her lighter – her illegal lighter from the back of the drawer – she placed the scrunched-up sheet in the sink before rolling the flint and touching the flame to the letter of goodbye to her darling friend. It smouldered, sending a soft plume of smoke upwards, as a gentle flame flickered up into the air. There was no whoosh, nothing dramatic, and Bess stared at the sink with a feeling of contentment and her hair still intact. She ran her fingers through the blackened ash of her words. It felt like a most satisfactory farewell to one of the great loves of her life. With a push of a button, she selected her eighties mix on Spotify and sung her heart out as she danced around the kitchen, beating out a rhythm on the countertop, performing her much-practised side-arm Soft Cell dance and shouting out the words to 'Tainted Love', caring little who heard. When it ended, she slumped into a chair at the kitchen table and cried, great, gulping tears that left her spent. It was her goodbye and the ending that meant she could move on to her next chapter, one she was excited to write.

More and more, she thought about Ellory, as if now that her daughter was no longer a secret, she could allow herself to picture her and talk to her in her mind. Was she married? A mother? Bess knew she could quite possibly have a grandchild in their teens already – a thought as weird as it was wonderful. She had registered her desire to be contacted by her daughter with an agency, and all she had to do was sit back and wait to see if Ellory had done the same. If she had, then she could write to her, or Ellory might choose to make contact.

Oh my goodness!

The thought of sitting down and putting pen to paper for the child she had last seen when she was but hours old – how and where in the world would she begin? How could she write all that she had contained for the past thirty-six years, five months, two weeks and three days . . . ? Ridiculously, she also wished her handwriting were better. *Penmanship and literacy* – she quaked at the memory. Having lodged her request for contact, she woke each day with a small bubble of excitement in her stomach, wondering if this might be the day she heard that Ellory wanted to get in touch. The truth was, her daughter might decide she did not want contact of any kind – the exact opposite, of course, of what Bess wished, holding dear the thought of reunion and picturing herself handing over the thirty-six cards that sat in a box at the top of her wardrobe. Each one was a birthday card with the same simple message, often written hurriedly in a darkened room:

> *Happy birthday, Ellory, my darling daughter.*
> *Please forgive me and know that you were the great-*
> *est gift.*
> *Mum X*

But if no contact was what Ellory decided, it would at least be the end of this chapter too, which in itself could bring peace.

Bess's thoughts were broken by the sound of the door of the waiting room opening, and suddenly all the hours of loitering on uncomfortable chairs dissolved into seconds and all the angst and chit-chat disappeared from memory, because in front of her stood Jake and Dan and in her son's arms lay a tiny bundle wrapped in a soft blanket. The family gathered round, faces beaming, and quite at a loss as to who should move first, all seemingly and equally as overwhelmed as Bess.

Jake couldn't speak for the tears coursing down his face.

Daniel, while choked with emotion, managed to get some words out. 'Here he is! This is Mario Jack, who has just weighed in at seven pounds six ounces. His mum is doing really well, and we, his daddies, are as you can see, absolute wrecks!'

Bess fought the desire that urged every fibre in her body to rush forward and take the baby in her arms. She wanted so badly to meet her grandson!

'Can you believe it, Eddie?' Mario said softly, putting his arm round his father-in-law. 'Your first great-grandchild!'

'Well, the first that we know of,' Bess's dad said, reaching out to grip her hand, and it was this gesture that set her off crying.

'Would you like to hold her, Mum?' Jake asked now. He stepped forward and placed his sleeping son in her arms. Bess peeped inside the blanket at the scrunched-up little face, red and squashed, not yet fully popped, and with such an impressive mop of straight, dark hair. He was the most beautiful baby! Her heart lurched at the scent of him, the weight of him in her arms! She knew she would never tire of holding this child, spending time with this child.

'He's only hours old and already he needs a haircut.' Jake ran his finger over his boy's head.

'Jake, he's beautiful – so beautiful!' Bess studied his tiny fingers, gripping the edge of the blanket. 'Just perfect . . .' Her joy filled her up.

'You know, Mum, Dan and I were saying, we've been on this journey with Gigi, who has worked so hard to bring him into the world, and we can't imagine what it must have been like going through what you did, all on your own. I mean, Gigi has had counselling and talked for days about the mechanics of it all, and yet you just . . .'

'I just left her in a hospital like this one and her new parents arrived and took her home. I walked to the train station, and that was that.' She shook her head at the brutality and sheer tragedy of it. Philip's muffled sob behind her drew her gaze, and she turned to acknowledge his presence both then and now and how truly grateful she was. They shared a knowing look. 'Here you go, Grandad!' Bess said, changing the tone. She didn't want to linger on thoughts of that, the saddest of days, not right now. Reluctantly she passed the sleeping baby to Mario, who seemed unable to speak or see, tears fogging his eyes and clogging his throat.

'Well, you've done a grand job, boys – he's a right little bobby-dazzler!' Bess's dad said, wrapping Jake and then Dan in a warm hug. 'Now, if you don't mind, I'll be getting home. I need a decent cuppa in a china cup and one of your nan's sandwiches.'

'I think you're coming back to ours, Dad, for chips?' Bess said, reminding him of the plan.

Everyone said their goodbyes to the new dads, and it was time to leave the little family in peace. Bess stood next to Mario as Jake and Dan disappeared behind the swing doors of the maternity unit with their son in their safe care.

'What a day!' Mario said, smiling at her.

'One we won't forget.'

'That's for sure.' He took her hand in his. 'He's a lucky little boy. Those two will give him a wonderful life.'

Bess smiled. 'They really will.'

Natalie chatted to Philip, as her nan and grandad put on their coats and gathered up their prized shopping bag.

'It's strange, Bess, isn't it?' Mario said. 'I don't think either of us could have imagined how far we would have come from when we got the news of the baby, but we have. I'm proud of you – proud of us.' He put his arms around her and she kissed him, burying her face in his chest, inhaling the scent of the man who had pledged to love her for better, for worse, for richer, for poorer, in sickness and in health.

'I'm proud of us too.' Bess bit her bottom lip, thinking of that afternoon at the Glade and how close she had come to losing everything. It was as if her husband could read her mind.

'I'm glad they're moving, the Maxwells. It's a relief, not only because it's awkward when I see him, what with me having given him that black eye . . .' he said. Bess winced at the thought of the altercation she had, luckily, missed. 'But also, it means some other poor sods will have to suffer their Christmas party.'

'I'm glad we can talk like this, Mario, really glad.'

'Yep.' He shifted to put his arm around her shoulders as the two walked off down the corridor. 'I was thinking, it's been a while now. Do you think you'll ever get to meet your little girl?'

'Oh, Mario, fingers and toes and everything crossed. But who knows? She knows I want to make contact and has my details, but the ball is entirely in her court. She might never make contact or refuse my letter. Or she might jump at the chance to meet me and even then, it might only be out of curiosity and to tell me to leave her alone. She might want only to know who her dad is.' The thought filled her with dread, knowing now she would do her very best to keep this particular grenade from Michelle's door. 'The permutations are many and not all have a happy outcome, no matter how much I pray for it. But it's out of my hands, so . . .' She let this trail, once again not wanting the jarring disappointment to cloud this magnificent day.

'What will be will be, eh?'

'Yup.' This much she knew.

The family said their goodbyes to Natalie, who was heading home to catch up on work. Mario insisted on driving, so Bess sat in the back of her little Nissan with her mum, while her dad climbed in the front.

'Let me know when you get home safe, Nats!' she yelled through the window. 'There are idiots on these roads!'

Natalie grimaced and gave an awkward thumbs-up.

With the engine running, Mario waited while Jeannie and Eddie clunked and clicked. Just before they pulled away, Bess's dad reached back between the seats and took her hand.

'You were wonderful today. I'm very proud of you – proud of you both.' He squeezed Mario's shoulder. 'Giving up is easy. It's finding a way forward that's tough.'

'Thank you, Dad.'

'And your mum and I have discussed this, and so I don't want to hear any refusal, but that little girl of yours has missed out on a lot in our family's lives, so many celebrations, and when and if you see her, we want you to give her this.'

He reached into his pocket and Bess shook her head. 'No, Dad, you really don't have to give her money. And you know, I might not even get to see her, not ever.' She tried to manage their expectations, the words bitter on her tongue.

'Money? It's not money, love – it's far more precious than money.'

Bess looked down at his shiny harmonica as he pushed it into her palm. '*If* you get to see your little girl, tell her her grandad sent her this.'

Bess couldn't speak, emotion stoppering the words in her throat. She nodded and sat back in the seat, as her husband drove out of the car park. They made the journey back to her house in silence, all a little exhausted and her keen to get back to Chutney, who she found snoring, oblivious to all the drama of the day. Mr Draper had very kindly let him out for a pee.

'Right then, who wants fish and chips? Come on, we need to celebrate! My treat – I'll take Chuts and run up the chippy,' Bess said, clapping for hush so she could take their orders. 'It's not every day we become grandparents.'

'Smashing!' Mario rubbed his stomach as he lowered his voice. 'And then an early night, I think. There might or might not be a card waiting for you on your pillow, Mrs Talbot.'

'Any ducks?'

'No ducks,' he said, kissing her.

Her dad shouted, 'I'll have a saveloy, no salt and vinegar, and I'll share chips with your mum. They always give me too many.' He sat in front of the TV, channel-surfing. The phone rang in the kitchen. Her mum was at the counter, reading the front of the free paper that was spread out on the work surface.

'They're opening a new Aldi!' she said, tapping the paper.

'That'll be nice.' Bess paid little attention to her mother's news about the superstore and went to grab the phone. 'Hello?'

'Bess?' Her daughter used her name, and this was usually a clue that Bess was in trouble with her child – what had she done now? Certainly not smoked – not that Natalie knew of anyhow. She smiled, happy that her darling girl, an auntie now, had made it home safe, knowing this would enable her to settle.

'Hello, love, all okay?'

'H— hello?'

'Nats, are you all right?' Her daughter's tone was odd – tentative, faltering. She wondered what was wrong and her heart gave a little skip.

'Bessie?'

And hearing her name for the second time, she realised the voice was at once strange to her and yet familiar, a voice with the same quality and pitch as Natalie's, but not quite. A voice *like* Natalie's, but older. Ten years older, to be precise.

'Bessie, erm . . . this is a strange call for me to make and I'm sure a strange call for you to receive. You don't know me but, erm . . .'

I do know you! I do know you! I do, I do, I do . . . ! You're the missing piece . . . You are my baby – my baby girl. My oldest child, my daughter . . .

Bess slumped over the countertop, the room spinning around her. Her voice failed and she could only squeak a small reply.

'Yes . . . this is me. I'm Bessie.'

'Oh! Hi, Bessie.' There was the sound of a girl taking a sharp breath. 'It's me. It's Ellory.'

ABOUT THE AUTHOR

Photo © 2012 Paul Smith
www.paulsmithphotography.info

Amanda Prowse is an international bestselling author of twenty-seven novels published in dozens of languages. Her chart-topping titles *What Have I Done?*, *Perfect Daughter*, *My Husband's Wife*, *The Coordinates of Loss*, *The Girl in the Corner* and *The Things I Know* have sold millions of copies around the world.

Other novels by Amanda Prowse include *A Mother's Story*, which won the coveted Sainsbury's eBook of the Year Award. *Perfect Daughter* was selected as a World Book Night title in 2016. She has been described by the *Daily Mail* as 'the queen of family drama'.

Amanda is the most prolific writer of bestselling contemporary fiction in the UK today. Her titles consistently score the highest online review approval ratings across several genres.

A popular TV and radio personality, Amanda is a regular panellist on Channel 5's *Jeremy Vine* show, as well as featuring on numerous daytime ITV programmes. She also makes countless guest appearances on national and independent radio stations, including LBC and talkRADIO, where she is well known for her insightful observations and infectious humour.

Amanda's ambition is to create stories that keep people from turning off the bedside lamp at night, that ensure you walk every step with her great characters, and tales that fill your head so you can't possibly read another book until the memory fades . . .

Did you enjoy this book and would like to get informed when Amanda Prowse publishes her next work? Just follow the author on Amazon!

1) Search for the book you were just reading on Amazon or in the Amazon App.

2) Go to the Author Page by clicking on the Author's name.

3) Click the "Follow" button.

If you enjoyed this book on a Kindle eReader or in the Kindle App, you will be automatically offered to follow the author when arriving at the last page.

LAKE UNION
PUBLISHING